It's 1966...

...a time in America when parents wake sleepy children to watch early morning rocket launches. We're going to the moon as a nation and 11-year-old Walter Hudson reads about all the space missions and clips pictures of the astronauts to tape on his bedroom wall in Brooklyn, New York. He's a big city kid — until his mother makes him pack up for a move to Mackinac Island, Michigan, where she needs to take over her father's weekly newspaper. Walter makes a special new friend on the island, but refuses to unpack. He thinks nothing interesting will ever happen on an eight-mile-around dot of land where they don't even have cars. But soon he's witness to a plot to bribe Governor Romney to stall housing integration, his mom goes to jail to protect his identity as the source of this scoop, and he has to run the newspaper. While grappling with the bad guys, Walter has to make a white-knuckle escape by helicopter. The pilot is Jane Hart, the senator's wife, who's trying to become an astronaut while space is still a men-only club.

Readers who did not live

in the Sixties are invited to

consult the glossary in the back

of the book when encountering

the unknown.

WALTER HUDSON

AND THE

MACKINAC ISLAND AFFAIR

🚲 🚲 🚲

Diane Petryk

ISBN: 978-0-9959629-0-3

Big Bang Tango Books, Lansing, Michigan/Stratford, Ontario

BBTBooks@outlook.com

Cover and illustrations by Tiffany Petitt

TGDraw@gmail.com

For Walter,

as what is not?

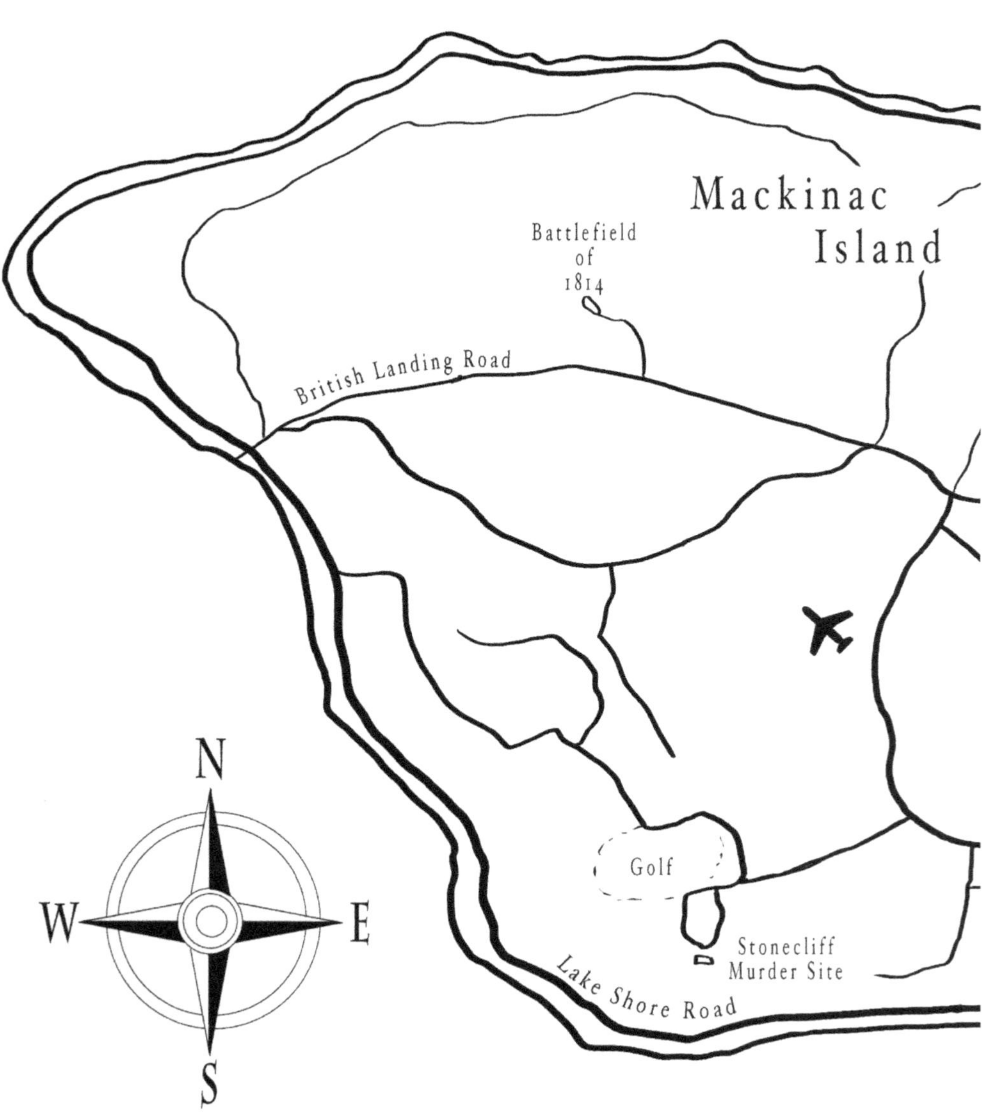

Mackinac Island
Battlefield of 1814
British Landing Road
Golf
Stonecliff Murder Site
Lake Shore Road
N
S
E
W

Mackinac Island

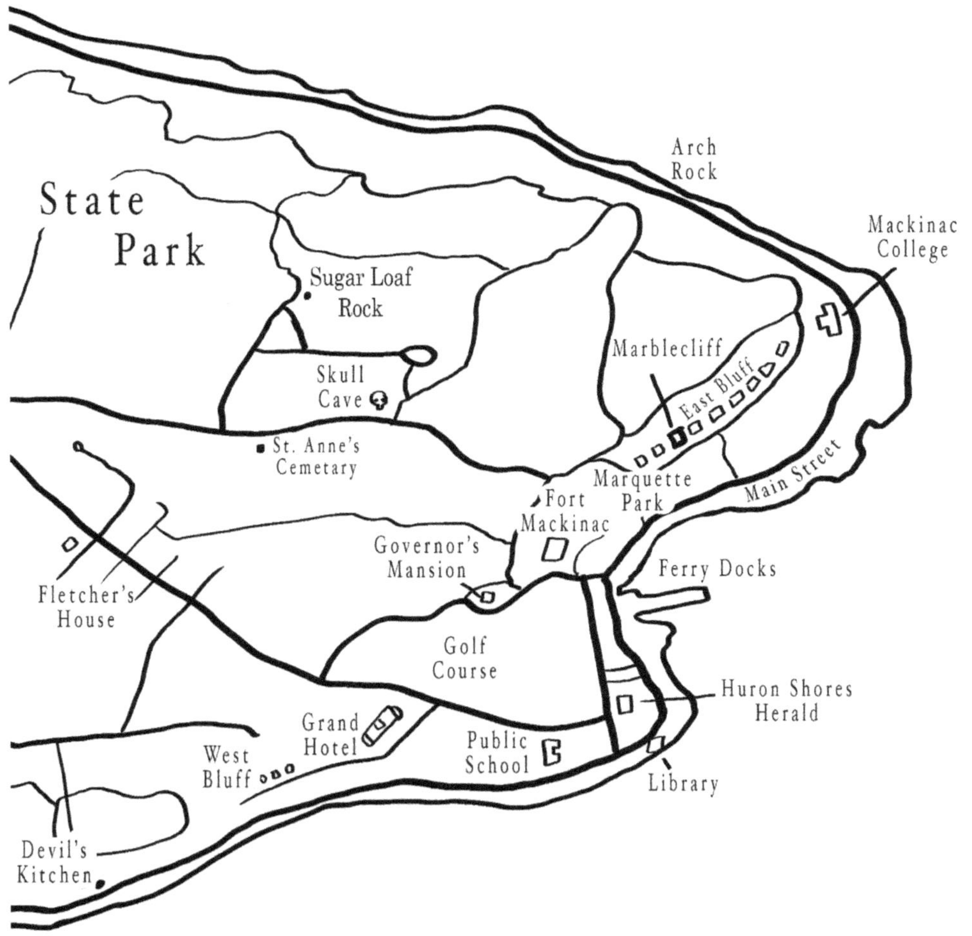

"A thousand years from now, historians

will mark this time as the beginning

of the greatest age of exploration ever."

– Tom Brokaw

"To find anything comparable to our

forthcoming adventures in space we must

go back far beyond Columbus, far beyond

Odysseus, far, indeed, beyond the first

ape man. We must contemplate the moment,

now irrevocably lost in the mists of time,

when the ancestor of all of us came crawling

out of the sea."

– Arthur C. Clarke

"Like all living systems, cultures cannot

remain static; they evolve or decline.

They explore or expire.   ...Beyond all

rationales, spaceflight is a spiritual quest

in the broadest sense, one promising a

revitalization of humanity and a rebirth

of hope no less profound than the great

opening out of mind and spirit at the dawn

of our modern age."

– Buzz Aldrin

Illustrations

Skull Cave

1 – THE KURYAKIN MANEUVER

June, 1966, almost 9 p.m.
Mackinac Island

I WAS LYING BLEEDING in Skull Cave.

It was almost dark and instead of getting home like I was supposed to, I was flat on my back in the dirt, out of breath, and hiding out from two bullies.

I wiped spiderwebs off my nose with my steepled knuckles, one brush left and one brush right. My wrists were still bound, but at least they were out in front now.

These two kids – they knocked me down on Fort Street, opposite the governor's mansion, where I was riding my bike. They tied my hands behind my back and stuffed a balled-up red and white cowboy neckerchief in my mouth and tied another one around my head and mouth to keep me from spitting it out. I got away and ran, but not before tripping once and cutting my forehead on a sharp rock or something.

I'm a pretty fast runner. I won third place in the 50-yard dash at our Fourth Grade track and field day last school year, but it's hard to run with your hands tied behind your back. You can't balance as good and I got winded trying to take in deep breaths through the gag.

When I stubbed my toe and fell, I remembered that *U.N.C.L.E.* episode where Illya Kuryakin was forced to run with a large target painted on his back. He was being pursued by a bunch of nasty guys with bows and arrows and his hands were chained behind him. He was having the same problem running, so he sat down and scooted his hands under his butt and around the bottom of his

17

feet and got his arms out front.

I was afraid to stop, but afraid to fall again, so I did that. Really fast. As fast as I could I sat down and got my arms in front. Then I ripped the gag tie down and pulled the cloth out of my mouth and jumped up again almost simultaneously.

And then I really ran. I made up for the delay. With my hands in front, I could balance and run faster and I could take deep breaths. I was a horizontal Saturn 5 rocket.

I couldn't keep up that pace all the way home, though. I needed to rest. So, when I saw the cave, I dove in. You can't go in standing up. It's too low.

Skull Cave is that sorry excuse for a cave tourists are always shown, about halfway between where I was attacked and our cottage on Huron Trail. I hit the ground on my left shoulder, almost scraping my head on the top of the cave's very low, wide opening. I wanted to get my wrists untied, but first I needed to calm my racing heart before it pumped all my blood out the cut on my forehead. I laid on my side and listened as I caught my breath. Did they follow me?

When I didn't hear anything, I let myself think. First, that something smelled of horse poop. My shoes. Yuck. Then I mentally gave credit for my fast escape to the "pure presence of mind," as Illya would say, that allowed me to get my hands in front. Well, I'll just call that the Kuryakin Maneuver.

I didn't hear anything, but I felt the warm trickle of blood take a left turn at my eyebrow, and run down the side of my head. It seemed to go behind my ear and then get sopped up by the one neckerchief that was still around my neck.

I wriggled my wrists. It was still not completely dark outside, but the cave didn't let in much of the twilight. It was as dark as our old brownstone's basement in a blackout.

I was supposed to be back at Grandpa's cottage by now – Mom could be freaking out already. But I hesitated. They might have followed me. And I had to leave my bike behind. They still had theirs. So staying in Skull Cave seemed smart for the moment.   I used the heels of my shoes to push myself in as far as possible. I hated that my Gemini 4 T-shirt was getting dirty, but I hoped to keep the blood off it.

The sky went from dusk to dark pretty fast. The cut on my head stung and my left shin hurt.

In the cave I couldn't see my leg or my shirt. It would have helped to get up so I could see to work the wrist ties, but that would have required coming out of hiding. Skull Cave is just a pickle-sized hollow under a big rock. You can't stand up in it. There are no skulls in it, either, if there ever were. They say, 250 years or so ago, a man fleeing from an Indian massacre at Fort Michilimackinac, just across the straits on the Lower Peninsula, rowed over to Mackinac Island in a canoe and hid in this cave among human bones and skulls. That's why it's called Skull Cave – not because it looks anything like that cave in *Peter Pan* or anything.

Apparently, it worked as a hiding place back then, or there wouldn't be stories about it.

I hoped it would work for me. I promised myself if I ever figured out who they were I'd get back at them somehow. But that was for later. Right now I needed to get home. Mom would be getting frantic. I'd just take another few seconds to make sure they weren't following me. I continued to listen...

PROLOGUE

March 12, 1966
Cobble Hill, Brooklyn

WALTER'S ROOM WAS ALL packed. He stood among 33 boxes and his two Samsonite suitcases that were colored like French vanilla ice cream with marshmallow swirls.

The boxes were taped, the luggage locked, his shoulders drooped.

Out one back window he could see the fire escape landing and a small patch of grass below where his playhouse stood abandoned. It took up nearly half of their pizza-box size yard, but his mom wouldn't be stopped from having it built once she saw the picture in Country Living *magazine. It was the year after his dad didn't come back.*

He sighed. The fun he and his friends Doug and Frank had out there was already in the past. He was going to turn 12 friendless, a stranger in a strange land.

His grandfather died and left his mom his weekly newspaper on Mackinac Island. This was seriously near the Arctic Circle as far as he knew. She couldn't be persuaded not to go there and take it over. Walter had tried.

Yesterday he packed his comics, marbles, baseball mitt and baseball cards, Monopoly and Clue, and miscellaneous old school papers and projects. All was ready for their departure from Brooklyn tomorrow evening, but there was one thing he still had to do. He looked at the wall above his bed. He'd kept putting it off. He still needed to take down his space pictures – the collection that had been growing since he was six.

He started it in 1961 when his mother said he could cut up the copy of Look *magazine she had brought home. He cast aside his blunt First Grade scissors and took up his mother's pointy ones. He carefully cut out the head of a grinning Yuri Gagarin, the first-ever man in space.*

Gagarin's broad smile had been high over Walter's pillow for five years, but he wasn't alone up there for long. Alan Shepard and his Freedom 7 capsule joined Gagarin less than a month later. In a few more months, he snipped from the Saturday Evening Post *a picture of John Glenn, first American to orbit the Earth. Then there were diagrams of alternate flight modes to the moon from* Scientific American. *There was a picture of President John F. Kennedy giving his speech about making a moon landing by the end of the decade – "not because it is easy, but because it is hard."*

Since his mom brought it to him, he even put up the picture of Valentina Tereshkova, the first woman in space – or so the Russians said. He wasn't at all convinced she actually went into space. After all, his cousin in East Lansing told him McDonald's restaurants wouldn't hire women "because they couldn't stand the pressure," so how could a woman be an astronaut? Shortly after her supposed space flight he started letting other clippings overlap her face – until she wasn't seen at all. So when he peeled off a picture of America's second man in space, Gus Grissom, he found her. He shrugged and decided to save it for awhile.

Balancing on tip-toes on the bed, he had been pulling off the taped corners of each picture and taking them down, then removing and discarding the tape so it wouldn't stick them together in a pile.

Then only his favorite picture remained. It was above all those.

He needed a step-stool when he put it up there. It was an autographed photo of Col. Edward White floating in space, tethered to the Gemini 4 space capsule. Walter met White last summer.

Shortly after becoming the first American to walk in space, White was honored by his fellow University of Michigan alumni at a banquet in New York. Walter's mom got him in on the strength of her press pass from Scientific Digest. *The Gemini 4 mission was a big deal for Michiganders. Both White and his partner in space, James McDivitt, went to U of M.*

There was to be a news conference just before the banquet and Walter slipped in with his mom. They both thought he'd just get a glimpse of his newest hero, but it was better than that.

Two TV technicians accidentally smacked their 310-pound video camera-on-wheels against a wall and it had to be fixed. While all the press people were hovering around or giving advice or complaining, somehow they lost track of their guest of honor. White sidled over to the only person not moving frantically – Walter, who was just standing there kneading his Silly Putty.

"Hi," he said.

"Hi" Walter said.

"I'm Ed White," he said. Walter just looked. "The guy who walked in space," White continued, while straightening his skinny maize and blue tie.

Then White saw that the boy's hesitation was from awe, not non-recognition. Finally Walter said: "I know. Twenty-one minutes. I know all the astronauts."

"You do? I'm quite sure we've never met."

"I mean I read about all you guys."

White let his head rotate, indicating around the room."You here to interview me for your school paper?"

"No. I hate that journalism stuff. My mother's here cause she works for a magazine."

"Oh." he said. "Then what do you like to do?"

"Science experiments. Study about going into space. Ride my bike. Read Tom Swift *and* Hardy Boys *books. I plan to help us get to Mars."*

"That'll be about 1980 or '85. How old will you be then?"

Walter didn't hesitate there. He'd already thought about it. "Thirty," he said. "And you?"

"Oh. I'll be grounded by then, but I'll be watching you go."

Walter thought. "I might not go," he said. "I'm not sure about the flying part. I might just help engineer it, or be part of ground control."

"As long as somebody goes, right?"

"Yup. Are you going to the moon?"

"Absolutely. First we have to finish the Gemini missions. Then the Apollo three-man crews will make it to the moon. I look forward to walking on the moon. I keep thinking about how great it will be to jump up and bounce like a rubber ball on Earth."

"Yeah, that'd be cool." Walter took a little light greenish-blue plastic egg out of his pocket and put the Silly Putty inside.

"Neat stuff, huh?" White said.

"Yeah. You can copy comics out of the newspaper by flattening it and pressing it on them, then stretch the faces into funny shapes. Sometimes I stick stuff up on the wall with it – when I imagine my bed's a space capsule. The tools don't float around. I stick 'em to the wall with Silly Putty."

"What kind of tools?" White asked.

"Well, little screwdrivers. I borrow the one's from my mom's sewing machine tool kit... and my toothbrush."

"No one's needed a toothbrush in space yet."

"But they will, won't they?"

"No doubt about it," White said, grinning.

"Well, then, you could stick your toothbrush up with Silly Putty so it won't float around."

"I'll remember that."

Walter changed the subject. "Do you worry about sinking into the dust? When you land on the moon, I mean."

"Nah...."

"Well, how was it out there walking in space?"

"Floating above the world... What do you think?"

"Amazing," they both said simultaneously, and laughed.

"Too bad that Russian guy, Leo Nov, got to walk out there first." Walter knew he was showing off his knowledge.

White was amused. "You mean Alexei Leonov? Well, when you get to do something as rare and incredible as that, quibbling about being second by 23 days would be absurd, don'tcha think?"

"Yeah... I'd be glad to be second or two hundred and secondth."

White pursed his lips, raised his brows, and nodded.

"Did you really have to be ordered back in by ground control?" Walter asked.

He shook his head. "I really REALLY didn't WANT to go back in, but the story about Mission Control having to order me back in isn't true. That would have been unprofessional. An astronaut would never do that."

"But going back into the space capsule," he added, "as I told McDivitt when I sat down in it, was the saddest moment of my life."

"At least you got 21 minutes, that was almost twice what Leo-O-Nov got," Walter said, correcting his pronunciation of the cosmonaut's name.

White smiled. "The next guys are going to be out much longer. We need to learn how to work outside the spacecraft. And docking, that's critical."

"I know. 'EOR - Earth Orbit Rendezvous.' So you don't have to get so much payload up at once. Wernher von Braun said that's the only other way to get there. Other than a humongous rocket."

"You really are following this stuff, aren't you? But don't count on Von Braun being right all the time."

Walter made a mental note of that, then said that it must have been hard to control movement out there without gravity. "After all, Newton said every action has an equal and opposite reaction. So if you touched the ship you'd go..."

"Hey," White interrupted, still smiling. "Who's the spaceman here? You're stealing my banquet speech. Anyway, give me your address and I'll send you an autographed picture." He took a narrow notebook from the young Free Press *reporter standing nearby and tore a page out for Walter to write on. Walter handed him the address, then the camera was finally ready.*

"You'll have to have a better camera than that if you want us to film the first steps on the moon," White said good-naturedly. "You'll have to make it tougher... and a whole lot smaller."

"Yeah," someone yelled. "That camera's as big as the Lunar Lander's supposed to be."

"Westinghouse is working on that," somebody else called out.

White sent Walter not only the promised autographed picture, but a Gemini 4 T-shirt. It was white with an enlarged picture of the mission badge. And he sent one of the actual mission badges as well. It had a red background with a white-stitched astronaut floating, tethered to the space capsule. The names McDivitt and White were also stitched on, at right angles. "Jim hates it" he wrote. "So wear it proudly!"

Walter treasured the shirt, the badge, and the photo. He recalled White saying that if we don't make it to the moon by 1969, the target date set by President Kennedy, the country might lose interest.

"That would be perverse," Walter responded.

White raised his brows. "Perverse? Yeah, maybe it would. How'd a kid like you get such a vocabulary?"

"My mom says it's because she read lots of books to me every day. Now I keep a word collection notebook. Because you can think more thoughts if you have words for them."

White nodded his agreement. "But I don't think they will. Lose interest, I mean. Because there's still the Russians. There's national pride and national security to think about."

Many Americans were afraid of what the Russians would do if they became more advanced in space. Then they might impose communism on America. Communism was supposed to be this terrible thing. Walter read a book he found in the library about it and couldn't see what was really wrong with everyone owning equal shares of everything. It was based on the ideas of a German economic philosopher named Karl Marx, who said government should be based on the idea "From each according to his ability, to each according to his need." That actually sounded good. But why then, he wondered, were his Ukrainian relatives, who lived under a communist system, because the Ukraine was one of the Soviet Socialist Republics, always writing letters asking for things they needed? And why weren't they allowed to come over and visit? Mom said Grandpa never even met one of his brothers who was born after he left to come to America. Why couldn't communism come with freedom? He thought he would have to learn more about this.

After the reporters questioned White, the hero was led off to the banquet. Walter didn't have another chance to talk with him, but observed that he was probably 5 feet, 11 inches tall. (He would have guessed 6-feet, but knew 6-foot tall astronauts were not allowed.) White was thin, with light brown hair and a nice smile, a smile like what Walter imagined his father must have had, although he didn't really remember. No one had seen him for seven years.

Walter's thoughts were brought back to the present by his mom calling from beyond the bedroom door.

"Are you finished gathering up everything?"

"Almost, Mom," Walter said flatly. He reached for White's spacewalk photo, but could only grasp the very bottom edge. It was too high for him to get his fingers behind the taped upper corners, so he tugged on it. The tape was stubborn and he tugged again. That was a misjudgment. The tape didn't yield, but the photographic paper did. Ed White's photo tore – down to the middle and then to the right, the direction Walter was pulling, almost taking a large portion clear off.

Walter grabbed both sides and finished pulling it off and held the torn artifact almost in disbelief. Then he collapsed onto his knees, then sat back on his legs. Tears welled up in his eyes – partly because a cherished memento was damaged, but deep down he knew it wasn't just that. He sensed something else, although, despite his beyond-grade-level vocabulary, he might not have known to call it symbolism. His life was being torn apart.

His mom heard the faint sobs of her son and stepped quietly into the room.

She knelt down on the floor beside him and put her fingers on his shoulder as gently as a butterfly landing. She looked at the torn picture, then spoke:

"You remember what President Kennedy said?"

"What?" Walter asked, in the angry, sad, and pouty way perfected by little boys over the centuries.

"We choose to go...not because it is easy, but because it is hard."

Walter wiped a tear with a violent sweep of his arm and gave an exasperated exhale.

"That was about going to the moon, Mom, not Michigan!"

She stood up slowly and left the room silently.

The next evening, after dark, they left the house, heading to the subway to go to New York's Penn Station, each carrying a suitcase. When they stopped to rest their arms, they looked up. The lights of the city obscured all but the brightest night sky features.

Walter's mom turned to him. As if consoling him over a broken toy, she said:

"From Mackinac Island you can see the stars."

2 – DASH FOR SAFETY
9:30 p.m. June 16, 1966
Skull Cave

I PEEKED OUT INTO the blackness while twisting the rope that bound my hands. Just where were the stars? The dark set in, a perfect background for stars, but a fog floated over the island from the lake. I slid on my back to the edge of the cave opening, but couldn't see any sky features, or very far down the path, for that matter. So I continued to listen. While I lay there, I thought about how I had been having a pretty good day, considering, up 'til that mysterious ambush. It was a sunny Saturday and the start of school was still more than six weeks away. I had my bike out for a spin and I accidentally won a stuffed animal contest in Marquette Park.

I didn't plan to enter any contests, but I had my platypus puppet and my skateboard, which were about the same length, tied to the carrier on the back of my bike. I got an ice cream cone on Main Street and rode up to Marquette Park. I wondered why a bunch of kids were gathered in front of the big black Father Marquette statue. They were all carrying Teddy bears and stuffed cats and puppies and stuff, which seemed weird. I put my kickstand down and just stood there licking the cone and watching. Then I heard the announcer making fun of one little girl's well worn bear, calling it "bearly-there" and making jokes about this and that. He was calling for last minute entries in the "stuffed animal contest." He was clearly running out of jokes, when he spied my platypus.

"Hey," he said, "and here's a skateboarding platypus!"

He thought that was such a clever idea, I did not want to disappoint him and tell him I had no such idea.   I just went along with him and gave my name

QVETTE
37 - 1675

then finished sucking melted ice cream from the bottom of my sugar cone. Next thing, I heard my name called. Surprise. I won first place and a lot of little kids were saying "Awww" and "Geez."

The prize was a coupon for two pounds of fudge.

Thankfully, there were second and third prizes and all the kids got something or I would have felt really rotten.

I went home, which was way up the steps at the back corner of Marquette Park and a little ways east on Huron Trail. They call the area the East Bluff. Mom wasn't home. Our housekeeper, Mrs. Kwashneetski, was mopping the kitchen floor in a dark purple dress that made her look like a mushy eggplant.

I went into Mom's library and watched a *Spin and Marty* re-run until the TV got only static. It's usually the 6SN7 tube, so I took that out with the idea I'd take it to the tube tester at the drugstore later.

The scruffy stray orange kitten, who greeted us when we arrived on the island, was on the back patio, so I fed it some Tabby Treat and it hung out for while. I made it chase some string I used for Cat's Cradle. That was not a "Happening," as they say in Greenwich Village, so I went back out on my bike. I decided to ride around the entire island. First, I rode from our house to the top of the steps leading to Marquette Park. Up near there is a memorial – a sculpted plaque attached to a rock. It shows the figure of a woman. It's called Anne's Tablet, named after a book called "Anne" someone wrote long ago.

In spite of a mental flash of Professor Fate driving down the Montmartre Steps in Paris at the end of the movie *The Great Race*, I ignored the impulse and carried my bike down all 144 steps. Then I went from the back of the park to Main Street, across from the Coast Guard Station, and could ride towards what they call 'town.'

On Main Street I ran into this kid, Fletcher Auginash, the only local kid I knew so far. I met him at the main horse stables after a carriage ride. His father's job is to help take care of the horses for Carriage Taxis & Tours. Fletch had been showing me places where tourists don't usually get to go. He said he lived in Harrisonville. That's the area locals live in if they're not rich or in business, he told me. Many of the kids who live there are of Ojibwa or Chippewa Indian ancestry. I didn't ask him if he was, but I guessed he must be. His hair was straight, black as licorice, and his eyes were brown and shaped like almonds.

Anyway, seeing him in town, I invited him to come with me to redeem the fudge coupon. That wasn't much of an incentive, I guess, there being no shortage of fudge on the island. He just said he had to get back to help his dad clean some horses or something and "catch ya later." So I took the coupon by myself into one of those shops where they make the stuff right in front of you on a kitchen-table-size slab of gray marble.

After watching a maple-colored bucketful of sticky ooze get folded over and over with a big paddle until it was fudge consistency, I selected four half-pound bricks from the display case – maple walnut, cherry, chocolate, and pistachio – which they gave me in two boxes, two rectangular hunks in each box. I ate about a third of the maple one, then closed the box and put it in my right back pants pocket, only sticking out a bit so I didn't sit on it. The other box I put in my left back pocket, the same way. Then I rode off again. (After you've eaten as much fudge as you can stand, there isn't much else to do on the island except ride a bike. Alas, not like in Brooklyn, where there's gobs of stuff to do all the time.)

I started going west on Main Street, then turned up to Market Street where Mom's newspaper office is, near the corner of French Lane. I stepped into the newsroom, which is behind a front reception area, and before I could ask anything they said: "Your Mother went to interview the new college president."

They being Britt Niagara, the one reporter on staff, who was sitting at his desk holding a phone, and Laura Kelly, the lady who retyped news releases and took classified ads and was always asking to write real news stories but never being allowed to, at the desk opposite him. Megan Nichols, the secretary-receptionist, who usually sits behind a counter facing the front window, was in the morgue, a little side room where extras of old issues of the paper are kept, along with the master set of bound copies (that you're not allowed to clip!) and old reference and photo files. It sounded like she was helping a visitor find an extra copy of last year's graduation issue. Not present were Mr. Orville Trivelpiece, who Mom called "Orrie" and I called "Mr. T," the business manager and display ad salesman, who has his own office to the right of the front door, and Mr. Vince Huggins, the part-time photographer/dark room guy. Mr. T didn't work weekends and Mr. Huggins was presumably out shooting "wild art." That's what they call pictures of just stuff going on that didn't go with stories. Well, those guys, plus Mom, who had a cool glass-enclosed office facing the newsroom, were the whole staff.

"Where is this interview?" I asked. Miss Kelly stood up, put a nail polish brush carefully back in its little red bottle and walked to a map of the town on the wall behind Mr. Niagara, her high heels clicking on the linoleum. The map was up high and while she pointed she had to get on her tiptoes and that made her dress rise a bit showing the lacy edge of her white slip. It was a full skirt and she had a tiny waist. "Here's the college," she said, turning her head and smiling back at me. "The eastern end of town – as far you can go before the road curves north. 'The Point,' they call it."

"No, that's where the new college is going in," Mr. Niagara said, in that kind of tone adults use when they want to make you feel dumb, "but they're meeting at the Grand." She flashed him pursed lips, rolled her eyes, and shrugged at me.

Mom had told me there was going to be a college opened on the island's east side. There was something freaky about it, but I forgot what.

"Anyway, kid, don't go over *there* and interrupt her," said Mr. Niagara, talking down to me, too. "She's busy."

He seemed annoyed.

"There" being the big, ritzy "longest front porch in the world" Grand Hotel everybody walked around in, I didn't see any reason not to go there.

I flashed him a look of my own.

It's no Prospect Park like in Brooklyn, but in a pinch, the Grand Hotel grounds make for a nice playground. I had already mastered the art of getting into the pool without being a registered hotel guest. You just put your swim trunks on under clothes, take them off down by the lake and get wet. Put your clothes in something that looks like a beach bag. Then you walk up the hotel grounds and go into the pool clubhouse or go directly past the white fence to poolside, hopefully still dripping a bit. Flop on a chaise like you belong there. Jump in the pool, whatever. No one will ever guess your parents aren't registered there.

From there you can tour the fancy gardens or set up a game of bocce. It's pronounced "botch-ee" and is some kind of Italian lawn bowling or something. The balls are very heavy and are only to be rolled. Then you can walk up the center staircase to that humongously long porch where you can sit in a rocking chair or flop on a chaise lounge overlooking the lawn and garden below and the lake out as far as you can see. It's a great view. You can even see the Mackinac Bridge. The Grand Hotel itself is up high, but then many places are, like Fort Mackinac and our house. All the land on Mackinac Island slopes down to to the lake shore. You're supposed to picture the island looking like a turtle's back.

Britt Niagara responded to my look by gesturing upward with the phone receiver, held in one hand, mouthpiece covered with the other. "I'd love to talk," he said, "but I'm on hold with a reference librarian in Lansing. Trying to get some facts for an obit."

Miss Kelly had her nail polish brush out again and while finishing a little finger offered to teach me to type classifieds. She didn't seem annoyed at all. I said a quick "no thanks, I don't do jerk-nal-ism" with a wave and backed out. And I liked advertising stuff even less than news stuff. It was bad enough Mom trying to teach me how to write newspaper stories, with Who, Whatzit, When, Wherefore and all those facts, but all that play on words stuff in ads? I can't do that. Anyway, everyone knows I'm going to be a scientist and Mom can care about fish wrappers. I don't.

I didn't tell Mr. Niagara, of course, but I had no intention of going to interrupt her interview. I got back on my bike and rode to where Market Street ends at Lake Shore Drive, and turned right. In just a minute I was passing my school-to-be and its playground. It was a new building, but it was the playground that impressed me. Schools in Brooklyn just don't have big expansive playgrounds like that, if any at all. Basketball they play in gyms or on rooftops. So I stopped for a quick swing facing the lake and the Mackinac Bridge. You couldn't see for miles like that in Brooklyn either, unless you went to some 20th floor balcony. This everyday, ground-level spaciousness, that was weird.

Anyway, then I rode past the Grand's tennis courts. You can't see the big porch from the road at the water's edge – Lake Shore Road. That's the eight miles of mostly blacktopped path that circles the island at lake level. In distance, it's about like going to Coney Island from my old neighborhood, Cobble Hill.

Mercifully, it's flat, so I wasn't tired at all, but I stopped at the halfway point, where British Landing Road intersects and they have a refreshment stand. I bought a Faygo Rock 'n' Rye and parked my bike near the historical marker. I had to go back to use their bottle opener, but I kept my eye on the bike. It's the only one of its kind on the island. The radio is built into the cross bar. And it's red, with a rocket-shaped front headlamp that's so cool.

It was also kind of special because my mom says my dad bought it the year I was born. That was 1955. It was a new model and he had this thing about owning the latest things. He drove all the way to Dayton, Ohio, to get one right out of the Huffy factory, Mom said. Then it stayed in storage until year before last when Mom thought I was old enough to handle a 26-incher. I remember her pulling it out of the huge flat box and how my lower jaw dropped like Howdy Doody's. Only she bit her lower lip to stop from crying because my dad wasn't there to give it to me. He was lost at sea, somewhere on assignment for a science magazine he worked for. It was a ferry boat accident and everyone died. They say. Mom doesn't like to talk about it much. I was too little to remember anything. When I think about him, it's mostly the feeling I had being awakened early and carried in his arms, my hands around his neck, as he took me downstairs to watch a rocket blastoff. I'm sure it was Alan Shepard's launch, because I looked it up and it was at 7 a.m. New York time. All I remember is he told me over and over we were watching our first man in space. And my pajama shirt had a glow-in-the-dark rocket ship on the front.

I put the kickstand down near the historical marker and stepped back and looked at the bike. It said "Huffy Radio Bike" on the side and you could see the chrome dial with numbers 5, 6 , 7, 9, 11, 14, and 16 in a semi-circle. Inside there are radio tubes that I can replace if I ever need to. That's why I call it "Robbie" – the tubes remind me of Robby the Robot. Only I spell it differently. I'm proud of Robbie. His red paint is still all shiny and new. But I'll keep it forever even when it isn't. Anyway, then I read the historical marker. It tells why the road that goes up from the shoreline there is called British Landing Road. The English soldiers came from Canada and snuck up that way to take Fort Mackinac at the start of the War of 1812 – and we were surprised and had to surrender. Mom said, even if teachers don't mention it, we were trying to take Canada, so it was only fair. Both sides claim they won the War of 1812, but after a lot of battles nothing much changed. And we got Fort Mackinac back. I'm going to have to try to explore up that road someday on the way home – because it, too, will take you to the East Bluff, just east of the fort. But not with the bike. It's too steep!

I turned on the radio and laid down on my side in the grassy area there between the road and the lake. With my knees pulled up I must have looked like click-clack blocks frozen in motion. I listened to "Sherry" by the Four Seasons and the Beatles' new "Yellow Submarine" song that makes no sense. Then I got up and got on Robbie again.

I could feel the breeze pushing up my bangs as I rode. You can pick up some speed when you don't have to stop all the time. To go around Mackinac Island it seems like you're just riding in a circle, but if you look at the island on a map, it looks like the head of a fish with its mouth open.   The boat docks sticking out look like its teeth. Along those docks are private sailboats and yachts. But mostly it's where the ferries park when they come in from mainland Michigan, either from the Upper Peninsula town of St. Ignace or Mackinaw City, the little town at the tip of the Lower Peninsula – the tip of the "mitten" as they say. The peninsulas are linked by the Mackinac Bridge, which you can see from the island. When on the island, a couple ferry docks can be seen from Marquette Park. It's a good view because the park is already up the turtle's back a bit, with Fort Mackinac behind it up even higher, like New York's West Point or Fort Ticonderoga.

You can't get to the island any other way but by boat, except fly. Then they are only very small planes, Mom said. I have never been in a plane, but I imagine a small plane would be scarier than a big one that had more than one engine.

Anyway, soon I was practically alone on the Lake Shore Road on the far side of the island from town, just a horse-drawn carriage passing once in a long while and a few bikes coming the other way. You don't have to watch for car traffic, so you can stare out over the lake for long stretches of time. And it's quiet, except for the distant squawk of seagulls. So you can hear the quiet lapping of lake water on the pebbly shore. Nothing at all like the noisy boardwalk at Coney Island where you bump into people most of the time, cars are everywhere, and planes constantly overhead. I admit I sometimes liked getting far from city noises. The smell was also different than New York. Air with just a dash of seaweed smell.

This was the quintessence of Mackinac Island, I thought. (I had just added that word – quintessence – to my word collection notebook and was itching to use it).

I was glad I had a lot of words to think with. At the very least you could annoy lots of adults by saying things they didn't understand. Especially teachers.

I pedaled and pedaled. The unpopulated far side seemed to go on forever. Then I saw Arch Rock and rounded Mission Point, where that college will be.

After that there's a bunch of private homes and you come back to Marquette Park. To get home, I decided to ride past the park, and skip the steps again, 'cause carrying the bike up would be worse than carrying it down. I'd go back up to the East Bluff via Fort Street. Well, it's like, almost vertical there, but at least you can roll the bike up when you can't pedal anymore. It's quite a slog. Only slightly better, I suppose, than carrying a bike up 144 steps.

I started riding up the hill fast as I could, for momentum, but by the time I was opposite the governor's mansion, I felt like I was pedaling through cookie dough. Then it happened. I can close my eyes and see it all unfold:

A girl yells "Hey, Brooooklyn Boy" and I stop and get off my bike. I'm going so slow I'm having trouble balancing anyway. I look at her standing on the left side of the road. And a taller boy on the right. They both have dark hair. I'm curious. How could she know I'm from Brooklyn? She's dressed like an Indian, all tan chamois with fringed poncho, and I think she might be a girl I met a few days ago during a tour of the new school, where Mom told people we moved here from Brooklyn. Then a guy, shirtless, with a bow and arrow and red and white and black "war paint" all over his face and chest, comes from the right, but behind me, and pushes me down.

Robbie falls. "Hey" is all I can say as I fall, too, trip and try not to step on the spokes, concerned more about the bike than myself. Suddenly, he's got a knee on my back. The girl pulls a rope from under her poncho and ties my hands while he's saying "Ojibwa knot, Ojibwa knot" and is pressing his full weight on me, so I can hardly breathe.

This is really unfair because I could see he was taller and heavier than me, being, maybe, a few years older.

I stand up, even though it's hard to balance without free arms. I say, "Okay, Okay, Tonto. Let's smoke a peace pipe." I think maybe they've watched too much *Lone Ranger* as kids and if I just look unconcerned and play along they'll stop bullying me.

But my words seem to anger the big guy. Maybe they were real Indians and I offended them. He holds out his hand to the girl – this must have been planned because she hands him a cloth right handy. He grabs my wrists from the back with one big hand and stuffs the cloth in my mouth with his other. She then ties another cloth around my mouth, tight like, reaching my back teeth.

He lets go and looks at me, inches from my face, with a real mean expression, but kind of fake mean, you know. There's something about that face....

But I'll think about that later. "Hey," I say, in "no more mister-nice-guy" tone, "you scratch my bike and…" but I'm just getting the cloth sucked further in my mouth.

In a fake deep voice he says, "No one's going to heeaaar you." Out of rising fear and anger at the same time, I try to jerk myself away from him by wrenching my shoulders back and forth. This makes me lose my footing. I struggle to stabilize myself with a step back, but he uses my temporary imbalance to push me down again – this time I roll some ways down the steep street.

My hands aren't free so I can't break the initial fall. I try to land on my shoulder, but I fall hard and my forehead gets cut by something in the road – broken glass or sharp stone – and my shin hits a rock. They're running toward me so I stand up fast. All I can do with my hands tied behind my back is reach my back pockets.   I bend my right wrist and grab one of the fudge boxes sticking up out of my pocket – by weight, I think it's the one with the part eaten maple walnut and chocolate. I turn sideways and manage to fling it round my left side with a wrist motion like you're supposed to use with one of those new Frisbee things. It worked. I hit him in the chest. But it didn't do much good. He laughs; she war-whoops.

I grab the other, heavier, box with my left hand, bend my knees, and fling it hard, but on a higher trajectory. That works better. The corner of the box hits him right under the eye! He screams and puts his hands over his face. I know it's just dumb luck. You couldn't land a throw like that again in a million tries. But I'm grateful for dumb luck and I don't wait around.

I glance at my bike, but decide not to risk going up past them, so I take off running. The girl starts screeching and throwing stones, so I dash into the woods.

There's a path off the side of the road. It smells like a horse trail, so I follow it. Too late I see the pile of fresh horse poop. My right foot lands in it and slides out from under me like I'm on ice. I can't break my fall by putting my arms out because they're tied and I land on my other knee on a sharp stone, but I don't stop to worry about it. I get up fast and keep trying to run. Then I come out at a blacktopped road.

That's where I do the fast Kuryakin Maneuver and jump up and continue running.

I follow the road all the way to Skull Cave, running as fast as I can.

Well, that's how I got here. I didn't sense they were following, but thought, if they were up on their Indian heritage, maybe they were tracking me all quiet-like.

So I listened from the cave, heart pounding, chest going up and down. When I didn't hear anything for a few minutes, and had caught my breath,

I began to work on the rope that bound my hands. It was pretty simple really. Relax your wrists, it gets slack, wiggle it some. Ojibwa knot! They were idiots! I pulled the gag tie, now down around my neck, over the top of my head and used it to wipe the blood that wasn't dried yet. The bleeding seemed to have stopped anyway.

Again I listened. Nothing. My tennis shoes stunk with horse poop. Well, I didn't want to be fooled, so I continued to lay silent, even though I knew it was getting late and my mom would sure say something severe. She worries.

After another five or ten minutes, I rolled out and brushed myself off. But Robbie! I couldn't go back now. It was too late. I started off in a sort of limping walk-run towards Marblecliff, our "cottage."

Cottages – that's what the Mackinac Island people call the mansions on the high cliffs with great views, the bluffs. The West Bluff was on the other side of the Grand Hotel. Our East Bluff overlooked Marquette Park and the ferry docks and yacht slips. Marblecliff was in a row of about 20 houses on Huron Trail, any number of which could have been the setting for the movie *Psycho*. But ours was weirder still.

The siding was lilac and gray wood, four stories tall with an even higher turret. The second and third floors had awning-covered verandahs – yellow and orange striped. Then there was a round two-story orange stucco wing to the left, with an outdoor twisting staircase of stainless steel. To me, it looked like a huge jar of Tang punctured to the hilt by a sword.

I tramped up the road, trying to hide the limping as I came up our front steps to the main porch, under the first verandah. The screen doors were not modernized. They were wood and I knew they banged. I held them until they closed quietly. I knew I would have to get upstairs surreptitiously (another cool recent addition to my word collection) and clean up before my mom saw me. I took my smelly shoes off on the porch.

I came inside, into a living room the size of the Henry Ford Museum, with its gargantuan fireplace to the right, and Mom sitting on the green leather couch in front of the raised hearth, with a newspaper open.

She must have burned the equivalent of a full size oak tree in that fireplace in just two weeks. She loved that thing and would light fires even on warm summer evenings, even if she had to put on the air conditioner. I had mixed feelings about the fireplace. It was great to warm up by. You could use the hearth, which was about 10-12 inches high, as a seat. But it had a five-foot wide mouth that could probably dispose of bodies for any number of hit men from Detroit.

Looking left, from the hearth along the East wall, you could see clear through to the back of the dining room, past French doors into the screened back porch and outside. The porch was huge, too. It wrapped around the back of the house and along the side. Sure, it's lots of handy space compared to our old apartment in Cobble Hill, Brooklyn, which was sandwiched between others just like it, with no side windows, but what good is it? You could roller skate on the porch I suppose, but you can't be at a store in half a block's distance like in Cobble Hill. Here, if you run out of food, you can't just get more anytime. You have to plan to have everything you need in the house way in advance. And it's eerily quiet at night – at least past the bedtime of our summer neighbors, a family with lots of children and teenagers.

Spookiest, how do you get off the island in an emergency, after the ferries stop at 10 p.m.? Or worse, after the lake freezes in winter? I worried about those things. Because I certainly didn't plan on taking any flights.

Logs were crackling. "'Bout time," Mom said, not looking up from her newspaper. Would she be mad?

I had a choice. Face the music or delay and camouflage. I looked at the curving staircase to the far left of the dining room. Its steps are all triangle-shaped tiles of black and white and three shades of green, even the railing, so when you go up it feels like you're climbing the back of a giant anaconda.

Could I make it?

3 – MARBLECLIFF

I DASHED BEHIND THE the couch, grabbed the banister end post and used it to propel myself up, multiple stairs at once, narrowly missing Canaveral, one of my cats, sleeping on one of the pie-shaped stairs where the snake's back twists to the right.

At the top, I bolted for the bathroom and shut the door so fast it banged. Cronkite, my other cat, jumped off the counter into the bathtub. I didn't mean to bang the door, but it must have sounded intentional downstairs. I cringed and listened for yelling. Nothing. So I washed my face in the all-white marble sink, attached to a counter big enough to make fudge on. But it wasn't gray, it had the trademark Marblecliff tiles, various shades of green with white and black. "Reptile fudge," I thought, for no reason other than the image popped into my head. What flavor would that be? Pistachio vanilla lime mint chocolate?

Ow-wee! The cut hurt when I washed it, but it wasn't that deep. I'd seen worse. I got all the dried blood off my temple, ear and forehead.

Luckily, I wore bangs on the side with the cut. My trademark half-bangs. One day, when my mom was only half done trimming them – I'm like seven – I grabbed her wrist with my hand, like a lobster snaps his claw. I don't know what made me do it. I just decided to say "stop." She tried to continue, and insist she wasn't finished, and got exasperated, but the more she did, the more stubborn I got, until she gave up. I went around with half bangs and got teased for a few years. Now they're me. I was half Beatle before anyone saw the Beatles.

In luck. The cut was angled and completely hidden by the bangs. I tipped my head back, covered my eye, and drizzled peroxide on it. It stung a bit. The Mercurochrome Mom usually uses on me would have left an orange stain, so I skipped it. You never know when a mom is going to brush your hair aside and kiss your forehead.

I ripped off my socks and jumped up on the counter and put my feet in the sink. I rolled up my pant leg and looked at my shin that landed on the rock. I rinsed it off quickly and rolled my pant leg back down, jumped down and put my socks back on. My right forearm arm had a red mark and itched a little, but I didn't pay much attention to that. I brushed and smoothed my shirt. My pant leg over the knee was dirty and scraped, but that was nothing unusual.

I came back down and went to stand by the fire. Mom looked up over the top of the *Free Press*. "You're la…. Glad you're back," she smiled. Mrs. Kwashneetski's kept dinner warm for you."

Oh, good. She wasn't going to blow up because it was probably about 10 o'clock already. If this was Brooklyn she'd have had the entire 76th Precinct looking for me by now. I forgot: 'Nothing criminal ever happens on Mackinac Island.'

Deflect to the food. "What is it?" I ask, groan-like, feeling that the pertinent question really should be "How much fat is in it?" Mrs. K, who usually cooked for us, was fond of fat. There was nothing she knew how to cook that didn't include gobs of hot runny globules. I hate fat. My mom, however, has no objection to a modest amount of it. She says it's what makes the food taste good.

"Whitefish and kraut," she said. "It's good. And salad."

Good? What is this obsession with Whitefish ever since we got here? It's yucky. Their reasoning is, it's been swimming here, we're here, so we have to eat it here. I like the kraut if it isn't too greasy. Mrs. K fries it in Crisco. Tons of Crisco. And always salad. I think to myself: "You know, I wouldn't die if a day went by without salad."

I changed the subject. "What are you reading?" I limped over to the couch.

"Freya interviewed Mayor Cavanaugh," she responded thoughtfully, turning pages of the paper. "She did her best, but I couldn't read half his bullschloggen."

Freya Firestone was her friend from college who worked for the *Detroit Free Press.* Jerome Cavanaugh was the mayor of Detroit. The paper was opened to the editorial and op-ed pages. Some parents have *Family Circle* or Agatha Christie books around the house. My mom has op-ed pages.

"You should start looking at these," she said. "It wouldn't hurt you to read some Sydney Harris and Drew Pearson."

"I prefer Spider-Man." I said.

"Please," she said, "At least Superman works for a newspaper.." She started to look at me like she knew something.

"I fell off my bike on Fort Street," I blurted. "It's so steep, I..."

She held up her hand like a traffic cop. "Walter, sweetheart, you have to be more careful," she says in her reasonable tone. "You have to keep control of the bike. There may be no cars to worry about here, but you could just as well get run over by a carriage or trampled by a horse."

"Or wind from a flying saucer could knock me down," I say, flailing my arms.

I shouldn't have pressed my luck. Sarcasm never pays. It just turns her into General Patton:

"If it's too steep, walk it."

"Yes, Mom," I say.

She stood up and kissed me on the forehead, bang-less side. Then she looked down at my shirt.

"Lemme have that shirt, I'll wash it." She looked again at the shoulder, before moving to lift it off me. "What are those spots?"

Drat, it did get on my shirt. The shirt Ed White gave me! I looked at my shoulder, where she was looking. By this time the droplets had dried and they looked as much like Bosco as blood. That was good. I didn't want her to know I'd been in a fight.

"I dunno," I said. "Chocolate milk.... Do you think we could go back for my bike?

"What? Why didn't you bring it back?"

I had to think of a quick lie. "Well, when I fell off my leg hurt and I couldn't ride it."

"Why didn't you walk it?"

I was getting in deep.

"I ....c..couldn't."

She wasn't buying it. Moms always know. It was just like the time when I was in First Grade and I said I loaned my blue and orange New York Knicks basketball to some boys at school for the rest of the year. I loved that basketball, so she knew I wouldn't do that. She kept asking, "Why would you do that?" I was too scared to say. So she went flying in to the school next day to demand

Miss Schwede get to the bottom of it. They started an inquisition and found out those boys took it from me and threatened to beat me up if I told. Between my mom and Miss Schwede, those boys got more grief than they gave.

"Well," I ventured, "after I fell off it, there were some weird guys standing around and I was afraid to go get it from in front of them." – which wasn't too far from the truth, actually.

"Really? Walter," she says, "You're not in Brooklyn anymore. There aren't 'weird guys' here."

"SOooo can we go get it?" I asked.

"Heck no! It's too late," she says, in the tone she always uses to indicate something's impossible before agreeing to it. "Besides, nobody steals anything big as a bike on the island. And if they did, there's no way to get it off. They'd be caught at the ferry."

She looked at my face. "Put your shoes back on."

I ran to the front porch and banged the shoes a bit on the side of the steps to get off more of the poop that stuck in the grooves of the soles and then put them on. Mom came out while I was tying them.

"What happened to the fog?" she asked. I looked out toward the lake. Even concern for Robbie couldn't prevent a Mackinac night sky from diverting my attention. The fog blew away as fast as it blew in. Stars hung over the lake like remnants of sparkler bursts.

Mom sure had been right. On Mackinac you can see the stars. More than anywhere. They were brighter and there were more of them that I could ever have imagined. Oh sure, they show you as many at the planetarium. But it's not the same when you know they're not real.

It's very cool, don't get me wrong. I love planetariums. But you don't really believe you could actually see them that way. Then when you do see them, that many, that intense, you think, wow, it's really true. There are a bazillion stars. And that's just our galaxy. People used to think that's all there was until the 1920s or so when astronomer Edwin Hubble proved that the universe extended beyond the Milky Way galaxy. Now we know there are millions of galaxies.

"See? Your initial," Mom said. That's what she always calls Cassiopeia, the constellation that looks like a big W. "It's out earlier than a month ago. And there's the Big Dipper."

"Okay, let me find the North Star," I said. "Follow the the two stars that make the outside of the dipper pan from pan bottom to top and then – there it is

Mom."

"Right," she said. "And the North Star is the tip of the tail of the Little Dipper. See it?"

"Yes." I remembered the first night we were up north. It was about a month ago. I still couldn't believe it. We had just crossed the Mackinac Bridge into St. Ignace and Mom stopped the car.

"I thought we were going straight to the ferry," I said, waking up in the backseat.

"We can't," she said. "It's 1 a.m. The ferries stopped hours ago. We'll spend the night at the St. Ignace Inn. But, look. Here's what I promised you. Come and get out."

I unbuckled myself and crawled out of the backseat, still rubbing sleep from my eyes. We were parked by the water. "What's that?" I asked.

"The Straits of Mackinac," she said, "where Lake Huron and Lake Michigan meet. Now look," she said, pointing up.

The sky was filled with so many points of light. My jaw dropped so far down a pelican could have flown in it. It was my first sight of a night sky not obscured by lights.

I imagined a giant hockey skater had stopped sideways, like they do on Canadian TV, and a spray of ice crystals went up and populated the sky. Or some giant, chopping wood, made sparks with his ax and they shot up and caught on floating gauze – the Milky Way.

Which itself could have been a giant's smoke ring – that's our galaxy, M-36.

She grabbed my shoulders and faced me north, towards the island. To the right, about halfway up from the horizon was Cassiopeia. To my left, or northwest, was the Big Dipper. The Little Dipper was high above and there were dozens of other bright stars, amid lots of smaller ones.

She turned me east and there were five really bright stars. High above, Andromeda. And then four that make up the Great Square, and that helps you find Pegasus, the flying horse. Later I memorized them by thinking they spell SAAM. Scheat, Algenib, Alpheratz and Markab.

That night we just stared up. I must have said 'wow' over and over. She told me never to lose my awe of it. I pointed to a really bright star. "What's that one?" I asked.

"Not a star. I think that's Jupiter," she said. "Here's a hint. Stars twinkle, planets glow.”

After a minute, like she'd been thinking, she said: “Your Uncle Brian once had a telescope. We could see the craters of the moon right from our own backyard in Dearborn.”

“Does he still have it?” I asked.

“Nope,” she said. “He gave it away. I was so mad – he didn't ask me if I wanted it first. But if he could make one we could too. I read in *Sky and Telescope* magazine about making one.”

“Make one. Wow. Really? You can make your own telescope?”

“Sure. Well, we'll look into it,” she said. “So, okay, let's go. I just wanted to show you what I meant when I said from Mackinac Island you could see the stars.”

“We're not even on the island yet,” I said.

“Well, I don't think they get any better over there. It's just three miles across the straits.”

I didn't care. I was still looking up.

And after two weeks I was still staring at stars and constellations.

Then I came back to earth, now, and worries about my bike. We walked down Huron Trail and around the back of the fort and to Fort Street and down. I saw Robbie on the ground and ran like a parent runs to a fallen child. I picked it up and looked for scratches on the fenders and crossbar. The power pack was still on the carrier. The platypus was still tied on. but the skateboard was gone.

“My skateboard!” I said. “I thought you said nobody steals anything on Mackinac Island.”

“No place is perfect,” she said.

But I was mostly relieved. The skateboard was nothing compared to the bike. Mom put her arm around me and we walked back home without saying much. When she went inside the house, I took the bike into the shed, locked it despite the island's reputation, and started to walk back inside. On the porch I heard a little meow from the little orange kitten that's been hanging around. I looked down at it. It looked like mashed apricots in Maypo.

I went into the kitchen and poured a little bowl of milk and got some of Canaveral and Cronkite's leftovers from the fridge and took it all outside. I watched it gobble the food and it let me pet him before scampering under the porch.

By the time I got back in, Mom was in front of her typewriter in the library. Bookshelves went around the room from ceiling to floor. We brought lots of our own books, but the old ones were mostly my grandfather's. Only Mom pushed them back on the shelves in places so her rescued Teddy bears could sit in front of the books here and there. She liked to pick up orphaned Teddy bears, like from second-hand shops and garage sales, even peoples' trash, and give them a home or adopt them out. So the library was mostly books and bears, with an old oak rolling ladder around three fourths of the room. There was a desk at one end and an old blond-cabinet Dumont TV from the 50s and a saggy-cushioned two-seater couch at the other. Oh yeah – and Voltaire. There was a bust of the philosopher Voltaire on a tall pedestal table at the entry to the room.

But the desk was just about her favorite thing. It had been shipped from Brooklyn with our boxes and the cats! We only took my bunk bed, hand made by a Japanese carpenter from Park Slope (next neighborhood over from Cobble Hill), painted red and silver by me, our low, round dining room table with the marble square inset in the middle and the desk. It was Scandinavian and she bought it at Macy's last year. The top sort of floated on top of the drawers on one side and the other side had a low bookcase and the legs were recessed, too, so the bottom looked like it floated as well. Like a lot of our things, it didn't really match the Victorian house. She said that made our style "eclectic."

"Bike stowed away?" she asked.

"Yep, in the shed."

She had her typewriter on a lower table at right angles to the desk. She had been spending a lot of time there lately working on her Ph.D. dissertation. Before we left Brooklyn, I tried arguing that she should stay at Columbia University and finish it, but she said the research was done and she could do the writing anywhere. It was some study of science news reporting in regular daily newspapers. She'd been working on it for a couple years.

Nevertheless, I noticed the TV was on. She stopped typing to look at it. "I thought you always told me not to do homework and watch TV because it distracts you," I said with a bit of sarcasm. "So how can you work with the TV on?"

"Well, I wasn't paying attention a minute ago, but Walter Cronkite's got these two scientists on. It's a special show on extraaaaa....terrestrials." She stretched the word "extraterrestrials" making it sound like a Halloween joke, but then used her science voice. "That one guy from Cornell, his comment just before the commercial got my attention.”

“Ooooo Martians?” I said. I pushed the rolling ladder for fun, a Teddy bear that had been sitting on one of the steps fell down, and I plopped down on the couch while they were still singing about Lucky Strikes. “Walter Cronkite is talking about aliens?”

“Well, everyone's seeing UFOs these days,” Mom said, standing up and replacing the Teddy bear on his riser. “Remember all those sightings around Ann Arbor? You should listen to this guy from Cornell,” she said, pointing at the screen and joining me on the couch. The faces appeared. “He's been saying interesting things. Like the fact that many of the stars have planetary systems where life could have evolved naturally. But he doesn't think any extraterrestrials have come here.”

Walter Cronkite asked the guy, then, how do we explain the fact so many people say they're seeing UFOs?

“We live in unsettled times,” he answered. And I heard him say “It used to be ...”

Then Mom said: “He's really cute.” So I said:

“Mom! I want to hear this.”

The guy was saying – the name Dr. Carl Sagan was under his picture on the screen – that most people don't believe in a personal savior-like God anymore. That science has destroyed a lot of the traditional religious stuff.

“The flying saucer myths are really a clever compromise,” he said. That way, as he explained it, we can still have beings that come from the sky, that want to take care of us. And we feel good because they're going to prevent us from destroying ourselves, and yet it's still all under the “cloak of science.”

But it isn't really science. It really derives from religious hopes because the alien visitors are usually all-powerful and wear long white robes, so this Dr. Sagan said. Then Walter Cronkite repeated that there is no evidence anybody who may be out there has come here, and signed off the program. Mom sprang up and turned off the set.

“Why don’t you go upstairs and read?” she said “Although you might have to open a box to find some of your books first.”

She was being sarcastic now. After yelling at me to unpack my boxes didn't work, she moved on to sarcasm. What would be next? Reverse psychology? I wasn't going to bend for any of it because I had to convince her to move back to New York. Had to. There was more at stake than she knew. There were facts about my dad that I was promised and I wasn't going to get them staying here. I felt if I unpacked, it would mean I accepted the situation – and I would never see Brooklyn again. We were living with that stalemate. That didn't stop us from exchanging remarks about it – like she'd say "Go visit the cardboard decor in your room" and I'd say "Canaveral and Cronkite have to have somewhere to play mountain cougars" – stuff like that. There were 33 boxes stacked in two rows six-high, three rows four-high, and a couple two-high in front and a stack of five on the other side of the room. Except for a couple large boxes that contained board games and other long things, they were mostly boxes we gathered from the little grocery store near our apartment that originally contained six half-gallon size milk cartons each. I used a black Magic Marker to put a number on each box and made an inventory so in case I needed something I could find it.

As for the TV, the reason Mom's usually snapping it off is because she doesn't want me to see the news full of soldiers getting shot in Vietnam and stuff. That's silly because it's in the newspapers, too, and they're all around. I turned it back on "just for the weather." Grandpa's extra high super-duper antenna on the roof reached some far off TV stations. If I could last through five minutes of sports and commercials I might make it to "Here's Johnny…"

"Can I stay up and watch Johnny Carson? School won't be starting for a long time yet."

"No," she says, faster than the car behind you honks when the light turns green (which Johnny Carson once said is the only thing faster than the speed of light). "You don't need to get into staying up late. Besides, Uncle Brian and Aunt Yoshiko and the kids arrived. They'll want to do some things with you starting early tomorrow, I'm sure. It's probably their last trip up for the summer. Aunt Yoshiko really can't stand the smell of horse poop – and tries to keep their trips up here to a minimum."

I stood up.

"They're here…?" I asked slowly, with eyes widening appropriate to a news flash announcing a Martian invasion.

4 – TWO COUSINS

"YES, THEY'RE HERE," MOM said, like I should have known. "And it's good timing, too. I have to go to the State Democratic Conference at the Grand all day Saturday. So you'll have someone to keep you company."

I ran my index finger along the top of the reptile fudge-tiled mantle. Felt the depressions between the little triangles one by one…

"They got here about five," she said. "But you were nowhere to be found. I told them you were riding your bike somewhere."

"Probably too fast down Fort Street," she added, all snippy-parent like.

It became all too clear to me. Those bullies were no native kids from Harrisonville. They were my very own darling cousins, Jeffrey and Alyce!

Jeff's three years older than me, Alyce nearly two. Of course! With their half-Japanese coloring, they probably looked more like Fletch than me.

"Where are they now?" I asked.

"Well, I haven't seen them in hours," she said. "They're staying in the annex. I think they all went to bed early. You know it's a four hour drive from Lansing. And they always stop at antique shops on the way to accommodate your uncle Brian's never-ending pursuit of classic comic books."

"And for ice cream about five times if I know those two," I added. "No, that's me. But, anyway, kids don't get tired this early."

"They do if they've been traveling and out playing all day. I wouldn't try bothering them this time of night."

I smiled to myself. Did she think I'd want to?

The Annex. That's what my mom called the Art Deco wing. It was built onto the cottage by the second generation of our family that owned it.

The "cottage" was originally built in 1888 by my great-great-grandfather Theodore Hodiak, who came from the Ukraine and worked installing railroad ties. His latter years he spent in Chicago, as a crew boss for the Chessie Railroad and he bought stock in the company. He did quite well with that, and after a while built the house on Mackinac so his family, as the story goes, could vacation in the fresh air. They would come up on the Lake Michigan steamers for long summer stays.

His son, my great-grandfather, Nicholas Hodiak, stayed in the railroad business for a while, then he went and did something in California for a while, and then came back and lived in the cottage as sort of a hermit for 20 years. Nobody knows why.

He had two sons: Taras, and my grandpa, Wolodymyr, who I'm named after. (My grandmother Americanized it to "Walter" long before I was born. She got tired of hearing people call him "Watermelon.")

"Okay, I'm going upstairs to read that robot book you got me. It was in the suitcase." (I didn't want her to think I was opening boxes.)

"Oh, good," she said. She likes to hear I'm reading. She says that's why my vocabulary tests beyond 12th Grade level. "I'm going to read too, here by the fire," she said.

I climbed the winding stairs again, this time avoiding Canaveral by a wider margin. She was still curled up on the stair, blending into the tiled steps, being a tuxedo cat with lime green eyes.

In my room I saw an inanimate furry thing perched on top of the boxes.

"You found another homeless bear?" I yelled down. There was no answer.

This one was light brown, had a chipped gray nose that looked like a brachiopod and overall resembled Peter Lorre. "It's outta here," I said, tossing it down the stairs.

I picked up the *I, Robot* stories book, flopped on the orange leatherette scoop chair, startling Cronkite again, who was under it. I put my feet up on a stack of boxes. I opened the book to where the two "Mighty Mac" Mackinac Bridge postcards stuck out.

I was supposed to mail those to Doug and Frank back in Cobble Hill. I'll think of something to write tomorrow. Hmmmm. Maybe I should look for Skull Cave postcards. They won't believe I had to come to Mackinac Island to get mugged.

I started to read, but my mind soon wandered again and I was just staring out, punching holes in Box 28 with my pencil.

My Great Uncle Taras was a labor union leader, but had an artistic side. He did wood carving and oil painting. He loved the Art Deco style which he discovered in 1939 when he took my Great Aunt Olga on a transatlantic crossing on a big ocean liner called the S.S. Normandie. The ship had been decorated in this new streamlined, space-age looking fashion thought up by some artists in France, Mom told me. She said the ship launched the style.

That's why there's an Art Deco annex on the cottage. Mom says the check-in desk in the lobby of the Grand Hotel is Art Deco. I don't know. It just looks like plastic stuff to me.

Well, even though Grandpa Walt objected to violating the original style, he and Great Uncle Taras inherited the cottage jointly and Grandpa Walt couldn't stop Taras adding the Art Deco wing.

Mom says she'd like to have seen how her uncle got approval for it from the island's planning commission, which normally requires builders to conform to the early developers' Victorian or Edwardian style.

Great Uncle Taras and Grandpa Walt were rivals in other ways. Walt got to go to college with his brother's financial help, so it became university learning versus street smarts.

Canaveral came in and climbed the boxes, then took a leap onto my lap.

As I petted her and she purred I kept thinking about my family's past. Grampa Walt became well known in the newspaper business. He was an editor at the *Detroit Free Press* for a while, then went back to Michigan State University to teach. He never made as much money as his brother did as a leader of the United Automobile Workers union, but by then the house on Mackinac was paid for and worth a lot. Walt mortgaged his half to start a newspaper on the island.

It became the *Huron Shores Herald*. Mom said her father always "told the truth to power" and wrote for the people. He taught his students to do the same. That's the main reason she didn't want the newspaper to fold.

Earlier, Mom wanted to follow in her dad's footsteps – in a way. She studied journalism at Michigan State University, but intended to specialize in science news. After World War II and the Manhattan Project, science was all the rage, she said. She studied biology, microbiology, physics, astronomy, and geology as well as the other stuff. And she joined the *State News*, the MSU student newspaper where the campus editor, Freya Firestone, assigned her to as many science-related stories as possible. At MSU that usually meant covering agricultural research and 4-H club shows at the stadium. Nevertheless, Mom and Freya became best friends.

Freya would have made a good editor-in-chief for the *State News*, Mom said, but that position never went to a female. It's 1966 and it still hasn't.

After graduation, Freya went to work for the *Free Press,* but Mom wanted to see new places. She went to Columbia University in New York City for her master's degree.

She said she liked the excitement of the big city. So why can't she understand that I do, too? Anyway, the war, World War II, opened up jobs to women that had traditionally gone only to men. Women worked in the factories making planes and tanks, and flew the new planes to where the men in combat needed them. Mom found she could finally cover real news instead of women's pages stuff. Front page news, like the first use of the polio vaccine and the discovery of DNA, like that.

It was there in New York that she met my father. He was a professor at Columbia University and a science writer for *Scientific Digest*. He was somewhat older and not, she said, in danger of being drafted into the Army. They settled in Brooklyn, where I was born.

I thought about how little I remembered about him. Most of what I knew was just told to me. My mom said he often traveled on assignments. I know he interviewed Albert Einstein once and people like Dr. Robert Oppenheimer. Then when I was about six, he went to New Zealand for an article on high altitude work or something like that. There was a ferry accident between the north and south islands – in Cook Strait they said. My mom says she doesn't know exactly what happened.

But I think somebody does. This guy I met, an archaeologist who works at the Natural History Museum in New York, told me he knew my father. He asked how old I was and when I said 11, he laughed and said "Well, come back and see me when you're older and I'll tell you a few things about your dad."   I asked him if he meant that and he said "yes."   His name is Dr. Parker Ripley and he said he's from Edinburgh, Scotland.

I closed the book, not even bothering to put the postcards back in. Canaveral jumped away as I stood up to go to the bed. I laid down on my back, looking at the ceiling. The Straits of Mackinac, Cook Strait. I looked up "Strait" in the dictionary. It just means a body of water linking two other larger bodies of water. In New Zealand, Cook Strait links the Pacific Ocean and the Tasman Sea. Here, a series of narrow waterways, the Mackinac Straits, join Lake Huron and Lake Michigan.

Canaveral curled up behind my back. She started to purr like she always did when she cuddled. Cronkite, the brown tabby, didn't like to be petted as much. I mean, you could pet his head, but if you stroked too far down he'd nip. Usually he was nowhere to be seen, but he'd always turn up in the kitchen begging food and Mrs. Kwashneetski would always say "shoo, shoo" and "no!" and swat at him with a dish towel, then break down in less than half a minute and give him little bites of pork chop or whatever she had. Cronkite will eat anything, while Canaveral will act insulted if you offer her human food.

For some reason Mom never took my dad's last name—Mangoustino. Maybe because it was too long or hard to pronounce. But she didn't keep her own, either.

It was part of the rivalry she had with Freya. Freya always bragged that "Freya Firestone" was a great by-line name. Mom would say, "It's not the by-line, Freya, it's what you put under it," but that didn't stop her from wanting a great one too. At least she turned Hodiak into Hudson, saying it sounded better.

While "by Freya Firestone" has been in the *Detroit Free Press* for years, "Alexis Hailey Hudson" has been a byline in many New York papers, the *Herald-Tribune*, the *Journal-American* – even the *New York Times* – and assorted magazines. And I guess Walter Hudson is better than Walter Hodiak would have been, although some people ask me if I'm related to the department store guy, J. L. There was a movie star in the 1940s by the name of John Hodiak, but I don't know if there's any relation. All I know is he was from Detroit and starred in three movies with Clark Gable and his father's name was Walter.

Mom interrupted my thoughts. "Don't fall asleep without brushing your teeth. And do it now because you want to get to sleep early enough not to be tired tomorrow," she said softly, peeking round my door. "I know Jeffrey and Alyce are excited about going to the Marquette Park Games with you."

If your eyes could get stuck in the back of your head when you roll them too far, mine would still be back there.

I got up grumbling to go brush my teeth.

She continued, following me. "Jeff's brought his Frisbee and I know Alyce wants to enter the hula hoop contest."

"Hula hoop? Nobody does that anymore, Mom."

"You want to get together with them, don't you?"

"Sure, Mom," I said, between clenched teeth, as she she disappeared down the hall. "Just like the crickets like to get together with Doug's lizard."

I finished, rinsed my mouth, and came back and got into pajamas. Canaveral jumped in front of me. I rested on my left elbow, holding the robot book open with that hand, and petted her head with my right hand. I noticed she'd lost a little patch of fur on the top of her head. "You being attacked on this darn island, too?" I asked.

My thoughts moved to food. I sure wished I had that fudge back. I sighed, looked over to the book again, read, and petted. But my mind soon wandered to the evil cousins.

I'll tell you one thing. Jerk Jeffrey and Aggravating Alyce would not be attacking me on Henry Street where we used to live, or any other street near my old neighborhood. It just doesn't happen. For one thing, it's an Italian neighborhood and there's no messing around with people. Cousins! And my friends would have been with me, anyway.

Doug Mocha and Frank Angelino. Geez, I wonder what Doug and Frank did today. They probably played baseball in Carroll Park. I would have loved that. I watched Mickey Mouse Club reruns and got beaten up.

This island has ruined my life.

Why are we here? When Dad didn't return, Grandpa asked Mom to come and work on the island, but for the past five years she always said "no way." We lived, just the two of us, in Brooklyn and it suited me fine. Now Grandpa died and she suddenly got excited to come here and keep the paper going – this dinky no-wheres-ville paper. Why?

I like the bigness of New York City. There's always stuff going on and you can have every kind of everything. And there's the museum and, yeah, the planetarium, too. Even though I like seeing the stars for real, I was learning about the stars and solar systems and galaxies at the planetarium. Maybe I will be an astronaut and maybe not. But I'll be one of those people who find out about space and help us get there. Get to Mars. After the moon, and that'll be this decade. President Kennedy said so. Mars'll be a cinch by 1985 or so.

I suddenly thought of the homeless kitten outside and went downstairs. Mom was asleep on the couch. I put a blanket on her and went out quietly, careful not to bang the screen door. The wooden porch was cold on my bare feet. The kitten was there, hiding under a lilac bush. "I guess you really don't have a home," I said as I picked it up.

I took it to the kitchen for more leftovers. When I took it onto the back screened porch Mom was standing behind me with her hands on her hips. I looked up at her and didn't have to say a thing.

"Well, if you name it Sevareid," she said groggily.

I started back upstairs and turned. Why not "Eric"? Why not "Analysis?" Or "B-Quiet" as in "Be quiet, I want to hear Eric Sevaried's analysis?" He's a CBS commentator Mom likes. He mostly explains what's going on with the Vietnam War and stuff. Mom always wants to hear him when he's on. But why can't it be Bergman? As in Jules. Jules Bergman explains the space launches. Jules, I like that.

I went back to the kitchen for a couple Pecan Sandies, remembered I had brushed my teeth, and went back upstairs without them. I picked up the book again, but my thoughts drifted. It was sad Grandpa Walt died last year. He left the cottage and the newspaper to both Mom and her brother. Uncle Brian's a professor at Michigan State University, in the Economics Department. That's where they put labor and industrial relations, his specialty. He said he had no interest in the paper, she could have it, but she'd "probably run it into the ground." He said just being a good journalist, that she might be, had nothing to do with running a newspaper, that it was a business and "women know nothing about running a business or handling money." To which Mom said "because their husbands don't let them" and "he was the worst of the lot, with a Japanese wife who he treats like a servant.....or....or... a door mat." They don't usually pull punches with each other.

In a way she's right. Aunt Yoshiko really wanted to name Alyce "Akiko."

Uncle Brian was in the Army after WWII, and, while stationed on Okinawa, he met Yoshiko and later brought her to the states, where they got married. They live in East Lansing, where his hobby is collecting old comic books. Doug's dad likes model trains. He has an awesome set-up of cars, rails, and bridges in their basement.

Aunt Yoshiko does clothing alterations for Jacobsons, a ritzy store on Grand River Avenue in East Lansing. When she had just arrived in this country and didn't speak much English, Mom was going to speak for her at the job interview. Then it turned out the boss was Japanese, too. I guess all Japanese girls learn how to sew really well. My uncle's family comes up to the Island several times each summer to use the cottage, despite the fact Aunt Yoshiko really – really – can't stand the smell of horse poop.

It was Mom's idea they take the annex.

To which Uncle Brian said it was "the more tasteful" wing anyway. The kids liked the modern shower with the glass door with fish etched into the glass. So "that's the way it is," as Walter Cronkite would say.

The kids – my evil cousins. I had only three days. I took one postcard in my hand and imagined the words "murder, mayhem and misery" in the voice of Ed McMahon. I put the card up to my forehead like Johnny Carson doing Karnak the Magnificent, who came up with funny questions to go with off-the-wall answers he was given by Ed. I imagined Ed saying, "Murder, mayhem and misery...."

I smiled: "What do I want to happen to Jeffrey and Alyce?"

5 – SEEKING REVENGE

FLETCH ASKED ME BASICALLY the same thing later the next day. After I told him the whole story about the bike ride, the attack, the fudge throw, running away, sliding on horse poop, and hiding in the cave. I even told him about the Kuryakin manuever.

Of course he knew exactly what Illya move I was talking about. He even named what *Man from U.N.C.L.E.* episode it was from. *"The Virtue Affair,"* he said. "Illya was being chased by these guys with bows and arrows."

"You remember the names of all the episodes?" I asked incredulously.

"Almost," he said. "I write them down. But that one was particularly memorable because of the bows and arrows. You know, my name is the name for someone who puts the feathers on arrows."

"I didn't know that," I said.

"Yeah, that's what Fletcher means. It's quite an exacting occupation. The feathers have to be exactly evenly spaced or the arrow won't fly right."

"Naturally, you're into archery," I said.

"Not really," he said. "I started to practice with this little bow and arrow set I got when I was seven, but then I shot my sister Ayashe in the foot and they took it away from me. They said I couldn't be trusted with..."

"You shot her in the foot?"

"Well, she was always following me around."

"How old was she?"

"She's three years younger than me."

I thought for a few seconds. "She was only four years old and you shot her?"

"Well they weren't really, really pointy arrows, you know."

"I see. So she's eight now. Does she still follow you around."

"More than ever."

"Remind me not to look to you for solutions," I said.

We sat and thought in silence for a bit. Then I hit my palm with my fist and said: "To the Moon, Alice!" like Jackie Gleason always does on the *Honeymooners*.

~~~

Saturday arrived and with it the "Games." When I left the house Mom was out front trying to console a little girl who had fallen off her bike. She asked the girl if she'd like to come in and pick out a Teddy bear.

I met Fletch at Marquette Park. We did a lot of dumb arranged gym-like things like long jump and high jump and tug-of-war. I avoided Jeffrey and Alyce as much as possible, but I got close enough to Jeffrey once to see that he had a little purple and black bruise under one eye.

Fletch and I rode off early on our bikes when Ayashe wasn't looking. He had a Schwinn. His eyes got really big when he first saw my bike. He said he never saw anything like it and thought it was "way cool" and "like so space-age, man." So I was ready to be friends with him.

Only he said he prefers to ride horses. Horses! The idea makes me shudder. Horses are huge! Like 2,000 pounds-each huge. I once knew a kid who went riding in Prospect Park in Brooklyn and fell off the back end of the horse, landing right on his butt. He had to wear a back brace for nearly a year. It was white plastic and went all around his body. We called him the Abominable Horseman. I guess if you grow up with them, horses, like Fletcher did, you get used to it. His dad's job is to take care of the Grand Hotel's carriage horses, Carriage Taxis & Tours' horses and some of the horses people board there. Fletch sometimes exercises the boarded horses if their owners haven't been riding them. He's been around horses a lot. I wouldn't ride one anymore than I would fly.

We stopped in Marquette Park, overlooking some of the docks. We sat on the steps of the broad pedestal below the huge blackened bronze statue of Father Marquette at the center of the park. Marquette stands in long dress and cape – typically with a pigeon on his head. He's staring at the bay like he's looking for the next ferry to arrive. I'm told that really he's depicted as he was discovering Wisconsin or something about 300 years ago. That must have been tough and scary back then, but the white pigeon droppings on the dark stone seem to take a
~~~

little of the solemnity away, seriously. Then we walked up the steps to the monument, sat back against its concrete platform and surveyed the park in silence.

I watched little kids playing. Dropping balls, running. A kid ran away from his Mom and then she squatted down and put her arms out and he came running back into her arms and she hugged him. It reminded me of when Mom used to do that with me when I ran around Carroll Park in Cobble Hill. One time I ran towards her open arms and then at the last second veered off. Mom ran after me and scooped me up. "I Grinched you!" I said, and she laughed and kissed me.

The Christmas before – I was two then – I got the book *The Grinch Who Stole Christmas*. It was my favorite book. Well, no, my favorite book was *The Sailor Dog,* but it doesn't matter. I loved the Grinch. So I invented "Grinched" as a verb. That was the first time I said it – when I ran away from her hug.

My thoughts returned to the present.

"The real question, Fletch," I said, "is not what I want to do – which is cause them pain – but how?"

My mom was always telling me everything, in newspaper reporting and life, comes down to the 5 W's and H – Who? What? When? Where? Why? and How?

I think she said the idea came from some Rudyard Kipling poem about his servants. I don't get it, but, anyway, I knew the *Who*: Jeffrey and Alyce. The *What* was pain. *Why?* Because they abused and scared me. That's why. And, because of it, I lost my skateboard. *When* had to be in the next three days. *Where* was optional. *How* was, indeed, the only question that remained unanswered.

Fletch, who was starting to seem like a real friend, since he helped me avoid the dangerous duo earlier in Marquette Park, stroked his chin. "There's always chewing gum in the hair – that's good for girls!"

"Yeah," I said, steepling my fingers and putting the thumbs between my teeth.

"Earth worms in the bed?"

"My mom would kill me."

"Silly Putty in a sandwich?"

"No opportunity. Mrs. Kwashneetski makes the lunches."

"Little colored soap balls – you tell 'em it's candy. I always liked that one.”

"They'd taste it and spit it out.”

"Not before the soap gets embedded in their molars – trust me, it lasts for days.”

I sighed and scratched my arm.

I think this is a question for MontesQ,” he said.

“What?”

“Who.”

I looked perplexed. “MontesQ is a ‘who’,” Fletcher said.

“I'll have to introduce you,” he said. “He's this guy who lives in the Grand Hotel. He's a certified genius.”

“And he lives in the Grand Hotel?”

“Yep. Up on the fourth floor. He's been there for 16 years.”

“Sounds like he's in a rut. Every summer?”

“Nope, every day, 365 days a year.”

“Go on. Nobody stays at the Grand Hotel 365 days a year. At those room rates. I think my mom said they're $150 a day – that's why the hotel can put nice big expensive ads in her newspaper.”

“Well, all I know is, he rents an executive suite. Permanently.”

“What does he do in the winter, cross country ski the state park?”

“Never leaves the building.”

“I thought the Grand closed in the winter.”

“There's always a skeleton staff to look after the place. And MontesQ doesn't leave. Never ever.”

“Fletch, that can't be true.”

“It is,” he said. “MontesQ – he spells it M-o-n-t-e-s- capital Q. I think his real name is Archibald something, but he took the name MontesQ for himself after the great French philosopher Montesquieu. That was way back when he was about 20-something years old. He came here for a big anthropology conference in 1950. He was giving the keynote speech on mass behavior of primates or something like that, looked around the big Grand dining room and collapsed.”

“Before or after the speech?”

“After. But then he was taken to his room – executive suite actually. He's been there ever since.”

“Funny it didn't happen to Mark Twain when he spoke there.” I muttered.

Then I looked up. "No way. Sixteen years!"

"Absolutely true. I got the whole story from Tenacity Jones who's worked at the hotel the whole time. He was just the doorman then. Now he's the concierge."

"What is a con-see-air-ge?" I ask, feeling annoyed he knows a word I don't.

"I thought you said your vocabulary was 'off the scale.' It's a person in charge of extra special services for guests. Tenacity calls for carriages when they want one, gets them ferry tickets, or riding lessons, or sends their clothes to be pressed."

"You mean he's a go-fer."

"Not exactly. Because the hotel pays him a lot of money to do it. Only they don't have to pay him to work for MontesQ. He's just personally very dedicated to him. He admires his genius. He'd do anything for him. He looks out for him."

"Doesn't this MontesQ have any family? Why didn't they take him home if he was sick?"

"He only has a brother. This brother's a doctor in Minneapolis. When MontesQ refused to leave the room his brother said he was faking it for publicity and hasn't talked to him since. His friends just call it agoraphobia."

"What?"

"Ag-or-a-phobia. It's what he's got. Means you fear going outside, being in crowds stuff like that."

"Geez. How can you be a genius and fear just going outside?"

"Genius doesn't have anything to do with being a normal person," Fletch said. "Often quite the contrary. Geniuses, they're often self-absorbed and don't have good everyday manners and such.

"You mean they're narcissists."

Fletch looked at me. "Okay, one for you. But two for me."

"So why do you like him?" I asked, changing the subject from vocabulary jousting.

"Well, a genius is smart for one thing, so you can learn stuff. And often they have other traits that make up for the ones they lack. Like MontesQ seems to be a good friend. He'll do anything he can for you – if he likes you."

Then I thought. Agoraphobia. Maybe that makes sense. Maybe it's even smart. It's a dangerous world out there. Even on Mackinac Island. But I just said:

"What happens if you do, if you have that Ag-gor-a thing, if you do, go out, I mean?"

"Panic attack. Some people pass out and die."

"Geez. "

"How do you get it?"

"No one knows. Anyway, with no family to go home to, he just stayed there. He has visitors. Lots of visitors. Anybody important who comes to the Grand. Sometimes real important people like scientists and professors and authors come just to see him. Isaac Asimov came once."

"No kidding?   Did I ever show you Asimov's 1964 predictions for the year 2014?"

"No."

"Remind me to. He really came here, Isaac Asimov?"

"Yep. MontesQ never goes to them."

"How can he afford it? An executive suite at the Grand? If he doesn't go out and work…."

"Well, he got some big science prize for ideas he comes up with. They give you lots of money for that. He used up a lot of his money on doctors and medical tests and stuff, but then he wrote a book. That was after he had his scientific research books shipped in and did a lot of reading and, they say, drove several reference librarians crazy with questions. Then he thought up a lot of stuff to write. The book is called *The Devil's Doctrine*. Heard of that?"

"Never heard of it. And My mother always has the *New York Times Book Review* around."

"It was an international best seller about ten years ago…"

"Well, gee. I was almost two then."

"But it's still in print and still sells lots of copies. Only mostly it's college students and smart people who know about it. It doesn't sell like *Valley of the Dolls* or *Sex and the Single Girl* or anything."

"Do you have THAT book?"

"NO!"

"What's it about?"

"There isn't any sex in it. The title's a big cheat. It's all about make-up and hair-styles and exercise."

"Oh," I said, feeling a little disappointed. "How about MontesQ's book."

"No sex."

"I mean do you have it?"

"I don't have sex!"

"The book, dodo. Do you have it?"

"Sure I have it. I have an autographed copy. It tells us why humans are violent and why they make war and what to do about it."

"Well," I said, "If so many people read it, why do we have this little thing called the Vietnam War going on?"

"He tells us that, too. We evolved that way. It's in our nature. It's hard to fix."

"I can see that. Boys going from trikes to Little League to graduation ceremonies to flag-draped coffins. Mom had a picture editorial like that last week – when the latest war statistics came out," I said. "That was really sad. But have you actually read it—his book? I mean, personally?"

"Yep. It's easy to read. He designed it that way, so anybody could read it. You don't have to be a scientist or anything. You should read it. Go to the library and ask for *The Devil's Doctrine* by MontesQ. The librarian, Miss Suzy, will have it. If enough kids our age read it, maybe we can design a peaceful future."

"So why should I go see him?"

"Because he could help. He's not just an anthropologist. He's, like, memorized all of human knowledge that's all. If you've ever heard the term 'walking encyclopedia...'"

"EN-C-YC-LO-PEDIA," I said, in the sing-song way I learned from Jiminy Cricket on the Mickey Mouse Club.

"Yeah, only he really knows it. Sometimes he goes on the radio – WJR brings the broadcast stuff right up to his room. People call in but they can never stump him with questions. He knows everything, believe me. History, science, everything. If there's something he doesn't know, he hasn't been asked it yet."

"He should go on that quiz show-the Six Thousand Dollar Question."

"Sixty-four. Sixty-four thousand."

"Whichever."

"He can't GO anywhere. Besides, fraud."

"MontesQ?

"No. The Sixty-four Thousand Dollar Question!"

"Yeah?"

"A man cheated. He had the answers in advance. And then that Dr. Joyce Brothers. No one knows about her. She was the only woman to ever win."

"That's proof it was cheating. If a woman won."

"Especially since she answered questions about boxing."

"Maybe she just studied up. Maybe that's how this MontesQ does it."

"How?"

"People look things up for him in the encyclopedia."

"He *is* the encyclopedia. No one could give him answers fast enough. Besides, I see him for real, talking to real people. Answering questions on the radio. Questions he couldn't know in advance."

"Well, let's see if he has the "R" volume in his head."

"What?"

"R for Revenge," I said. "Do you have to call in for an appointment?"

"Not usually. I just go up there. When he allows visitors. About four o'clock in the afternoon."

6 – MEETING MONTESQ

I WAS READY TO go see this strange MontesQ guy right away, but Fletcher said it wasn't time yet. He decided to show me what it's like to ride a bike down British Landing Road. Ayashe, who had caught up with us on Market Street, followed us past Fort Street, but we made a quick U-turn and went up Fort. We really pushed it going up hill, alternately riding and walking our bikes. She couldn't keep up. Yeah, we were being mean to her, I guess, from her perspective. But we didn't always have to have a little girl tagging along, did we?

She gave up. We saw her, down below, a little forlorn thing, really, turning her back and returning to the park. I felt bad for her for a minute, 'til the prospect of meeting this genius guy occupied my thoughts. If I couldn't meet Wernher von Braun, it might be the next best thing. We hooked up with Garrison Road out behind the fort and went left. We passed Skull Cave, and rode between St. Anne's Cemetery and lots of horse trails. We didn't stop until we got to Four Corners. That's where you can see the Mackinac Island Airport to the left, but where Garrison turns into this infamous British Landing Road. Fletch pointed to a plane on the runway.

"That's Mrs. Hart's plane," he said.

"How do you know?" I asked.

"'Cause she keeps a couple horses in the stables where my dad works – rents the space from Carriage Taxis & Tours. She likes the way my dad takes care of the horses. Well, once she flew him out East to take care of The Senator, one of their horses. She flew him there in that plane."

"Your dad didn't mind flying with a woman pilot?"

"No. She must be a good pilot. She flies Senator Hart to all his campaign stops and back and forth to Washington in the summer."

"Really?" I said, looking skeptical.

"Haven't you ever heard of Amelia Earhart?" he asked, sounding kind of exasperated with me.

"Sure," I said. "Everybody's heard of Amelia Earhart. But she didn't come back. Makes my point. Her plane went down over the Atlantic Ocean. Bermuda Triangle wasn't it?"

He tipped his head and looked pityingly at me. "It was the Pacific, dodo, and her plane was probably shot down because she was on a spying mission."

"How do you know it wasn't the Atlantic?"

"Because when they talk about she was maybe spying on the Japanese, where would you find them?"

"Oh," I said, humbled.

Fletch got back on his bike and I followed. He turned onto British Landing Road, then stopped again, opposite the Wawashkamo Golf Course on the right and a historical marker on the left that commemorates a battlefield of 1814.

"Here's where it starts to get steep," he said. "I like to coast down fast. We won't be able to stay together. Just don't go too fast or you'll wipe out. And never try it on a horse."

"No worry about that, Fletch," I said facetiously, but I don't think he got my meaning. He went out ahead and I yelled after him: "Horses are huge, Fletch, HUGE. What if you fell off and the horse trampled you or, worse, fell on you?"

"That doesn't usually happen," he yelled back, then stopped to let me catch up. "I'm an experienced rider. I know how to manage a horse. *You* might fall off if you tried to ride one down British Landing Road, though. The horse will know it's too steep and might start going side to side, or stop suddenly and put his neck down and you'd fly off over his head."

"I'll file that," I said, "for when I ride a horse." I could hear my mother in my head: "Keep your bike under control." But I wanted a fun ride. But I didn't want to scratch the bike. I was torn. Did ambivalent apply here? Or was it schizophrenic?

I let Fletch continue on ahead. Then I let it roll. In seconds the wind was hitting my face like when you stick your head out a car window on I-75. The speed increasing rapidly as you went down. Down was a real happening. Your stomach feels like it does when you're in the fast elevator at Macy's, when it's stopping – but over and over again. How much speed would I pick up? I knew I would have to start braking soon.

I thought of Ed White and the too-short space walk. I didn't want to slow down, but my inner Mission Control ordered me to brake.

But the road was still downhill. The bike picked up real speed again. It was like it had a mind of its own. I could feel the wind blowing my bangs totally off my forehead. It was a real "whoopee" ride.

Too soon I saw the intersection with Lake Shore Road coming up fast ahead of me. Left and right on the road was visible and I couldn't see anyone coming either way, so I let her rip right across the road, whizzing past Fletch, and going bumpety-bump on stones until I hit the lake and fell off the bike as it plunged into the water.

Fletch had his hands on his hips, standing by the historical marker, looking at me.

"Wow, that *is* cool," I said, sitting in the water. Fletch waded in and extended a hand.

"Well, I've never seen anyone land in the lake before. You've got style."

"I didn't plan on it!" I grabbed the bike up and hoped I got it before water could seep into the radio.

"Don't admit that," Fletch said. "It takes away from it."

"Okay... Give me your shirt."

I wiped the bike dry with Fletch's T-shirt.

He put it back on after a disgusted look, then we turned left and rode Lake Shore Road to the south, then east. Fletch leaned toward my bike. "This is about the time MontesQ'll accept visitors," he said. "He keeps to a very strict schedule. He always sleeps, eats, and works at the same time. At 4 p.m. he'll see people for about an hour. Then he answers letters or calls people back on the phone."

We turned up at that Devil's Kitchen landmark and made our way through to Grand Avenue and followed West Bluff Road to the front of the hotel. We parked our bikes by the hotel's outdoor central staircase, where the six foot-wide red carpet begins, a level under the porch. The wind had dried me. We got a wave-in from Tenacity Jones as he was giving directions to some other guests, but he pointed at Fletch's shirt with squinty eyes. He was a tanned, stocky guy who never stopped moving, which was exceptional for someone with a job that entailed standing at his post a lot. He had a smile like a Moon Pie. He didn't stop talking to guests while he gestured to us, a thumb aimed in. He was accustomed to Fletcher's visits by now and they were busy. Guests were just finishing High Tea in the Grand's formal lounge. We lowered our voices. A pianist was tinkling out some quiet tune and people were telling each other where they went that day.

Not everyone can get into the Grand Hotel – or even onto the porch. If you don't look dressed well enough, say, they might turn you away. But that's if you approach it the usual way, from Cadotte Avenue, the second to last turn off Market Street. If you come up from the gardens, like we were, you're an assumed guest. If you're not dressed up, they just assume you've been on the tennis courts or playing bocce or just coming from the pool.

There was also a rule that after 5 p.m., ladies have to be dressed in dresses, no slacks, and men in formal wear. But it was only approaching 4 p.m. And, besides, we were kids.

We took the elevator up to the fourth floor and Fletch pointed the direction toward MontesQ's room, past the stairs to the center cupola.

We knocked. This MontesQ guy flung the door open in stride and kept walking. He was a small man, pale, thin, no more than five feet-six or five-seven, wearing headphones, a white terry-cloth bathrobe cinched around the waist with a 4-inch wide brown leather belt, and white socks. No shoes. Hanging off the belt were some gizmos I didn't recognize, but hanging on a strap from his shoulder was what appeared to be a reel-to-reel tape recorder.

"Hi Fletch," he said. "Still doing my exercises, but come in. I have to keep walking. I'm on 168."

We sat on wood folding chairs on the opposite side of a king-size bed. Fletch bent close and said he does 200 laps around the suite everyday. As a confidential aside, he said: "A man who can't go out and do normal things has to keep his body in shape."

I watched. MontesQ looked like a cross between Barney Fife and a sock puppet.

"Is he recording us?" I asked.

"No, he's probably listening to some scientific journal. Tenacity sent him this Ojibwa woman who couldn't walk – I know her. She lives near us. Her name's Molly. She couldn't get any other type of work, see – and he sends her books and articles every week and she reads them onto tape. Then he listens to them while doing other things. He's always taking in information."

I raised my eyebrows. This *was* weird.

MontesQ walked as briskly as a man rushing to the subway just before 9 a.m. when he had to be at work at 8:30, circling the bedroom and the adjacent sitting room in a figure eight formation. Both rooms were cluttered with books, magazines, newspapers, and assorted dirty dishes on trays, and piles of clothes.

MontesQ's hair was the color of roasted cashews. Although it was crunched down on top by the headphones, many of its deep coils had escaped this way and that, as if they didn't want to stay in their own sprockets, like semi-coiled pipe cleaners.

When he got to 200 laps he still had pushups to do. I used the time to look around the room. There were stacks of reading matter. The *Journal of the American Medical Association* and something called *Lancet. Scientific American* and *National Geographic.* Psychology, anthropology, history, sociology, art, music, theology, biology, geology and every other "ology" you could imagine were represented, too. Some books were propping up the terrarium that, if I wasn't mistaken, held an ant-farm.

The typewriter was impressive, an IBM Selectric, extended over the bed on a wheeled table like one of those they use for meals in hospitals. All over the room were papers, envelopes, manila folders, typewriter ribbons, and carbon paper, along with a few elephant ear plants. It was cluttered. It was chaos.

I looked away, out the window. That was a contrast in calm. The view was the same panorama as the one I'd seen from the West Bluff when Mom took me to see the hotel the first time. It's basically the Straits with the Mackinac Bridge as the focal point.

Between the hotel and the bridge I saw a westward moving freighter gliding on the water, with containers on deck that looked like detached rail cars. It was probably heading for the locks at Sault Saint Marie.

Looking down one sees the formal Grand Hotel grounds. Mom told me those bushes trimmed to look like horses and ducks and stuff are called topiaries. Flowers were still in bloom. The gardeners cleverly plant flowers so there are some blooming in spring, summer and fall, she said. I saw a family playing bocce, down front, just below the red carpeted steps, where the horse-drawn carriages stop. And people were still using the big dog-bone shaped pool off to the right. There were the white cabin dressing rooms and below that, tennis courts.

I turned my attention back to the room. MontesQ was now doing push ups. He stopped at 38.

"Ah, well, two more tomorrow," he said. Then he used a towel, one end in each hand, and moved it right and left behind his back 25 times. Then he flopped on the king size bed and looked at one of the gadgets on his belt.

I must have looked curious because he said: "Pedometer. Records how far I walk each day."

I didn't ask why. He said:

"What can I do for you today, Fletch? Who's your friend?"

He had a large nose and a voice that boomed.

"This is Walter Hudson," Fletch said. "He just moved to the island. His mom inherited the *Huron Shores Herald*. Now she's the editor and publisher."

"What's her name?" he asked me.

"Alexis Hudson," I said.

"I've read her stuff in the *Times*," he said. "I always read her pieces to the end. She likes to come full circle on things. Smart. Why's she giving up science writing?"

"She inherited the paper."

He nodded as if he understood all.

"But she hasn't given up on science news," I said. "She's writing a big paper on it. How to do it better. For a doctoral degree."

"Your mean a dissertation?"

"Yeah."

"Walter has a problem," Fletch put in. "He wants to get back at his cousins for doing something awful to him. They pushed him down and tied him up and so he fell and cut his head and..."

"Tsk," he said, not indicating if it was for the act or the desired revenge. "What about turning the other cheek?"

"I've heard of that," I said. "Something religious people say to do. But isn't that just stupid? It's inviting more abuse."

"Sometimes," he said. "Though sometimes it's the wisest thing to do, religion has nothing to do with it. I mean I'm a set-in-stone atheist, but I often turn the other cheek. It saves a lot of energy and time. And then when the abuse is coming from religious people, you can point their hypocrisy out to them."

"I know what you mean," I said. "Kids from the most church-goingest families make fun of you and sometimes even throw rocks and stuff if you don't go to church."

"That's because they're told people who don't go to church have no reason to be good – fear of God – so they mistakenly assume that makes them bad people."

I paused just for a second. "Really, isn't it better to do good because you think it's the right thing to do, rather than do good only because someone will punish you if you don't?"

"Hey, Fletch," MontesQ said. "You bring me a man after my own heart." Fletch was studying the ant farm.

"A lot of people look to religion for how to act, though," Fletch said absentmindedly, a finger on the terrarium.

MontesQ shook his springy hair. "Right and wrong should be decided by thinking about what does the best, or the least harm, not from old words written by people who lived in primitive times. Alas, today's religious leaders require morality to be their exclusive franchise. It's their reason for being."

"I know," I said. Well, I really didn't know what franchise meant, but I thought I knew what he meant anyway. "When I told my Fifth Grade teacher I didn't believe in God, she said 'then you must smoke.' I didn't get what the they had to do with one another."

"They don't," MontesQ said. "Your teacher is reasoning by inference, but that often leads one astray. To quote Elbert Hubbard, 'There are men who assume that men who do not go to church play cards; those who play cards chew tobacco; those who chew tobacco drink whiskey; those who drink whiskey beat their wives; therefore all men should go to church.'"

"You remember all that?"

"Well, it's one of my favorite quotes on a favorite subject."

"Who's Elbert Hubbard?"

"A disarming writer who was popular about 40 years ago. So you see, if your teacher believes only religious people obey rules, then a kid who's not religious, in her mind, would automatically be expected to break rules. And it's a rule kids can't smoke. But it doesn't really work that way."

"You know," he continued, "some of our best thinkers couldn't stand school. Don't tell your mom I said this, but Edison – he flunked everything because he was off thinking. You know Einstein…." MontesQ paused, lifting papers and books on the table beside his bed. Then he opened its drawer and then closed it.

I jumped in, "No, but my father interviewed Einstein once. He wrote for *Scientific Digest."*

"...once walked out of the house in his pajamas." MontesQ continued like he didn't hear me. "Can you imagine Einstein walking down the street in his pajamas? You know, Walter, a couple years before he died Einstein wrote to a philosopher friend of mine. He said he thought the concept of God is an expression of human weakness. I can assume you're strong minded. What else are you?"

I thought only a second. "Well... I'd like to be an engineer or astronomer or something. I follow all the space exploration news and watched all of Dr. Von Braun's Disney specials. I want to do something about helping to get us to Mars."

"Aha!" he exclaimed loudly, as if my statement was cause for great excitement. "This is admirable. Much better than wasting time on revenge. But everyone's interested in space now." He kept looking around. "Unfortunately the attention span of the average human is very short. Oh..." He picked up the tall drinking glass on the table. It was what he was looking for – a toothbrush head that he then inserted in a fat handle.

"Sorry," he said. "I can't go out to the dentist so I take very good care of my teeth. Brush after every meal. Doctors will make house calls, dentists won't." He turned it on. A battery-operated toothbrush.

During the buzzing – I'd never seen such a gadget – Fletch and I conversed close to each other's ears.

Then MontesQ rinsed the brush end in a glass of water while holding it 'on' and then turned it off and left it on the bedside table. "We will get to Mars," he said. "It's man's nature to explore."

"If we don't each kill each other off first," he added. "That's also man's nature."

We talked on for at least an hour, until I said I had to get back home, 'cause it was getting late. He told Fletch to bring me again and seemed to genuinely mean it. He said next time he'd show me his remote-controlled Lunar car. "Lunar Rover they're calling it." He nodded toward a big wheeled plastic thing on a shelf.

"Cool," I said. "How'd you get it?"

"Helped design it," he said. "Grumman was up here once and..."

"The engineering firm?"

"Yup. Had to help them with a weighty matter."

I got it. They had to reduce its weight.

"But there isn't anything like that going to the moon," I said, looking at the model.

"Not yet," he said. "But we're thinking ahead."

He walked us the short distance to his room door. We were turning to leave.

"You'll have to show me some of the articles your father wrote sometime," he said, lifting my right forearm by putting his palm underneath it. In one spot it looked like a pink Petoskey Stone. Then he dropped it.

"Have them play with your cat," he said.

7 – REPTILE FUDGE

I HEARD THE ADVICE, but "Grumman" dominated my mind. We were only a door or two down the hall outside MontesQ's room, Fletch ahead of me, when I tugged him back and stopped. "Fletch, Grumman is designing the lunar excursion module!"

He nodded and raised his eyebrows in the way that means "I told you so."

Tenacity Jones was still on the porch monitoring the central entrance as we left the Grand Hotel. We waved and said "thanks" as we descended the steps. He smiled at us even though he was standing guard in his red tunic, like a British Revolutionary War soldier.

We got our bikes and rode below the hotel porch to Cadotte Avenue. We had to part there. Fletch needed to take his turnoff home to Harrisonville. He mounted his bike and looked back to wave.

I almost forgot. "What did he mean about the cat?" I yelled.

"Just do it," he shouted back, and turned, pumping hard up the road.

I stood there for a minute. Cadotte Avenue is right angles to the hotel and goes uphill to meet the hotel's east end. There's a chain fence that follows the road and curves sort of serving as a barrier in front of the steep downward sloping hotel grounds. Below are the hotel's gardens and pool further distant. On the spur of the moment, I put the kickstand down on my bike and parked it off the road. Then I jumped that about two foot-high barrier chain and tossed myself lengthwise on the grassy hill. With arms extended, I let gravity roll me down like a pencil off a sloped school desk. Over and over I rolled. I felt happier than I had in many, many weeks.

Sunday is a lazy day around Marblecliff, just like back home in Cobble Hill. Mom watches *Meet the Press* and *Face the Nation* and stuff like that on TV and reads the *Free Press,* those op-ed pages especially. I read the comics section. "Peanuts" first, then "Nancy," "Terry and the Pirates," "Dondi," and "Gasoline Alley." I avoid "Brenda Starr." If I want scrambled eggs Mom makes them for me. I like the part she scrapes off the pan and calls "the scrap."

This Sunday I was sitting on the floor and had breakfast on a metal tray with fold-out legs. We put the tray on a big patchwork blanket of dishtowels sewed up by Mrs. Kwashneetski and I sit cross-legged on the floor. The tray has a map of the United States painted it. The map was a game when I was a little kid. There were three dotted routes and different colored magnet cars. I guess we lost the cars.

"Milk?" Mom asks.

"Tang," I say, 'cause John Glenn drank it in space. I flipped the newspaper pages, noticing ads. "It's Father's Day," I said.

"I know," she said, walking back to the kitchen. Then she came back and knelt down with me on the floor. "I love you as much as 10,000 fathers."

Sundays also include playing with the cats and saying "yes, my homework's done" when it isn't. Only school hadn't started yet, so I didn't need to do that. I checked Robbie's radio and it still worked, despite the dip in the lake. Mom saw my arm and said "come here" and put some cream gunk on it from the bathroom medicine cabinet.

The cousins came over from the annex. They were going home Monday. I had just one day.

I asked Alyce if she would "please help me" find the apricot kitten and bring her to the porch, where Canaveral was already splayed out in the sun. Cronkite, as usual, was off somewhere. I gave Jeffrey a ball of yarn and told them both the cats needed exercise. "Play with them," I said.

When I saw Alyce cradling the kitten in the crook of her arm, I smiled like the Grinch just before setting in motion his plan to destroy Christmas.

Then I went to the bathroom to make "Reptile Fudge."

Strictly speaking, it was Fletch's idea, one I had rejected at first. But I so improved it! I got the idea after Mom told me the history of the Bridge Walk. The walk tradition started in 1957, the year the bridge opened.

The guy who was governor then cut the ribbon and led a walk across. So it became tradition to do it every year, with the governor leading. Only this guy's name was G. Mennen "Soapy" Williams. He was nicknamed "Soapy" because the Mennen family made soap products.

So what would be better than a mixture of Mackinac Island fudge and soap?

The day before, I bought a brick of vanilla and a brick of chocolate fudge. In the bathroom I cut triangles out of Mom's green soaps. She loves green, so I figured there'd be green soap in there somewhere and I wasn't disappointed. Only the soaps were from New Zealand – little green Maori heads with their tongues out an an angle. How appropriate, I thought.

I took the little pieces and pressed them into the fudge. Wa-LAH Waltah! Reptile Fudge for the snakes of East Lansing. I laid the pieces carefully in the fudge boxes. I'd give it to them just as they leave for the ferry.

By afternoon, Mom was making BLTs and all was calm until Britt Niagara beat on the door. I opened it and he was standing there with his yellow plaid button-down-collar shirt casually open, hands in the pockets of his mustard-colored corduroy pants and rocking back and forth on his brown loafers. I gave him the look of a displeased elementary school principal.

It must have been something big to bring him to the house on Sunday. Despite his relaxed act, it was clear he'd been running – probably all the way from Market Street, across the park and up the Marquette Park steps.

"Mrs. Hudson," he breathed (everyone calls my mom Mrs. Hudson, even though she isn't and never was because, as I said, she made the name up), "We got a tip."

"What is it?" Mom asked.

"A telegram… It said a man from the island is working with another man who works in Governor Romney's office in Lansing and he's got $500,000 to pay Romney to make sure the state police cooperate in making sure this Negro doctor doesn't move into a house he bought in Bloomfield Hills....

"…and he says Romney will take the money and do it because he wants to run for President in 1968 and he needs their backing."

Mom squeezed her eyebrows together a bit. "Whoa, wait a minute." she said. "How?"

"I'm not sure. He could tell the police to let protesters get away with violence and intimidation. Doesn't he control the state police? A pay off..."

"Yeah, but that would be a violation of the Civil Rights Act. You have heard of the Civil Rights Act of 1964, Mr. Niagara?"

"Besides," she said, "Romney marched in 1963 for desegregation of suburban Detroit housing. He helped write the new state constitution. It would be extremely hypocritical of him."

"Unless all that was a ruse. To mask how he really feels." Mr. Niagara said, pursing his lips together. "He does live in Bloomfield Hills...."

Mom glared.

"Besides," he said, "Isn't that what people do when they run for President – get hypocritical? It's a lot of money he could use in the campaign."

"George Romney has worked for housing integration for... I suppose this telegram wasn't signed?" she asked.

He nodded yes. "But everyone knows he wants to run for President."

"And how would it enhance his candidacy to have been caught taking a bribe?"

"Well..." He didn't have a ready answer for that. "Maybe he doesn't plan on getting caught."

She put her thumb and middle finger on her forehead. "George Romney is a white elitist, with a religion wackier than most, but no fool. Did the telegram identify the member of the governor's staff who is conspiring to do this?"

"No. Do you want me to write a story about it?"

"About what, Britt?" Mom asked. "You have an anonymous tip about an unnamed person and unfounded accusation. What do you propose to write about?"

"That somebody is planning to stop this Negro from moving into his house."

"And we know this how?"

Mr. Niagara hesitated. "By...the telegram...."

I could have pitied him at that moment, but I didn't. He was always too condescending (a recent word book addition) towards me to deserve it. And, see, he had no reason to be uppity. He was a 23-year-old graduate of Central Michigan University. His only other newspaper job before Mom hired him was working for the *West Branch Gazette*. That's a town in Michigan and let me tell you, West Branch is even more nothing than Mackinac. I think they have a gas station and coffee shop off I-75. That's all. I know that because he told me so. He also said his father, who lives in Livonia, near Detroit, refers to a job on

Mackinac Island, as "working in the attic."

"WHICH IS UNSIGNED!" Mom said forcefully. "No, I want you to do something else," she said. "I want you to take that telegram and shove it in the first available … crevice in your desk and keep it there until you get one single concrete fact to back it up."

Mr Niagara's eyes got wide and he started taking backwards steps toward our front door and Mom moved toward him. "Yes, Ma'am!' he said. The door strip caught his heel and he stumbled backwards, turned, and hurried down the front steps.

"Novice reporters," Mom grumbled. "What DO they teach them in journalism school these days?"

She stood in the doorway, following him with her eyes. Then she looked up. "Still, if it's true, it would be a big state story. 'Governor takes bribe.' Or even just 'Attempted Bribery of Governor.' So big I'd have to give it to Freya. After I broke it first though."

I looked down the street at Mr. Niagara, walking away obviously slower than he arrived, looking at his feet. I wanted to offer him a bear.

8 – MISSION TO LANSING

DAYS PASSED BUT NOTHING new came up on the alleged attempted bribery. Mr. Niagara said nothing about it. Mom seemed to forget about it and started to think about improving the office equipment for writing stories about bicycle safety and lilacs.

She was in a good mood because her dissertation writing was going well, she said.

Fine for her. I was pretty bored and generally uncooperative. Then I got a letter from Doug.

He said he went to the museum and asked for Dr. Parker Ripley like I requested, but he couldn't get a home mailing address for the guy because they wouldn't give out that information.

"They said I would have to talk to him personally about that," Doug wrote. Then he said he'd be happy to do that, but the guy is soon to leave on an archaeological dig in northern Scotland. "And they said he's going to be gone for two years!"

I was frustrated and angry. If I'd been in New York I could have gone to find him. But I was helpless. Maybe I could get a phone number. I went down to Mom's library. There was a phone on her desk.

I was going to call long distance information when I saw Mom's dissertation notes and reference articles copied from microfilm and her work in the typewriter, complete with carbon copy.

I sat there for awhile

Then I started to read it:

A Content Analysis of Science News
in 12 Metropolitan Dailies

*The widespread dependence of science
writers on press releases, conference speeches,
and journal articles is evident in the near
disappearance of independent digging in the
laboratories and campuses where scientific
work is taking place.*

*On the surface, it seems that science
reporters are waiting for the news to come to
them, unlike their brethren in politics, economics,
and crime. But closer inspection of the
circumstances they are up against relieves them
of some of this responsibility. The fault often
lies with peer review journals that embargo
science news until their publications are
distributed. This leaves science journalists in the
mainstream press devoid of opportunity for real
scoops of any kind.*

How bad is this situation.....

This stuff went on for pages and pages. It looked like she had about 50 pages finally written up discussing the research statistics that were set up in tables and diagrams on another four or five pages.

Something gripped me from the inside. It was like a spaghettification machine was making its way from my stomach to my throat. I took the finished work, carbons and all, and started cutting it up in little pieces. The moment I started I knew I was in big, big trouble, but somehow I couldn't stop. The more I cut, the more I wanted to cut. I cut and cut and cut.

I cut it so small it could never be put together. It would have to be rewritten as well as retyped.

When I had piles of slices and dices of her work, I found a manila envelope and put it all inside and taped it shut. On the outside I wrote: "From Walter. I want to go home."

Then I hid in my room and cringed under the covers.

I heard Mom come in that evening. It was a long time before she came upstairs. She said simply:

"I got your message. I think we both need a break. Let's go to Lansing and do some shopping this weekend."

While I started to cry into my pillow she launched into a monologue about there not being any stores with good cameras and typewriters and stuff nearby. She wanted to go shopping where there were big stores and the closest place she could think of was Lansing. Traverse City might have been okay, she said, but if she was going to go that far she might as well go to East Lansing, visit old friends, and use her brother's house instead of a hotel. "What do you think?" she asked.

I sniffled, wiped an eye and nodded yes. Then she flipped my light off and went downstairs.

I stared into the darkness. Was that all she was going to say? "Let's go shopping?"

Perhaps she was trying to make me suffer with kindness until I broke. Oh well, it would give me a chance to see first hand how it was going with Cuz 1 and Cuz 2. I fell asleep.

Next day it occurred to me how we'd have to drive across the Mackinac Bridge in Uncle Brian's old '55 Nash Ambassador he gave us when we came to Lansing on the train. I liked it because it had reclining seats – I mean they went flat and you could sleep on the passenger side. But it was getting clunky. But that wasn't the point. The car was parked at the newspaper's printing shop in St. Ignace. That's Upper Peninsula. So she'd have to drive across the bridge.

Mom must have forgotten how it was when we came up for the first time.

We had taken the train from New York to Lansing. From there she was driving the old Ambassador and even from the back seat I could see her grip on the steering wheel tighten as we got closer and closer to the bridge. Her knuckles started getting white somewhere around Gaylord.

I was in the center of the back seat, strapped in by all three seatbelts. Mom had to dig them out from the crack between the seat and the seat backs. "Nobody uses those things," I protested.

"Uncle Brian sure didn't," she said. "I had to dig them out from far enough down to reach China.

Only thing not immobilized was my voice.

You see the bridge from miles away. It's really, really high.   There's no stop or toll booth or anything coming north. You just start going up. Pretty soon it feels like you're in a plane. At least, I think so. I've never been on a plane. There are two lanes in each direction. Normally, Mom likes to drive on the far right of a road. But on the bridge she wanted to avoid the low railing edge.

On most bridges you feel protected by a high railing, but on this bridge the railing is as low as a grasshopper's eyebrow. Even I could agree with her there. So she drove in the left lane. Only in the center two lanes you get onto the open grate.

I learned that the bridge designer made those grates so the wind goes through instead of hitting the bridge and pushing it around, but it isn't much of a leap to think about a grate falling out. I mean, I have more faith in the engineers than that, but Mom... Mom's not very trusting. So it's a choice between low scary railings and holey panels you think might fall out and drop you down a million feet. And when you choose the grates as the lesser of two evils, the openings cause your tires to make a weird spooky noise, reminding you there's water below – WAY below.

I didn't mind it, really. I mean, how can you even think of going to Mars if you're afraid of the height of a bridge? Well, I was afraid of flying, but I was going to work on that later.

So this Monday, when she said we were going back to Lansing to shop for cameras and better typewriters, I said we can't go to Lansing because we have to cross the bridge.

She just looked at me. I suggested we could take the ferry to Mackinaw City, which is south of the bridge, and take a bus to Lansing.

I didn't say anything more. Well, except, did she know the bridge was 200 feet high at the peak? I'd read about it since we arrived.

Apparently, though, the prospects of shopping make moms overcome most fears. Come morning we took the ferry to St. Ignace and walked to the car. In a few minutes we were starting up the ramp to the bridge.

Mom just inhaled and said: "I can do this. I'll just say, 'I'm not on a bridge. I'm not up high.'"

"I am not on a bridge. I am not up high. I am not on a bridge..."

I listened to her repeat that about ten times and then I said: "YOU ARE ON A BRIDGE."

So she kept saying louder and louder "I am not on a bridge" and I kept saying louder than her, "YOU ARE ON A BRIDGE!!!!!"

We increased the volume as we yelled back and forth over the five mile span. That got her over okay. She was so busy trying to drown me out she didn't worry so much.

When we were coasting down into Mackinaw City she said: "Thanks a lot, Walter. I was so distracted by your yelling I didn't notice I WAS ON A BRIDGE!"

"You were on a bridge," I said.

"I know," she said. "I said I know I was on a bridge."

"I know you say you knew you were on a bridge, but I think you really were," I said.

"That makes no sense, Walter," she said.

"ON A BRIDGE!" I yelled.

And then there was a moment of silence before we both broke out laughing and didn't stop until we saw the turnoff for Petoskey.

We passed that and headed straight south to Lansing. We were making good time, but when we were about at the city of Clare, Mom saw a flea market sign in time to make the exit for it.

We pulled in and parked. There were lots of tables so I wasn't too reluctant to spend some time there. But then I knew we were doomed. I saw them first. Teddy bears hanging by their ears on a clothesline. A few on an old dresser and a couple propped on some rolled fencing.

There was also a barrel filled with stuffed toys of various types.

"How much are your bears?" Mom asked.

"Fifty cents each," the woman said.

Mom started to act like she was browsing, but I knew she was out to rescue the bears. There was a tan bear with a white snout and green ribbon around its neck; a black bear, like a grizzly, small; a chocolate-colored bear, large; a light brown bear with short cropped fur; a white Teddy bear; a white polar bear with a red ribbon around its neck; and one that looked like it had been swimming in oatmeal.

Mom started to unclip the clothespins, as if she felt being hung by their ears was hurting them.

I was looking around. Mom was checking the bears' conditions.

I heard her say: "I'll give you $2 for all seven. That's more than half price."

"No, I couldn't do that," the woman said, "but how about $3? That's one for free.

"No. Thanks anyway," Mom said, turning her back on the woman. She was trying to make the seller think she wasn't going to buy any. I knew better. I waited. The seller didn't say anything more. Then Mom turned up the pressure. She said: "Walter, are you ready to go?"

That did it.

"I'll tell you what," the woman said. "I'll split the difference with you. $2.50."

"Well, maybe if you throw in something else."

This was my cue. My eyes were seeking like lasers. Mom said:

"Walter, do you see anything you need?"

"Yeah," I said. When she first started to look I saw a stuffed camel that was real cool, in the barrel of toys, while other people were going through it. "I want the camel in that barrel." My taste in stuffed animals was a little more exotic than Mom's.

"There's no camel in there," the seller said.

"Yes there is," I said. "I saw it."

"No, sweetie. No camel. Never had a camel," the woman said.

"Well, Walter, let's go," Mom said.

"Mom, there's a camel in there. And you know, I need a baby camel for my big mama camel."

Actually, I did have this stuffed camel from when I was about four.

"Well, you can look," the woman said. "But I'm sure there's no camel."

So I started to empty the barrel, putting the animals in a cardboard box she gave me.

Sure enough, about halfway down there was a camel. And it was a GUND.

"See," I said.

"Well," the woman said. "He was right. I sure thought there was no camel in there. But I can't just let it go for nothing."

"Three dollars... and two quarters... that's all I've got," Mom said.

"Deal," she said.

So that was the original price, but we got the camel thrown in. "Mom, you have more than $3.50," I said as we walked away.

She put her finger to her lips. We went to some other tables and left with the menagerie, a couple Percy Faith records for Mom, and some poster paint for me.

After we were driving again for awhile, I asked: "What is it with you and old Teddy bears? Why not just buy new ones?"

"Everybody buys the new ones. It's the old, lost or abandoned ones that need homes."

"Some people just throw them away. They're just fake fur and stuffing."

"I know, but once they have faces, it seems like they'd know if they were thrown out. Or lost."

"Really mom...."

"Well, maybe it's because of this bear I had once. It was a pajama bear....you know it had a zipper in its tummy and you stored your pajamas in there. Well, I loved that bear. It had a sailor shirt and one of those hats that had two ribbons hang down the back. I named it Fauntleroy because it reminded me..."

"Of the movie *Little Lord Fauntleroy.* I get it."

"Well, Fauntleroy was the coolest bear because he had an expressive face. If you threw him high in the air he would always land with a different expression on his face. His ear would curl or his hand would land under his chin. So he would look surprised, or sad, or coy, it was different every time. So I was throwing him up over and over again in the back seat of the car one day when we were driving to Belle Isle. My dad was driving and my mom was up front and my grandmother was in the back with me. It was our big Packard so I had room to sit on the floor and throw the bear. Well, it was annoying my grandmother, but I kept doing it. She pinched me once and told me to stop, but I had to do it once more and that time Fauntleroy landed right on her hand holding a cup from the top of our big therms. The hot coffee spilled and stung her hand.

"What was Fauntleroy's expression then?" I asked.

"I guess he looked surprised, but not as surprised as I was going to be. Nanny grabbed him and threw him out the window of the car!"

"You're kidding."

"No, she really did. And I screamed for my dad to stop and all that, but he said there was too much traffic to turn around and if he did someone would probably get run over trying to get the bear off the road. I folded my arms and pouted the rest of the way..."

"Then what?"

"Nothing. I just stayed mad at my grandmother and then I was sad whenever I thought about Fauntleroy. So I guess I hoped someone picked him up and gave him a good home. That's why I adopt homeless bears. Because it makes me think someone might have saved Fauntleroy the same way."

~~~

We got there about 6 o'clock. East Lansing, actually, where *they* live.

First we went out to dinner with Uncle Brian, Aunt Yoshiko and Target 1 and Target 2.

Aunt Yoshiko said: "Brian-san want go Tiffany."

"Oh, sure, great," Mom said. "You mean Jim's Tiffany Lounge on Michigan Avenue?" and Aunt Yoshiko said "*Hai.*"

"*Hai*" sounds like "hi" but doesn't mean hi or hello in Japanese. It means something like "yes" and "okay" and other things similar to how we use "cool."

Once we were in a booth at the restaurant, under a fake Tiffany lamp, I could see Alyce and Jeff were looking a little blotchy on their faces and arms. I smiled to myself, looked up, pressed my palms together and made an ironically religious-like homage to that self-described "stone-set" atheist, MontesQ. Having memorized everything in every text book and encyclopedia, he recognized that somewhat Petoskey Stone-pattern on my arm as ringworm. Highly contagious. You get it from your cat.

Watching them itch, I, at least, had a delightful dinner of steak and fries. Jeffrey and Alyce and I got to have cherry pie ala mode. Mom said no to my request for double ala mode, but that was okay. I knew mine wouldn't have the residual taste of soap, I thought to myself, and chuckled. Alyce kicked me under the table a few times, but it was worth it. I kicked back once for my missing skateboard, but I only hit the central table leg.

Best thing was, at first they didn't even connect me with the splotches. After Mom put the stuff on my arm she said she thought it was ringworm. Most moms aren't that far behind geniuses after all. I figured I got it from the stray kitty now becoming thoroughly confused by being called Jules by me and Sevareid by Mom. But my splotches had faded by the night of the dinner. While Mom explained to Uncle Brian what the cousins had, I grinned the grin of the Cheshire Cat. Then they knew how they got it and knew I knew they knew.

It was SWEET revenge. Yes, I paused to think how I didn't deserve the satisfaction for cutting up Mom's dissertation typing, but rationalized that that
~~~

was different.

I was, for the moment, content and sat through Mom and her brother talking about Vietnam and labor unions and all that.

Mom said the Vietnam War was a waste of lives and money and it wasn't going to assure democracy for anyone because if the majority of the people want something else that's what they'll have.   No debate from Uncle Brian, who'd been in the army, but not Vietnam. He talks more about unions and workers because he's a professor of that stuff. I remember he said the auto companies aren't being fair to Negro workers. He said they only hire them for unskilled jobs, even if they're better qualified than white guys who get the better jobs.

Mom said the Negro workers should make their displeasure known when they vote. Women, too, for that matter. Whenever women get jobs, they're paid less than men doing the same work.

"If get them at all," put in Aunt Yoshiko.

Everyone looked at her. She didn't usually speak up in conversations like this. She continued. "My boss, Hiromi, she say she apply at McDonalds in East Lansing. She told they don't hire women because 'women can't stand the pressure.' Ha!"

Aunt Yoshiko seemed to notice how loud she'd spoken and looked down, not to say another word.

Mom took up the issue. "See?" she said. "Women can't stand the pressure? I'd like to see those men stand childbirth."

"Don't start," Uncle Brian said, changing the subject back. "Who are the Negroes going to vote for? Negroes usually vote labor and that's Democrats, but even the Democrats don't get tough with the companies and union bosses. They need their endorsements."

And by the way, did she think Governor Romney would run for president?

It depends on how well he does running for re-election this November, she said. "And let me tell you about a mysterious tip we received at the office..."

It went on like that for awhile and I was getting restless. Besides, Alyce was again kicking me under the table. Finally, they split the check and we walked out into the parking lot.

Uncle Brian opened the passenger side front door of his new car for Aunt Yoshiko and she said, "Thank-you Brian-san." That car was a real cool dark turquoise '65 Olds 98 Luxury Sedan he just bought marked down when the new

'66 models came out. He showed me how you can even open the trunk by pushing a button inside the glove compartment. As we walked to the Ambassador, mom waved and said: "We'll see you in the morning." Of course we would. We were staying at his house on Orchard Street in East Lansing.

I got in the front passenger seat and Mom didn't object. I fastened the seat belt without being asked.   She just said she wanted me to see the State Capitol lit up at night, so we drove down Michigan to Capitol Avenue. Michigan Avenue ends at the Capitol building, the skinny-domed thing. There you have to turn left because Capitol Avenue is one-way.

Mom tried to turn back east by making a left turn on Allegan from the second lane from the left and a police car stopped us. The officer said she was making an improper turn, she needed to be in the far left lane. She sweetly said she was sorry and, being from out of town, was unfamiliar with the roads. He still gave her a ticket.

Then she kept driving around until we were going the completely wrong way again and found ourselves on the near north side of downtown. I saw a sign over a concrete arch that said Durant Park.

I sneered. "What do they think this is, Grand Army Plaza?"

Then the rocks started to fly.

9 – RIOT

August 7, 1966

T HE BRICK-SIZE STONE hit the hood of the car without warning.

The loud thud caused us both to jump back in our seats. It was as anonymous as a meteor falling through the Earth's atmosphere.

"Oh! What the…?" Mom said, moving the gear shift to 'park.' Suddenly we were in the middle of an angry mob. Or, rather, between a white mob and a Negro mob.

"Get down!" she said, pushing me to the floor. She changed her mind and decided to drive off, but forwards or back? She looked out the back window then a bunch of smaller stones rained down on the car and she changed her mind again and threw herself over me on the floor.

They kept coming in batches – about 10 seconds apart – then the rain of pebbles tapered off like the end of a Jiffy Pop.

Mom looked up and saw something that made her duck down again. A beer bottle hit the window like a missile. A loud blam, crack.

"Stay down" she said while she got up and started to drive. Any direction, she said, just to find a store open or cops or something for protection.

I think we were both pretty scared. People were bumping into the car. People were shouting at each other across the hood. They didn't seem mad at us, but some of them started to shake the car like a mechanic does when testing your shock absorbers. The Negros shouted "whitey go home" to the whites – and the whites answered. Both used nasty words I'm not allowed to repeat on penalty of having my mouth washed out with soap – and that was too ironic at the moment.

Mom opened the glove compartment and scrambled the contents until she found a box of film. Her camera was on the seat. She had to sit up to load it with film and that released me to rise up and peek out a little. "I told you to stay down," she said. I crouched lower and she got behind the wheel again and started snapping pictures! Then she drove forward and I could hear the camera clicking. I could feel her making a U-Turn. Then there was a bump. She had to drive up over the curb and on the sidewalk to get around them and more people were coming up behind us. Mom was driving with her left hand and clicking that camera with her right.

I heard "coons get out" answered by "we'll smash your honky white faces any day." I peeked out again. The crowd started moving like two separate mobs, but away from us.

"Boy, I didn't expect to see that in Lansing," Mom said. "I need more film," she said. "They only put 12 on the Tri-X rolls. Reach into the glove compartment...."

"Mom, your newspaper doesn't cover Lansing," I said.

"Right," she said. "But I can't not... Someone has to document things. Maybe somebody will need these pictures."

"Yeah, like the cops."

"That never," she said. "The minute we work for the police we lose our sources."

We saw another crowd in Durant Park, but by this time there were also police sirens.

Are the cops coming?

"I hope so. Somebody's got to have called this in."

"But you said...."

"I said we don't give cops our pictures. I didn't say we don't let them protect us."

"Pigs! Pigs! Pigs!" The chant was coming from both camps.

"The cops have arrived..." She opened the door to step out with the camera and, while pointing it at one group, an open beer can flew in from behind, crashing on the inside passenger window and nearly missing my nose. "...but it looks like they're going to be occupied."

"Yeah, especially with those people breaking into that gas station across the intersection," I said.

The cops surrounded them and it was over fast. Mom kept taking pictures.

Eventually police came up to our car to get our names and damage report. After we told them everything we saw and they wrote it all down, they left. I thought the beer smell inside the car would impress Uncle Brian.

Mom studied the old Ambassador, Pentax camera around her neck, arms akimbo.

"Well, Walter," she said, "These little dents have a rather moon-crater look don't you think? And a cracked windshield is a journalist's badge of honor – and I never had a car in New York so...."

"You didn't need one," I said. "We had that clever device known as a subway."

"True," she said. "But we never could drive up to an A&W and order ice cream sodas from our car. Let's go."

I rolled my eyes, but enjoyed the late night ice cream after we got to East Lansing. She could have just let me have that double ala mode at the restaurant and skipped the night drive.

In the morning she called over to the paper and told Mr. Niagara to "just get the paper out" because we might be delayed for car repairs if it took more than a couple days. She told the *Free Press* Capital Bureau they could come and get her pictures. Over breakfast, Uncle Brian said white people will have to start giving fair treatment to the Negroes or there will be more violence. He looked at me, I don't know why, and asked: "Did you know Malcolm X lived in Lansing?"

"Who's Malcolm X?" I asked.

"He's the Negro leader for violent protest. Martin Luther King is the non-violent one."

"Wait," Mom said. "He's not for violence. He said he's for Negroes defending themselves if whites start the violence. I think it's good for King's group to have Malcolm X followers waiting in the wings. It makes King's demands seem like the better choice."

"You're probably right," Uncle Brian said.

"More scramble egg, Brian-san?" Aunt Yoshiko asked. "Walter?" I said "no thanks." That morning she served breakfast with no opinions.

We read about the riot in the *Lansing State Journal* under a banner headline: **Police Curb Rioting Youths.** There was a 3-column wide picture of a woman and man looking at a car with the windshield broken completely out. It said "Riot Victims: Mr. and Mrs. Clark E. Baker of Flint stand beside their car which was damaged by rioters Sunday night. The Bakers were driving through Lansing on their way to Missouri. Mrs. Baker was cut on the arm, shoulder and head by glass from the windows hit by clubs and bricks."

"She doesn't know when to duck," I said. They listed these other injured:

> *"Francis E. Cutler, 500 S. Verlinden, cut*
> *to the left ear and shoulder; Robert E. Beck,*
> *226 W. Jolly Rd., severe cuts*
> *to right wrist; Michael A. Roat, 19, of*
> *Nashville, cuts to left eye and neck; Clark*
> *E. Baker, 50, and his wife, Dorothy, of*
> *1172 E. Orton St., multiple cuts to their faces*
> *and upper parts of their bodies.*
>
> *"June Torok, 2508 Park Avenue, was hit*
> *on the head with a brick while driving*
> *in the 1100 block of W. St. Joseph*
> *St; William C. McCallum, 218 S. Sycamore*
> *St., was cut on the left side of the face*
> *when attacked with bricks and stones*
> *by motorized Negroes as he drove on*
> *Chicago Ave., near Oakland Ave., a*
> *good mile from where the rioting was*
> *in progress.*
>
> *"Gary E. Bauer, 308 Ferguson St.,*
> *was hit in the back with a rock while*
> *walking on the 400 block of North*
> *Washington Avenue; Michael Stark, 3628*
> *Sumpter, and a group of friends,*
> *walking in the 100 block of West Genesee*
> *Street, were accosted by Negro*
> *youths who hurled rocks. Stark was hit*
> *on the right leg.*
>
> *"Walter E. Dick, of R. 1, Lansing,*
> *suffered neck and facial cuts from flying*
> *glass from his car, and Richard Murray,*
> *832½ N. Capitol Ave., was hit on the face."*

Mom glanced at the rest of the front page. She saw the one- column, three-line headline to the right of the picture, sort of in the center of the page:

U.S. Plane
Loss Sets
Record

She shook her head, like she does when she sees stupid things in newspapers. "Plane" and "Loss" should not be on separate lines, she said. "We call that a 'bad split.'"

I could see what she meant. Because I really didn't understand that headline until I saw the smaller "drophead" below it:

**7 Aircraft Downed
in N. Vietnam
In 107 Missions**

The story was from Saigon, the capital of South Vietnam. She scanned down. Only two out of nine pilots were rescued. She folded the paper with drooping shoulders and a sigh.

"Well," she said, pointing to the paper's main picture. "Their car looks much worse than ours."

I reached for the paper. She put her hand on it and looked at me. "I want to see it," I said. I know she didn't want me to read about Vietnam.

I looked at the broken windshield picture, but my eye was quickly drawn to the headline immediately beneath it:

Moon Orbit Launch
Slated for Tuesday

It was datelined CAPE KENNEDY. I swallowed the remaining half-glass of orange juice – Aunt Yoshiko didn't buy Tang – in one gulp. They were going to launch an unmanned lunar orbiter spacecraft to transmit pictures of nine potential moon landing sites.

"Get me some scissors," I said.

10 – GIRLS CAN'T

"Not my scissors," ALYCE said while pushing on her hair and looking at herself in the mirror. "He'll get cooties on them!"

Everyone ignored her, including me, except for the way she was... well, what she was doing to her hair. She was using the comb backwards and the hair was getting all tangled! It was sticking out and up. I was transfixed and nonplussed. Nonplussed. I knew the meaning of that word before Mom did because I used it once and she had to look it up.

"Doesn't mean like it sounds," she said. True. It means "reduced to hopeless perplexity." I was that. Alyce was just plain hopeless.

"Don't stare at me!" she said.

"Well, if you don't want to be stared at, maybe you shouldn't be using a comb like a retard," I said.

"It's called teasing," she said. "It's styling. Everyone does it."

I must have just had my mouth open. "Be careful, a bird could fly in there," she said.

"What do you do it for?" I said at last.

"It makes your hairstyle bouffant, stupid," she said.

"Okaaay. Why do you want it boufy? Cause you're goofy?"

"It's the style. Mom, Walter's bothering me."

"Be nice," Aunt Yoshiko said, to which one of us I wasn't clear.

I split, making like to look for my shoes. I found Mom's briefcase, and grabbed her thin metal pica pole. It's like a ruler but also has the printer's unit of measurement, picas, opposite the inches side. It had a nice, thin straight edge and I used it to tear out the articles. Alyce could keep her scissors.

Mom said: "Okay then, lets get going." She looked at her brother. "I can borrow your car, can't I? Triple A picked up mine to fix the windshield and stuff."

"Go ahead. I can walk to work," he said. His house, at Orchard and Ann streets, was only two blocks from the MSU campus.

While I was tearing out newspaper articles, Mom said she needed to buy some new cameras. "Don't forget to put that back," she said, eyeing the pica pole, "and we need some film and maybe an IBM Selectric. Laura says we need another one. Britt's monopolizing the one and she has only a manual Royal."

"I think they should write things out by hand," I said, waving the pole like a conductor's baton.

"You're going to spoil them," Uncle Brian said. "And spend more than you earn the first year for sure. You know how much those carbon ribbons cost for those IBMs? And you can't rewind them and use them over and over like you can with regular typewriter ribbons."

"But maybe they'll be more efficient with better equipment," she said. "Like our cameras – an old Argus C3 and a Kodak. A couple new 35mm Pentaxes ought to get better pictures."

"So would teaching them to focus," I said.

"Yeah, that too," she said. "Let's go, Walter."

I ran my clippings to my suitcase, put them inside a thick magazine, and got in the car. We drove back down Michigan Avenue and stopped at Mark's Photo. Mom took notes on models and prices of different cameras and then we went downtown to Knapp's, the department store in the yellow tile building. Yellow tiles, glass bricks making a rounded front corner. "Art Deco," Mom said, pointing. I got to look at some tape recorders. I had been asking for one. I looked at a very small one – perfect for spying. I even tried to put the tape back on the end of a reel. Mom wasn't too impressed. They were annoying to thread, she said, and the sound wasn't that good.

We drove back down Michigan to Frandor shopping center to check out Sears. At Sears the cameras and tape recorders were in the same place and there was a woman behind the counter. "Do you wish to be helped?" the woman asked. I thought the wording was odd and she sensed it. She leaned in and said "We're not allowed to say 'May I help you?'"

"My son wants a tape recorder and I need a couple of good cameras – Pentax or maybe Canon," Mom said, "depending on the features and prices."

The woman showed Mom some cameras. Mom liked the price of the Pentax at $249 compared to the other stores. Then the sales clerk looked at me.

"What do you want a tape recorder for?" she asked.

"Oh," I said, "I want to carry it around and tape people."

"Then you don't want a big one," she said. She smiled. "Let me show you this Norelco."

She pulled out a rectangular thing about the size of a box of macaroni – maybe a little longer.

"Look at this," she said. "It's the Norelco Carry-Corder 150. This is the tape..." It was a little thing enclosed in plastic – no bigger than a pack of cigarettes and much thinner.

"It's called a cassette," she said. She unsnapped the recorder's leather case and opened a cover on the plastic body of the machine.

"It goes in like this...." She snapped the little rectangular thing in, closed the cover. "You don't touch the tape," she said. Mom and I looked at each other.

"How do you re-wind it if it comes off the end?" I asked.

"It doesn't come off," she said. "It will stop when the tape comes to the end, then you flip it over." While you use the other side it's rewinding. Or, rather, just using the other side rewinds the first side."

"Wow," Mom said. "That is really nifty. I've never seen anything like that. That is really space age. How much is it?"

"Ninety-nine dollars," she said.

"Will it tape the space launches off TV?" I asked.

"Sure," she said. "Well, the audio. Just set the microphone up in the hole in the side of the separate microphone case – and the case holds it up. When you're traveling it slides onto the recorder's carrying-case strap."

"Cool," I said.

The woman said you could get tapes that were a half hour on each side or an hour. They were about $1 each. You could record things and keep the cassettes, as they were called, in their cases.

"Wow. I can record my favorite TV shows and keep them!" I said.

"If you can afford the cassettes," Mom said. "But it is so modern, so futuristic." She thought a bit while I stared at her with big pleading eyes. (That always works.) "I guess you can have it," she said.

"Yippie," I said, jumping up a little. I gave her a sideways hug. "Thanks, Mom."

"And," Mom said to the sales clerk, "I'll take that Pentax camera and about 120 boxes of Tri-X black and white."

"Well," the sales clerk said, "I can sell you the film, and the tape recorder, because they are under $100 each, but I can't sell you the camera. I'll have to get a male sales clerk for that."

"Why's that?" Mom asked.

"Women aren't allowed to sell 'high ticket' items at Sears," she said, "which means anything $100 or more. Only men can sell those." She pursed her lips, as if in disgust.

"What?"

The woman sighed. "Yes, high ticket items are only for men to sell."

"And that would be because why?" Mom asked.

"We work on commission," the woman explained. "They think only men are supporting families so they save the expensive items for them so sell. We women can't sell cameras or furniture or washing machines and dryers. They don't even let us work in the appliances department. It's like I said, all the high ticket – high commission – items are reserved for men. Of course they have all sorts of excuses. Like a woman couldn't sell a complicated machine like a washer." She leaned in and whispered. "As if a man has ever used one."

"Naturally," Mom said. "Well, you ought to protest that."

"We do, frequently. But we don't have a union here, so..." She rang up the tape recorder and film. "Will that be on your Sears charge?"

"Yes," Mom said. "Why don't you get a union?"

"Ha! We try. But it gets voted down. People say they don't want to pay union dues."

"I see," Mom said. She looked at me. "Your uncle Brian could teach them something about the history of collective bargaining. Young people have no idea about child labor. Why, even the concepts of weekends and vacations came from union..."

"Don't start, Mom," I said.

"I'll get someone to ring up the camera," the sales lady said.

"I ought to protest and not buy it," Mom muttered as we waited.

On the way back to Uncle Brian's, Mom stopped at a rummage sale on Grand River. She bought some books and a couple homeless bears. I found some comics and something called Stadium Checkers.

That night Alyce and Jeffrey went to mutual friends' houses and, while

Mom and Uncle Brian continued their endless debates, and as Aunt Yoshiko worked at her sewing machine, I made an expedition into Jeffrey's bedroom. It didn't take me long to find my skateboard. Under the bed. How imaginative is that?

When we were leaving the next morning I carried it out under my arm, walking with my best swagger. And I looked back at Jeffrey to make sure he saw me smirk.

And when Uncle Brian gave me a stack of comic books, ol' Jeffy-boy said, "Hey, those are mine." That was the whipped cream on my sundae. Mission accomplished.

I had the Norelco on my lap all the way home.

I practiced pushing the red button down and the record lever in at the same time, which you could do without opening the case because there was a cut out in the leather, and plugging in the microphone and setting it standing in its own little case. Then I attached the little case to the leather shoulder strap on the recorder's case. When you needed to insert, remove, or flip over tapes, the case could be snapped open, no need to take the recorder out. When you took it out it was dark gray and light gray plastic. But usually you'd use it in the case. It was so cool.

Once we got past city traffic and it was just two-lane rural highway with few stops, we were both quiet for awhile.

"I'm sorry I cut up your papers, Mom," I said.

"I know you are," she said. "I know it came from your hurting."

I didn't say anything.

"Are you willing to provide some restitution?"

I thought a moment. "Yessss," I said slowly. "Like what?"

"Let me think about that."

When we started on the approach to the Mackinac Bridge, Mom made a deep sigh and gripped the steering wheel with enough force to choke Dracula. I turned on the recorder. Then, our "I am not on a bridge/You ARE on a bridge" duet was captured as it got louder and louder, until we started down on the north side and we laughed ourselves silly.

11 – 'IF THERE ARE NO CARS ON THE ISLAND, WHY DID THEY BUILD THE BRIDGE?'

THERE WAS A LETTER from Doug Mocha when we got back to the island. I tore it open. He had gotten my postcard of the Mackinac Bridge. He had three questions.

One, "Why, if there are no cars allowed on the island, did they build the bridge?" Two, "When are you coming back to Brooklyn for a visit?" And, three, "Have you unpacked yet?"

"Ahk!" I said to no one in particular as I walked upstairs. "Everyone I know from New York asks the same question!" I sat down in my scoop chair between the box towers, with Canaveral looking down from the highest one, six high, and little Jules, a.k.a. Sevareid, staring from boxes stacked about four high. There were other stacks at heights in between, so they could play mountain cougars if they liked – and they often did. I propped a clipboard on my knees and started to write:

*"One: Because the bridge links the Lower and Upper Peninsulas of Michigan. It **doesn't** go to the island. You have to take a ferry boat to and from the island. I'll show you when you visit someday....*

"Two: AS SOON AS I CAN!!!!!!

"Three: No and Never."

I went on to explain that the confusion is probably due to the fact the bridge and the island have the same name.

Doug knew about my refusal to unpack protest and I had talked to him about the guy at the museum, Parker Ripley. The protest hadn't gotten me anywhere yet with Mom and I didn't want to tell her about facts I might find out that may or may not be true. I didn't want to upset her.

Doug said he and Frank were going to a game at Yankee Stadium. "Say 'Hi' to Frank," I added. I started to write "enjoy the game," but realized it would be long over before he got the letter. I could call, but Mom didn't like me running up the phone bill on long distance calls. I wished there was a fast way to communicate that didn't cost a lot. I settled for writing: "I hope you had a good time at the game. Up With Yankees. Will write again soon."

I sighed. I always went with Doug and Frank to baseball games. They were bigger fans than me, but I went and they always went with me when I wanted to go to a new show at the planetarium. Besides, I liked the hotdogs. Frank's dad, who drove a subway train, usually could be off in the daytime to come with us. He'd just volunteer for a night shift when necessary. Doug's dad was a city engineer, but he could get off sometimes. Sometimes Mom would be the chaperone. But we had been starting to get to do more stuff on our own. Like go to the movies on Court Street. But Doug and Frank always liked it when their dads joined us.

Thinking about all that was making me feel trapped again. I took out another piece of paper. "Listen, Doug," I wrote. "I need you to do me a favor. When you can, go to the Museum of Natural History and ask for the mailing address of Dr. Parker Ripley's dig in Scotland. I know they wouldn't give his home address, but tell them this is business." I inserted that page in the envelope and sealed it and took off for the post office on my bike.

From Market Street I decided to go up to find Fletch at the stables. I knew he'd be getting off soon. We were planning on getting together Saturday, but he might be free this afternoon, too, I thought. We knew school would be starting all too soon and we wanted to make use of every minute of vacation we had left.

I caught up with him coming down Harrison and we went to The Big Store. After annoying staff by playing with toys, toy bows and arrows and tomahawks, and trying on souvenir T-shirts we weren't going to buy, we were asked to leave. "If you boys aren't buying anything..." the clerk said. It was then I spied the rings with the big red stones.

I looked at Fletch.

"Waverly rings," he said.

"Just what I was thinking," I said.

They were $1 each. I was afraid of that because they were in a case. If they had been cheap, like 10 cents, they would have been out where they could be handled. But this was too good to pass up. We asked to try them on and each found one that fit. Then we turned out our pockets and counted change. We had just enough, if Fletch owed me 60 cents, that is. We bought the rings and strode out. To the relief of the store clerk, no doubt.

"Just remember," said Fletch, always ready to quote U.N.C.L.E. shows, "a Waverly Ring commands instantaneous obedience no matter what creep appears to be wearing it."

It was late afternoon, but still warm enough to get wet in the lake and high tail it up to the dog bone (what we called the Grand Hotel pool because of its shape).

Later we got into the library just before closing, in time to pester Miss Suzy, the Zazu Pitts of librarians. But she's okay. I've only known her for a few weeks, but she hasn't ever stopped me from checking out books because they appear to be advanced for my age. The other day I got *The Count of Monte Cristo,* and not an abridged kids' version, and she just smiled. And she didn't laugh when I checked out *Little Women.*

Saturday we went into the cleaners, looked around, and said we were looking for the entrance to U.N.C.L.E. Headquarters.

"Who do you like better, Napoleon or Illya?" Fletch asked.

"Illya," I said. "He's not the lothario Napoleon Solo is."

"What's a lothario?"

"Someone who chases women then throws them off," I said. "Illya wouldn't do that."

"That sounds right. He had more education and accomplishments – more of a sense of right and wrong and responsibility."

"Probably because he's a Commie," I said.

"He's not a Commie."

"Of course he is. He's Russian. He'd have to be if he's their representative in U.N.C.L.E."

"I suppose that explains what he said when they went to that party on Long Island," I said.

"What did he say?"

"You don't know? You're the U.N.C.L.E. encyclopedia."

"No," Fletch said. "I don't know. What did he say?"

"He said the rich people there were all dopes."

"That's because he doesn't think money is the most important thing in life."

Hmmmm," I said. "That would be the Commie view. But money does buy happiness."

"Does not."

"No – but it'll buy a good double scoop cone at the walk-up Dairy Bar on Market," I said.

"That it does, my boy," Fletch said, brightening, "and you happen to have some, so let's go."

We stopped to buy some new comics on Market Street and got the ice cream. I got strawberry on the bottom and chocolate on top. Fletch got two scoops of fudge ripple. "It's going to be too hard to ride one-handed," I said. "Let's go read and eat in the morgue." I nodded to Mom's nearby building.

We parked our bikes outside the newspaper office and I took the skateboard off the carrier with one hand and rode it in. I smoothly popped it over the door ridge by pressing on the back to raise the front and pressed down on the front to raise the back and sailed in holding the ice cream in one hand and steering with my other arm and my feet. Only I went in too fast, whizzing by Mr. Niagara and Miss Kelly's desks – but they were in the back doing paste-up.

They looked up from a light table and saw me coming at them. "Whoa, kid," Mr. Niagara said, holding up his hands. I tried to stop, but I was passing them when my toe hit a depression in the linoleum and jerked me back. The top scoop of my ice cream flew off the cone onto a page on the table. I stopped without falling by jumping off the board. The page was almost complete, with copy and a three-column picture. Miss Kelly swiftly picked up the blob of ice cream and ran with it to a sink. Miss Nichols, who was standing there with pink slip phone messages in her hand, ran and got paper towels and started dabbing, but the chocolate stained the copy and the page was ruined.

"Your mother is going…." Mr. Niagara started to yell. "We're going to have to re-set all that copy!"

"And replace the picture," Miss Kelly said. "It was brought in. We don't have a negative for that one."

I looked at it. "It isn't really in focus anyway."

They gave me dirty looks.

"Honestly," I said, "and you're better off without that 'grip and grin' anyway." It was a check passing picture. Charities love those when they give money. Sometimes they even make phony giant-size checks for the purpose.

"Get a real news photo," I said. "Mom will thank me...." I pivoted on the skateboard towards the front door, but turned left to the morgue.

Well, that rendered them speechless, since they really couldn't do anything to me, being the owner's kid and all. But I was right. I've heard Mom say over and over the problem with small town newspaper photos is that they're usually staged – like handshakes (the "grip and grin") at charity check-passings or rows of people at grand opening ribbon cuttings, where the photographer has to get way far back to get them all in the picture, so they're so small you can't see their faces. "Get faces!" I can hear her say.

Fletch was already sitting on the morgue floor. He had made his way in there during all the commotion. I started in on finishing my remaining scoop of ice cream; Fletch had his double scoop intact, though somewhat diminished. Looking back into the paste-up area I saw Mr. Niagara grab a ruler and pretend he would throw it at me.

We read our comics. No one said anything else until we were ready to leave about an hour later. Miss Kelly, speaking to no one in particular, said: "Where will we get a better photo by morning?"

I grabbed a camera off Mom's desk and stopped at the front door. "That's easy. Just get out of the office!" Mr. Niagara threw the ruler down to the floor. "Don't worry, I'll get you something," I said, raising the camera above my head and pushing on the floor with one foot to get the skateboard going.

Ayashe was sitting on a curb outside. I parked the board and re-attached it to the bike. "Bobby wants you over at the Big Store," she said.

"Bobby? Who's Bobby?" I asked Fletch.

"A kid I know from school. He knows about you."

We all went to see what he wanted. It was a baseball card swap. Tigers.

When I walked up Bobby was trying to trade short stop Dick McAuliffe for a fairly new pitcher, Denny McLain. Everyone wanted an Al Kaline or Norm Cash card. I just shook my head and blew out a puff of air. "Got any Yankees?"

"Yankees?"

"Yeah, everybody knows those are the only cards worth having," I said.

"G'won, get outta here..." the other kid said, then, "You got a Mickey Mantle?"

"Sure," I said.

"Well, I might trade an Al Kaline for a Mickey Mantle..." he said.

I laughed in derision and he punched me and we started wrestling. Fletch pulled him off me.

Then we just hung around the park, avoiding Ashe, but she dogged us.

"Girls," Fletch said.

"Yeah," I sighed. "Say, Fletch, do you think the Russians really sent a woman into space?"

"Probably. Maybe not. They lie about a lot of things."

"Why would they?"

"I think it has to do with communism."

"What? Lying?"

"Well, yeah, because they want everyone to think they're fantastically successful. But they might have sent a woman into space because under communism all people are supposed to be equal. Even women."

"But maybe they can't stand the pressure," I said.

"Pressurized suits?"

"No, the work pressure. Anyway, that's what my aunt said about women not being allowed to work at McDonalds in East Lansing. Not that she agreed with it. She just said that's the reason the manager said they won't hire them."

"Well, if they can't even work at McDonalds, how are they going to work in space?"

"Yeah right. Except...."

"What?"

"During World War II, didn't women work in airplane factories? Rosie -the-Riveter and all that? And my Mom, and her best friend, Freya, they work under pressure a lot. When something's happening – like a fire or something. They have to go and get the facts, even if people don't want to talk to them, and the pictures and then they have to write it real fast, and make sure it's right and all the names are spelled correctly and meet the deadline so the papers get delivered on time."

"I don't know, Walter. Maybe they're exceptions."

"Maybe. But then an EXCEPTIONAL woman could be an astronaut, right?"

"Even the men have to be exceptional," he said

"Can we head over to the Grand now?" I asked.

We were too early to see MontesQ. It was about 3 p.m., but I had a picture to take and that seemed like a good place to find one.

We got there and picked up a basket of bocce balls on the Grand's front lawn and set up a game. Then up comes this young guy in a sports coat and tells us to go away, he and his "friend" – a girl – are going to use the set. He just ordered us to get away!

We walked up the red carpeted middle stairs and found Tenacity. "Did you see that?" we asked.

"Just a minute," he said, and told someone he was taking a break.

He took us up to the hotel's cupola that was centered on the roof, rising a bit above it in a sort-of circle. It was a dusty hollow under the top dome of the hotel, but fairly large, at least 15 feet in diameter, and with windows on all sides the view was spectacular.   Tenacity often snuck us in there. He said there was some talk of making it a piano bar but nobody, meaning the owner, Mr. William Woodfill, wanted to spend the money. He was too busy collecting old carriages or something. That was okay with us because we didn't drink (ha ha) and we liked having the place to ourselves. Sometimes Tenacity let us stay there when we had to wait for MontesQ to be accepting visitors. Anyway, from the cupola you can see in all directions – over the straits and the bridge in the distance. You can look down over the Grand Hotel lawn and gardens. I pointed out the guy and told Tenacity what he did, grabbing the bocce game from us.

"Oh, that kid," he said. "I'm not surprised. That's the governor's son, Will...ard."

When he said the name he curled his upper lip and puckered like he was holding back spit.

"Willard, what kind of name is that?"

"Dunno, but they call him Mitt."

"There's something about him..." he added. "The glassy eyes... he looks like a lot of those new college students that are pouring in. They stare out into space. Last summer he took a young girl out in a canoe all the way under the bridge. Mighty dumb. They could have easily been capsized by the wake of a freighter. They could have been swept out so far they couldn't paddle back."

Fletch and I were silent, gazing out, and he continued.

"Oh, but they weren't," Tenacity said. "They had dinner here in the hotel that night. I heard His Ivy Leagueness tell the girl he wouldn't have to go fight in Vietnam. That he'd get a deferment as a Mormon missionary. He'd go to France! But then he said it would still be "dangerous" over there – being a missionary."

"Was that a joke?" I asked.

Tenacity laughed. "Oh no. He was being honest. Imagine trying to convert French people into giving up wine!"

Fletch didn't get it. "Mormons don't approve of alcoholic beverages," Tenacity explained. "Most French people drink wine."

"And that girl," he went on, "I found out she was just 16. I don't how her parents let her come. I supposed they thought it was safe – the governor's place and all that. Maybe they even sent a limo. So, yeah, I'm not surprised. That's the governor's son, Mitt.... If only I could slap him, just once. France, indeed. It'd be one thing if he was protesting the war like other kids. But a few weeks ago he was at Stanford, protesting the protestors.....Chicken Hawk."

"What's that?" I asked.

"That's what you call someone who's all for a war but won't think of going to fight in it himself."

I looked down at the lawn. "Who's he playing with?" I asked.

The idea struck like lightning. I looked at the camera around my neck then ran down the cupola stairs to the fourth floor, took the elevator to the ground level and ran down the red carpeted stairs to the lawn. I went up to where they were playing the game and snapped pictures of him, sometimes getting real close to his face. I kept taking pictures until he was real annoyed. I didn't stop until he stomped his foot at me.

~~~
~~~

MontesQ flung the door open with his hair in full Phyllis Diller. He said "Aha!" in his usual way when presented with good ideas or visits from people he liked. At this point, I knew he liked Fletch and felt fairly certain he liked me, too.

He was wearing a robe of some kind of fancy shiny material trimmed in fur around the collar and cuffs, but then it hung open and he was only wearing striped boxer shorts underneath. When he flopped on the bed he was all fur and skinny legs.

"Did you kids hear about the Lunar Orbiter success? Now NASA has some fascinating pictures to study."

We talked about that for awhile then I reminded him he promised to show us the remote-control Lunar Rover model.

"Oh, yeah," he said. "Where's that remote?" He took the buggy off the shelf and got it moving around the bedroom with the black box that had a lever and two buttons. Then he directed it into the living room area. It hit stacks of manuscripts, mail, and books. A wheel fell of and MontesQ had to stick it back on twice.

"That going to happen when it has to go over some moon rocks?" Fletch asked.

"We've got time to fix stuff like that," he said. "This baby comes first. It's the Lunar Lander." He pointed to a model that looked like it was made mostly of tin foil. MontesQ said that was because that's about what it will be made of. It doesn't need to be strong.

"But that window isn't to scale," he said. "It'll be much smaller. They thought they needed a window that big. So the pilot could steer the ship visually. Well, it would need to be that big if he's sitting. But I thought, 'Why does the pilot have to sit? The window can be much smaller if he stands. So they shrunk the window and saved gobs of weight."

"So they can bring back more moon rocks?" Fletch asked.

"I think it's more to have enough fuel to land and take off," I said.

MontesQ rubbed the top of my head.

At first I thought we shouldn't visit him so often. I worried that we might be using up time he needed for thinking and writing – and talking over the radio. But he always seemed so grateful for our visits. Us dumb kids. I finally figured he was lonely a lot. When we listened to him it fed his hunger for companionship, apparently, because he always told us to come back, that our visits are a gift.

The first time I went back I thanked him for the tip he gave me to get the cousins to play with the cats. He just smiled and laughed a little. We didn't discuss it.

Today, he nodded toward the ants.

"Look at them," he said. "They have 'revenge' too. One ant will kill another for stealing, for instance. And they can't do anything about it. They are programmed to do that for their own survival. And if they don't need to kill – say they have an ample food supply – they can't learn to turn it off. They can't learn NOT to kill under certain circumstances because the ants that came before them couldn't leave written information about what they learned – that revenge is no longer necessary. It's just an endless cycle of aggression, retaliation, and revenge." He sighed. "And it's the same with people. For now. But people *can* learn. They can do research and leave behind the results in books and libraries. I'm going to include that in my 'grand synthesis of human behavior and everything in the universe.' I might call it social biology or sociobiology."

"What if revenge does solve something?" I said. "What if getting revenge means you won't get picked on again?"

MontesQ tilted his head and the wiry coils danced a bit. "Aha!" he said. "You are thinking. Yes, for a while that seems correct. But you only get delayed revenge on your revenge. It's a never ending cycle. Will be until we understand it."

"It sounds very hopeless," I said, thinking of Vietnam.

"Not at all," he said. "Because we recognize the problem and can start to direct our own evolution. Evolve the way we want to."

Steer evolution, I thought. Now that was an idea.

He explained what his ant farm was teaching him about the way creatures act – and to him that was a link to the secrets of human behavior. He said some ants would sacrifice themselves for the good of the group. I learned the word "altruism." It means allowing yourself to take less for the good of another person or group. "Most often observed in parents," MontesQ said.

"And communists," I said facetiously.

"Well, yes, sometimes," he said. "Although it isn't something you can say in public in America. The Blacklist may be over, but the intolerant have other means of retaliation."

I changed the subject to *2001,* the movie everyone was talking about.

They weren't done making it, but there were pictures of its sets in LOOK and LIFE magazine and everywhere else. Its full title is *2001: A Space Odyssey* and it was written by a top science fiction writer, Arthur C. Clarke. I was interested in it because it was about space, but it seemed more important than any movie I'd ever heard of. It was being talked about so much. Just the idea of a year called 2000-something seemed fantastic. Mom said she'd never live to see the year 2000. I'd be like over 50...

"The movie is important," MontesQ said to me. "It's going to give people the first realistic look at what the future might hold. Oh, not the fictional part of the story – the monolith and the sentient computer. That's just a story. But the idea of an orbiting space station and travel to the moon. A television telephone! What a spaceship might look like that has artificial gravity."

"*What* kind of computer?" Fletch asked.

I kinda knew what he meant, but I let MontesQ answer.

"Sentient. It means being aware. It's aware of its own existence." Well, that was MontesQ. He was not only the encyclopedia of human history, he was a dictionary as well.

"You mean the computer knows, like a person knows, that it exists?"

"Exactly. Like the one in the story. But we don't have any computers like that yet." he said.

"Will we?" I asked.

"I don't know. Some people think so."

"Do you?"

MontesQ looked at the ceiling. "Possibly. Arthur says if a competent scientist says something is possible he's probably right, but if he says something's impossible he's usually wrong. But if we ever do have sentient computers that means they have become a life form and we have to figure out how we will interact with them. Would we own them because we made them or would they have rights?"

Fletcher looked up from the ant farm. "You mean if they decide to kill us?"

"Well, yeah."

"But Isaac Asimov already has the answer," I said. "In *I, Robot* he says a robot, and that would be a computer inside, right? Well, a robot may not harm a human being. It's in the Three Laws of Robotics."

"That's fiction, dolt," Fletch put in.

"Yes, but what Walter's observing is right," MontesQ said. "Isaac is saying we'd better build that 'law' into the design of artificial life as a safety precaution."

"Right," Fletch said. "Because when the machines decide they're smarter than us, we're roadkill."

"Space debris," I corrected.

"Well, we'll see how they deal with the problem in *2001*, MontesQ said. "You will tell me after you see it. I won't be able to..."

"G'wan," Fletch said. "You've probably already talked to Arthur C. Clarke about it."

"Well, just a little. But even he doesn't know. Stanley Kubrick – the director – isn't making a movie directly from something Arthur wrote. At first he thought he would. He looked at six of Clarke's stories, but didn't pick one. He just wanted to make a movie about space because the timing is right. They'll cash in on the intense interest people have in the race to the moon."

"You mean Arthur C. Clarke doesn't know the ending?" I asked.

"Neither does Kubrick," MontesQ said. "I think they're making it up as they go along."

~~~

I ran my film down to Mr. Huggins at the paper and left cutline information before I went home. That night I decided the space pictures could go back up. But that didn't mean I was capitulating. They were educational. The boxes stayed unpacked, even if I had to dig inside them once in a while for scissors and colored pencils and clothes and stuff. I also decided to start a space exploration time line right on the wall. Well, maybe not right on the wall. Maybe Mom could bring me an end roll of newsprint paper. I got tape and tried to put the pictures up the way I had them in Brooklyn. I put Ed White in the middle again.

Then I got Mom's *LOOK* and *LIFE* magazines and cut out the *2001* movie pictures. Over the next two days, I made a big scrapbook about the movie. There was a picture of the actor Gary Lockwood jogging around a spaceship centrifuge, the stewardess in space, and Hal, the computer, watching Gary Lockwood and that other actor, Keir Dullea.

I kind of wanted to keep it, but I gave the scrapbook to Mrs. Kwashneetski to send to her nephew Stephen. He's a corporal in the Marine Corps, stationed in Vietnam. I went into the kitchen that night. "Mrs. K," I
~~~

said, "I made this scrapbook about the movie *2001: A Space Odyssey* that they're making. Do you think you'd like to send it to your nephew? Didn't you say he liked science fiction?"

"Oh, Walter, let me see it," she said. She thumbed a few pages and said she thought that was just something he would like.

"Mrs. K," I said, "You know the governor's son, Mitt?"

"Not personally," she said. "Well, he's going to graduate from college soon, and Tenacity Jones said he plans to go to France as a Mormon missionary – to avoid the war, Tenacity said. How do you feel about that?"

She said something that sounded like a Ukrainian curse, but I wasn't sure. Then she said: "It's always the sons of the poor who go to fight the rich men's wars."

I was in the newspaper office the next afternoon when they were giving the new issue a staff review.

"That headline on two stinks," Miss Kelly said pointedly to Mr. Niagara. "Without a verb it's a label not a headline." She flashed her tongue and wrinkled her nose at him. Mom missed it.

"Well," Mom said, trying to be diplomatic. "A head with an active verb should be the first choice. I like the picture of the governor's son and the girl on four."

Mr. Niagara scowled.

I winked at him.

"Next time ID the girl," she added.

Mr. Niagara smirked at me and I shrugged.

12 – STEP DWELLERS THREE

THE LAST DAY IN August, Fletch and I met early in the morning at Anne's Tablet, near Marblecliff. Ayashe was tagging along already. She was there with her 20-inch bike with the pink handlebar streamers. She parked it, sat on one of the benches, and started taking off her Keds and socks.

"Waltie," she said, "do you want to see the mark on the top of my foot where Fletcher shot me with an arrow?"

When did she started calling me Waltie?

"Sure," I said. She pointed to a little white circle that was, indeed, on the top of her foot.

"Ashe," Fletcher said, "we need a note delivered to Tenacity at the Grand Hotel, but the messenger MUST NOT BE FOLLOWED."

She jumped up. "I can do it!"

"Okay, if you're sure you can handle it. Put on your shoes."
She did, quick as a bunny.

"You need to use Evasion Pattern Eight," Fletcher said. He started to draw in her notebook.

He leaned in to me and whispered: "Mandy, the *Never-Never Affair...*" while he kept sketching. "First, go to the end of the ferry docks and come back to town. Buy some chewing gum. Here's 10 cents. Then turn around and ride your bike past Arch Rock to Sugar Loaf hill."

"That's NOT the way to the Grand," she said.

"Not directly, of course," he said. "It's so they don't catch you?"

"Who?"

"The s-p-i-e-s."

"Oh!" she said wide-eyed, so excited to be asked to help.

"So go to Sugar Loaf Rock, then double back to Garrison. Stop at British Landing Road and go as far as the golf course. Then go back to Annex Road and down to the Grand."

"That's Evasion Pattern Eight?" she asked.

"Yes. Don't deviate," he said emphatically, handing her the map.

"I won't," she promised as she started off. Then she stopped. "What's the message for Mr. Jones?"

"Tell him..." Fletch paused and I was sure he was making this up on the spot. "Yellow lamp at 9 o'clock. Say it."

"Yellow lamp at 9 o'clock."

"Okay, don't forget."

"I won't," she said.

"Then wait in the lounge for at least a half hour before you leave – to make sure."

"Make sure what?" she asked.

"That you weren't followed!" he said.

She nodded pensively, as if this was a desperately important assignment.

"But give me the ring," she said.

"What?"

"Give me the Waverly Ring."

"Why?" he asked.

"That way they'll know I'm official," she said.

He just grimaced and took it off and gave it to her.

She peddled off on her bike. "Don't lose it," he called after her, "or you won't get another assignment." After a pause he yelled: "EVER."

"Okay," Fletch said as she faded from sight. "We're rid of her for the next three hours at least. We can go downtown and buy some snacks of some kind that we won't have to share with a girl."

Halfway down the Marquette Park steps we saw some really big pine cones. We thought we could put glitter on them and sell them for Christmas ornaments later so we were collecting them in my rucksack. Then I slipped on some moss, against a wooden support wall under the stairway. At least, it looked like a support wall.

It wasn't supporting anything anymore, if it ever did. When we moved it, it revealed a small interior space under the stairs. It was about three feet by five feet. We crouched down and supposed no one knew the space was there. It was full of moss and spider webs. We started to speculate. Maybe it was an Indian hideout from the old days. But no, the steps wouldn't have been there then. Well, no, it could have been a little cave, then the steps were built and no one noticed it anymore.

The ground was damp so we didn't sit on it. We dragged some rocks in to use as stools. We let our imaginations run. We were hiding from the British. Then we were hiding from Thrush agents in the *Bat Cave Affair*. A few times we were hiding from Mackinac College students who were following us with little Bible tracts.

"We could make this our regular hideout," Fletch said.

"Yeah, way cool," I said.

We decided to bring a lantern and some plastic lawn pillows.

"It'll be like a clubhouse," I said.

"Whenever we don't want anyone to find us, we come here," Fletch said.

"We could call ourselves the Step Dwellers Duo," I suggested.

He looked up in thought then nodded. He liked it.

That decided, we went to the store for snacks. Fletch had just enough money for a pop and Hostess Cupcakes. I got a Faygo, Hostess Cupcakes, too, and a big bag of New Era potato chips to share. We walked across Main Street, intending to consume our goodies while sitting up against the front of the Coast Guard Station. I ripped open the cellophane and started in on my first cupcake. Fletch grabbed some chips. He said he was saving the cupcakes for last. We watched the passing scene for a while. A Grand Hotel carriage passed, a bunch of bicyclists, and assorted pedestrians stepped over our legs. Then a group on horseback. A girl riding a dappled gray horse slowed the horse by pulling its reins. It surprised me that she stopped in front of us. The horse neighed and she said "Hi Fletch," looking down at him and throwing her long ponytail off her right shoulder onto her back with a toss of her head.

He looked up at her. "Oh, hi, Carlee," he said. "Want some cupcakes?" he asked while standing up and reaching into his bag before she even answered. He extended his hand with the unwrapped, saved-for-last, treat.

She reached down and took them with a smile, but without a word. Then she just twisted her ankle inward, tapping her boot heel into the horses belly, and rode off to catch up with her companions.

Fletch sat back down and I looked at him. "So much for snacks we don't have to share with a girl.”

“I know her from the riding stable,” he said, looking down into the chips bag. “She could have stopped to talk.”

“Yeah...” I didn't say anything more. It wasn't my desire to mix with horseback riders. But if she was going to take his cupcakes, I think she should have stayed a bit longer .

He was quiet, pulling out grass with one fist. I was quiet, not wanting to rub it in. “Let's get some milk,” I finally said, patting his back. He shook both shoulders to reject my sympathetic touch.

A rush to gather supplies for our dwelling provided distraction. We ran to Marblecliff and grabbed old vinyl-covered seat cushions from the back porch, a flashlight, potato chips and candy bars, plastic dishes, an alarm clock, writing paper. We went to the food market and made a secret insignia for the Step Dwellers Duo from Twin Pines milk carton emblems. Two pine trees, two members, it was perfect. We spent some time cleaning the cave out and went back to Marblecliff to get an old canoe tarp I remembered was in our shed.

When we got back we slid open the panel and Ayashe was inside, grinning at us.

I looked at Fletch. “Step Dwellers Three?”

He shrugged and sighed. “Trio... Ashe. What are you doing here?”

“Please! Please!!” Ayashe said. “Can I be your look-out?”

“Okay,” he relented. “IF you take a vow of secrecy,” he said, looking at me for a nod of agreement. I gave it. He continued: “You can be a member if you promise to never tell anyone this is here.”

She nodded. “Raise your right hand,” I said. “Do you solemnly swear...”

When she did, she hugged her brother. I thought she was so pleased to be included I don't think she would have told about the hideaway under any circumstance, up to and including Gestapo questioning.

Later Fletch and I were at Mom's office reading comics in the morgue, with the homeless Teddy bears that lived there, when she started a “budget meeting.” Only a newspaper budget meeting isn't about budgeting money. It's about budgeting stories. Like planning what they had and what they would use in the next edition. I could hear every word.

“Well what do you have for the paper this week, Britt?” Mom asked.

"Preview of the Bridge Walk. They expect 10,000 this year. Routine."

She waited for more.

"They've announced the faculty of the new college. That'll be long."

"Why should I devote space to that college? They're not advertising in my paper," Mom said.

"Because it's big news," he said, astonished that she would question it. "These people are pretty big deals."

"Yeah?"

"Yeah, like they're from the Sorbonne and Harvard and Princeton and Oxford and the like and every country you can think of. And the president, S. Douglas Cornell, is from Yale with loads of science credentials like the National Academy. And the Moral Rearmament angle is big. These folks think they're going to teach us all stuff."

"And this bag of pretentious academics," Mom interrupted, "who've probably never done a day of real work in their lives, are going to tell us how to mind our morals? Bah humbug."

"That makes it more of a story," he said, but timidly.

Mom appreciated universities and the learning that colleges offered, but was unimpressed with those who teach without first going out into the world and working.

And the new college on Mackinac had an aura of what was not right with the world, she said. It was founded by people who believed in absolutes.

"Well, perhaps in this loooong story, Mr. Niagara, you'll tell me if these people are all kooks or fascists or what? Or are they Ku Klux Klan? And do they want to take over this idyllic island as their own headquarters for spewing that junk? Just what are they? Is your long story going to tell me that?

"I don't think so."

She glared.

"I'll try."

Mom poked her nose past the archway to the morgue. "Walter, here's something for you, since your picture of the governor's son came out so well. Can you take a picture of the dedication of the refurbished Indian Dormitory? They're having an opening ceremony."

"Sure, Mom," I said.

"Dr. Eugene Peterson will be giving a speech. See if you can take a few notes and write it up. Just a short."

"Argh," I said, "but yes."

"Hey, photographers have to come back with information, too," she said. "I'll do the Police Chief's resignation. That's got to be politics."

When Fletch went home, I decided to go to the library before they closed to see what historic facts I could dig up about the Indian Dormitory. I parked my bike and saw Ashe's unmistakable little bike with the pink handlebar streamers. I thought she might be inside the library, but then I heard little gasps.

I walked up the steps. She was sitting on the library porch, back against the wall, head down, clutching her knees.

"Hi, Ashe," I said.

She looked up with wet eyes and a face of dried tear streaks, visible because they were mixed with dirt from her hands.

"What's the matter?" I asked.

She started sobbing. She told me, in fits and starts with words punctuated by sobs, that she lost Fletch's Waverly Ring.

"And he'll kick me out of the Step Dwellers Trio, I know it..." she sobbed again. "I want to be in the club."

"Well, maybe we can find it," I said. "Whenever I can't find something my mom asks me to think where I was when I last used it and then go back there and retrace my steps. That usually works. Where did you last have it?"

"I had it doing the Evasion Pattern Eight," she said. "I was riding my bike the way Fletch told me. I don't know where I lost it."

"Well, I'll ride the same way. It's probably just on the ground."

"Would you?" She said, brightening a little.

"Yeah, sure." I said. "I'll try. But it's going to get dark soon. I might have to finish looking in the morning. So meet me here tomorrow about noon. Now tell me the way you went."

Well, it was hard just getting her to remember what Evasion Pattern Eight was. I tried to retrace it. I got to Arch Rock and decided the effort was ridiculous.

She was waiting at the library next day before I got there. I held up the ring the minute I saw her and she ran to me with such acceleration that I had no choice but to grab her up off her feet as she hugged me. I swung her around in a couple circles.

"Wherever did you find it?" she asked. I told her at the Grand. No need to let Fletch know I bought it. He still owed me 60 cents for the first one.

INTERLOGUE

MACKINAC COLLEGE WAS READYING to open on September 14. In the words of its new president, S. Douglas Cornell:

> "The Mackinac concept is that education has
> two roles to play. One is the imparting of
> knowledge, the training of the intellect, the
> sharpening of the mind. The other is the
> building in men's lives of an adequate framework
> of purpose and moral responsibility... "

Moral Rearmament, the religious movement upon which it was based, cited "absolutes" in the matter of honesty, unselfishness, purity, and love.

But then, whose morals were they?

The college stood on a 21-acre site which had served as a conference center during the past decade for Moral Rearmament devotees. Two years of "careful" research, the group said, showed there was a market for an institution dedicated to learning based on both knowledge and a "devotion to moral disciplines and larger motivations."

Funding came in from right-wing groups of all kinds, and rich individuals, including Mrs. Henry Ford, who had suggested the site, so an impressive faculty could be hired. They came from top institutions of higher learning across the globe. The college was designed to equip students "morally, spiritually, and intellectually" to push back against just about everything ushered in by the Sixties so far.

The philosophy was particularly that of Dr. or Rev. Frank Buchman, a Protestant Christian evangelist from Pennsylvania who founded the Oxford Group, in England about 1928. There, Buchman would host house parties to get young people together to encourage their religious practice and promote theocracy as a solution to the world's problems. In 1932 and 1933 he sought, unsuccessfully, to meet with Adolf Hitler. Nevertheless, he would write in 1936 that he liked what Hitler was doing to save Europe from godless communism.

Every country, he said, needed a moral and spiritual awakening. He blamed "materialism" for the evil societal changes he saw and preached against it.

13 – BRIDGE WALK

SUDDENLY IT WAS SEPTEMBER and we played like there was no tomorrow – because the start of school was almost upon us. Sunday before Labor Day Fletch and I acted out U.N.C.L.E. versus Thrush all day. He was Napoleon, I was Illya. We acted out parts of the *Finny Foot Affair.* That was the one with the old age formula and the kid who follows Napoleon Solo onto the plane to Norway because he thinks he might get him interested in his widowed mother. We pretended we were rapidly aging, Marquette Park substituting for a village on the Scottish coast. In the lake, we pretended we were in waters off Norway. Anne's Tablet was the stand-in for The Maid of Norway statue. "Marry the Maiden" was the big clue. In the show a clue was a big ring that fit on the statue's finger and pointed the way. We put Silly Putty on top of Anne's ring finger, since it was not a complete free standing statue like in the show and didn't have a backside.

Then we sat around and talked at the Tablet site until the fireflies could be seen blinking on and off above the forest grass. I got home just in time for dinner. Next day was going to be the Bridge Walk. For almost ten years this had been Michigan's big Labor Day celebration for adults, but Fletch said it was depressing for kids. It meant school would be starting the next day.

Mom asked if I wanted to go on the Walk. She would be walking next to Governor Romney.

It is the only day of the year anyone can walk across the bridge, she said, but I didn't see it as a big deal. I walked across the Brooklyn Bridge lots of times.

"The Brooklyn Bridge is a lot shorter than Mighty Mac," Mom said.

"I'll think about it," I said.

Freya came to cover the Bridge Walk for the *Free Press*. She normally wouldn't cover something frivolous like that, because she was a serious reporter, but she wanted to see Mom and, nowadays, being the girlfriend of the city editor, she could just about name her assignments. The city editor's name was Karl Lovekey. How did I remember that? How could one forget, ha ha ha? I walked in when she and Mom were talking in the kitchen. I left the Norelco recorder on the counter with the microphone standing in its case, and surreptitiously turned it on.

"So you know we have John S. Knight's grandson working in the newsroom?" Freya asked.

"The founder and publisher's grandson? How's that working out?" Mom asked.

"Weird. See one day Karl needs him to go to Toledo to cover a plant strike and he says he'll take a cab. And Karl replies: 'That'll cost a fortune.' John S. Knight the Third replies: 'I have a fortune.'" Freya gestured bending her wrist down.

Pretty soon she and Mom are both laughing so hard they're stomping their feet, bending and holding their middles, gasping and and tromping all over the kitchen.

"Oh, Freya, you are really bad," Mom says. When Freya laughed her long wavy hair bounced. It was the color of that rusted anchor by the Arnold Ferry dock.

When they stopped laughing, I was opening the fridge. As I was perusing snack possibilities, Freya asked Mom:

"So how's your dissertation coming?"

I tried to retract my head into my shoulders like a turtle.

"Oh, you know how dissertations go," she said. "What you think will take a month takes six, and what you think will take a year takes two. But the research is done. I'm writing now."

"That's good. I'll be having to call you Doctor Hudson soon."

Mom waved her hand as if brushing that thought away. "So what's new in your newsroom?" she asked. Whew. She wasn't going to bring up my recent *help.*

"Well, remember Barbara Stanton?"

"Sure, knew her when she was getting her master's at Columbia."

"She's on the copy desk now."

"Really? She was such a great beat reporter. Why would she want that?

"She didn't."

"Then why? Wasn't she uncovering all that juicy stuff covering Wayne County Courts?"

"Yeah. Great stuff. Only then she married a judge."

"I see the conflict of interest. But copy desk? I mean, they could have given her Education or something."

"Taken."

"City?"

"That's mine."

"How 'bout your city editor?" Mom raised her brows. "He yours, too?"

Freya looked up and sighed.

"No, I mean it. How's it going between you and Karl?" Mom asked.

When women start talking about boyfriends they don't notice much. I seized the opportunity to go after ice cream. I was right. Mom didn't see a thing.

"Well," Freya said, her voice going low. "Great. Except people in the office are a bit stiff about it, you know. They think there's favoritism now." She faked a snotty voice: "'Mr. Lovekey gives all the good assignments to Freya.' Honestly, Lex, it's just the opposite. I get all the bad shit that happens."

"But isn't that the good shit?" Mom asked. "Journalistically speaking, of course."

"We'll sure, but sometimes I'd like to just cover a Hudson's parade or something."

"Well," Mom smiled. "That's why you're here, to cover the Bridge Walk. Besides, it's good exercise."

"You don't think I'm going to walk five miles, do you?"

"Why not? In New York I could walk from Central Park to Battery Park in an afternoon. That's about 90 blocks."

"No way. You go walk from St. Ignace in that crowd. You know they're expecting 10-15,000 people? I'll drive over to Mackinaw City after the traffic dies down and I'll just talk to the governor a bit there."

"He might leave right away."

"He'll wait for me. He needs the *Free Press*."

"Even so, isn't that phoneying it up? You're not actually covering The Walk. What if he says something important midway? What if he stops at the high point on the bridge and says: "We should commit ourselves, before this decade is out, to put a woman on the State Supreme Court..."

"And bring her safely back to the kitchen later?" Freya quipped.

They started laughing again. Brought themselves to tears.

"You know what I mean," Mom said.

"Like what's he going to say? He's going to start a Peace Corps? That was the last time any politician said anything spontaneous, when JFK blurted out 'Peace Corps' when he was campaigning at U of M."

"I don't know. Maybe he could say something about desegregation or executive job opportunities for Negro auto workers."

"Like did they have that when he was CEO of American Motors?"

"Times are a-changin'."

"You so sure? Well, maybe for Negroes. Oh, sorry. Floyd McKissick says they don't want to be called that anymore."

"What do they want to be called?"

"Blacks."

"Blacks? How's that better? Anyway, what about women?"

"Yeah, what about us?" Freya asked. "When is Sigma Delta Chi going to admit women?"

I swallowed a cold glob. "What's Sigma Delta Chi?" I asked.

"It's a professional organization for journalists with one major membership restriction," Mom said. "You have to be a man."

"Yeah," Freya said. "Dickey Chapelle – a woman – was killed in Vietnam last year taking news photos. I suppose they think that wasn't practicing journalism." Palms together she looked up. "Aren't I a journalist?"

Mom said: "Sojourner Truth." I looked up from the ice cream carton. Nobody noticed. I put the spoon back in. Freya kept talking.

"Karl and I walked into this nice restaurant in Southfield the other day and I was wearing this really dressy pants suit – I mean a nice Givenchy suit from Jacobson's. It was navy cashmere. The jacket was long and fitted at the waist and had crystal buttons all the way down." She gestured from her neck to her hips. "It also had a satin trim collar and cuffs. But it was unacceptable. They said I couldn't come in wearing pants!"

"I can just hear you giving them a piece of your mind, Freya," Mom said.

"Nope." She smiled. "I said 'okay.'"

"You said 'okay'? You? You just walked out? Karl didn't say anything?"

"No, we didn't walk out! I said 'okay' and took the pants off!"

"You what?"

"I took the pants off and then I was wearing a crystal-buttoned mini-dress. A short, short dress, but a dress. Well, the rules didn't say how long of a dress you had to have. The jacket was just long enough to cover my butt, but, then, that's today's minis. Good thing they invented sheer-to-the-top pantyhose."

"And you have great legs."

"Thanks.... A lot of people think the mini dress is scandalous. Well, if they're going to bar pants suits! I let everyone know, too. I said it real loud. 'Oh, so you don't let women coming in wearing pants, do you'.... The maitre-d's eyes just about popped out of his bald head."

"So what happened?"

"We got seated real fast."

They started to laugh and hug.

"You're amazing, Freya," Mom said.

"Hey, so are you, kid. Giving up New York City for this...."

"This is pretty cool, Freya. It's a great life. No pollution, no crime, no cars, and," Mom looked at me spooning ice cream, "plenty of stars!"

"Well, I guess it's great for the kid," she said, "as opposed to dirty old Brooklyn."

"No!" I said, swallowing a huge lump of ice cream that was so cold it made my head hurt. "It's not."

"What don't you like about it?"

"No cars!" I said.

" But you have no objection to the stars?" she asked.

"Well, no...they're pretty cool."

"And I hear you're going to build a telescope," she said.

"Yes," I said. "If the parts come in the mail. If the post office can find this place."

"Bedtime, kiddo," Mom said.

I started for the stairs. Freya grabbed my arm. "Walter, don't forget to come to the mainland and see my new car tomorrow," she said. "You'll love it – It's a Thunderbird Apollo. It's a concept car. That means, well, it's just to show off ideas. There were only five made – but Henry Ford junior gave one to me to drive. It's metallic royal blue with a metallic blue vinyl top and blue leather bucket seats and that super cool landau emblem." She made made a stretched out 's' in the air with her finger. "And suicide doors," she said. "They open like this..." She showed me by putting her knuckles together then opening her arms, but I knew what it meant anyway.

"And get this," she continued, "a power-operated sun-roof. It just slides open to the sky! Have you ever heard of such a thing? No, no one has. And in the back seat there's a folding table built-in to the front seat's back and there's a telephone and television!"

My eyes did widen a little. "Wow, cool," I said, meaning it.

"Freya," Mom asked, "Where do you park a car like that in downtown Detroit?"

"Anywhere I want to," she said, grinning. "Nobody would ticket a car like that. Tonight it's in St. Ignace, at the ferry dock."

"Walter, get to bed," Mom said. "We have to gather at the governor's mansion by 6:30 a.m. He leads the Walk and we go with him. You might find it fun."

Fun? Nothing could be fun at 6:30 in the morning.

"You can decide later," Mom went on. "If you don't want to go with us you can just walk home. But this year they're going to have a Marquette's Landing pageant, too."

"Oh," I said, already half asleep walking upstairs. As I brushed my teeth in a daze I was wondering what's a Rockette's Landing. That's what I thought she said. I thought of the Rockette's Christmas show in Rockefeller Center. I visualized dancers in short red and white dresses trimmed in white fur. It didn't occur to me to question "landing." I thought about them all landing on the bridge in a giant helicopter and getting out with their bare legs... Then my head hit the pillow and I fell asleep.

That's why it was so funny in the morning. I was still not fully awake when we started walking towards the governor's mansion, but I grabbed my recorder because I took it everywhere. We were opposite the house on Fort Street, same as a number of other people, when we heard a helicopter. Of course we all looked up because it was really loud. The helicopter's bubble cabin reflected the orange and lavenders of the early morning sunrise over the lake, so it looked like a *Mysterious Island*-sized, dragonfly as it landed. Everyone who had already arrived seemed to be watching the landing. "Is it the Rockette's

Landing?" I asked Mom.

"What?" she said, perplexed. Then I heard someone say: "Senator Hart's on time."

We watched until the people got out, with that slight bending motion people do when they're under helicopter blades. But the blades stopped and the pilot got out last and flipped the sunglasses onto the top of his head.

Only it was her head, I soon learned. She was tall and nicely slim, but no Rockette, if you know what I mean. She was wearing plain blue trousers and a man's type polo shirt. Her hair was short. The man was greeted as "Senator." She was "Mrs. Hart." The first thing I noticed, when she got close enough, was her huge wristwatch.

"The pilot's a girl?" I whispered to Mom.

"Yes, well, not 'girl' exactly," Mom replied. "Since she's the mother of eight. That's Mrs. Hart. She's Senator Phil Hart's wife. She learned to fly helicopters to take him on his campaign stops when he ran for senator in 1957."

Oh, so those were our neighbors down the street, I thought. In the summer, when they're not in Washington.

"She was the first woman in Michigan to get a helicopter pilot's license," Mom added.

I just looked.

"There's something else I have to tell you about her later," Mom said as the door was opened by a woman with an apron. A fancy dressed woman stepped from behind us as Mr. and Mrs. Hart approached.

"Hello, Lenore..." said several of the arrivees. I knew Lenore was Mrs. Romney, the governor's wife.

We were offered a standing breakfast out on the front porch. Choices on the table were green Jello and Utah scones, a hot puddle of fried dough drenched in butter and honey. I hate honey, so I only took the cup of Jello. I was going to come back for the canned pineapple. Lenore Romney didn't look anything like Mrs. Hart. Mrs. Romney was on her way to becoming an MGM movie star, they say, when she met George. Well, she looked to me like she thought movie cameras were on, like everyone was supposed to look at her. She was wearing a navy blue dress with red collar and red pocket flaps, red and white scarf and pearls. She said she would change from her high heels to walking shoes and disappeared. Mrs. Hart was already wearing loafers. Lenore Romney and Jane Hart looked at each other once and then, almost instantly, looked away.

Mrs. Hart leaned casually against a wall, sipping coffee from a tea cup. She had short, straight, blondish hair, thin lips, and eyebrows that turned down rather than up, which kind of gave her a tired look – until she smiled and then her eyes looked like tiny sparklers. She had no jewelry on except for a wedding band and that big watch.

"Janey, I want you to meet my son," Mom said.

I looked up from my wiggling Jello.

Mrs. Hart smiled. "Well, hi, Alexis. I heard you were now ensconced in the Hodiak cottage. And took over the paper."

"Yes. I don't think you've ever had a chance to meet my son, Walter."

"Walter! That's my father's name and my oldest son's name," Jane Hart said, smiling large, igniting the sparklers. "Welcome to the island, Walter." She extended a hand and I shook it.

"Thank you," I said, "But I don't..." I stopped. I felt like saying "I don't want to be here," but knew that would be insulting and Mom wouldn't like it.

I learned later that her father was Walter Briggs, who owned Tiger Stadium.

"Walter's interested in the space program, too," Mom said then, looking at me, she said:

"Mrs. Hart has passed all the tests to become an astronaut. She could actually be one of the first women to make it into space."

"Well," Mrs. Hart said, "If the men ever get over themselves. We're still waiting to hear."

"I hope you make it," Mom said.

"And this is Phil Hart, Walter," she said, "He's our senator. The Harts live in Washington most of the time, but they have a cottage on the East Bluff too, just down from ours and before the Lehman's."

"Cool," I said, not meaning it.

"But Marblecliff is so much more interesting than Ann's," Mrs. Hart said. Ann Bronfman is the granddaughter of Arthur Lehman, Mom said. That didn't mean anything to me, but later she told me he founded Lehman Brothers, a big Wall Street investment firm.

Mom then started to talk to the senator about Vietnam, war protests on campuses, and the next move in Civil Rights. I backed away.

I went back to the food, took some canned pineapple, and heard one woman say: "Mormons use canned pineapple in just about everything." Others muttered other things about the food. I was pretty much deciding I wasn't going to walk the bridge. I didn't like crowds. I could just see people pushing. A fist fight breaks out. Those low railings... I shuddered. I went back to Mom and told her, interrupting her talking to the senator, that I was going to go home. She just nodded and said, "Be careful."

I couldn't push through the crowd to the porch doors, so I started to look for another way out. The porch hooked up with some kind of room, a living room of some kind. I saw a formal dining room. Nobody was in there. I wandered off and opened a door. A bathroom. I saw the kitchen, opened a pantry door and another bathroom door. There were people going back and forth quickly and did not stop to question me. After two bathrooms I decided to see if I could find all nine that they said it had. I tip-toed upstairs where I was pretty sure I wasn't supposed to go... four, five... six... I went into a bedroom. Seven... eight. A uniformed woman, a maid or a caterer, asked me what I was looking for. I said, "Ah... they told me there was a library...."

"Downstairs, right door," she said. I went down. I was still wondering where the ninth bathroom was. I found the library, though. It was away from the buzz of voices coming from the side porch. There was a potted palm by the door and a tan leather two-seat couch at the center of the room with its back to an irresistible landing up half a flight of stairs – what they call a mezzanine at Macy's in Manhattan. I always go up stairways and walk along railings. I went up there and sat down. I started looking at books. The Michigan State Constitutional Convention. Bleh. Really boring stuff.

I laid down and put my head on one of the big books. I knew I got up too early, but didn't think I'd fall asleep. But I did.

It was a minute. Or a few minutes. Or maybe half an hour. I don't really know for how long. I woke up hearing the door to the room click shut. The buzz of voices from the side porch were gone. The walking party must have left for the ferry dock and the governor's special boat to St. Ignace, where the Bridge Walk would start. Since I had gotten where I wasn't supposed to be, in the governor's house no less, I didn't dare stand up, but peering through the railing, I saw seven people enter the room.

There was a solid wood panel of about 12 inches at the base of the mezzanine railing. That was the reason the four men with guns didn't see me.

14 – WITNESS

I COULD SEE THEM between the railing slats.   Four men in police uniforms. They were standing. There were others.

"Are we all here?" said a man with a receding hairline, a big flat nose, and reddish dark circles around his eyes that made me think of a raccoon. One of the officers walked to the other side of a couch and turned his back to the railing. He was so close I could have touched his Michigan State Police arm patch. I looked down right at the butt of his holstered gun. I tried not to breathe.

The other police were standing. One mimicking the potted palm on the other side of the door and two facing the couch. Two regularly dressed men were seated in chairs opposite the couch. They wore charcoal gray suits with white shirts and narrow blue ties. One was plain looking, the other had a beard and a big nose. He was a real troll.

Raccoon Man took charge. "Is everyone else gone from the house?" he asked in a British-like accent.

People nodded. "Except the household staff," someone said.

"Shut the door. Then we can talk freely," said the bearded troll.

"Let's just not be overheard," Raccoon Man said.

Naturally, that made me want to record what they were saying. If Mom did it, it would be good reporting, but she might say I was invading privacy. I set the book I was holding down quietly and pushed down on the red button on the Norelco, but hesitated over pushing in the record lever because I knew it does make a slight click when it engages. But the plain man started to clear his throat while he grabbed for the ashtray, joined by the cop with his back to me, and that's when I did it. No one heard above the coughs. I looked, five of seven them were smoking. I had no purpose for my recording at that time. Just wanted to know if I could do it secret like.

"Okay, we have the money. Is the governor with us?"

"I believe he is," said one.

"Sometimes we're not sure," he said. "He was out there marching for god-damned integration a few months ago."

The door opened. A young man in a sports coat, turtleneck shirt, no tie, came in and closed the door with a soft click. He moved next to the palm. "That's just politics," he said.

The palm tree was in the way so I couldn't clearly see his face, but he seemed familiar. "Marching was for the press, you know. I know how to deal with the press. Privately, the governor is a devout Mormon and..." His voice slowed down. "Mormons believe.....Mormons know ...." Then it sped up like a record: "Negroes are a people cursed by God and it is not for man to remove God's curse."

"Great kid. Whatever works for you," the raccoony guy said sarcastically. "We just don't want Negroes, cursed or uncursed, in our white neighborhoods around Detroit, going to shopping centers next to our wives and schools with our kids, 'cause they'll be datin' our daughters next."

"I saw a big 'ole Nigra boy holding hands with a white girl once," the bearded man said. "Next thing you know ..."

"Shut up John," he continued. "We got real estate agents and mortgage bankers mostly all on the same page. Negroes walk in to a real estate office, the agents say nothing's for sale. If they find anything on their own, the banks steer clear of making them loans. But we don't want any slip-ups and now we got this one about to happen. Some turncoat son of a bitch decided to sell his home privately and this Negro doctor, he had cash to buy it, see. Soooo we're not gonna let that happen. We can't let it happen. They're not going to move in. 'Cause when one Nigger gets in, others follow. We will do what it takes—harassment, threats if necessary. We just want the state police to look the other way."

The young man laughed. "The state police are completely controlled by my dad."

"We know," said the troll. "That's why you can pinch a state police uniform and drive around stopping cars and harassing girls and get away with it even though impersonating a cop's a felony."

"Yeah, well, I wouldn't say any more."

"Sure, kid. Daddy's gonna protect you if anybody blows the whistle."

The kid glared. Then I recognized him. That's who that was. Wil-lard Romney, a.k.a. Mitt. The boorish bocce player whose picture I got in the paper.

"Hey, lay off the kid," Raccoon Man said. "We'd all do it if we could. Who wouldn't want to employ a red flashing light on the top of the car when we want to stop chicks? What a scam."

"We don't care about that," the troll said. "What we care about is this Nigra doc, one Dr. Clifford Mongabay, bought a home where he shouldn'ta outta have. Bein' a cardiologist at Providence Hospital is gettin' him beyond his place. Made too much money already. Buys a house in Birmingham! Your neck of the woods, kid."

"You mean Bloomfield Hills," said the governor's son.

"Yeah, Bloomfield, Birmingham, Grosse Pointe. What's the diff? He ain't gonna move into it."

Mitt Romney backed out of the room. "You guys talk among yourselves," he said, closing the double doors in front of himself with a smarmy smile.

"We have the bucks to stop it," Raccoon man continued.

"It isn't going to be easy," said one of the cops.

"Yeah," said troll man. "The doc's got his own bucks and he's probably seen *Raisin in the Sun*. We can't just buy it from him and tell him to stay out of Livonia, too, while we're at it. He can buy anywhere."

"Not really," Raccoon Man said. "Like John, our lawyer, said, we've got the bankers and the realtors. And now," he said, nodding to the bearded guy, "We got 500,000 bucks says it isn't going to happen. We send it to the Governor's 'Presidential Exploratory Committee.' He tells his state police to back off. Quid pro quo, his campaign gets a big boost. City cops, we know how to handle them. Our protests will be huge. We got whites from all over willing to make sure. We just don't want state cops comin' in." It got quiet.

Raccoon Man continued. "Okay. I think the kid knows his old man. We can talk the tough shit now. You know what we have to do. Municipal red tape. Fire code violations. Drag it out. Then you call when this Mongabay tries to move into his new house and we'll persuade him that wasn't one of his best ideas."

"He's got some NAACP connections. He won't be persuaded easy," the plain guy said.

"Then we'll persuade him hard," he said, smacking his left palm with his right fist.

Smoke had been getting to me, wafting right up from the cop near me. My eyes were watering and finally I had to cough. They might not have noticed it wasn't one of them coughing, but it made me move my leg and I accidentally pushed a stack of books and the top one fell through the railing. I clenched my teeth.

The book dropped behind the couch the men were sitting on.

"What the Hell?" someone said, and all the heads turned toward me and Raccoon Man walked closer. For a terrifying second I was nose to nose with him. We were staring into each other's eyes. I started rubbing mine, pretending to be just waking up.

"I'm sorry," I said. "I fell asleep here."

"Come down here," he demanded. I walked down. "Who are you? What is that?"

"Oh, that's my new transistor radio," I said, sidling toward the door. I thought I'd better play stupid.

"What are you doing here?"

"Sorry, I fell asleep. I just woke up. I was supposed to go on the Bridge Walk." I rubbed my eyes and stretched my arms.

One of the officers grabbed the Norelco's black strap. It was still recording. I pulled away and turned smack into the bearded guy. He fumbled about and said "Stop him!" as I bolted.

People ran after me. I bounded out the front door and down the porch steps and into the street and when I glanced back it was two officers and Raccoon Man, but he stopped on the porch.

One officer caught the tail of my shirt, but I twisted free. He didn't seem to be taking it too seriously. He just laughed and yelled after me. "Better watch out, kid." The other one stopped while Raccoon Man yelled "Catch him!"

"We can't shoot him!" the officer yelled back. "What can a kid do?" I glanced back as I went out the front door. One officer was still running after me, and he seemed to be taking it seriously. "Better stop kid," he yelled.

I glanced back. The one officer gave me breathing room by debating with the guy yelling orders. I'd already crossed the road and dashed into the bushes. A thorny branch caught my arm. Normally, you would stop and pull it out so it wouldn't rip your skin, but I just plowed ahead. And it tore my arm, but

I didn't have time to look at how bad.

I thought I could out-run him; like I said, I'm fast. But he was taller. Long legs can catch kids. But when I hit the horse trail I had an idea.

I remembered where that horse poop had been before and had high hopes for a fresh pile, nothing being more assured on Mackinac Island. Yes! It was there. I scooped up a handful with my left hand. (When you're desperate you don't think about yucky.) It was just the right consistency. Mushy, but sticky. I grabbed a tree with my right arm and swung around behind it. When the pursuing officer started running down the trail I waited for just the moment intuition told me he would be opposite the tree and, hanging on to the tree with my right hand, I swung out and pasted him in the face with the contents of my left. He was running full bore. Obviously, he didn't imagine I would stop. So he smacked into it hard, lost his footing, and swore.

"Damn!" he said. "My eyes!" I could hear him swearing and yucking, but I just poured my energy into my feet. I took the only route I knew. My arms were pumping as I disposed of the trail and got to Garrison Road.

My left hand was sticky with poop and I kept shaking it to get the stuff off. But I kept running.

15 – SCOOP

I WAS LYING BLEEDING in Skull Cave – again.

Again I waited, heart pumping. This was what they call D-jayvoo or something. Feeling like you've done this before. But it wasn't exactly. This time I'd been chased by bad state cops, not my irritating, but fairly harmless, Eurasian cousins. This time my arm was cut.

Mom was probably somewhere out on the lake in a ferry or walking the Mackinac Bridge by now. They were to walk south, from St Ignace, she said. I could try to find the local police chief. Good he wasn't state police, but I think he left the island after his resignation – something about garbage pickup schedules. Anyway, would he or anyone else challenge state troopers? FBI agents maybe. But I didn't think any of those guys were around. I could try to find Mr. Niagara, but no, he'd probably help the cops. Hey, wait a minute, I thought. Freya's press pass would trump any cops trying to nab me for dubious reasons. And she has that cool car phone. But I had to find her. Where did she say she'd be? Driving to Mackinaw City to meet them. She said she parked the car at a St. Ignace ferry dock. That covers a lot of ground. And I'd have to get there. Hopefully she wasn't in a hurry – no, she said she'd ride over to Mackinaw City after the traffic dies down. The walkers have to have time to go five miles. I hurried to the dock. A ferry was loading.

I didn't have any money, but Captain Rhodes was there. He just smiled and waved me on like he has been doing since we got here. When we came out of the harbor I walked up to the boat's upper deck. I paced as we passed the West Bluff and the bridge came into sight. I paced stern to aft the whole 18 minutes. I knew Freya said she parked it anywhere she wanted to, but most parking spaces were filled up today. I disembarked and walked among the rows of cars. I didn't see anything like a fancy metallic royal blue Thunderbird in front of the docks, so I started walking along Main Street, dock-side. There was a crowd of people in front of the pancake house! Sure enough, they were gawking at a car parked along the street city-side. It was a Thunderbird.   Around the sidewalk side, Freya was sitting side saddle on the front passenger seat with the door open and her feet on the curb. She was talking on the phone. Then she saw me.

"Gotta go, Karl. Talk to you tonight."

She smiled at me. "So, kid...you decided to come see my car? Your mom's still on the bridge."

"Yeah, I know, listen," I said.

She looked at me questioningly. "You look kind of messed up. What's that on your shirt? Blood?" She grabbed my arm and twisted it to where it was sliced by the thorn. "How'd you do that?"

"Listen..." I said.

"And what is that smell?" She sniffed and her nose went to my left hand.

"It's horse poop. Listen...."

"Horse poop! What have you been doing? You fell off a horse?"

"No, I wasn't on a horse. Listen!"

"Okay," she finally said. And I told her the story while she dragged me into the pancake house *girls'* bathroom and washed my hands.

"Then there WAS something to that telegram your mother got..."

"That's what I'm trying to tell you … and now they're after me."

"Goodness," she said and took my hand. "We've got to find your mom."

"Yes...and get out of *here.*"

We rushed back to her car. I got there just ahead of her and picked up the phone, but I really didn't know how to work it.

"Open Channel D?" I queried.

"Give it here, Solo." She grabbed the receiver from me with a smirk. "Firestone N-1149. Patch me through to the governor's security detail," she said. She tapped the receiver while waiting. Then someone came on. "Where's the governor's party?" she asked them. She found out they were over the half way mark descending into Mackinaw City. For them that was still about a hour's walk. "We'll drive," she said, pointing. "In and seatbelt." She went around to the driver's side. We headed to the south-bound bridge approach and up we went.

Only one driving lane was open that direction. And there was a backup of

traffic. Freya just drove on, passing cars, getting in the way of opposing traffic, and flashing her press pass Brenda Starr-like at anyone who moved to stop us.

"See if you can see the front of the column or spot your mom," she said. She pushed a button and I heard a soft motor sound above me. It was the roof opening up.

"Stick your head out the sun roof and look," she said.

"Can I stand on these leather seats?" I asked.

"No! Oh, what the Hell?" she said. "Of course."

I unbuckled the seatbelt, quickly loosened my shoe laces and kicked my shoes off. Then stood up and stuck my head out.

We were angled up. I put my hands on the rooftop. The wind whipped my hair. That was cool. We were going faster than Mom ever drove it and it was kind of exhilarating. Now this was the way to be on a bridge!

It felt as windy as it was on that ferry coming across the straits, only with a better view. I could see over the sides – how the waves of the straits peaked and fell.

We leveled off in the center, then we were coming down and getting over land again when I saw Mom. Well, not specifically, but the governor's party, because that's where all the photographers were and people carrying boom mikes. And the "secret" security agents. You couldn't miss them, they were so obvious, with dark blue suits and walkie talkies. I sat back down.

"They're just up ahead."

"Well let's interrupt them!"

She turned suddenly and whipped that car around facing the other way, right beside the governor's group. A number of officers started to yell, "Hey, you can't park there," but she parked, blocking half a walking lane and half a driving lane.

Freya told me to stay put and got out and waved a press pass at the approaching officer waving his arms. He was too late. Governor Romney was shaking her hand. After a few exchanges, she whispered in Mom's ear and Mom looked up towards me, my head again out the hole in the top of the car. Mom's eyes widened. She nodded and both of them marched towards the Thunderbird.

"Got enough to write a Bridge Walk story?" Freya asked when they got to the door.

"An hour ago," Mom said walking around to my side. "I can give you yours, too."

I was still standing half out the roof. "Say....you can't stare at the sun, but you could look at the night sky all you wanted. Why not call it a moon roof?"

~~~

After we got the car off the bridge, and I must say I was mad Mom made me sit down, we got out at the first diner in Mackinaw City. "My treat for coffee," Freya said, dashing toward the place. We followed and all sat in a booth. They had coffee and I had a Faygo Red Pop. Freya and I filled Mom in on the bribery plot and my hairbreadth escape. Mom's eyes kept widening. She put her hands on my cheeks. After she checked me out for damages and found nothing major, they talked about the story this *would have* made.

"If only we had proof," Mom said.

"We have a witness," Freya said, directing her thumb back at me.

"I..." I started to say.

"He's a kid. Since when is a kid going to be considered a credible witness?"

"With the telegram it's two pieces of...."

"You should always have at least three..."

"I...." I started to speak.

"No, we need proof."

"We could say it's an anonymous source."

"Without proof?"

"We say we have it, but we are protecting our source."

"They'll never...."

"Mom, I..."

"We gotta put it out there. Maybe someone will come forward..."

"Mom...."

"You hope."

"MOM."

"It's too damn weak."

" MOM!"

I finally got their attention. Sometimes you just gotta raise your voice.

"Remember the Norelco?"

"That cassette recorder? Sure ...."

Freya continued as if she hadn't heard me: "This is such a big story, if only..." Then she pulled a handful of her wavy cinnamon hair 'til it was stretched straight. Then Mom suddenly grabbed her arm so hard she said "Ow."
~~~

Mom and Freya looked at each other then at me. Freya looked perplexed, but Mom had finally got her bulb lit.

"Walter, you mean you..."

"Yep!" I smiled.

"My kid. My kid!" Mom grabbed my head between her hands and kissed me. She ruffled my hair. She looked at Freya. "What a great kid this is!!!!!!! Is this a great kid or what?" She must have kissed me a dozen times. People were starting to look.

~~~

Well, we were all pretty revved up. We climbed back into the Thunderbird, locked the suicide doors, and huddled. I described the man who seemed to be in charge, balding, with flat nose and those raccoon eyes. I played the tape for them. They noticed the English accent, but couldn't explain it. They were silent for a few beats, then they looked at each other and went nuts laughing and screaming. Mom wrote the story for the next edition of the *Huron Shores Herald*. The Bridge Walk story was played page one, but below the fold. "First time in history," Mom muttered, Bridge Walk goes below the fold. Freya broke the bribe attempt story the same day in the *Free Press*. In journalism parlance, it was a scoop.

They both used the same headline:

Attempted Bribery of Governor

And the same drophead:

Aim is to Stall Housing Integration

And a smaller drop:

Where is the $500,000?

Governor Romney denied knowledge of any of it.

There was an uproar in state politics. Of course, more people read the
~~~

story in the *Free Press*, but it was credited to the *Huron Shores Herald*. I was kind of proud, but they didn't name me. I was the protected source.

Of course, I couldn't identify Raccoon Man by name... or any of the men for that matter. Mom and Freya kept asking me if I saw anything… a hat, a briefcase, a ring on a hand, ANYTHING that would be a lead to identifying them. But I hadn't. We knew there was a lawyer named John, but so were half the lawyers in the world. I hadn't seen anything that could identify anybody. Except Mitt Romney, but he left early. I had never seen the older guys before. They showed me pictures of all kinds of well-known people, Ku Klux Klan members to prominent Detroiters, but none of them were the guys.

Mom tried to call Mitt Romney, but he was back at Stanford, according to the governor's office. People at Stanford University said they couldn't reach him "at this time." Mom and Freya decided not to name him at this point. After all, he was not a public official. When we were still in the car, Mom explained libel law involving government officials. So that people won't be afraid of criticizing government, the law allows you to say anything about politicians and government officials. You don't have to be able to prove it as long as you didn't have reckless disregard for the truth. The Supreme Court said you can be completely wrong as long as the other side can't prove you were reckless or acted with malice (*Times v. Sullivan*, 1964).

"Karl's thinking about writing a novel with a plot about that," Freya said. He'd call it something like – she looked up dramatically – *Without Malice*."

"Great. Let me know when it's made into a movie," Mom said. "So the governor's fair game. Mitt is a little more dicey. It gets more risky to talk about private individuals – people who haven't 'thrust themselves into the limelight' as the courts say. Arguably, though, Mitt did that by protesting war protesters."

She explained he wasn't an elected official, but he was the governor's son and he was involving himself in public affairs. He got his picture in the paper out at the Stanford anti-protest. But his just being in that room where the bribe was discussed wasn't a crime. The extent of his being "in on it" was just speculation. He could say he didn't know what they were planning. Freya and Mom decided to play it safe for now and not name him.

Both thought such a bribery attempt was dumb. After all, Governor Romney had called for a Civil Rights Commission for the State of Michigan in 1963. And in his State of the State message in 1964 he said that "Michigan's most urgent human rights problem is racial discrimination – in housing, public accommodations, education, administration of justice, and employment." He supported the federal Civil Rights Bill that same year.

But they left open the possibility that was a ruse, asking themselves which was the real George Romney, the civil rights supporter or the man who went along with the Mormon Church's refusal to let Blacks become priests and didn't even criticize it, at least not openly.

Regardless, Mom said, the story wasn't about Governor Romney but about the people who wanted to block civil rights and integration and bribe the governor into helping. But who were they?

With luck, they were having the same trouble trying to place me. Mom said I shouldn't worry. Just because they stooped to bribery didn't mean they'd resort to violence. But I know she was thinking one crime can lead to another.

Those men all saw me, but I was new on the island and they probably didn't live on it. We hoped they thought I was just one of tens of thousands of kids who were on the island for the Labor Day weekend and somehow got invited to join the governor on the Bridge Walk. A Boy Scout, perhaps. Those little do-gooders are always on the island.

The bribery conspirators will focus on the paper now, Mom said. They'll want the tape. Now that we've printed the story, they will forget about me, she said.

That was comforting. I guess. Mom thought about putting the tape in a bank safety deposit box, but if anyone knew she had one its contents could be subpoenaed. We decided "hide in plain sight" was the best idea. We stapled the tape into a manila file folder and put it inside another one and put it in the morgue in a folder among old clippings and pictures from more than two decades ago. I labeled it "File 40."

"What does File 40 mean?" Mom asked.

16 – FANTASY AND REALITY

I DIDN'T HAVE TO explain "File 40" to Fletch. Quoting Napoleon Solo, he said: "'Mr. Waverly himself can't take anything in File 40 out of the building.' *The Waverly Ring Affair*."

"Okay, cool," Mom said. "File 40 is our stash. But you kids should know something."

"What, Mom?" I asked.

"U.N.C.L.E. is impossible."

"What!" I said.

"Well, yeah," she said. "It's impossible because it's a global organization.

We can't even get 50 states to agree on laws and policies under the same federal Constitution."

"Please explain, Mrs. Hudson," Fletch said.

"Easy," Mom said. "U.N.C.L.E. is supposed to include people of all nationalities. Now, even supposing you could get brilliant, like-minded people from all nationalities to agree on what to do, you have their governments... a democracy here, a monarchy there, and a few communist governments here and there. Not to mention a bunch of petty dictatorships of all kinds. They all have different laws and customs."

I'm quoting Mom from memory, but I think I pretty much got it:

"So, to do what it says it does," Mom said, "U.N.C.L.E. would find itself maintaining the 'legal and political order' of truly awful governments. For instance, in some countries it's not legal to speak or write whatever you think. In another, they'll chop off the hand of a thief, put a homosexual to death. Countries often make up excuses for invading their neighbor's territory. Which legal order would U.N.C.L.E. choose to protect? Nope, this global cooperation is probably several hundred years ahead of its time. Maybe a thousand years."

"Take Illya Kuryakin for example," she added. "He seems to be on good terms with his government. Does that mean U.N.C.L.E. would help the Soviet Union send dissidents to the gulag?"

Fletch wanted to know what a gulag was but I thought she was getting too carried away.

"Mom," I said. "It's just a TV show."

~~~

Despite her reassurances that I was safe, Mom still made sure I was absent from school when the class picture was taken, just in case. Then she ran the picture in the paper like they always do. And she walked me to school and picked me up.

"So, Mom," I said on one of those walks home. "You weren't walking me home from school in Brooklyn."

"I did when you were little."

"So we had to come to nowheresville to get into 'danger.' How about sending me home to live with Frank? His mother would..."

"Forget it," she said. "This will blow over."

I wasn't serious about that, of course. I really wouldn't want to live without Mom. I just didn't want to keep missing out on things in New York – or
~~~

anything anybody was going to tell me there.

Mom was right, for a while. It did blow over. Auditors were trying to trace the $500,000 that supposedly went into the governor's fund for running for President. The governor denied knowledge of any of it. The State Attorney General was demanding Mom reveal her source and produce the tape. So was the NAACP. They wanted the racist "bad" guys revealed. She was refusing and had to repeat, because people kept asking why, that no one would talk to reporters if they couldn't protect the identity of their sources. The weeks and months dragged on.

Most tourists left by Labor Day weekend, but there were still some fall activities. People did come to the island to walk in the state park and look at the coloring leaves, ride bikes in the cooler weather, etc. Restaurants still had some business. There was one on Main Street where we would go to to listen to the piano player. He played requests and Mom would ask for songs from her era like *Smoke Gets in Your Eyes.* I just had to tug on her when she'd decide to sing along. "This is what we did before we had TV," she'd say.

The piano player had butch-cut white hair and his fingers looked gnarled, but he was always smiling and seemed to know everything without looking at any notes. I asked for Mom's favorite, *Theme From A Summer Place,* because I knew she'd like that. He knew it of course. That wasn't much of a surprise. But when I asked for *I Get Around* by the Beach Boys he knew that, too! So I was impressed and it made me want to play piano again.

Shortly, Mom found a piano teacher so I could resume lessons I'd started at the Brooklyn Conservatory of Music when I was eight. The teacher was in St. Ignace, though. It wouldn't be long before the ferries stopped when the Straits iced over. But we went to see her anyway. She was a white haired lady with a black Steinway grand piano in her living room where she gave the lessons. You could see the Mackinac Bridge from her picture window. Her name was Mrs. Burgess and she played beautifully. She said she would give me enough assignments to last the winter! So there was now a need to get a piano, quick.

No one was advertising one for sale and it wasn't looking good when we bumped into one in the thrift store in Cheboygan (Yeah, Mom drove over the bridge again). It was an old oak upright Gulbransen piano. It was $50 and they agreed to find some guys who would deliver it to the ferry in Mackinaw City.

We waited for it to arrive on the Mackinac side. It took a huge industrial-size flatbed cart with four horses to haul it up to the East Bluff and into our house. We put it out in the big wrap-around back porch area I previously eyed for roller skating. It was okay for the piano since there are storm windows and it is heated in the winter.

I started practicing *The Entertainer* by Scott Joplin. Mrs. Burgess said to get that ready for a recital in the spring. I also had lots of other songs to pick from. Mom unpacked a bunch of old piano music from the good old days. I sighed. Well, Mrs. Burgess seemed nice.

My regular teacher at school, Mrs. Nelsen, was nice, too, but she had several ages in one class and was always busy with other kids. We were divided into groups of four – our desks were pushed together in squares, which we called tables, and we worked on projects cooperatively. The idea was, the older kids could teach the young kids the lessons and they'd reinforce their own learning that way.

For my part, I found it really a pain not to be able to blend into a crowd when necessary. In Brooklyn schools, you can always hide among the throngs of kids. Here, you were always noticed.

Fletch was at my table to start, but I guess we talked too much about U.N.C.L.E. plots, impossible or not, and other non-school stuff, and laughed too much, so we were separated. I ended up sitting with Naomi, Linda and David. Fletch got moved over to the group with Debbie, Irene and, sigh, Carlee Rhodes.

I often found myself looking over at Carlee. She usually wore her straight apple butter-brown hair in a pony tail tied with a long ribbon – but a different color to match each new outfit. She was the girl every other girl envied because she always had something new to wear. She had those fluffy angora sweaters in every color. She must have had a plaid wool skirt in every Scottish clan pattern. And shoes and boots of every color to match as well. Her eyes were blue or green or turquoise depending on what she was wearing. Carlee Rhodes was the granddaughter of Captain Grandon Rhodes, owner of the Harbor Ferry Line, and her father was the city attorney for St. Ignace, Grandon Rhodes II. If you wanted to know who owned some major thing it was usually the Rhodes family – the gas station, the marina, horse and bike rentals, you know. Above all, Carlee had her own horse.

Horses were all she ever talked about. If we had to do an art project, she drew horses. If we had to write about something, she wrote about horses. A book report? She'd pick *Black Beauty*, or *Black Stallion*. She walked around with *Misty of Chincoteague.* I'm sure if she had to devise a math problem it would involve bales of hay divided by feed bags or something. And she never talked to me because I had never ridden a horse and therefore was beneath contempt.

Oh, I could read about them. I actually read *Black Beauty* once. I liked it because it was from the point of view of the horse. I once told Carlee that Black Beauty would have loved having her as his rider.

"He was a cart horse," she said dismissively.

Well, I knew other horse stories, but that wasn't enough if you couldn't ride. I could say my Ukrainian Cossack ancestors were great riders, but that didn't matter if you didn't ride. Nothing mattered if you didn't ride. And Carlee could ride. Not just trotting slowly on the trails like most people, but – well, once I saw her on her horse, that dappled gray I learned she called Snoopy, galloping along the west shore. I don't think even Fletch could have kept up with her, but I'm not sure. Even on the playground at school, she had a way of running that mimicked a galloping horse, with her arms up in front like she was holding invisible reins. On the swings or merry-go-round she was always humming a tune – It went like, Doo do do doot-doot do, doo do do doot doot do, doo do do doot doot doot doot do do do. It sounded familiar....

School was blah and it was still just September. After school was another thing. No one ever threw a rock at my head in Brooklyn.

17 – MORE ROTTEN APPLES

THIS BIG ROCK, ABOUT the size of my fist, whizzed past my head.

I had just left school and was walking along Lake Shore Road, between the school and Market Street. There wasn't much there. I looked back and this kid was standing on a high rock, about 20 feet behind me.

"Can I ride your bike?" he asked.

"What?" I said. "No, you can't ride my bike."

"I'll pay you," he said.

He came up to me and extended a hand with a couple dollar bills folded.

"No, sorry," I said. He was rough looking, but not too much bigger than me. "And you almost hit me in the head with that rock. You should watch what you're doing."

I turned away and walked my bike trying to be nonchalant about it, but glancing back I could see he was following me.

"I need to ride that bike," he called, ominously.

"Go home," I said. "Go home and tell you mother she wants you."

He seemed to disappear and I relaxed for a second or two only to have this bike skid in front of me on a sharp turn, kicking up dust. It was the same kid.

"I just wanted to give you some money," he said. "You look like a poor person."

"I don't want any of your money," I said. "Go away."

He got on the bike and rode away and then circled back.

"I'm going to have to take that radio," he said, pointing to the Norelco. I had it hanging by my left hip with the strap across my body. Well, he wasn't about to get that, I thought. He didn't even know it was a tape recorder. I didn't recognize the kid. I didn't think he was from our school. Such is luck, he wasn't a cousin either.

"Go away," I said. "Before you get in trouble."

"I just wanted to help you," he said, getting off the bike and putting forth the money again. He was alternately threatening me and offering money. Weird.

"Look, I don't want to fight with you. Just go home or back to your hotel or where ever you're from. What do you want to become a criminal for?"

"Okay, sorry," he said. He turned and I turned, again letting myself feel relieved. Then in a split second I felt a kick to my butt. He had turned around and kicked me! I fell on my hands and knees. When I looked up he was running down the road away from town.

Then I saw the blur of a person come from the school field and cut him off, tackle him, and punch him. He pulled him up by his jeans belt and said: "You'll get worse next time," and let him drop.

Fletch?

It *was* Fletch. He walked toward me.

"Fletch," I said, "where'd you come from?"

"I was watching him follow you for awhile. I thought he might be up to something."

"You know him?"

"Yeah."

"He's a local?"

"Yeah. He's one of the kids who lives up by Stonecliffe, part of the Moral Rearmament compound. You know, those people backing the new college. They own a lot more than's obvious around here.   And they have kids and that guy's one of their kids. There's a bunch of them in the MRA. We call them More Rotten Apples."

"What? Are they a gang? Should the police know about this? My mom should know about this. She'd write about it."

"The police know – but they can't do much unless they see an actual crime committed. Your mom can't write about it because what can be proved? Let me tell you something...."

He led me by the arm toward town, past the patio at the Iroquois Hotel down to the lakeside. No one was around. We sat in the grass.

"A couple years ago I was coming out of school. I was walking by the

Grand's tennis courts. You know, these kids don't go to public school.”

“Years ago? I thought they came to start the college just now.”

“The college is new, but these people have been around for a long while. Well, a couple years ago, I was seven that year, I had a friend named Mark Klapper. He was a little blond kid, small for his age and a bit of a scaredy cat. But we all were at that age, more or less. We were just second graders. Well, this one day these MRA kids had Mark trapped up against a backboard – you know, where the tennis players practice. They wouldn't let him go. If he went left, there were guys there stopping him by throwing tennis balls; same thing if he went right. He started to say he was going to tell his dad, or mom, I forget, and they taunted him – called him 'momma's baby' and stuff. He screamed and they taunted him more. They said they would have to keep him so he could never tell. They threw more tennis balls at him. First they were just throwing at his legs.... and he was just saying 'cut it out' and stuff.”

I had never heard Fletcher's voice so trembly.

“I was watching from behind some trees near the courts,” he said, nodding his head in the direction of the Grand Hotel. “There were five of them. One on each side, so little Mark couldn't run away and three in front throwing balls. They had a bucketful and kept retrieving them.”

Fletch continued: “They were standing only about 10 feet away from him and throwing real hard. I watched them hit his body and he dropped and tried to cover himself with his arms. Then they threw at his head. They kept throwing and throwing. Then I heard them say 'Now we're going to cut your ears off.'”

“Oh my,” I said, horrified.

“I should have run for help, Walter. I should have run for help right then,” Fletch said, slapping his thigh.

“Mark was just crying and sobbing curled into a little ball.”

Fletcher's own voice broke into a sob. “I didn't do anything. I was only Mark's age and maybe a little bigger, but there were five of them and they were older, maybe 11 and 12.”

“But he got away okay eventually, right?” I asked.

“Not really. When they got tired of the balls they started hitting him with their rackets.”

“Oh no...” I said.

“They just started in on him and started smacking him with the rackets. On the legs. On his shoulders. He was trying to cover his face with his hands, so one boy poked him in the crotch with a tennis racket handle and when he moved his hands there they they hit his face.”

Fletcher started to sob harder. “Then they started to use the wood edge of the rackets.”

“What did you do?”

“Nothing,” he sobbed. “I was afraid if I ran they'd see me. Mark put his arms over his forehead and stayed curled up. I could see the blood running out of his nose, between his fingers – and I didn't do anything!”

I was horrified. I didn't know what to say. Finally, Fletch continued. “It's just that I didn't do anything to help. I ran to Market Street to try to get to the police station or the first officer I could see.”

“Well, you ran for help. That's all you could do,” I said.

“It took so, so long. By the time I found a policeman. By the time I made him understand and believe me... By the time the police got there, little Mark Klapper was beaten unconscious.”

I inhaled.

Fletch's chest was heaving up and down. I held his shoulders and let him sob it out.

When he quieted, I said: “Was he all right after that?”

“He had a broken arm and broken nose. He was black and blue all over. He recovered from the physical injuries, but I don't know about... Well, the family moved away.”

“And....”

“The boys denied everything and got away with everything. They said they were just teasing him and trying to get him to say he accepted Jesus, or something. They all said when they left he was okay and they don't know who beat him. You know... They all stuck together and the Moral Rearmament adults 'couldn't imagine' any of their kids could do such a thing. Naturally. As if it wasn't their typical behavior. Everyone else knew it.”

“And then?”

“I didn't eat dinner and I didn't sleep at all that night. I just kept seeing those tennis balls pummeling this little kid and then the rackets. I... I stood there, afraid. I should have run for help earlier. It haunted me for months. I still think about it.”

“You couldn't know how crazy they were going to get. Who would have?”

"I should have. Now, I watch. I watch them. I know who's a Rotten Apple. I'm not going to let them… I'm not going to let them hurt anyone if I can help it."

I hesitated because I didn't really want to know. "Are they after me? I mean, once in awhile some kid asks me what church I go to."

"I don't know. Depends on what they know. If they know you don't go to church, maybe. As if they need a reason to be bullies. They just think only they can be good because of their religion, like MontesQ said. Monkeys are more moral. They torment anyone they feel like tormenting."

"Maybe they don't get that savage usually," I said, hopefully.

"I think they can even do worse," Fletch said. "I mean, there was a murder up by Stonecliffe in 1960. That's where they found Mrs. Lacey's body."

"Body?"

"She was murdered," he said. "Mrs. Frances Lacey. She was from Dearborn. She was a widow, 49 years old. It's been six years and police still haven't got a clue. Most regular people think the Moral Rearmament folks had something to do with it. Stonecliffe is their mansion, off the usual path of tourists."

I could picture that English Tudor-like building. I had often ridden my bike around there. It was at the end of the airport, opposite the end you can see from British Landing Road. I had no idea...

"Murder on Mackinac....?"

"Yep."

It was impossible to think my mother didn't know about it, but if I ask her, I'll bet she'll just call it an anomaly. An exception. One murder on Mackinac versus murders every day in NYC. That's what she'll say. But that beating of the little boy? Fletch seemed to think violence like that was just waiting in the wings. Who did these MRA people think they were anyway?

"Why don't you come home with me for dinner?" I asked. "My mom will call your mom."

I walked my bike and we headed for Marquette Park. We didn't say anything for a long time.

Just before the park steps, we stopped.

Fletch grabbed my arm and looked at me. "Where's that God everybody talks about? Where was He when little Mark was being tortured?"

“I don't know. They'll tell you man was given free will.”

“Man! Sure. What about a little boy who's the victim of some gang's free will? Did he have free will?”

“Obviously not,” I said.

“People are always coming to our door asking us to accept their version of God who they say is good. God could save innocent victims like Mark. If He doesn't, I don't think He's good.”

“Maybe it's better to believe in Spider-Man,” I said. "Remember that comic book *Amazing Fantasy* you gave me? There's a story that ends with Peter Parker, the kid bit by a spider who becomes Spider-Man, feeling just as bad as you do now because he didn't stop a burglar who later killed his Uncle Ben. As I recall, he was realizing that with great power comes great responsibility.”

“Wow, a comic book character gets it and God doesn't.”

“Some people will say God was looking for man to help himself.”

“Well He misjudged what an eight-year-old kid can do.”

“He's not supposed to mess up. He's the 'all-knowing, all-powerful' God.”

“He messed up!”

“If he exists. But even if He doesn't we have to do God's work. Try to.”

“So you think we’re like... Spider-Men?”

“Not with web shooters. Just with choices.”

We carried my bike up the steps and then got to my house. Mom listened to the story with even more sadness and distress than I had, possibly.

She said she would talk to Chief Holden, but didn't hold out much hope anything would change. Then she got on the phone and got permission for Fletch to spend the night. We watched TV to distract our minds and Mom made us macaroni and cheddar cheese. We were soon really tired. We got halfway up the stairs on the way to my room when Mom asked Fletcher if he would like a bear. She didn't wait for an answer, just told him to pick one from the library. He turned and mechanically started to walk that way. I stayed on the landing.

“But not the one that looks like Peter Lorre....” I called.

~~~

I went back to concentrating on the space program. On September 12 we took another step toward learning what we would need to know to go to the moon. Between Gemini 11's launch on September 12 to its splashdown September 15, NASA achieved a record high orbit, a first direct-ascent docking,
~~~

and a bit of artificial gravity by spinning the capsule and target vehicle connected by a tether. Gordo – astronaut Richard F. Gordon Jr. – walked in space twice for a total of two hours, 41 minutes. I was sad to see him best Ed White's record, but what the heck? The job was to get better at it.

I tried to concentrate on my science and math, but I'm sure my test scores would have been higher in Brooklyn because of all the competition.

Before they moved back to Washington, the Harts gave a big picnic. Mrs. Hart would give me a few dollars to run down to the store for something she forgot to get now and then – when her kids were nowhere to be found. I liked her. It was a nice, informal picnic and everyone had a good time because they could relax and be themselves. Then the Harts left the island.

Fletch and I took to meeting after school in the newspaper morgue to do our homework. Often we let comics distract us, but Mom didn't mind. I know she liked it better having me and Fletch there when she was in the office, rather than having me go home alone. When we were leaving one evening she told us about a new TV show she knew I would like. She said she had seen the first episode last week when I was at a volleyball game. It was called *Star Trek*. It was about the crew of a space ship supposedly on a five-year mission to "explore new worlds and seek out new civilizations."

Well, yeah, that sounded exciting.

The first episode I saw was September 15. It was called *Charlie X*. This guy was a Billy Mumy type character. You know, in *Twilight Zone*, Billy Mumy played a kid who could "wish people into the cornfield" if he didn't like them. Charlie X was a teenager who could wish people off the starship.

The communications officer on the ship was a Negro woman named Uhura and she wore this short, short, very short dress. I mean, I hope Freya's top was longer than that when she took her pants off at that restaurant. You couldn't get a skirt any shorter. Anyway, I thought the show was cool enough to invite Fletch over to see it the next week. Besides we had better TV reception with our tall aerial. At his house TV was fuzzy, especially when a freighter went by.

When Fletch first saw Kirk and Spock, he said, "Hey, those are the two guys from *The Strigas Affair*."

William Shatner, who played Kirk, and Leonard Nimoy, who played Spock, were coincidentally cast together in an U.N.C.L.E. episode two years before *Star Trek*. Leave it to Fletch to spot such a thing. He was a *Man from U.N.C.L.E.* encyclopedia.

He wouldn't become a *Star Trek* fan until *City on the Edge of Forever,* early 1967. That really did it for both of us. I just liked the plot. He said he liked the time travel plot, too, but I'm not completely sure it just wasn't that the actress who played Edith Keeler was from U.N.C.L.E.'s *The Galatea Affair.* All U.N.C.L.E. episodes are an "Affair." Mom liked *City on the Edge of Forever* and when she saw the author's name, she said, "Of course. Harlan Ellison. My friend Nancy and I met him at a party in New York. A real out-of-the-box thinker."

Because of *City on the Edge of Forever* I started to record the episodes with the Norelco cassette recorder and then I would transcribe them on my father's old Royal typewriter. "Are you nuts?" Fletch said. "That's a lot of work." It was, but it was fun, too. I had to learn to describe the things that were only visual and not revealed in the dialog. After I did a few, I saw a *Star Trek* coloring book at The Big Store. It was for little kids, but I bought it and used the faces and outlines of ships and stuff to combine in ways that made my own illustrations of the episodes.

And I was, after all, learning words from Mr. Spock. Like "symbiosis." It was the episode called *Metamorphosis.* I played my recording where he said "a symbiosis of some kind" and didn't know the word or even if it was started with a "c" or an "s," so it was hard to find it in the dictionary. But I finally tried all kinds of spellings until I found a word that made sense in the story. Symbiosis means a close and long term interaction between two separate biological species who come to depend on one another. So when I read that definition I knew it fit Zefram Cochrane, the main character in the story, and the cloud-like entity he called Companion. I made entries in my book-bound word collection notebook after almost every *Star Trek* episode. Spock taught me "parolation" and "plethora" and "subcutaneous" and many others.

But in fall, 1966, our days were divided into the worlds of School and After School. After school, I usually got together with Fletch, usually at Marblecliff, because we had more room than at his house and better TV reception. Fletch looked at my tape recorder one day and said, "Norelco. I thought they just made those twin-headed electric shavers."

"Apparently not," I said.

"Well, maybe it makes sense," he said. "I saw this TV show where the spy took apart one of those shavers and the twin heads were really tape reels. It WAS a miniature tape recorder. Do you think the Norelco company could be a supplier of spy equipment?"

"Is now," I said.

18 – MACKINAC COLLEGE

By LATE AUGUST, MOM had changed her mind about not covering the college in the newspaper. She decided it was important to examine the type of people who were attempting to influence the community. As 115 students came to town, she kept interviewing faculty members from those places like Oxford and the Sorbonne and Harvard. She said she was just trying to find a definition for "Moral Rearmament."

I told Mom I kept running into the new students here and there. They were usually smiling, but kind of weird like. Like they were androids or something. If someone asks them directions, they might just smile and hand you a flower and say "Jesus knows."

I was down Main Street one morning, by the library, avoiding these Heaven's Hippies, when I heard "Jesus Knows" as the response to a tourist who wanted to know where the Grand Hotel carriage picked people up.

"Jesus may know," the man retorted, "but I'm the one who needs to get back to his room to pack."

"Good one," I said to the guy, laughing. Then I told him to just head up Main Street and look at the dock opposite the park.

Once I had to cross Market Street three times because this guy was following me with a flower in his hand trying to get me to take it. He was yelling Jesus something or another as I pushed off on my bike. It was enough to make even Robbie cringe.

I kept thinking of those kids as grown Billy Mumys.

Anyway, after interviewing President Cornell, Mom said he had impressive credentials in the science establishment, but his views on human behavior were troubling.

For instance, in his opening address at the school on September 17, he promised that in addition to academics, which everyone was emphasizing after Sputnik, Mackinac College would teach "moral clarity."

MontesQ was reading Mom's coverage of the speech when I next visited. He was sitting up in bed with his legs outstretched as usual and he folded the paper and threw it down on the bed. He clapped one hand on top of the paper as if that would keep the ideas from escaping. "People shouldn't read this stuff."

"Well, Mom has to write what he said. She can't change it."

"I know... I know... but someone should write an editorial exposing this kind of claptrap that masquerades as thinking. 'Moral clarity?' Whose moral clarity is it he's going to teach? What is that? The world is full of moral dilemmas, moral arguments, moral platitudes, and moral indignation. But moral clarity, no!"

He continued: "We can't even get 'thou shalt not kill' defined. Does that mean never kill? Even in self-defense? Only if we think it's justified as a punishment? To save other lives? Because it's war?" I could tell he was going to give a speech so I turned on the tape recorder:

"Consider the dropping of the atomic bombs on Japan," MontesQ said. "That killed about 200,000 people. But some say it prevented a couple million more people from being killed in a land invasion. So President Truman didn't lose any sleep over it, he says. Other people saw the devastation and say there must have been another way. Heck, some people even say Japan was close to surrendering anyway and we just did it to let the Russians know what we had and that we weren't afraid to use it. A lot of carnage for a teaching moment.

"And if you go on the other side of the world, like to the Moslem countries, what they consider moral includes beating your wife, keeping sex slaves, and ordering 'honor' killings. They look at us and think a short skirt or a woman's uncovered hair is immoral. And they are absolutely sure they're right. I wonder what Dr. Cornell would say when confronted by a Moslem and *his* absolute moral clarity? And the fact they far outnumber his little gang?

"No, it may be that someday 5,000 years from now mankind, if it survives, will reach a consensus on moral issues. It won't be in Dr. Cornell's lifetime. And it probably won't be his version of right and wrong.

"First we have to find a scientific basis for what we decide. It can't be based on old religious doctrines that, at best, conflict with each other and are accepted largely on a geographical, rather than logical basis.”

“Can we even have a scientific morality?” I asked.

“I think so,” he said, “but it will take a lot of work. I think it might start with tabulating how much what we do hurts other living, feeling beings. And recognizing that all people, maybe animals, too, have the same rights. Something is moral or immoral, I would think, based on the degree of help or harm it does to others.”

He slouched down a little and put his arms behind his head. “Maybe it's as simple as the Golden Rule.”

“You mean 'Do unto others as you would have them do unto you?'”

“Yep.”

“Hitler sure didn't do that, killing and imprisoning innocent people,” I said.

“That's an obvious one,” MontesQ said. “Greed is more insidious. It drives man's inhumanity to man, but they make you think it's for the greater good.”

He went on: “Cornell says, according to your mom's article, that the man who would serve his nation must want nothing for himself. But he, Cornell, wants contributions. He can say they're for a cause, but no chance he doesn't skim the top for himself personally. They all do, the evangelical class. No, I'm very much afraid the moral rearmament they talk about is designed to maintain control for one old religious philosophy that's past its day.”

Later, I told Mom how upset MontesQ was about what Cornell had to say.

“Tell him to write a letter to the editor,” she said.

“He doesn't write to newspapers, Mom. He writes books.”

“And those are mutually exclusive?”

“No, but he ...”

“He's harmless, I suppose, but a bit off the deep end.”

“He's not, Mom. He's just different. Moral Rearmament, he said, was nothing more than another attempt at religious control.”

“He's nailed it there,” she said. “Control people and keep them poor. While the leaders get rich.”

She'd get Uncle Brian riled about that college every time she talked to him on the phone. All she'd have to say to him was "and they're anti-union." Despite all the support the college had in the community, she decided to write an editorial about it. When she finished it, she ripped it out of the typewriter. "Orrie, here it is," she said, handing it to him. I read over his shoulder:

> *Moral Rearmament, now in the guise of Mackinac College, wants our children to abandon "materialism." Let's examine this from both sides.*
>
> *Oh, you didn't know there were sides? Yes, Moral Rearmament is backed by the monied elite, like the Ford family. Mrs. Henry Ford II, who's bankrolled some of this MRA preaching, does not exactly eschew materialism – at least for herself and her family. Neither did MRA founder Frank Buchman and the upper echelon of his flock or its current leaders.*
>
> *Lowly followers, whose numbers give the group its power, are supposed to be humble and poor. Nothing new about that.*
>
> *Henry Ford the First recognized that you have to pay your workers enough to buy your product. So this anti-materialism seems ill-conceived spewing from a Ford and the manufacturing class.*
>
> *For the rest of us, is it evil to want a comfortable life for your children? A good home, nice, safe neighborhood, and enough money to buy nutritious food?*
>
> *Is it wrong to seek recreation, entertainment, and art?*
>
> *To pursue goals, like a professional career, which often costs money to obtain?*
>
> *To expect a fair day's pay for a fair day's work?*
>
> *This is what Moral Rearmament followers call materialism, including the ability to pay a doctor or the right to compensation if injured on the job, or having a retirement fund.*
>
> *Importantly, is it materialistic to pursue happiness, a fundamental right according to our Declaration of Independence? MRA: A yoke by any other name is still slavery. Religion has long been used to keep the poor quiet while empowering kings, nobles, and priests to keep fruits of others' labors for themselves.*
>
> *Is Moral Rearmament training our youth to support a new aristocracy? Not that the corporate fat cats have ever left us. But*

Mr. T looked up over the glasses that were way down on his nose, and rolled the typed pages. "Lexie!" he called – he only called her that when he was agitated about something – "you are going to bring forth a firestorm with this editorial. One you won't be able to contain."

He looked at her through the glass walls of her office, like a curmudgeon straight off the pages of a Dickens novel. She came to the door.

"The college has widespread support," he said. "People are going to pull their ads and you are going to go bankrupt." He squeezed the rolled pages.

"I think you're exaggerating, Orrie," Mom said while he was wrapping her fingers around the crushed tube of paper.

"At least run it by the Grand," he said. "Make sure they won't pull their ads. We couldn't survive without the Grand."

"And old Woodfill can't survive without us. Not for long," she replied. "You know in 1962 they lost $55,000..."

"Don't be so sure," he called, walking back to his front office. "I know they lost it. I mean don't be so sure William Woodfill can't keep his Grand Hotel going without your little newspaper. They can go to radio and direct mail. And that loss was due to over-booking, not under advertising. They're not going to do as much over-booking. The advertising, well, when they read this.....they'll crucify you."

"It's truth to power like my dad taught me," she called back to him. "I have to be true to my conscience."

"I have to meet payroll," he called back.

Miss Kelly and Mr. Niagara remained silent, but I think they agreed she should stay in business to write another day – and pay them another week.

Mom smacked the rolled copy in Britt's palm.

"Run this as the editorial next edition," she said and walked away. He put his forehead down on the desk. I just hoped Billy Mumy wasn't out there.

I handed my pictures and copy on the Indian Dormitory and started to leave on my skateboard.

"Hold it," Mom said. "Now that you're taking pictures I want you to know how to use the sizing wheel."

She motioned for me to follow her into her glass enclosure. She picked up the plastic disc – two different size wheels fastened together. "Look..."

I played along – like I was interested. Mostly because I think she considered journalism lessons my restitution for ruining her papers.

The wheel directions were something like, measure your picture and line up the width on the large disc with the depth on the smaller one. If you want to increase the width, without moving the original alignment, follow the numbers on the disc to the width you want and see the corresponding number on the other wheel. That number will be the new depth.

Then you can design your page, because you know how deep, or long, the picture will become when re-sized.

"Okay, Mom, great," I said, turning on the skateboard.

She grabbed my shirt. "There's a way to do it, even if you don't have the wheel."

I looked with infinite patience.

"You just put the picture on the page dummy. Say it's a two-column and you want it to be enlarged to a three. You take the pica pole, or any ruler, and run it diagonally from corner to corner on the picture. Then, where the ruler intersects three columns, that's how much longer it will be.   You can tell Vince to make it a three column and he'll figure it out in the darkroom. You'll already know the length from the ruler mark."

"Great..."

"But," she said, "before all that make sure you have CROPPED the picture down to its most important parts. You don't want a lot of wasted stuff taking up space in the paper. Crop off all dark spaces, useless sky and stuff. Even legs....because it's faces that matter. Sometimes it's almost just the eyes..."

"Great... I'm going to the...."

"Wait, I have to read your story on the Indian Dorm."

Mom started to read what I wrote:

*About 35 people were on hand Monday
when the Mackinac Island State Park
Commission dedicated its newest museum
at the Old Indian Dormitory adjacent to
Marquette Park.*

"Good lead....." she said, nodding.

*The building was built in 1838 for
visiting Indians conducting business with the
government's Indian agent. It had been used
mostly as the local school, however, and
generations of children studied there until
the new school was opened in 1960.*
*The restoration was part of the Parks
Commission's commitment to preserving
the rich history of the straits, said
Eugene Peterson.*
-30-

(I liked to end with " –30– ". I thought it made me look like a pro. That's
how professional journalists indicate "the end.")
I was at the door as she read the last word.
"Don't forget to ID Peterson," she called out after me.
"He's Director of the Parks Commission," I yelled back.

19 – DR. RENDEZVOUS

Even the straggler tourists were gone by Halloween. The few strangers we saw were construction workers or oddballs of some kind. We year-round island kids Trick-or-Treated on Main Street and Market Street and at the Grand. Fletch and I were Napoleon and Illya, respectively. Ayashe came out wearing a wide brimmed hat and a beige trench coat and white vinyl boots. She had a little gun that was really her dad's cigarette lighter.

"Who are you supposed to be?" Fletch asked.

She twirled around and said "Honey West."

Fletch shook his head.

"She fights, too," Ayashe said.

Yeah, Mom confirmed that. She said she was the first female on TV who fights like a man. She said she was tired of women standing and cowering while men fight when, as anybody could see, the sensible thing would be to crash a lamp over the bad guy's head. Well, perhaps Honey West was first female character on American TV to fight, but a little later we got the *Avengers* from England, which had been running for quite a while over there, and we saw Mrs. Emma Peel. I think she was a better fighter than Honey West. Her karate looked more real. And I really digged the actress Diana Rigg!

I still didn't think American women generally were very useful. Except Mom and Freya, of course. And Mrs. Hart. Maybe Mrs. Nelsen. She had some nifty ideas. We were doing a Michigan unit and she told us about Michigan, mostly Detroit really, being the "Arsenal of Democracy" during World War II. This was really amazing: at Willow Run, a factory complex just outside Detroit, Henry Ford converted a vehicle factory and they produced one bomber airplane every 63 minutes, she said. It was the first time airplanes were made assembly-line-style. And most of the work was done by women. I didn't believe it at first, but it's apparently true. And women pilots ferried the new planes to the war zones. So, maybe the Russians *had* sent a woman into space.

Things got really boring in November. We stayed inside more. It was too windy and cold to ride bikes or do much of anything outside. No one was in town. People talked about the "Gales of November" on the Great Lakes.

Mom put a Percy Faith record on and played the side with *Theme from A Summer Place* over and over by leaving the stacking arm over to the side instead of down the middle. I don't know why that makes the needle arm start over but it does. So we heard the song over and over and now I can hear it in my dreams.

"Get up," she said. "Let's dance."

"I don't know how to dance," I said.

"One of these days there's going to be a dance at school and you're going to need to know how," she said. "I'll teach you a simple box step."

She said to think of it as drawing squares with your feet.

"You move your right leg over a step to the right and then your left leg over to join it. Then you move your right forward a step and your left leg up to join it. Then move your left leg left a step and your right leg over to join it. Then move your left leg back a step and your right leg over to join it. There's the square. If you have a partner, she does it backwards. Then you do that over and over while moving around the room. Voila! You're dancing!"

So we danced a few "boxes." Then I sat down and she picked up the back pillow on the couch and danced with that.

On November 11, I got to watch news about Gemini 12 on TV. It was the last Gemini mission. I remember because we had a Veteran's Day assembly that day and Mrs. Nelsen stopped to say a word for "our brave astronauts launched into space today." Mrs. Nelsen was okay.

After November 19, Uncle Brian kept calling because he ran out of people in East Lansing to talk to about that day's Michigan State versus Notre Dame football game that ended in a 10-10 tie. It was talked about endlessly by everyone because the Notre Dame coach, Ara Parseghian, chose to run the clock out and settle for the tie rather than play on and risk losing. That meant both MSU and Notre Dame ended the season 9-0-1. It was already being called "The

Game of the Century." Uncle Brian wasn't usually that much of a sports fan, so I guess it was a big deal.

Mom was busy as always, but at the end of the month she had to write about – she'd say "cover" – the sinking of the SS Daniel Morrell in Lake Huron. First, word came from Mrs. Hart, calling Mom from Washington. She had heard from her Civil Air Patrol contacts that the ship was lost in a gale. There were 70 mph winds in the early morning hours of November 29. Winds that raised 25 foot waves. Then there was a great human interest story. All but one of the crew were lost. It was the story of the the miraculous rescue of a 26-year-old sailor named Dennis Hale. He was found nearly frozen after spending 40 hours in a life raft wearing only boxer shorts and a pea coat and a life vest. His three crewmates on the raft were found dead.

Then she had to write about the cause of the wreck. The Morrell broke in two in the storm. The aft section continued under power of the ship's engines, but later collided with its other part, like a decapitated body slamming into its severed head, she said. In that forward section men were waiting to launch a raft as soon as the section reached water level. Instead they were killed in the collision. The reason the ship snapped in two, according to a Coast Guard investigation, was because the steel used for her hull was too brittle – a common problem, they said, among ships built before 1948. Mom said it was important to always give the reasons for things happening if possible and if it was because of someone, name names.

What saved November for me was all the talks I had with MontesQ about Gemini 12. It was the last of the Gemini missions and probably the most interesting and important.

I had read about the Gemini 12 team's underwater preparation for EVA (extra vehicular activity) in *Scientific Digest* and I couldn't wait to talk to MontesQ.

"You know," I said, "that Buzz Aldrin guy is going to fix all the problems Cernan had with working in space. He's invented hand holds and foot restraints and..."

"Aha!" MontesQ said. "You see it too. And, he's going to vastly improve rendezvous techniques and how we can work in space. Cernan did one good thing. He proved that poor planning makes you sweat. He couldn't see for the sweat in his eyes and he couldn't move without flailing around."

Eugene Cernan was an astronaut from Chicago, who, despite the accomplishments of Mrs. Hart and other women who were pilots, didn't think women were qualified to be astronauts. "I heard that Alan Shepard called him a blind and boated rag doll out there on Gemini 9," MontesQ said.

No doubt female pilot Jerrie Cobb enjoyed that description. She tested for the astronaut program with Mrs. Hart, and ranked high at every challenge, but ran into the brick wall that John Glenn, Cernan, and others held up with their backs.

Gemini 12 was commanded by James Lovell, but Aldrin, the rookie on board, designed most of the mission. It was important because it had become obvious that Wernher von Braun's idea, one big rocket that blasted us all the way to the moon from Earth orbit, wasn't the best way. Too costly fuel-wise. It looked like a lunar orbit rendezvous and a very light landing vehicle would be better. At any rate, the "meet-up" would require docking in space, and that's what Buzz Aldrin worked on at M.I.T. It's not as easy at is looks.

MontesQ explained it to me. First he asked if I knew what "counter intuitive" meant. I didn't. He said intuition is just feeling you know how something should work. Like, intuition on Earth tells you if you jump out of a tree you will land on the ground. Intuition tells you of you throw a ball at a wall it will hit that wall. But in space, he said, things operate "counter intuitively." In other words, if you aim your space ship at another spaceship and "step on the gas," figuratively, with the intention of meeting up with it, you will end up somewhere else. Fire a thruster thinking you'll catch up and you go up, up and away.

It's true and Buzz Aldrin was the guy who figured it out – how intuition goes wrong.

MontesQ grabbed a large newsprint sketch pad from his over-the-bed desk and drew it out for me on a piece of paper with a thick black pencil. It was from Buzz's 1963 doctoral dissertation that he did at Massachusetts Institute of Technology. It seems that MIT had invented a new program – astronautics – just for Buzz Aldrin.

"Buzz worked this out," MontesQ said, drawing a circle with big swoop of his arm. "This is Earth." Then he grabbed a red pencil and drew dotted lines to indicate orbits. "Say you and the spacecraft you want to dock with are in this orbit. You're behind and you want to catch up, what would you do?"

"Go faster? I guess I already know that's the wrong answer..." I said.

"It is. If you went faster, you'd end up above it in a higher orbit. See, there is no 'up' or 'down' as we know it on Earth. Buzz realized he'd have to be able to control centrifugal energy.

"A pilot who speeds up to catch another craft in a higher orbit will end up in an even higher orbit, traveling at a slower speed and watching the second craft fly off into the distance."

It made my head spin. But it was fascinating, as Mr. Spock was always saying.

Anyway, space docking required new orbital mechanics and procedures and Buzz Aldrin figured out how, so we could use docking to get to the moon. For that, they gave him the nickname Dr. Rendezvous.

20 – CARLEE

I'M GLAD I WASN'T born in December. Being born near Christmas is really crummy because you really get less presents even though they deny it. Think about it – parents having to buy all those presents at the same time. For sure you get shortchanged.

But that was the least of Naomi's problems. She was a girl in our class and she wasn't really very popular. She was kind of awkward and chubby. Actually, she looked like a puddle of orange jello when she sat down, but was that her fault? The other girls tended to stay away from her. I felt sorry for her. You could see she was lonely. I didn't go out of my way to talk to her, but when she talked to me on the playground, I talked with her. Other kids would walk away or taunt her. Like when she wore a checked-pattern sweater they called her "Chubby Checker." Cruel stuff like that.

Problems started for me when I got an invitation from one Miss Naomi Martin. It was to come to her birthday party on December 4. It was going to be held at the Island Ice Cream parlor and then there would be a special showing of *The Ugly Dachshund* at the Main Street Theater just for the party goers. Well, that seemed a fair trade to me – ice cream and a movie, and Mom would do the work of picking out a present, so I said I would go to the party. Apparently, the ice cream and movie weren't enough for some people in the class to go against peer pressure to ostracize Naomi and they turned her down. That was bad enough, but kids were starting to pull me aside. They'd say: "Don't go to Naomi's party." I didn't see any reason not to, and if people weren't going to like me if I did, well, too bad. I didn't want to be friends with people like that.

One day we were out on the playground and Naomi tagged along with me as usual. I was up on top of circular monkey bars and she was below when a bunch of kids started taunting her by chanting: "Don't go to Naomi's party; You'll get cooties. Don't go to Naomi's party; You'll get cooties." One kid went right up close to her face and said it and she covered her eyes.

Then I saw Carlee walk up. Well, she strode right up in her take charge sort of way. She turned a hip out and swung her ponytail. She didn't see me, because I was high above. I looked down at her suede boots. They were the color of boiled shrimp. She tossed her ponytail to the other side and said, looking left and right twice: "Oh stop it you stupid, uncouth people. I'm going to Naomi's party and we're going to have a great time without you all – right Naomi?"

Well, Naomi had started to cry by this time. So all she could manage was to spread her fingers so her eyes showed and nod. Carlee stood by her side, arms akimbo, and glared at the others with her blue/green eyes. They all walked away without another word.

The bell rang and Carlee said: "See you in class, Naomi," and galloped off.

I climbed down. "Sorry about those kids, Naomi," I said. "But that was nice of Carlee to say she's coming."

"Yeah," she said. "And I didn't even invite her."

~~~

Carlee did come to the party. She brought Naomi a pink cashmere sweater set – a pullover and cardigan. In large. I don't know if Naomi ever gave her an official invitation or not. At least a few other kids came because Carlee came. There was maybe eight of us. I enjoyed the ice cream and the movie. I think Naomi liked my present. Mom picked out a soft mermaid island for her gift. It had lots of little two-inch mermaids that could be placed about a placemat-size spongy green "island" and a couple plastic palm trees, also removable, and you could play with it in the bath. She got some games and art stuff from the other kids.

With Carlee, I talked about cats versus dachshunds and other dogs. I was just sorry I had nothing to say about horses.

The rest of December we weren't really weather shut-ins like most people I'd known up 'til then. Up that far North people get used to going outside whether it's freezing or snowing or whatever. But it helped that Mom decided we should go ahead with the telescope project and ordered all the parts.
~~~

The packages for the lenses, eyepieces, and the telescope tube and its base had come in the mail a few weeks earlier. Mom ordered them from Scientific Instruments Company. We set up in the back porch using the pedestal table Voltaire had been on. He got put on the floor behind the rolling ladder in the library. We put the round clouded glass on the pedestal top, affixed with clamps. The lens grinding process was sort of like cleaning the bottom of a frying pan with a scouring pad and cleanser by walking around the pan and rubbing.

The work was good when I was lonely. I walked around that pedestal so many times. It was like I was a clock hand, rubbing the lens as I went around, seeing into the living room, then out the big porch windows to the sky out back. If it was daytime, I looked at clouds. At night, the stars.

The Mackinac winter sky was sometimes cloudy, but often crystal clear. Those nights I could see Mom was right. New Yorkers could see nothing like it. A clear night sky over the Straits was magnificent. Mom and I would put on our coats and walk out of the house and our shoes would make crunchy noises on the frozen top of the snow as we walked out to the road. She'd be behind me with her hands on my shoulders and we'd look up. "There's your initial," Mom would say, like always when she saw Cassiopeia. And usually then we'd see Orion and the Big Dipper and then compete to see others first. I was pretty good at finding the Little Dipper because you use the North Star. The Big Dipper is always easy to spot. So you use the stars on the outer edge of the Big Dipper pan. They're Dubhe and Merak. If you visualize a line from them the way out of the pan, they point to Polaris, or the North Star. And the North Star is the end of the panhandle of the Little Dipper. I can always find it – if the night is clear enough. I couldn't wait to take a closer look at the moon and planets, though. That's what the telescope was for.

It was about 8 p.m. three weeks before Christmas. Mom was stringing some Christmas lights along the porch rail. The snow was sparkling and, I discovered, the good packing type. I rolled a snowman's head and midsection. When she was done she helped me roll the body. The snowman had to be placed where we stopped with the body because neither of us could lift it. After we put the middle and head on we plopped on the ground and made snow angels. Mom went in and got big buttons for the snowman's eyes and a carrot for the nose. "Pipe?" I asked. She raised her shoulders and shook her head. I took the little cat's brush off the porch and that stood in for one.

Next night Fletch came over and we walked down the steps to Marquette Park. We made some snow angels on the upper platform of the Father Marquette monument and while still laying in the snow looked up at the sky. I was picking out constellations and pointing them out to Fletch. Cassiopeia was high in the sky facing north. Facing East you could see Orion. I pointed up. "He's always easy to spot with those three stars making up his belt," I told Fletch.

"Yup," he said.

"I think I'm in love with Carlee Rhodes," I said, letting my arm flop down.

"What for?" he said.

Facing the opposite way, I could see half of the Great Square. I remembered the Great Square from my book *The Stars, A New Way to See Them.* And it was the bottom half of Great Square that made the wings…of Pegasus….a horse.

An idea popped into my head and I sat up suddenly. I also had to sit up because the cold of the snow and cement was starting to come through my winter coat. We went home and I checked the book. The constellation Pegasus would be in the center of the sky facing west between 9 and 11 p.m. Dec. 1, getting a little earlier each night until Dec. 16. I asked Fletch how I could get Carlee to agree to come over to my house for some board games on Dec. 12. Maybe about 7 p.m.

"Let me help," he said.

Fletch arranged the date when they were out riding. I heard the doorbell ring right on time. I opened the door and saw Carlee standing there in a bottle green coat with a white rabbit fur collar up around her neck and ears. She was in front of Fletch, with one hand in her coat's pocket and the other around her neck, tightening the fur collar. Fletch smiled and didn't seem to be wearing a coat warm enough for the cold windy evening.

We played Sorry and chess for about two hours. Carlee was pretty good at chess for a girl. I was just learning it myself. When I was nine, Mom said she'd have to learn it first so she could teach it to me and we played off and on since then.

When Carlee won the third game, I suggested we warm up some pizza I had stashed in the kitchen. We ate and then it was good and dark outside. I said, "Carlee, I want to show you a horse."

"Where?" she asked skeptically.

"In my backyard," I said mysteriously.

"In YOUR backyard? YOU have a horse?"

"Well, come, I'll show you."

(Fletch's "help" included deciding to stay I the hose when I did this.)

Well, Carlee seemed excited to see the horse and went toward the back door without even stopping to put her coat on. So I didn't get one either. I took her by the arm and led her through the back screened porch to outside.

"First, look there," I said, pointing up, northwesterly. "See the constellation Cassiopeia?"

"Yes, I know it," she said impatiently.

"Well, let your eyes follow down from the end star in Cassiopeia to that really bright star – that's Andromeda and part of The Great Square. Look just at the bottom triangle of that square below Andromeda, a bright star to the left and a bright star to the right and one beneath, like an upside down pyramid. See?"

"Yes," she said, brushing aside her hair that had blown across her face.

"Well, just imagine that triangle is a wing, the wing of the flying horse in Greek mythology. Pegasus is that flying horse. The star at the peak of that upside down pyramid is where the tail of a horse attaches. Then beneath you can make out the horse, Pegasus."

"I don't see it," she said.

"The triangle," I said, repeating. "That's the horse's wing. In the old way of looking at constellations we used to just see the front part of Pegasus and it was always upside down. Now, according to H. A. Rey, who wrote this book I have about the stars, there are new ways to look at some constellations. Now, the way Rey describes it, we see the whole flying horse. Follow the stars below. The rectangle is the horse's body. Then there are stars that make the legs and head. Do you see it?"

"I think so," she said, holding her hair back.

I took her other hand and pointed up with it. "Trace it this way..."

I tried to outline the horse with both our fingers.

"See? Pegasus stands for beauty and strength and courage," I said. (I was either making this up or remembering some mythology I read.) "You see, in Greek mythology, Pegasus is a divine stallion – pure white. Look up at Pegasus and imagine a pure white stallion, rearing up its front legs."

"Pure white..." she said. "I always thought a pure white horse would be pretty."

I was getting to her, I thought.

"According to legend," I said, "his father was the king of the sea, Poseidon. Seeing that he is very fine and brave, Zeus, king of the gods, instructs Pegasus to bring lightning and thunder down from Mt. Olympus."

I waved my hand over the span of the sky and tried to be super dramatic about it.

"And he does! Thunder and lightning... He does everything Zeus wants. Once, he's ridden by a Greek hero named Bellerophon and together they defeat a monster – The Chimera."

I let go of her arm.

"After that and many other daring exploits," I said (alternately looking up and looking at her), "Zeus transforms Pegasus into a constellation and places him up in the sky as a reward."

I held my gaze on Carlee. She was silent for a few seconds.

"That's really stupid, Walter," she said, and walked back into the house.

21 – WINTER WONDERLAND

IT WAS DEEP WINTER now and it got dark early. In ways light years more than in Brooklyn, we had to make our own entertainment. I played the piano more. I perfected *The Entertainer,* with Mrs. Burgess' spring recital in mind. Then I learned a number of songs that were simple, but "lilting," Mom said. She said songs like that always made her want to dance, like *Once Upon a Dream,* the theme from *Sleeping Beauty.* Another was *Stranger in Paradise,* from the Broadway musical *Kismet,* but that was really a classical work by the Russian composer Borodin before it was used in the show, much like *The Blue Danube* was played when the space station went round and round in *2001: A Space Odyssey.*

We read a lot of books. I started *Swallows and Amazons* by Arthur Ransom and it made me think I might like canoeing.

On December 18 we got to watch an animated version of one of my favorites: *The Grinch Who Stole Christmas.*

Fletch and I played in the morgue after school. When we locked up, Fletch went his way and Mom and I headed home by the lake shore route. She gazed out over the water and said: "There's a tradition... After Christmas they will take the used Christmas trees and stick them in the ice making a path to St. Ignace. People will follow them either walking or on snowmobiles. The path marked by trees ensures they can find the shore if a blizzard or fog cuts visibility. So they don't walk out onto Lake Michigan and lose their way."

"Like forever you mean?"

"Yeah."

"And die?"

"Well, yes, they would."

"What if those who follow the trees fall through the ice?" I asked.

"That doesn't usually happen. It's usually solidly frozen after Christmas. But there are often areas that aren't frozen, due to underwater currents or whatever. Seems like Ski-Doos often find them."

"And what happens then?"

"It depends. They say you only have about four minutes in icy water. It depends on how fast rescuers get to you."

"Long time ago a whole carriage and horses went under," she added.

I was pondering. "Just walk to St. Ignace? Three miles? On the ice?"

"I've never walked it myself," she said. "But three miles isn't so much. Still, the Coast Guard doesn't condone it."

"Right." I said. "So we're trapped until the ice melts.... in… What? March...?"

"Sometimes April."

"Great..."

After a minute I said: "Mom. How do you stick trees in ice?"

~~~

I can't even find words for surviving a January on Mackinac Island. The quintessence of nothingness. But, fair's fair. In late January there was a Winter Festival on Main Street. They had an ice- sculpting contest, demonstration sled dog races, and fire pits for warming. The ice sculptures were huge. I had to admit they were impressive. There was a race car, an eagle, even Mickey Mouse and Donald Duck. I wondered why people would put so much work into something so temporary. But it's what people do here. Mom took pictures of them for the paper. I sure wasn't going to. It was more than 10 degrees below zero. To operate the camera she had to take her gloves off. After every few snaps she had to rush into a tent and go by a heater to warm her nearly frostbitten fingers.

"Do you think it could get any colder in Siberia, Mom?" I asked as we entered a tent again. We stood in front of an electric heater that was glowing like gold on fire.

"Yeah, just a bit," she said.

"Let's not go there."

"Roger that," she said.
~~~

By this time I was wearing a thick sheepskin fleece hat with suede on the outside and leather ties with round balls of sheepskin at the tie ends. Mom bought it at a store in Mackinaw City before the ferries stopped. She said I looked ready for an expedition to the North Pole. I thought the thick sheep nap in the hat would come in handy if you fell on the ice.

The Winter Festival included demonstration sled dog races. Kids got to say "mush" but they really didn't do anything but hold reins. The dogs knew the routine. It was fun anyway.

I also climbed up a mountain of snow the festival organizers constructed. At the top you could start down a slide going through the middle. The new police chief, Larry Holden, was catching the little kids as they came hurtling out. Mom said that was all she had to see to know he was a really nice guy.

At dusk Fletch joined us. He had his skates, so we stopped at the paper where we had ours stashed and we went skating on the frozen lake.

I used to go skating on the rinks in New York City, but this was not like that at all. There you went in circles with lots of other people bumping into you all the time. Here you didn't have to go in a circle. You could just skate like Hans Brinker... on and on. Little flakes of snow fell on our faces and I would look up, open my mouth and let the flakes fall on my tongue. We went a long way before we turned back. And we could hear some music coming from big speakers on top of poles. Usually waltzes. Some pop tunes. Some kids with hockey sticks came on the ice, but Mom kept telling them to put the sticks down because sticks were not allowed. It was too dangerous for the little kids. Heck, I didn't want my teeth knocked out either.

"No sticks!" she said, grabbing a kid way bigger than her by the collar after telling him several times.

There were big lights on poles around the shore, too, so we could and we did skate until after dark. Their yellow glow made the falling snow surrounding each light look magical and the newly fallen snow glisten on the mounds made when they plowed to clear the ice. The music transported us outside of ourselves. We were all having such a good time we skated past our hunger. We skated until our fingertips and toes were numb. Then we were ravenous. Mom said we could go eat dinner right away in the Grand Hotel instead of going home first and she invited Fletch. In a skate shack, Mom pulled my mittens off and rubbed my fingers. She had a couple pairs of dry socks and asked Fletch if he needed any. He said, "naw," but she made him put a dry pair on anyway. We changed back into our boots, slung our skates over our shoulders, and I said, "Let's go eat!" We walked across our schoolyard to Cadotte Avenue and up the street and into the Grand at the east end. Tenacity saw us in the main lounge.

"Your cheeks are red," he said to neither one of us in particular.

"Tell me about it," I said. "I just want a huge hamburger with fries."

"Check out the buffet," he said. "You'll change your mind."

We walked in and through the lounge and looked into into the dining room and there was a row of tables full of food, and another at right angles to it. Each had enormous ice sculptures intermixed with the dishes of meat, potatoes and salad. A pelican, a boat, a "Mackinac Bridge" and a moose, all hand carved in ice.

"Hey that wolf is salivating," Fletcher said, pointing to an ice wolf with melting fangs.

I gave it a good glance, but then started to fill a plate. A white-aproned server in a tall cotton white hat that billowed out at the top, cut me a piece of roast beef and I also took shrimp, sliced pork roast, and mashed potatoes. Fletch did almost the same. "Have some salad, boys," Mom said predictably, but I had to admit, even some of the vegetables looked good. I passed on the Whitefish, but took a big sprig of crab legs. We sat at a table and ate and ate and went back for strawberry cheesecake with whipped cream.

I was done and happy, but Mom was still having coffee when Tenacity came running with his transistor radio. He stopped in front of us and held it out in one hand and then the next, like a hot potato. It seemed like he couldn't get a word out. He looked at the radio and shook his head as if it had suddenly started broadcasting in Greek. Finally he said:

"There's been a fire at Cape Canaveral..."

22 – APOLLO 1

"GIVE ME THE RADIO," I said.

It was scratchy, but we listened. "Fire… Fire… Astronauts Grissom, White and Chaffee..." It was a test and there was a fire. "...dead...."

"No," I said. "It can't be. It can't be."

"But that's what they are saying..." Tenacity said.

"No. No. Not Colonel Ed White," I said. "No." I shook the radio as if to make it say it was wrong.

Mom was shocked too, but she said: "We'd better go home. There will be news on TV."

"No. No!" I said.

Tenacity tried changing the channel and we waited. Then a commentator on another station said it plainly: "A fire at Cape Canaveral has killed astronauts Grissom, White, and Chaffee."

"NO!" I yelled and I jabbed one of my skate blades into the Mackinac Bridge ice sculpture.

I remember chips of ice flying. It was kind of all in slow motion in my mind, but it must have been fast because it was all done before Mom yelled "Walter!" and she and Tenacity grabbed my arms.

I put my face in my hands. Mom put her arms around my shoulders. I heard someone yell: "What is going on here!" and it suddenly got quiet.

Tenacity picked up a water tumbler. "Well," he said . "What's the use of an ice block if you can't chip parts of it off into your glass?"

It was mostly a blur. I remember my mother saying sorry to the staff and she and Fletch sandwiched me until we got into a carriage out front. We rode home in silence. Fletch called home and got permission to stay over.

At 11 p.m. the TV news came on.

"This is Jules Bergman at Cape Canaveral…..A fire….has taken the lives of Gus Grissom, Ed White and Roger Chaffee during a 'plugs-out' test of the Apollo 1 capsule…."

"What's a plugs-out test?" I asked.

"Listen," Mom said. We listened until it seemed to be the same information over and over. It was a test to see if the capsule could operate on its own – unplugged from the launch tower. Mom finally told us to get to bed and pulled out an extra pair of pajamas for Fletch and he took them without a word. We brushed our teeth in silence and Fletch climbed up into my top bunk.

I fell into exhausted sleep. When I got up very late Saturday morning I was hoping it had been a bad dream. But I saw Fletch, already downstairs, and knew it was real. The TV news anchors were already at the story. "Tragedy at the Cape," they were calling it. We watched it all, again. Then Mrs. Kwashneetski offered us some waffles and milk. I only ate a little. She twisted her apron and stared. "But it's his favorite…" she said to Mom. Fletch and I went to my room. I threw a tennis ball at the wall.

"We've got to go see MontesQ," Fletch said. "Let's see if he heard anything from his science buddies."

Tenacity turned us away. He said MontesQ was on the radio. He was being interviewed about it by WJR.

So we bummed around the island aimlessly.

"People are starting to say maybe we shouldn't go to to the moon," I said dejectedly. "It's too dangerous. Why would they say that? What if they said that to Lindbergh?"

"Or Columbus?" Fletch said.

"They probably did."

"They went anyway."

"Exactly. But Columbus got money from Queen Isabella selling her jewels and Lindbergh I don't know, but he probably was rich and paid for his plane and fuel himself. But the space program needs money from the government. What if they take it away?"

"Why would they? We have to beat the Russians."

"Not everyone thinks so. MontesQ told me there's this Senator Mondale. WALTER Mondale, I'm sorry to say. He's from Minnesota and he's against funding the space program. He says it costs too much. What if people forget how excited they were about getting to the moon and agree with him?" Fletch just looked at me and we walked awhile in silence.

I'm sure I felt worse about Col. White because I met him and he was so nice to me. But it was sad about the other two.... They had families....

I remembered another thing MontesQ said once – about what would happen if we missed President Kennedy's deadline. People might lose interest, he said. This was bound to delay everything. What if the Russians beat us to the moon?

"Well, what if they do?" Fletch asked me.

I always took it for granted that Fletch understood about the importance of the space program, but then I wasn't sure.

"Well, for one thing, it would make us look second rate," I said. "For another, well, you know how everyone got so upset about Russian missiles in Cuba. What if they go to the moon and put missiles there and tell us they own the whole place? Wouldn't they be more powerful than us then? Wouldn't that matter to our nation's safety?"

"Yeah," he said. "That'd be bad. A Commie moon."

And I don't know that it wouldn't be as bad if we just stopped exploring. What would there be to look forward to?"

<center>~~~</center>

Finally, in a few days we saw MontesQ. We talked about what they knew about the cause of the fire. We talked about Grissom, White, and Chaffee. That, earlier, Grissom got a bum deal being suspected of panicking and blowing his hatch after splashdown in a Mercury capsule, but he didn't. The hatch was too easily sprung. They redesigned the hatch and that's why they couldn't open it in time to save them from the fire. And how awful it was that Chaffee didn't get even one chance to go into space and how White was a great hero for Michigan. Well, for the University of Michigan, anyway. He was originally from Chicago.

"You know, during White's spacewalk, they did have to order him in," MontesQ said.

"No," I said. "He told me himself. He wouldn't go against the flight director. An astronaut wouldn't do that."

"He was supposed to be out for 12 minutes. He was out 21," MontesQ said flatly.

"Well, he wouldn't have disobeyed...."

182

"No, not normally. But walking in space is not normal," MontesQ explained. "He was evidently mesmerized by the Earth floating by, being able to somersault and pirouette weightless. Even the strangeness of a glove floating past him – a thermal glove that he had left on his seat – pushed him into a sort of euphoria.

"Gus – he was Cap Com for the mission – was worried that White was showing signs of a sort of 'rapture of the deep' that afflicts scuba divers sometimes. It's when things are so amazing, I guess, that you lose your sense of reality.

"So, yes, he had to be ordered back in. Several times."

"Well, I'm glad he got to do it," I said. "The space walk. But I know he wanted to go to the moon."

Most of our worry was that the planned Apollo launch for February 21 would be postponed while they tried to work out what went wrong. That Mondale twerp was chairman of the committee named to investigate the tragedy, of all people. We had to wait.

Would the U.S. government fix the problem and go on or quit?

There were chunks of snow on Market Street. There was nothing to do. Fletch went home and I went home. I looked at the *Free Press* and went up to my room, thinking. Something must have been churning in my mind as I just sat and watched my cats on the boxes. If Cronkite moved close to Canaveral's position, she moved higher. If he persisted, she'd jump down.

I listened to records. I played *Blue Moon* over and over. After awhile I picked up a pen and paper and wrote. I hadn't planned to, but Monday I submitted what I wrote to the school newspaper.

When the next issue of the paper came out weeks later, it had my column in it on the editorial page. I took it home and handed it to my mom. She was surprised. There was a headline: "Great Place to Leave for an Adventure" (I didn't write that. Reporters almost never write their own headlines.) My name – no, my byline – was under the headline: By Walter Hudson.

I held the paper out in front of her and pointed to it. "What's this?" Mom said with phony pique. "You won't write for me except under duress, but you'll write for the school paper? What are you going to do, go into competition with me? Well, let me see it."

She started to read what I wrote:

*One of Man's basic drives – the hunger
for knowledge – often comes with tragic
consequences. This was the result on January 27
when three U.S. astronauts were killed during a
practice run of the Apollo flight.*

*Virgil "Gus" Grissom, Edward White,
and Roger Chaffee had one of the noblest
missions – to help mankind enlarge its
knowledge of space, space travel, and space
machines. Their deaths are probably the
greatest loss the people of the United States
have felt since the Kennedy assassination.*

*One of the seven original astronauts,
Grissom was the first man ever to journey twice
into space and the first to maneuver a capsule
from within. He came very close to drowning
in June 1961 on his suborbital Mercury
flight when his capsule's hatch blew off at
splashdown.*

*White became famous as the first
American to walk in space. For 21 breathtaking
minutes – nine longer than planned – he
romped outside the Gemini 4 capsule
and the story was often told that he refused an
order to get back in. I was privileged to meet
White at a banquet in his honor last year and
he told me the story was untrue. Experts now
believe he might have become mesmerized by
the awesome new experience. He did say
having to go back inside the space capsule
"was the saddest moment of my life."*

*Michiganders can be proud that
White earned his degree in aeronautical
engineering from the University of Michigan.
I know he dreamed of going to the moon.*

It is especially sad that Roger Chaffee,

*the newest astronaut, who had worked
nearly all his life for space flight and the day
he would set foot on the moon, died before
experiencing a single flight. He was born
in Grand Rapids, Michigan.*

*All three felt that "Earth is a great place
to leave for an adventure." They were aware
of the risks involved – it was what they wanted
to do. Grissom himself said, "If we die, we
want people to accept it. We are in a risky
business and we hope if anything happens to
us it will not delay the space program. The
conquest of space is worth the risk of life."*

*Their deaths, unfortunately, will
delay the space program, but they will not end
it. The Apollo flight, scheduled for February
21 before the accident, is now set back to some
indeterminate time in late summer. And, it
is estimated that U.S. plans for a lunar landing
will be set back for a whole year.*

*If one thing can be learned from this
tragedy it is perhaps this: Nobody gets
something for nothing. There is always a price
to pay for the acquisition of knowledge.*

*Americans have always paid the price
for progress. There is no other way.*

Mom looked up and smiled in a different way. The way she smiles when she's proud of me. After a while she asked if I wanted to do any assignments for the *Huron Shores Herald*. I said "maybe."

She started to teach me journalism basics like how to know the lead (pronounced leed) of a story, – that is, what you lead-off with. What "inverted pyramid" means – start with the most important or biggest thing and put the facts down in descending order of importance. That's why the biggest part of the pyramid is on top. The smallest part, the peak, the least important information, is last – inverted pyramid.

Mom also taught me to cover speeches. "Remember," she said, "don't start off saying someone gave a speech. Write what they said."

That's how I ended up listening to the Mackinac College president go on and on about education for Moral Rearmament at a banquet one day. She told me to cover the speech. It was blah blah blah. I was bored, so I looked around at the people sitting up on stage with him.

Behind him, one man turned to talk to someone next to him.

It was Raccoon Man!

23 – FEAR AND FEBRUARY

We could now place him.

By calling around, Mom figured out who the man was: Jasper Tarpoff who taught theology at the college and came from Oxford, England. That made sense, she said, because that's where the original Moral Rearmament people came from.

"But what was he doing opposing integration?" I asked. "Is THAT what he thinks is 'moral'?"

He didn't have any young children in the school, so it was unlikely he would be hanging around there. We decided to watch for signs he was looking for me.

Meanwhile, Mom and Freya were both being pressured more and more to reveal their source for the attempted bribery story. They were refusing, but were being threatened with a court order. The campaign officials wanted to know, Governor Romney wanted to know, and the state police wanted to know, or pretended they did, since at least some of them were involved.

Mrs. Nelsen thought the sled dog races in January were a lot of fun for us kids. So much so, she wanted to re-enact them.

Fletch piped right up: "But we don't have any sled dogs."

"I know," she said. "You're going to be the dogs."

Heads dropped on desks. Kids groaned. Mrs. Nelsen didn't stop.

"And a few of you are going to be the sled drivers."

She explained that we would race with sleds that we would make out of cardboard. Then one of each team would ride on the cardboard sled holding the reins of the "dogs" pulling it.

We got big pieces of cardboard from deliveries of new refrigerators that came for a new apartment complex in Mackinaw City. Mrs. Nelsen just saw them by quirk of fate one day and asked that they be shipped to the school and the builder was kind enough to oblige. The ferry lines were always sending our big supplies at no cost.

Carlee's grandfather donated some rope. Each team used the boxes and rope to design their own sled. Fletch and I wanted to be on a team together but we didn't get to. I think Mrs. Nelsen tried to balance the teams' sizes and strengths.

Since there still was a lot of snow on the ground, it turned out to be a blast. There were five teams. I ended up with Natalie Knight, David Pendleton … and Carlee. We picked Natalie to be the driver because she was smallest. Carlee, who I am sure would have rather been a horse than a dog, nevertheless was a good sport. She and Dave and I had ropes tied around our waists. When the race began we took an early lead. Every team was screaming. Drivers were yelling "mush, mush" and "dog teams" were yelling "pull, pull." It was pandemonium.

Our lead dissolved when we hit a depression in the field and turned over. We were all in a pile. I was face down in the snow, Carlee and Dave were both on top of half of me. "Get up, hurry," I said, "I'm smothering." They got up and I turned over and was looking up at Carlee's face. Her forehead was all snowy, but her cheeks were red like two Michigan McIntosh apples.

"Fix the sled," she squealed and we jumped into action, righting it and untangling the ropes. She glanced at me and said I looked like the Abominable Snowman. I didn't care; she noticed me. I threw snow at her and said: "So do you."

Mrs. Nelsen had invited parents to the race and some of them stood along the sidelines. Mom was there, cheering our team and taking pictures for the paper. Fletch's mother came, and Grandon Rhodes II, Carlee's dad. Naomi's grandmother was there and a few of the others. It was neat to have them laugh at us and applaud.

Our team came in second to last. I don't know what calamity befell the very last team, but before the finish line we were laughing so hard we could hardly run.

Fletch was on the winning team.

"Figures," I said.

~~~

Then came the day of the Congressional hearing on Apollo – really on the whole space program, because overall issues of safety and carelessness were being discussed.

You could see parts of it on TV news.

The next day I walked in to MontesQ's room and he said "Aha!"

"Don't say Aha!" I said. "Aha what? That Mondale guy is trying to ruin the space program."

"I say 'Aha' when I see you because I anticipate your inquiring mind, Walter," MontesQ said. "But, yes, he is a cause for concern. We're going to be months behind. Maybe not even make it to the moon this decade now."

"No!"

"Well, look at the facts. We don't know what caused the disaster, except general incompetence, design mistakes, maybe overall hubris."

"What's hubris?"

"Extreme pride or arrogance. Often with loss of perspective on one's own competence."

"Oh," I said, writing it down on a scrap of paper to add to my word collection later.

"They had a sealed cabin pressurized with oxygen and a lot of explosively flammable stuff in there, including that Velcro you think is so cool. It burns! They were worried about the hatch blowing open, like it did when Grissom landed in his Mercury capsule, but never thought about needing to open it quickly from the inside. It was heavy and awkward and opened *in* for Pete's sake. Fire? They thought the possibility was remote. They should have known better."

I looked downhearted.

"Don't look like that," he said. "That's what happens in exploration and experimentation. You don't know all the answers at the outset. There's a learning curve and, unfortunately, there's never a way to make it completely safe."

"But you know what people are saying?" I said miserably. "That space exploration isn't worth it. That it's wildly impractical and silly."

"You know," MontesQ said, (and I knew he was going to launch into an
~~~

verbal essay so I turned on the Norelco as always) when they built the first rail line across this country people said the same things. 'Who would ever want to go out there?' they asked. In 1866, just a hundred years ago, it was called a 'monstrous folly.' But they went on building it just the same. And, for at least the more dicey parts, it cost at least one human life a day. One a day! Building the Chicago World's Fair in 1892, which was just a temporary thing, cost many lives.

"Heck, five people died building the Mackinac Bridge right there outside this window. Look at it. Majestic as it may be, it will hardly compare to the awesomeness of a manned trip to the moon. They didn't wind up the suspension cables and say let's not build it after the first man died in a fall! Does Mondale have even half a brain?"

He paused and sighed, then gestured with his palms up.

"Look, every life lost is a tragedy. But if people didn't go and do, what would life be for? What happened at the Cape, sad as it was, was normal for exploration. No one was more surprised than Lewis and Clark when they didn't lose a man on a trek across the entire continent. We've got to educate Congress – and sometimes that's pretty hard to do. But I think they will muzzle Mondale and his ilk and continue to pay for the program as they should. So cheer up. People in the U.S. won't want to be seen as a bunch of quitters."

"But..."

"That accident was *nothing.* Oh, I don't mean it wasn't a tragedy for the men and their families. But in the larger scheme of things it wasn't much."

I just looked.

"People get killed all the time doing ridiculous nonsensical unimportant things. And people don't stop doing those things, like riding snowmobiles along that ridiculous Christmas tree trail, or skiing and horseback riding, and for sure driving. A pilot died filming *Flight of the Phoenix* last year. He risked his life for a movie. Just entertainment. But he chose to take the risk.

"Our astronauts are more likely to get killed in their Corvettes than in their space capsules. Here, look at this."

He went to one of his bookcases and pulled out a book and opened it. "This is Ralph Nader's *Unsafe at Any Speed* published last year. He predicted that about 50,000 people would be killed in cars in 1965. It turned out to be 47,089, nearly 4,000 a month, almost 130 a *day*."

"Compare that – useless deaths most would say – to three people dying in an attempt to further man's knowledge and capabilities – and fuel the imagination of a nation and the world."

"Here's another way to look at it," he said. "If we didn't attempt new things we wouldn't learn new skills. So danger is positive in that sense. I think it was Alfred North Whitehead who said..."

"Who?"

"Alfred North Whitehead, he was an English mathematician and philosopher. He said it's the business of the future to be dangerous and one of the merits of science is that it equips us for the future. Something like that anyway.

"Look, we've lost just three men so far. Gus, Chaffee and Ed White, they died looking the future square in the eye. They loved what they were doing."

24 – THE ICE STORM

WE KNEW BY THE end of February that our hopes for an American moon landing would not be dashed, at least not by the Apollo 1 fire or Walter Mondale's failure of imagination. It was Gus Grissom speaking from the grave that defeated Mondale and those others who had no sense of wonder. Astronaut Borman told the congressional panel that he and all his colleagues were in complete agreement with Grissom and they just wanted to get back to work.

The next few months were the busiest NASA had ever had.

That work was primarily done at Cape Canaveral, whose soft tropical breezes we on Mackinac Island could only imagine. For us, a winter storm was coming. It started with a warming trend. All of a sudden it wasn't biting cold outside. It almost felt like summer. Up to 39 degrees, 40 maybe. Fletch and I were playing catch in front of Marblecliff, until it started to flurry. But the snow flurries melted as they landed. Then it just rained. It rained for a day and a night. We all stayed home and read or watched TV, until we got tired of that. Fletch put on one of those yellow sailor's parkas and tromped through the rain to come over and we played so much Monopoly that, afterward, I was buying Boardwalk and Park Place in my sleep.

On January 27 the sun came out – which meant we would also see the full moon. We watched *Star Trek*. It was another time travel story, *Tomorrow Is Yesterday.* The Enterprise is accidentally sent back to the 1960s and is seen by a fighter pilot. The ship's tractor beam destroys his plane so he has to be beamed aboard the starship. Beaming is where they turn your molecules into energy and send them, to be reconstituted at the other end, like putting the water back in potato flakes. In this story Captain Kirk and Mr. Spock think they can't send the pilot from the 1960s back because he has seen the future and could then do something to change history. Spock researches the guy and says it's okay to keep him in the future because he didn't make any substantial contribution back in his own time. But later, Spock discovers the pilot's son had been on the first Mars mission. They have to send him back.

Well, it was pretty interesting, but if you think about it, stupid, too. A person could do lots of things that influence history without it being recorded in history books. You could be a lifeguard at the Grand Hotel pool and save some doctor's life who goes on to invent artificial hearts or something. And that changes history, but the lifeguard – he's just another anonymous chap. Spock should have known better in the first place.

Fletch didn't get home that night. When the ice started to coat the trees and wires Mom gave him a homeless bear, a pair of my pajamas, and called his parents. Fletch held the bear at arm's length and looked at me. "Another..."

"Give it to Ashe," I said.

You could go out on our back porch and see all the trees turned sparkly. I mean, coated with ice, they all looked like they were made of glass – a fairyland glass forest.

The ice would have made walking hard enough, but then we started to hear "crack" and "thud." It was like gunshots in the woods. Only it was tree limbs breaking from the weight of the ice. They broke everywhere and fell everywhere. The big limbs here and there blocked the trails so carriages couldn't pass. But the horses already weren't coming up and down the hilly trails because of the slippery ice. We were trapped.

Then the power went out.

The first night we spent in front of the big fireplace. Mom, Fletch and me, and Mrs. Kwashneetski, all wrapped in blankets with pillows in front of the fire. Our heads came together in front of the hearth like spokes of a wheel.

Mrs. Kwashneetski said it reminded her of the time it flooded when she and her husband lived in a cabin along Rock Creek Park, near Washington D.C. It was during the early days of World War II, she said, before they moved back to Detroit. Her husband was too old to be drafted into the military. He worked as a high school choral instructor. Housing in Washington was hard to find at the time, so what was available was expensive, she said, and so they took the cheapest thing they could find – a cabin on stilts without indoor plumbing.

"But, you know, we didn't mind," she said. "We had so much fun being young and swimming in the creek – it doubled as our bath – that we didn't notice. We caught fish this big...” she parted her arms wide “...and ate like kings.”

“And the songs we sang!” she said. “Every day we sang and sang and it lifted our hearts. I even sang when I was ironing his white shirts!”

“That's how I met the Kwashneetskis,” Mom said. “I joined a Ukrainian choir when I was living in Dearborn. We had to take a streetcar to downtown Detroit – but people came from all over the Detroit area. It was the best choir. We even sang over the radio.”

“Oh, yes,” Mrs. Kwashneetski said. “We were the best. We were invited to entertain at all the civic events.”

“And you and Mr. Kwashneetski were in it with Mom?” I asked.

“He was the leader!” Mom said. “He was our director.”

“There was the Depression, when we were kids, and then the war,” Mrs. K said. “And we never could have gotten through it all without singing. It uplifted us all.”

“And your mom played the piano, a bit. I always say, if you know how to play the piano you'll always be the life of the party!”

“I played a little, but Walter has surpassed me, Nina,” Mom said. “His piano lessons are working out real well.”

“Very good,” she said, looking at me. “But sing. Always, you must sing.”

“Well, we have a chorus at school, if I have time,” I said.

Mom went out for kindling and newspapers to ignite the big logs. We had plenty of those.

Next morning state forest rangers and city officials went door to door and told people to go to warming centers – they had generators at the fort, the Grand, and at the college. With our fireplace we didn't really need to go, but Mom thought it would be a good idea to interview people about their experiences in the storm. So we called Fletch's house to say he was safe and going with us, took our blankets and a couple books each and walked down the steps to Marquette Park. It was slow going. The wooden steps were covered with ice and we had to be real careful. We were grasping a railing that was covered with ice, too. We each slipped and nearly lost our footing a few times.

We decided to go to the college. People were camping in the gymnasium there. Mom started to do her thing talking to people and getting their stories.

It was human interest stuff. Who fell on the ice. What happened when they lost power. How they coped. While she was talking to one mother she noticed her little boy had a Teddy bear whose side seam was split open and had one felt eyebrow missing.

"My, he needs a stitch," Mom said to the boy. "What's you bear's name?"

"Bear," said the boy.

"Good choice," I said. I could tell Mom was getting an idea.

When we sat down by ourselves she told it to me: "Lots of kids' favorite stuffed animals need repairs, but their parents don't have the time or the tools to do it. So we should open a Teddy bear clinic at the newspaper office. We'll just need needles and thread and a few noses and eyes we can get from a doll maker... pillow stuffing... "

"Of course," I said. "That's just Journalism 101."

~~~

After a while I got bored and decided to walk around. I went out of the gym and into the hallway.

I was getting a drink of water at a drinking fountain obviously last used by an entire basketball team that had to spit out its gum. The flow of water must have been slowed by the freezing pipes, because it was hard to get a drink and I was thirsty.

"Hurry up kid," said a voice behind me. I ignored it and continued trying to lap mere droplets.

Then he tapped me hard a couple times on the sleeve. "Move it, move it." It was a man in a suit. "Hey," I said, turning around, "keep your mitts to yourse..." I looked up at him. That receding hairline. The brown circles... It was Raccoon Man!

Those big reddish droopy bags under his eyes were unmistakable.

First he widened his eyes. "Do I know you?" he said slowly. "Hey....Aren't you that spying little weasel who was at the governor's house?" He stared at me. "Brattiest kid on the planet..."

"That's a bit of hyperbole, don't you think?" I said.

"Oh, vocabulary boy. See if you have a word for this!"

He took a swing at me with his hand opened flat but I ducked in time.

At least we didn't have to wonder any more if they wished me harm.

"You'd better behave yourself," I said. "There are police officers here."

"Cops I got in my pocket, kid," he said. "But now I know you live on the
~~~

island."

"Perspicacious, aren't you?" I said.

"Perspe... Hell and damnation," he said, backing me into the wall. I twisted my body away from him and ran.

I dashed back into the main gym. He followed and wouldn't take his eyes off me, but couldn't touch me in a crowd. I couldn't go up to Mom. Then he'd find out who I was. I needed to get out of there before he could point to me and ask around. But I needed to get word to Mom. I saw Fletch. If I motioned to him Raccoon Man would see. But he turned his back long enough for me to catch Fletch's eye and point to him. I borrowed a pen and went into the mens room and wrote on a paper towel. "R man. Getting out. Tell M."

I tore it off in a hurry and passed it to Fletch via Ashe who was running in the hall. I hoped they could decipher that. I didn't think Raccoon Man would chase me through the ice storm. And he didn't. I made it home. In about an hour Mom and Fletch got back.

I ran and slammed her with a hug.

"Mom, he's here. He saw me. He knows I live on the island."

"Yeah, but... I don't think he'd dare... besides he still doesn't know you're my son or where you live."

"But he'll be looking."

"Don't worry."

"Mom! Don't worry?" My mother, who could barely bring herself to drive across the Mackinac Bridge, said 'Don't worry.'"

We went to see Chief Holden.

The Chief was a graduate of Michigan State University's Criminal Justice Department and he was up in Mackinac with custody of his two sons after a divorce. He was previously Chief Deputy in Owosso. He once saved two kids from drowning when a car went in Houghton Lake – and he was off-duty at the time. Since Mom wrote a nice feature on him becoming police chief, Chief Holden was willing to give us his time. Although, in fairness, he had time to spare.

We were in his private office. He had shaggy, sandy-colored hair which touched his shirt collar in back. I always thought that was forbidden for a cop. His hands were occupied playing with a circle of string. He gestured to me and we did rounds of Cat's Cradle while Mom talked. Finally, he missed a round and the string puddled on his desk. Then he talked.

"So where we're at is this: Walter is witness to a crime, or a conspiracy to commit a crime and the ringleader has seen him. The ringleader we have already realized is this theology professor, one Jasper Tarpoff, a.k.a Raccoon Man. He's seen Walter but doesn't know who he is or where to find him. We think."

"Yes," Mom said.

"I'd say he can find out," Chief Holden said. "It might take a while but all he's got to do is ask around long enough. And you say there were three, maybe more, state troopers in on this, but we don't know who they are. Walter might be able to identify them if he sees them again. Meanwhile, Raccoon Man will be reaching out to them in an attempt to identify Walter."

"What would they do?" Mom asked.

"That's hard to say. Corrupt state police...?" Holden tsked, raised his eyebrows, and shook his head indicating doubt. "They're in some jeopardy. Your son and your subsequent articles have put them at risk of being identified. Perhaps you should take Walter off the island, but....."

There it was. Mom looked at me. I could suggest New York...

"But," the Chief continued, "it's less likely we can ever catch them if he leaves." I felt like my head was in a vice. I heard myself say, as if from outside my own head, "I should stay."

"What's the risk?" Mom asked.

"Don't know," he said. "I can ask around and watch. But from what you say, I can't go to the state police for help. We have no idea who's in on it among them. Could be two, three officers or a whole battalion of them. Perhaps, then, just let things cool off. Most people who get mad about newspaper articles don't take revenge on the newspaper." He looked at me. "Or their sources."

I didn't know if he meant that or was just saying it to make me feel better.

"Besides," he added. "These guys are racists. That's their focus."

Mom said: "The governor's been offered a bribe. He wants answers. He doesn't want it left there. He wants to know who these people are to show he didn't work with them. "

"So...."

"They want me to reveal my source. They're not dropping it."

"So the good guys want to know and the bad guys already know. Why not reveal....?"

"Never," she said.

25 – HELP WANTED, MALE

IT WARMED AND GOT colder alternately. Chief Holden had Jasper Tarpoff under what surveillance he could manage with limited staff. I was pretty sure I was being watched by someone, too. We were in a "wait and see" time. It was gloomy and boring again, but tense. Even the night sky was more obscured by clouds than usual. Nothing going on, except Mom moved out of her glass-walled office. She put her office desk out in the newsroom, between Mr. Niagara's and Miss Kelly's desks – you can imagine how they liked that – and the composing area in the back. That's where there were a few light tables and wax machines and X-ACTO knives I wasn't supposed to go near. I never did, but I liked to dip my fingers in the pooled melted wax.

Wax machines were necessary for offset printing. Pictures and columns of type were stuck to layout sheets by having their back sides waxed. The wax would stick 'em down, but you could pick them up and move them elsewhere as necessary. Pieces of copy that ran too long for one column could be cut and stuck on the next column or on a "jump" page. "Jump" page just meant the page where the story was continued.

The wax machines were these table top devices with rollers the paper, cut in columns, or pictures, were put between. One side would come out waxed. There would be a little pool of wax after the machine was turned on and warmed up – ready for the paper, or finger tips. I knew to coat only the tips of my fingers. If I dipped them in any deeper it would burn me. I hadn't discovered a use for wax coated fingertips. It was just something to do. Like kneading Silly Putty.

I knew for Doug and Frank there was plenty to do in New York City, even in February. They wrote about a big anti-Vietnam War peace march and a weird thing called a Be-In. The Be-In was in Central Park in Manhattan. About 100,000 people showed up for no other reason than just to be there. I could taste the cart-vendor hot dogs from here. I wrote back about dodging horse poop on Market Street and checking TV tubes at the drugstore. The number 6SN7 might as well have been imprinted on my brain. There wasn't anything else to say, trapped on an tiny island in the dead of winter with about 200 or so other lost souls.

We watched TV weather every night – hoping. It got a little warmer in March, but the wind chill kept up and there was less sun than ever.

Oh, yeah, I forgot to say, the reason Mom moved out of her office was to turn it into the *Huron Shores Herald's* Teddy Bear Clinic. Mom advertised that subscribers or subscribers' children, could bring in their "sick" Teddy bears for an operation for absolutely free. Non-subscribers would be charged a nominal fee. It was a good will thing.

We stocked polyester stuffing, all colors of thread – but more of the various shades of brown – common sizes of noses and eyes, felt for eyebrows and sometimes lips, new ribbons for neck bows, etc. On March 10 we got our first "patient." It was Malcolm.

Strictly speaking, Malcolm was a mouse not a bear, but we didn't turn any injured companion away. Malcolm arrived cradled in the arms of Melody, Mrs. Nelsen's 7-year-old daughter. Her older sister, Michele, who I think was in 11th grade, brought them. I knew Melody from seeing her at recess. I didn't know Michele.

"What seems to be the problem?" I asked.

"Michele tore Malcolm's arm almost off," Melody said.

"Did not," Michele said, shifting her hips from left to right inside a pink and orange psychedelic dress. "You were the one who wouldn't let go of him."

"YOU tore him," Melody said. "She did, Walter. That's why Mom said she had to bring us here."

"We'll, can you fix him?" Michele asked, looking at me from under lids laden with thick black eyeliner. I looked at the mouse. The arm was ripped nearly off at the armpit, that was for sure.

"I think we can repair that," I said. "He'll have to be hospitalized, though."

"That's okay," Melody said. "Just as long as you can make him better." Then directing herself to the mouse, she said: "Don't be afraid. We'll be back for you soon."

"Give us a few days," I said.

"Sure," Michele said, taking Melody by the hand and heading toward the door. She stopped and turned. "Don't forget, Sonny and Cher are going to be on *The Man from U.N.C.L.E.* tonight."

I just looked, maybe a bit perplexed. Michele pointed at me with her free hand, made a click with her tongue and winked. "I got you babe," she said.

I thought: Who the heck are Sonny and Cher?

Malcolm survived his ordeal, got better, and word of mouth spread the news about the clinic. Soon we had a patient every few days. Sometimes more than one a day.

All staff members (well, except Mr. Trivelpiece) had to take a hand in running the clinic – whoever was least busy when a patient was brought in, unless no one had time, like when we were on deadline to get the paper out. Then the patient would have to be "hospitalized" overnight.

I, personally, saved a GUND lion from "starvation" by plumping him with polyester stuffing and I grafted a llama's ear.

After school, I hung around the paper a lot so Mom and I could walk home together. I'd hang around with Fletch some, but he worked at the stables several days of the week after school, taking care of the few horses that weren't taken off the island for the winter.

Sometimes I would see him and Carlee riding together, she on her precious Snoopy, he exercising a horse for some absent owner. Usually they were with a couple other kids with horses. Sometimes just them. Although Fletcher and I were friends, I wasn't accepted in that group because I didn't ride. I'd often look after them as they rode by and feel dumb and awkward and lonely. It was usually then that Ashe came and hung out with me. She was not a horse rider – yet. Sometimes she brought friends. I did stuff with them because, if I didn't, some days there would be no one to talk to. It felt awful not having kids my own age to hang out with. I had little kid followers. It was embarrassing.

Thank goodness for the telescope project. I worked on it at home and did a lot of reading when no one was around, especially on cold days. But winter began to melt into spring.

One warm weekend day, when I just finished *The Rolling Stones* by

Heinlein, I walked outside. I didn't dare go far, so I was kicking stones on Huron Drive when the entire Hart family came out. I didn't know they were back. The senator and all the kids were walking toward the Marquette steps and it looked like Mrs. Hart was the only one being left behind on the porch of their cottage. I looked at her and she gestured for me to come over.

"Walter, would you like a little job?" she asked.

"Sure, anything," I said.

She wanted me to blow up balloons. It was her youngest daughter's birthday and the family was up for a short spring visit. All but Mrs. Hart were going to the movies downtown. She had a surprise party to get ready – wrap presents, decorate the house, that kind of stuff. There were 40 balloons. "Do you think you could do 15 if I do 25?" she asked. "And if your mom says okay, you can stay for cake and ice cream."

"Oh, heck. I can do at least 20," I said. "Anyway, Mom says I'll do anything for ice cream."

She smiled and tore open the first plastic package with ten. We started blowing. She grabbed a yellow one and I picked a green one.

Some of them were round and some of them long.

"How hard do you want them?" I asked.

"Well, fill the round ones as much as you can. They can be tossed better that way. But leave a little stretch in the long ones – 'cause the kids can tie them into shapes."

"Right-O," I said. I blew up two and then had to rest. I inhaled and started in again. When I got five knotted I took a longer rest. She had five too and suggested we take a few minutes break.

While we caught our breath we twisted some crepe paper streamers and taped them to the ceiling. Then we went back to blowing. At 12 each we seemed to be racing each other. But then I blew up one purple one and instead of tying the knot, stretched the neck and let the air out slowly, making it squeak like... well, like air being slowly let out of the stretched neck of a balloon. Mrs. Hart made her next one squeak and then I did my next and we made quite a racket and then laughed.

"We better get back to work," I said, exhaling and inhaling rapidly.

"Take it easy," she said. "They aren't due back from the movie until after 7:30."

"What are they seeing?" I asked.

"Well," Mrs. Hart said, "There were several choices. *Fantastic Voyage* and *Batman* got the most discussion."

"I saw them both," I said. "*Fantastic Voyage* is so cool. These scientists get themselves miniaturized and then they get into this little submarine that's also miniaturized so they can go inside a guy's body to break up a blood clot he's got. Only when they're tiny they've got to fight with human antibodies and avoid gobs of tobacco pieces in the lungs that are so gross. It's great."

"I lobbied for *Batman*," she said flatly. "Phil was for *Fantastic Voyage*."

"That one's great science fiction," I said.

"I think he was more interested in Raquel Welch in a skin tight diving suit. No, I'm sure they went to *Batman*."

"Well, that's still okay for Mr. Hart then," I said,   "because in Batman Lee Meriwether has a skin tight cat suit. She's Catwoman."

Mrs. Hart narrowed her eyes, pretending she thought that was bad, then she laughed and her opened eyes looked sparkly as ever.

"Well maybe the Academy Awards will start a whole new category – *Best Clingy Costume*."

We got back to the balloons. Mrs. Hart finished her 25 and I was on my 15th when there was a terrible screeching howl out in the yard.   It sounded like some awfully mad cats.

We ran out and I saw one cat dash across the road and Canaveral howled in front of the house."

"Canaveral!" I shouted. And Mrs. Hart and I both went running for her.

She was a bloody mess. A flap of skin hung from the side of her head and the skin was all raw underneath. And her right front leg was stripped of fur as well for about three inches.

"Oh my gosh." I said. "Oh my gosh, she's hurt bad."

"Let's get her inside and see what we can do," Mrs. Hart said.

I scooped her up in my arms and we ran inside and Mrs. Hart led the way to her bathroom.

"Oh, that facial injury looks bad," she said. "Not much we can do but wash it and put antiseptic on it. The leg we can tape."

First we worked on her head. I held her tight over the sink, grasping her behind the neck. She didn't fuss. She's the best cat in the world. Mrs. Hart poured warm water on the wound. Then she took out Mercurochrome and dabbed it on.

"She'll lick it off as soon as she can," she said. "But it should do its work before that...now let's see that leg."

Again we rinsed it and put the antiseptic liquid on.

"This we can cover," she said. She opened her medicine cabinet again and took out a roll of cloth bandage about an inch wide. She held the end and then started to wrap the leg.

"You know," she said, "this reminds me of when my husband was first elected senator and I was pressured to join the Senate Wives Club. They wanted me to come and spend hours and hours rolling bandages dressed in a fake Red Cross uniform." She continued twisting the bandage around Canaveral's leg. "It was quite a scandal when I refused, but I found the idea outdated to say the least. I told Lady Bird Johnson – President Johnson was Senate Majority Leader then – 'You make the bandages and I'll fly them anywhere in the world you want in my plane.' There." She clipped the bandage to itself with a metal gripper thing.

I took Canaveral back to the living room and she seemed content to lay down quietly by the hearth while we finished our work. We didn't squeak anymore balloons. But we hung more crepe paper streamers. Mrs. Hart laid out the presents and stuck candles in the cake and returned it to its box to await the kids.

"I didn't call Mom, so I'd better go now," I said.

"Come back at 7:45," she said. "For that cake and ice cream."

"Sure," I said. I looked for Canaveral by the fireplace. She wasn't there.

"Where's Canaveral?" I said.

We saw her at the top of the cellar stairs, but she scooted down before we could catch her. We followed. When she went into the room with the shelves for homemade canned stuff and bags of potatoes and such, we followed her there, too.

"Come on, Canaveral," I said. "We have to go home now."

Then the door banged shut and clicked. It was pitch black inside. I tried the handle, but the door wouldn't open.

"Oh dear," Mrs. Hart said. "The house has settled and the door always tends to close."

"Yeah, whether you want it to or not," I said.

"And the handle doesn't engage the catch," she said. "I've been meaning to get that fixed. The family just usually yells for somebody."

"Yeah, but nobody's around now."

"Well, your kitty won't mind. She can see in the dark."

We tried fiddling with the latch with whatever implements we could find down there – a weeder, a pointy can opener. No luck. We were stuck.

"Well, I'm glad I didn't leave the coffee water boiling," Mrs. Hart said. "Phil and the kids will be back in about... What time is it?"

"Don't you have a big watch?"

"Yeah, usually I'm wearing it and it has a luminous dial, too. But I'm not. I took it off in the kitchen. It should be about 6 p.m. They left at 5. The movies started at 6 and 6:30, depending on which they went to… about two hours... Phil knows they have to come right back for the surprise party."

"I hope there aren't a lot of previews," I said.

"Yeah... There's a bench here somewhere," she said. "Let me see..." She bumped into it. "Here it is. Take my hand, I'll guide you."

She sat. I didn't have enough bench and almost fell off the end, but she still had my arm and pulled me back up and made room for me. She put her arm around me. "Not afraid of the dark are you?"

"Nope," I said. There was a long silence. Well, maybe a minute. At least 30 seconds. I felt like crying. Not because I was trapped in a cellar room from which I knew I would get out and about when. No. But because I thought about Fletch and Carlee out riding and other kids doing stuff with friends from our class and how I was alone without any kind of respectable friends I could be proud of having. That's why I was alone kicking rocks on the road and how I ended up here. Not that Mrs. Hart wasn't cool, but I wanted friends my own age.

Then Mrs. Hart said: "You know, this is like one of those astronaut tests I took."

"Yeah...?"

"Yeah. It was about four years ago. We were – thirteen of us women pilots – taken to undergo the same tests the Mercury 7 astronauts took."

She laughed. "They even called us the Mercury 13. I was the oldest tested, but I did it all. They put us in the centrifugal force machine – the 'vomit comet' they called it, and did those tests where they see how long you can hold your breath and how long you can run a stationary bicycle and all that. And one of the tests is the sensory deprivation test. You know, because space is supposed to be black and lonely. They put you in a black box – no light, not the slightest sliver, comes in. You can't see your hand in front of your face. And there's no sound either. All you have to rely on is your own mind. And you sit there until you can't stand it anymore.

"How long were you in there?"

"Oh, about 30 hours."

"Well, then, this is going to be a piece of cake," I said.

"With ice cream," she said, squeezing me around the shoulders. "When we get out." I liked Mrs. Hart.

She kept talking to make the time go faster. She told me about other machines they had to ride. One of them was an enormous thing – but really just a gyroscope. It simulated an out-of-control spacecraft.

"How'd you like that?" I asked.

"It was like a bucking stallion," she said. I felt she was smiling. Although I couldn't see her, there was just a hint of sparkle coming from her eyes.

She said she thought pilot Jerrie Cobb did the best on the tests in general. "She could ride the roughest stuff, stay sane longer than any of us. The doctors and scientists running the tests said she was 'an exceptional human specimen.'"

"I think we did too well," she said. "As far as we can surmise, women are being blocked because they're a threat to the men in some way."

"How so?"

"Only in the men's minds," she said. "As if somehow if we're good it means they're not. Why can't we all be good?"

"Mrs. Hart," I said. "Did the Russians really send a woman into space?"

"Absolutely," she said. "It's too bad it's another thing they beat us on, but, yes. In 1963, just about a year after we took the astronaut tests. Valentina Tereshkova. Too many people would have to keep it a secret if that was faked. Of course, she went. And she was just a parachutist. We have trained female pilots with lots of experience.

"Oh, not jet pilots, like they say we must be. But that's a phony argument. We could fly jets if they would let us. Woman aren't allowed to fly jets in the military, so of course there are no women with jet pilot experience. That's the only place you can get it. By every other measure we did as well as the men, often better."

"Which I didn't hesitate to point out to the members of Congress," she added. "They fund the National Aeronautics and Space Administration, you know, so they make the rules. So I wrote to every senator and congressman with the facts, suggesting women should be allowed into the space program. And do you know what the press asked me?"

"No," I said. "What?"

"'What does your husband-the-senator think of your petition to Congress?'"

"And what did you say?"

"I said: 'I never asked him!'"

"That was a great answer," I said. "I think my mother would have asked what you think Congress is going to do about it."

"*That* is the question," she said, "and the answer will affect more than just whether women can have a part in space exploration. You know, it's not just that women can fly planes, they can design them, too. A Canadian woman, Elsie MacGill, helped design and engineer machines to build the Hurricane, a plane that was very important in fighting World War II."

"No, I think this particular discrimination is bolstered by men who are scared," she continued. "They're scared of the competition. Look how quickly they sent women back into their kitchens after what they did during the war – making bombs in dangerous munitions plants, ferrying planes in dicey situations, taking risky jobs the men turned down. Even proving themselves as spies and saboteurs.

" That's why last year, at Betty Friedan's invitation – she's the author of a bestselling book on women's abilities and how they are wasted – well, at her invitation I became a member of NOW – the National Organization of Women. The organization is to fight that sort of thing. So women can be doctors and lawyers and astronauts and, well, anything a man can be.

"We might not get into space right away, but NOW's already had success in shaming newspapers out of gender segregated help-wanted ads."

26 – TURNING 12

THE WEATHER WARMED WAY too slowly. The Harts went back to Washington. Few people came to town. I was looking forward to the Grand Hotel opening again. Tenacity was still away on vacation. MontesQ was up there, of course, but visits were always limited so he could get on with his writing and researching – even though he always looked forward to seeing us.

Fletch and I were riding our bikes one chilly day and he pointed across Cadotte Avenue. "Rotten Apples at 3 o'clock." I nodded and we turned down Market Street, discretion being the better part of valor as the saying goes.

Canaveral's leg healed quickly. She worked the bandage off in a day. But for a long while her facial wounds were more striking. There was all the redness and this patch of skin just dangling from the side of her head. But it finally dropped off and healed.

May came and it was warming up just a little, not enough, but I looked forward to May 22, which was my birthday.

I wouldn't have had the nerve to invite Carlee, but, turns out, I had to. There was a new rule at school about birthday parties after word got out about the attempt to sabotage Naomi's. The rule was, if you invited anyone in your class you had to invite everyone in your class. So I invited everyone to a pool party at that motel with the indoor pool in St. Ignace. The weather was warm enough to get off the island. The ferries had been running for many weeks now.

Everyone who was coming from the class, and a few extra friends, like Ayashe, were to meet at 8 a.m. at the ferry dock. We had to wear wind breakers because it's really a lot colder over the water than on shore. The smart kids had hoods and they put them up when the wind whipped lake mist onto us while we were standing by the railing on top.

Those less wise about weather on the Straits stayed deep inside the boat where it was warmer.

It was only a 20-minute ride or so. First you curve out of the harbor and and see the Round Island Lighthouse on the left and the Mackinac Bridge way further out. It was a little choppy. In the morning sunlight, the water looked like it was woven with yellow ribbons. In minutes we passed in front of the Grand Hotel and West Bluff to our right.

Shortly we could see the St. Ignace shoreline looming larger by the minute. Once docked, we all got in a couple of courtesy vans to the motel, where they gave us breakfast.

Then we went swimming. Later we had cake and I got to open presents. No balloons. The cake had chocolate frosting with a Starship Enterprise outline on top. Mom got the basic cake from a bakery in St. Ignace, but drew the ship herself with a cake decorating tube of vanilla frosting. She said she went by the picture in that coloring book I got for illustrating episodes. It wasn't perfect, but a good try since that must have been pretty hard to do freehand from a tube.

Below the ship she wrote: "Beaming up to age 12."

I got a new board game called Battleship. Well, the box makes it look like a board game, but it isn't played on a board. It was in two plastic cases, one red and one blue. They opened up so the covers blocked your opponent from seeing what you were doing. Each player put pegged battleships in holes on a grid and each player had to guess where the opponent's battleships were by naming coordinates in turn. Each guess got a peg put in the board and if a ship got enough "direct hits," that is, all the pegs it could hold to "sink" it, well, that ship was sunk. To win you had to sink all of your opponents ships first. I got that from Fletch and Mom gave me a tennis racket and three Heinlein books, and some oil paints and canvases – she likes to encourage art stuff. Freya sent a Rollei spy camera and a few blank cassette tapes for my Norelco Carry-Corder.

We all had a great time in the pool. Ashe kept cruising the edge and splashing me when she saw me. I dunked her a few times. There was a ball people kept throwing around trying to arrange a game of water volleyball that never really worked and Fletch and I practiced diving.

Carlee didn't come.

27 – LILACS AND MAYHEM

At HOME MOM LOOKED at the Battleship box and said "typical."
"What?"
"Must have been designed by a man. Shows two boys playing the game and in the background, a mom and little sister washing dishes!"
"So?" I asked.
"So what are we supposed to infer from this? Boys are to enjoy recreation while women and girls do the housework?"
"Yeah, sounds great to me," I said. She threw a dish sponge at me.

~~~

In mid-May the summer horses returned. You could go to the docks and see them being unloaded from the ferries. Fletch and Carlee were helping guide them off. I watched with nothing relevant to say, except, when they were done, "let's get some ice cream now."

We were all getting spring fever. Raccoon Man was almost forgotten. Maybe not by the police, but I stopped thinking about him as much. The Teddy Bear Clinic was busy. We were anxious for school to let out. We wanted to just do what we wanted to do, free of cares. One weekend Fletch managed to lose the horseback riders long enough to schedule a canoe trip with me. I'd been talking about wanting to try canoeing since reading about the Walker children and their friends in *Swallows and Amazons*. Fletch's dad said he'd tow us by motor boat to Bois Blanc Island early in the morning and then we could canoe around the shoreline – long as we wore life vests and promised to get back to the rendezvous point by 7 p.m. Fletch's mom wanted us to pick wild baby leeks on the island.
~~~

Next morning I rushed down the Marquette Park steps when dew was still on the wood. I met them at the dock opposite the park, east of the ferry landings. Ashe asked us to bring back a butterfly cocoon. She handed me a large quart-size Mason jar. She said her mother filled it with milk, but when it was empty we were to get a cocoon and put it inside. I said we'd try. Her mom also sent a basket with lunch that was later to hold the leeks we were supposed to find. I put the lunch my mom made in the basket and we got in the canoe. Fletch's dad tied the canoe to the motor launch and towed us out.

I was a little nervous out on the water in a small boat that wiggled, but I figured Bois Blanc was only 2.5 miles out and we were getting nearer Round Island every second. If anything happened to the boats I figured we could swim to the lighthouse on Round Island – which was between Mackinac and Bois Blanc.   I have to admit I like the fact that, unlike going swimming off Coney Island or Manhattan Beach in Brooklyn, there are no sharks to worry about in the Great Lakes.

After a bunch of safety instructions, Fletch's dad left us at Bois Blanc and turned back to Mackinac Island. We started to canoe south-east along the Bois Blanc shore. Then Fletch told me, nonchalantly, about the Massasauga Rattler. I had no idea Michigan had a rattle snake. I thought that was stuff for people in Arizona and New Mexico to worry about. Didn't we have enough stuff, what with the gales of November and falling through the ice? But no, he tells me these snakes are on Bois Blanc! In the wetlands, mostly.

After awhile we paddled up to shore and tied up the boat. It was only about 10:30 in the morning but we were hungry for lunch. We traded half our sandwiches – one of my mom's peanut butter and jelly on Koeplingers raisin bread for one of his mom's liverwurst with lettuce on rye. We also had Fig Newton cookies from my mom and oranges from his. My mom probably figured I wouldn't stop to peel an orange. She was right. I would have preferred Hostess Cupcakes because we had the Mason jar full of milk. But the milk tasted good anyway. We walked and took turns drinking out of the jar. I spent a lot of time looking down – for snakes.

We passed an old sign that said "Struble" but it didn't occur to us that meant private property. We took turns on an old swing we found hanging from a tree limb, but I kept eyeing the ground. Fletch yawned and told me the rattle would be unlike the sound of a rattler in a western movie, more like a kid's toy.

Then he fell asleep! I climbed a tree branch and stayed up there 'til he woke.

He only slept about 20 minutes. Then Fletch decided to chase a frog. In the wetlands, of course. I was seeing things slither every few minutes, whether they were there or not. We didn't catch the frog. I hurried out of the swamp.

When we emerged we were spotted by a woman coming out of a cabin nearby. We thought we were going to get yelled at for trespassing, but she said hello and smiled and offered us some lemonade. She was about my mom's age, I think, with the ends of blunt cut brown hair showing under a floppy sun hat, the strands by her ears being longer than those in back. We said, "Sure, thanks," and she went in and got it for us in tall glasses with ice. While we drank, she picked up a hand spade and tied on one of those gardener's aprons. She said she was transplanting a favorite peony bush so it could get more sun.

"I'm Esther," she said. "You're not from Bois Blanc are you?"

We told her we lived on Mackinac, said we canoed over for wild leeks and a butterfly cocoon and were sorry if we walked on her garden. She said "don't worry, you missed the new tomato plants." Then she said we could use her dock to jump off of into the water if we wanted to. She said we could use her tire swing, too. We thanked her, although we'd already used it.

Most importantly, she told us of a nearby trail they called "Leek City" because it's loaded with leeks! She also tipped us on where to look for a butterfly cocoon – on the milkweed stalks. She said the proper term was chrysalis. And she was sure right about the milkweed stalks. We found one right away and broke off the branch and put it in the Mason jar.

When we got back from the great leek hunt we waved to her and pointed to the filled basket and held up the jar. She nodded and smiled. Then we jumped off her dock for a quick swim. As she saw us leaving, she said: "Come back anytime. Ask for Esther Struble's place."

We got back to the canoe and the trip back to the rendezvous point was uneventful, but we were tired so it took longer. Canoeing never seemed to be that exhausting for the kids in *Swallows and Amazons*. Anyway, tired turned to invigorated, somehow. Mom said exercise works that way. By the time we met Fletch's dad we launched into our adventure story with such energy he thought we wanted to row back to Mackinac. We had lots of leeks for Fletch's mom and the jar with the chrysalis for Ashe. She grabbed it and gave a little dance. Her mother said, yes, chrysalis was the right term and the butterfly would emerge in

8 to 12 days. Ashe started to watch over it like a cat with kittens. Mrs. Auginash started leek soup.

I didn't know it then, but, snake scares notwithstanding, those were my most carefree days. As much as I looked forward to the end of the school year, I didn't realize what was coming.

~~~

I was picking onions out of my salad one day in the kitchen while Mom talked about the paper's upcoming coverage of the Lilac Festival. That was always a big deal in early June. It had been going on since 1949 when some teenager and a carriage horse veterinarian had a mind meld of sorts. The centerpiece of it all was the biggest all horse-hitch parade on the planet, whoo-hoo.

I mean, really? Once you've seen the Macy's parade, just a few floats pulled by horses is not going to be impressive, is it? Yes, I'd go take some pictures, I told Mom. Carlee and Fletch were going to be riding in it, of course. I already knew that and that I'd be alone all day or dodging Ashe & Co. So why not? I was starting to get a lot of good pictures in the paper.

School got out. Ashe released her Monarch butterfly with great ceremony. I wish I could say that was the biggest news of the month, but far from it. Having nowhere to go on a daily basis anymore, I took to hanging out at the paper. Often Fletch was there, especially when Carlee was away at an equestrian competition or accompanying her family on their yacht to Florida or some such place. And we would check to see if any of the Rotten Apples were following us or watching the newspaper office at Market and French Lane.

We were there when Mom was having a budget meeting for the first June paper. It was going to be a big issue because there were a lot of ads due to the start of the busy tourist season. The more ads, the more pages, and more pages meant more room for news. Most ads didn't take up a whole page. What's left is "the news hole," the space we could fill with news and pictures.

So the news hole was big for this first June paper.

Everyone was throwing out ideas that were obvious things: preview of the Lilac Festival and parade; predictions of the number of visitors; who was playing at the Grand, etc. Mr. Niagara advised an editorial against additional snowmobile routes in the winter. This was pretty controversial, because some people thought they should be banned outright as "motorized transport" that has been banned since 1898, and others thought people should be allowed to use
~~~

them because they made it easier to get around in the winter. We started to argue amongst ourselves and then Naomi came in with her grandmother – and friend.

It was a stuffed panda almost as big as she is. "He needs a new nose," she said.

"I can see that," I said. "But we don't have anything that size in stock. He'll have to be hospitalized."

I thought she was going to be upset, but she just straightened her arms and aimed the creature at me. "Okay," she said.

I watched them walk to the door and Naomi turned back.

"Thanks, Waltie," she said with a little wave.

Oh, no. She'd been listening to Ashe. I had hoped that nickname wouldn't spread. I turned back to the budget meeting.

"So, how's the search for the new school superintendent going?" Mr. Niagara asked.

"You tell me, Britt," Mom said.

"Okay, I'll check it out, but we checked last...."

"We stay on top of things."

"Yes, Ma'am."

"By the way," Mom said, "I appreciated your story last week on the city council vote about bringing back the concession stand at Arch Rock. Where was the advance?"

Mr. Niagara looked perplexed. "What?"

"The advance story," Mom said. "You reported the vote, but who knew it was coming? Certainly not our readers!

"We need to tell people that the council is considering an issue and when they will be voting on it BEFORE" – she slapped her right fist into her left hand – "the vote. Preferably well before, so the public, some of whom are actually our readers, can attend the meeting and voice their opinions."

"Right," he said, sheepishly.

"From now on I want advances on every meeting."

"Right," he said again.

"I was doing the calendar..." Miss Kelly mused. "There's a convention of cardiac surgeons at the Grand Hotel starting this weekend. But there's not much we can say about that."

Mom paused a long time with her elbows on the desk and palms covering her cheeks. "Britt. Why don't you check and see if one Dr. Clifford Mongabay is going to be among them?"

He looked stunned. "That's a long shot, isn't it?"

"Well, probably. Sure. He's a prominent cardiac surgeon in Southfield... Why should he come to the most important state-level meeting of his colleagues?"

Mongabay was that guy the would-be bribesters didn't want moving into Bloomfield Hills.

"I'll check," Mr. Niagara said, neatening up his papers and pens.

I leaned in to whisper to Mom: "Fletch and I are going to get ice cream."

~~~

Turns out, Dr. Mongabay was indeed going to be attending that convention. Mom wasted no time setting up an interview for soon after his expected arrival.

Refreshing what we knew about him, it was basically this: Born in Greenville, South Carolina in 1926, he was the son of a grocer and oldest of five children. Showing an early aptitude in school, he was pushed ahead several grades and became the first in his family to be admitted to college. He attended Fisk University, then, as part of the Great Migration of Negroes to the North, his family moved to Michigan and he attended the University of Michigan Medical School, graduating with honors in 1936. He went on to specialize in cardiology at Harvard University before returning to Michigan to work at Henry Ford Hospital and Beaumont Hospital. He is now Chief of Staff at Providence Hospital in Southfield.

His house in Bloomfield Hills was reportedly still "undergoing renovations."

Mom thought that was just a ruse, so he could avoid confrontation while all the anti-integration agitation was still going on. Dr. Mongabay was more than willing to talk to the *Huron Shores Herald.*

Just so he wouldn't be observed coming to the office, she invited him over to Marblecliff for dinner; Mr. Niagara and Mrs. Hart, too. He was bringing a colleague, a general practitioner from Hamtramck named Dr. Ivan Fychenko.

I was glad the Harts were back for the summer. Well, Mrs. Hart and the kids. Senator Hart was still in Washington until the next recess. It meant lots of kids on our street, even if some of them were teenagers, and more people to talk to.

Since the dinner fell on the day of the famous horse-hitch parade, I asked
~~~

to stay out in town because it would be full of activities following the 4 p.m. event. I figured I could hang out with Fletch and Carlee after the parade ended. But Mom said, no, she wanted me at the dinner. Something about I could "learn something." But since she could use as many photos of the parade as she could get, she let me go for most of the day – with a camera.

Visitors were pouring off ferries every few minutes at several docks – much more than usual and that's nearly 10,000 a day in summer.

The town was more festive than usual, too. There was a mish-mash of sounds including kids' excited voices, the jingling carriage harnesses, horse neighs and the clomp of their shod hooves on blacktop, and bicycle horns of both the clink-clink and Clarabell-the-clown honk-honk variety.

It was hard to even walk on Main Street it was so jam packed. In Five Ws and H terms: **Who** – tourists; **What** – flooding onto the island; **When** – June 5 to 11; **Where –** downtown Mackinac Island and all the hotels; **Why** – because it was Lilac Festival time; **How** – they came by ferry boat. Add sights: masses of people walking with ice cream cones and cotton candy or chomping fudge; carriages with their yellow-fringed tops; thousands of bicyclists; and smells: horse poop and fudge. I could have written a "color" piece about it, as Mom would say. Miss Kelly was doing that while Mr. Niagara was going to get the "hard" news – anything that happened during the day. Plus, Mom was having him take notes at the dinner for a Mongabay story.

Earlier, I was asked to get some history on the Lilac Festival, so I looked in the old bound volumes of the paper. Vince came out of the darkroom and helped me look. He knew where the old photo features were. He told me the floats in the Lilac Parade are all drawn by draft horses such as Clydesdales, the ones with the big furry feet, and Percherons. The stores and organizations make up all kinds of historic and imaginative floats – with room for their advertising banners, he said.

I read in last year's paper that the parade has been popular for 15 years, the big signal of the return of the season of things to do. For me, sadly, it meant Fletch and Carlee riding more. I was a little downhearted about watching them riding in the parade together. The theme this year was Mackinac history. All floats told a historic tale – except the Lilac Queen's float. We kids at the public school voted for her. This year it was Loretta Cowell. Never met her.

Fletch was dressed as an Ojibwa brave and Carlee an Indian Princess, which was perfectly fitting for her. She had a beaded soft suede dress and soft boots. Her hair was in two braids tied with strung beads, although I must say my cousin Alyce's dark Eur-Asian hair would have suited the part better. Fletch had a painted deer-skin jacket and, over his shoulder, a bow and quivver. Their horses were saddled over red, white and black Indian blankets. Snoopy looked good in his. Well, so did the black horse Fletch was riding, for that matter. I took their picture. Ashe was waving from a float sponsored by the Drum and Fife Tavern. I snapped her picture and she waved and smiled.

Mrs. Hart rode The Senator, who was big, brown, and imposing. I took her picture, too, and she waved at me. On the brown and white horse next to her I recognized former Governor John B. Swainson. He lived on the island and they often rode together.

I watched from the other side of the road, opposite Marquette Park. I saw them all pass. At 5:30 I knew I'd better get going, but I wanted to get some cotton candy. I got in a long line in front of one of the fudge shops on Main Street and I started to have second thoughts about the pleasures of cotton candy eaten while alone.   I was standing, by necessity, in front of a parked Carriage Taxis & Tours rig – the usual three-horse hitch.

A state trooper was standing on the street side of the carriage, right near the horses' heads.

Our eyes locked for just a second.

He was one of the officers in the room at the governor's mansion that day!

Then it happened so fast.

He lit something. A sparkler right near the horses' eye and ear. The horse suddenly reared and spooked his two companions and they shook and lunged forward.

I was knocked down, my camera flew in the air, and all I could do was put my hands over my head and hope the horses' hooves landed elsewhere. The carriage lunged forward. I was underneath it, but not under the wheels. It just went over me.

Luckily, the carriage driver was aboard, and he was able to control the horses fairly quickly. But other people were knocked down and bumped and scraped. A child being carried by his mom hit his arm on a hitching post when his mother fell and a crew of first aid workers came to his aid. I was able to brush myself off and the trooper who spooked the horses was no where to be seen. I retrieved the camera. It had a dent in the side of the lens housing.

I knew I was lucky. I was going to tell Chief Holden about it later, but right then I had to get going home. I was late for the company that was coming. I brushed myself off in the entryway, removed a smudge I saw on my face in the mirror. Mrs. Hart, Mr. Niagara and Mom were sitting around the fireplace with two men I assumed to be Drs. Mongabay and Fychenko. They all had beverages in their hands and hors d'oeuvres were on the raised flagstone hearth. I sat down without being introduced because the Negro doctor, that would be Dr. Mongabay, was talking. His voice was deep and seemed to come from a big nose that looked like a flat anchor on the front of his face.

"..and they dragged the young man from his shoe store to the town square. I was afraid it was going to be a lynching. The men – the white men of the town, most of them – were yelling about the boy having molested a white high school girl. I don't think he even knew who she was, except she had come into the store.

" No!' the young man cried out, nervous sweat pouring through his white shirt. 'I did not touch her. She came into the store. Looking for shoes for a party she was... she said... I just...'

"You just laid your dirty black hands on her," a man said.

"Another: 'We'll teach you to raise your hands to a white woman.'

"Thankfully, the people of Greenville were past lynchings. But they tore his shirt off and punched him until his face was unrecognizable.

"I was hiding down a street, shakin' scared. I told myself I couldn't do anything to help, but perhaps I was just being a coward. The mob looked out of control...

"My uncle found me and insisted I get out of there, so I went with him, to the other side of the tracks."

"So," Mom said, "they weren't willing to have a Negro – ah, I mean a Black man, even speak to a white woman—or girl."

"No, that wasn't it at all!" Dr. Mongabay exclaimed. "They didn't really care about that – not a bit. That's often a ruse. Black men talked to white women all the time in business settings. What bothered them was that the young Black man's shoe store was selling shoes!"

I saw Mrs. Hart nod. Everyone was silent. Mongabay looked around the room as if to register everyone else's surprise.

"It was all about e-co-nom-ics," he said, emphasizing each syllable of the word while he moved his head to look everyone in the face. "There was a shoe store owned by white people on the same block. They couldn't tolerate customers going to the Black businessman's store. Especially white customers. That was particularly galling."

"So, what you're telling us," Mrs. Hart said, " – and I hear you prefer 'Black,' – is that a lot of the lynchings of Blacks in the South, the accusations of rape and molesting were..."

"Were a cover up for the real reason – money!" he said.

As if on cue, a log broke in the grate and settled in with a shower of sparks.

Mrs. Hart pursed her lips together and nodded.

"That's a revelation," Mom said, "but it makes sense."

Everyone was silent in absorbing this in their minds. Finally, Mom said, "Well, I have to see how Mrs. Kwashneetski is doing with dinner." Looking at me: "Doctors, this is my son, Walter. Walter – why don't you take Dr. Mongabay and Dr. Fychenko up to see your space photos while we get the dinner on the table?"

"Sure, Mom," I said. I wondered whether she was being diabolical or what.

"It's upstairs," I said, gesturing up. Both men stood.

"Please ignore the cardboard boxes up there," Mom called after us. "My son refuses to unpack because he preferred his life back in New York City."

When they went up ahead of me I had a chance to lean over to Mrs. Hart. "What movie did they end up going to see?" I asked.

"*No Deposit, No Return*," she said. "No wetsuit or catsuit."

"Clever senator," I said.

Standing in my room, where the ceiling was lower than downstairs, Dr. Mongabay looked very tall. With an African robe and spear he would have looked like one of those Zulu warriors. His skin was the color of caramel candy. Dr. Fychenko was Kuryakin blond. Ukrainian, I figured. Mom said those "ko" endings usually meant Ukrainian.

"These boxes here are my stuff from Brooklyn," I explained. "I am refusing to unpack them as a protest. I want my mother to take us back home."

"I see," Dr. Mongabay said, looking up and down the stacks, which made the wounded Canaveral jump down and flee.

"Well, there's my space pictures wall my mom wanted you to see. That's Astronaut Ed White," I said pointing up. "He was the first man to walk in space. It was during the Gemini 4 mission. I got to meet him."

I looked away. "He died in the Apollo 1 fire."

"Didn't he go to U of M?" Dr. Fychenko asked.

"Yes," I said. "So did McDivitt, who commanded Gemini 4."

Dr. Mongabay was silent.

"He signed that photo for me after his spacewalk," I said. "When I met him in New York. I was really sad that he – and Gus Grissom and Roger Chaffee – got killed."

"Yes," Mongabay said. "That *was* sad. But it is also sad they are spending money on a frivolous space program when there are problems on Earth to solve."

"What!" I said.

"Yes," he said. "As my friend, the Reverend Ralph Abernathy, has said, 'putting a few white men in space for fun while hundreds of thousands of little Negro children and poor white children go hungry and ill-housed represents an inhuman priority.'"

Dr. Fychenko shrugged and looked at me sort of apologetically.

I couldn't believe what I was hearing.

Then I said: "Inhuman priority...? With respect, Sir, that's wrong. You can't blame poverty and misery on the space program and NOT doing the space program won't solve those problems."

"Oh," he said in voice as deep as that visiting African premier in the U.N.C.L.E. pilot episode. "And how do you know this, a boy of…"

"Twelve." I said.

"A boy of 12. Uh huh."

"Well, I have a friend named MontesQ," I said. " I wish I could introduce you to him. He's a real genius like Einstein. We've talked about this. He can explain it with numbers, but, basically, he says there is so much money spent on poverty programs now, and relatively little on the space program, even though it seems like a lot, that taking it away and adding all of it into the poverty programs money would be like putting a drop of water in a bucketful.

"In other words, it wouldn't make any difference to the poor. But space exploration will make a difference for everyone. It isn't just for fun. MontesQ says exploring is essential to the human spirit. And the money used on the space program is providing all sorts of scientific advances regular people can use and it will provide even more once we get all the way to the moon and invent all the things we need to get there."

Dr. Mongabay just folded his arms and shook his head at me with that pitying look religious people give you when they find out you don't believe in God.

I went on: "I wish I could remember all of the specific medical advances and stuff MontesQ talks about. But I, personally, think about it like this – this I know – because I'm building a telescope now and grinding the lens myself. It's kind of an old fashioned method. Lenses were first made about 400 years ago. And 400 years ago there was even worse poverty and starvation than now and people were getting the plague and lots of other preventable diseases because they didn't know about germs.

"So, the first person who starts grinding lenses to allow him to see small things bigger – well, people could have said that was a waste of money and his money should be spent helping the poor and the sick. But you know what? The result of those lenses was more help to the sick than a billion dollars because they allowed the discovery of germs. For the first time germs could be seen because the microscope was invented!

"And the discovery of germs led to better sanitation and better care being taken around sick people not to give them germs or pass their germs on to others. It led to keeping the water clean so people wouldn't get sick from that. Not to mention eyeglasses that were to come from it. Eyeglasses must have allowed people to go on making things their families needed because they could see again. So you would have told this person not to spend money on lenses research? Not to... not to... strive to learn new things? How do you know we won't discover some things at least that important and useful out in space? I just know that exploration can lead to miraculous things. "

Well, Mongabay just kept shaking his head and smiling like I was an idiot.

Dr. Fychenko patted me on the shoulder and looked up at his colleague.

"I think he's got you there, old boy," Dr. Fychenko said. "Who knows? Maybe that heart transplant you keep saying is going to happen... Maybe we'll learn something about helping hearts where there's no gravity."

"Exactly!" I said, looking from him to Dr. Mongabay. "As a doctor you should at least acknowledge the medical advances of the space program. Miniaturization, monitoring telemetry, and all that." But, I thought, maybe he wasn't that smart when it comes to the big picture – MontesQ says most people aren't. They're locked in their own little worlds.

Dr. Mongabay moved back toward my bedroom door, as if to go. Then stopped. He said:

"And your refusal to unpack your boxes. Is this embracing the future?"

I felt like he hadn't heard a word I said about the space program.

Mom called from downstairs: "Dinner's ready gentlemen."

"Well," I said, "I guess the space program is just one area where we will have to agree to disagree. And I don't think the future is being made here on Mackinac Island. It's being made in New York and Houston and big cities like that."

"Well, we'll have to agree to disagree about that," Dr. Mongabay said. "Tell me, have you visited the Beaumont exhibit at Fort Mackinac?"

"No I haven't," I said.

"We went there on tour yesterday," he said. "Dr. Beaumont did something here that no one else anywhere in the world thought to do. And he changed medical science forever. Right here on Mackinac Island in the early 1800s. See, the future can be made anywhere. It doesn't have to be in outer space. Or even New York."

<p style="text-align:center">~~~</p>

At dinner Dr. Mongabay asked Mom how the state police were faring in their attempt to get her to reveal her source on the bribery story. Mom said she and her colleague were refusing, but admitted they could face jail time if they didn't. I set the Norelco's microphone up in the hole in its leather case and started the machine.

"Of course they want to interrogate our source," she said, winking at me. "But we can't give in to that. No one would talk to reporters if we did."

"Aren't you afraid of the consequences?" he asked.

"Aren't you, by integrating a white neighborhood?" Mom asked. He looked down. Mr. Niagara jumped into the conversation.

"We could go to jail protecting our source," he said, exaggerating his own jeopardy in the matter, "but you face people who aren't above getting violent about their racism, maybe even angry mobs, if you move into your house. And from the way it looks, the state police might not lift a finger to help."

"Or, they'll help the mobs," Mrs. Hart added, running her fingers through her short hair.

"Yes," Mongabay said. "I've often been asked that question. And my wife, she asks me that question. We have two daughters, you know... But look here. There comes a time when it is more dangerous to remain obedient and subservient. To stay a second class citizen. Because the first class will continue to demand more and more until we are back to slavery and have to fight the Civil War all over again."

Mom sipped her coffee.

"Consider Viola Liuzzo," he continued, "a white woman from Detroit, murdered just last year for going down South to help with voter registration. She went into danger even though she had five children ages 6 to 19. There are those in the country who think she shouldn't have gone because she had five children and those who think she should have – because she had five children. Who's right? It is very hard. But those children gave her a stake in the future. She went to make a better future. I don't want my two daughters to live as second-class citizens, who can't sit at a particular lunch counter or have a good education or live in a nice neighborhood."

Everyone looked in their coffee cups and said nothing so he continued: "Maybe I can explain it this way. As we speak, Robert Kennedy has just delivered a speech of great moral courage in Capetown, South Africa. He said each time a man stands up for an ideal, or acts to help others, or fights injustice, he sends forth a tiny ripple of hope, and – I'm paraphrasing here – those ripples cross each other and enough of them build a current which can sweep down the mightiest walls of oppression and resistance.

"So I say, if we each are responsible for just one ripple of hope, we can change the world."

"Your husband," he nodded to Mrs. Hart, "is a man of intelligence, idealism, and decency." She smiled. "You know that," he continued. "He led the way toward enacting the Civil Rights Act of 1964 and the Voting Rights Act of 1965. These were major accomplishments to the credit of every man and woman who voted for them. But we still need to rectify discrimination in housing."

She smiled again.

"And he's working on that problem, Dr. Mongabay. That I can assure you," she said.

"I believe you. I know Senator Hart will continue to help the cause of equality before the law. The Constitution is color blind. JFK said that, just months before he was killed."

Mrs. Hart nodded. "He also said 'Those who make peaceful change impossible make violent change inevitable.'"

"That seems to be the big worry among the general public," Mom said. "The growing militancy of Negroes – Blacks. Or, is this a myth fueled by reporters who need stories? Can you tell me, Dr. Mongabay, is our future going to be ala Martin Luther King or Malcolm X?"

He answered: "Malcolm X was not for Blacks starting violence, you know, only for not standing arms down while violence is perpetrated ..." He made a fist and pounded his own chest. "...on them.

"But I'm glad you asked that question and there is a simple answer. We ALL want to achieve equality by peaceful means. But an increasing number of spokesmen say we are not obligated to ask peacefully forever. That is where Black Power comes in. Last month Adam Clayton Powell Jr. told Howard University graduates that the only way to demand our rights is to 'seek Black Power.'"

"It's that Black Power movement that has people scared," Mr. Niagara said.

"What Black Power will mean depends on white folks," Dr. Mongabay said. "It means if peaceful requests are not enough, well... my people will not wait forever."

He looked at me. "Maybe not even until we send a man to the moon and bring him safely back to Earth."

Mom changed the tone: "Mrs. K has laid our dessert out on the back porch table, so everyone will you please meander back there."

I gobbled up a brownie, complimented Mrs. K on it with my mouth still half full, and asked Mom if I could go back to town and look for Fletch and Carlee and the other kids from my class who would be hanging out after the parade.

"No ice cream?" she asked. I shook my head and she said, "Okay, go. You can't keep a wave upon the sand."

I ran to feed the cats first. Then got on my bike, but it was funny. I thought I saw someone lead a horse around the corner and behind our house. I stopped to pretend to tie my shoe and listen more. I was sure I heard talking. It was a group of maybe four or five, just mumbling and hanging around. They were horseback riding – but stopped. I wondered what they were up to and had a sense of foreboding.

So I didn't go down the Marquette steps as I had planned. I waited quietly by Anne's Tablet and watched.

Then I heard soft crunching twigs and leaves behind me. I turned. It was Ashe. Pigtailed, big-eyed Ashe in pink Keds.

"What's going on?" she asked, as calm as if she was there to get instructions for Evasion Pattern Eight. She had her 20-inch bike, the one with the handlebar streamers. I didn't think I would ever be glad to find her stalking me, but I was. I crouched down before her, put a finger before my lips indicating she should be quiet, and whispered:

"Ashe, I think those people are up to no good. Either they're after me or following Dr. Mongabay or something. Can you turn around quietly? Roll your bike down the steps then ride like the wind and get a policeman." I counted on there being plenty of officers down by the parade, just in case they're needed to keep order.

She nodded and turned to pedal away, but I caught her shoulder. "No," I said. "They won't believe you. Go to your brother...."

She shook her head but spoke quietly. "He won't believe me more," she said with perspicacity beyond her age.

I had it in a split second. "Here," I said, tugging off my Waverly Ring. "Show him this."

She smiled, pleased to be trusted with another one after what happened with the first. She would take her task seriously.

"Tell them there's a criminal mob on Garrison Road and I'm afraid for … tell him lives are at stake! "

Any worry that was an exaggeration was quickly dispelled. No sooner than Ashe had turned and gone, I heard sounds from my house.

Someone opened the front door and the wooden screen door banged. All of a sudden you could hear lots of voices. One was my mom's. And I think I heard Mrs. Hart and for sure I heard Dr. Mongabay's really deep voice. Across from me the mob moved into the bushes. Mrs. Hart must have returned to her cottage the opposite way. Then I saw Dr. Mongabay and Dr. Fychenko coming down the road. I guessed they intended to walk back to the Grand Hotel.

They didn't get very far. The mob jumped out. I counted five people. I recognized some of them as part of the gang who plotted the bribe.

They were going very slow. I was watching while walking my bike some distance behind, staying close to the bushes. The dismounted riders split, two on one side and two on the other side, to let the doctors pass. Or almost pass them. Because then, well out of hearing distance of our house, one of them jumped Dr. Mongabay from the right and another jumped Dr. Fychenko from the left. I dragged myself and my bike into the bushes.

The doctors shook their shoulders in an attempt to wrest free, but soon their attackers were each helped by a few others who just emerged from the trail on foot. Two men held Dr. Mongabay's arms back and two men held Dr. Fychenko's arms back.

I almost gasped as one man socked Dr. Fychenko in the stomach. Then Dr. Mongabay. They did it again. Dr. Fychenko crumpled to the ground. "Get up. Our quarrel isn't with you. Our quarrel is with this uppity monkey."

"What have I ever done to you?" Dr. Mongabay asked.

So one of the men told him of his "no right" to buy a house in a white neighborhood. The shortcomings of the dark race he went into with great detail, almost spitting the words.

With that, the speaker punched Dr. Mongabay in the stomach again. He doubled up, then rose up and with expansive hands freed himself from the grip of the others, and roaring in that royal African tone of his: "You won't get away with this."

A man began to laugh. I knew the voice. I knew it was Raccoon Man without seeing him.

Dr. Mongabay slipped their grasp only momentarily. They grabbed him again on both sides and the next punches were more severe.

I didn't know what to do. If I rode for help it would take too long. I remembered Fletch said he felt helpless when the little boy was being brutalized by the tennis courts and he thought it would take too much time to get help. What did he vow? He'd step in and help somehow.

Then a cold shiver went up my spine. One of the men threw a noose over a tree branch.

28 – THE CHASE

I WAS JUST ABOUT to cry out, no matter what the consequences, just like I knew Fletch would.

I was afraid that noose might not be just a scare tactic.

Dr. Mongabay and Dr. Fychenko were being silently brave. I couldn't imagine what they were thinking. But when the dangling rope caught their eyes, even from my distance I could see the complete whites around their pupils.

The men were surrounding Dr. Mongabay and telling him he wouldn't be moving into any house in Bloomfield Hills or any white neighborhood.

And one added, "this side of Hades."

Another punched him for good measure.

They punched him and they slapped him, but they talked a lot about the desecration of white neighborhoods.

No one said "lynch" but they didn't have to.

I decided if they tried that I would yell, but they didn't move to do it. It was as if they were just as interested in insulting and taunting him as in hurting him. He bore it with great dignity, but then Dr. Fychenko said, "See here – you can't do this... the law..." and the fury of the men turned to him. They punched him and punched him and when he fell they kicked him in the lower back.

"The law isn't for coons like him, or white traitors to their race like you," one of them said, then stomped on Dr. Fychenko's leg.

It sounded like maybe his bone cracked.

When he tried to stand, holding the tree and bracing himself with the other leg, I could see blood coming from his mouth. Then one of them threw Dr.

Mongabay against a tree.

When both doctors were slumped at the base of trees, one man lit two cigarettes and passed one to another. The third man put his hand out, so he gave his over and lit another. Minutes passed, but maybe only seconds.

If I went down there they'd probably just hit me, too. I wondered if I could stay hidden and just make noise and scare them off. But a man can usually tell where a sound is coming from. If I had a stick and a big metal pot I'd bang the stick on the pot anyway. But I didn't. I could race past on my bike and yell, but they had horses.

Then one man kicked Dr. Mongabay in the foot. "Listen up, scum," he said, and started a lecture on white superiority. When they were talking they weren't punching as much. The man pulled Dr. Mongabay back up to standing. I could see the blood running out of his nose. They must have thought they had time to prolong this – that no one would be on the trail with all the doings in town.

If I made a dash for home, I'd surely be seen. Maybe that would be good. I could lure them off. My chances were better, being white. They were focused on hating Negro people so much.

I hoped they would continue the insulting remarks before doing any more violence. Then the first smoker pressed the lit end of his cigarette into Dr. Mongabay's cheek.

I was actually opening my mouth to make a desperate scream when, all of a sudden, Carlee came up behind me on Snoopy like a storybook Pocahontas, her braids blowing in the wind. Then another horse snorted quietly and I saw Fletch on a ridge above us on his horse. He had his bow in one hand at his side. He looked at me and understood what was going on in an instant. As the next guy lifted his arm to sock Mongabay's face, Fletch pulled an arrow from his quiver and shot it in what looked like one unbroken motion, impaling the man's sleeve to the tree.

I heard it whiz by and hit the tree with a THWATT – like a sound effect from *Robin Hood* on TV.

The man with the arrow in his sleeve was shocked, then tore himself free, ducked and glanced around. They all looked up and a few scattered on foot. Two mounted their horses in a dither. Another was trying to mount.

Fletch guided his horse down to the road. "They're running. We'll go for the police now," he said. "Get up on my horse."

I shook my head "no" and he shook his head in dismay.

"Didn't Ashe already tell the police?" I yelled.

"Don't know. She ran into us first on Fort Street. Gave me your Waverly Ring and said you needed help. We set right out to find you."

"Go!" I said, waving him on, "Go for help." He and Carlee took off through the bushes toward the fort. They knew all the shortcuts.

Two men were already riding off. The third turned toward me with one hand on his horse's reins and another on the saddle grip. Raccoon Man!

"I've seen you too many times," he said. "You're dead meat, kid."

I hopped on my bike and pedaled as fast as I could down Garrison. I glanced back as he was struggling into the saddle.

I knew a galloping horse could catch my bike no matter how fast I pedaled. But somehow I didn't think he knew how to make a horse gallop – or had the courage to gallop on a horse. But he kept up a good canter following me. I knew there was a gap in the wrought iron fence around St. Anne's Cemetery that I could get through on the bike, but a horse couldn't. I took it and cut through at an angle and came out on Custer. I had to hook up with Garrison Road again, but Raccoon Man was momentarily befuddled and didn't know which way I'd go. He turned back to go around the cemetery, but I knew which way I wanted to lead him. I took Custer back to Garrison before he figured it out. After that, he was slowly closing the gap between us.

I had an idea. British Landing Road. I just had to make it to British Landing Road. I sped across the airport property. Some grass slowed me up but didn't hamper the horse's speed. I stopped looking and kept pedaling as fast as I could. I heard the hooves getting closer. I started to think I might have to fight him and there was no one around to help. The airport was shut and there was no one else around.

He was closing on me. I reached the top of British Landing Road and glanced back to see Raccoon Man and his horse were just inches from my back fender. If he'd been a cowboy he could have lassoed me easy. I wished my bike had one of those oil sprays they put in James Bond's Aston Martin. But I had gravity. I picked up speed on the first downslope. The horse kept up. Then at the real steep decline after the Wawashkamo Golf Course I just let Robbie go and hoped Fletch was right.

I didn't have to wait but another few seconds to find out.

I heard a loud neigh. I dared a quick look back, and saw the horse's mane

shake left and right against its neck. The horse had had enough. It put its head down and put the brakes on. Raccoon Man flipped in the air. I stopped and saw him smack the blacktop road. I saw his face scraping the blacktop as he slid. "Ouch," I grimaced inwardly with misplaced empathy. But I hopped back on my bike and kept going.

I had to brake a little now and then on the way down, to avoid going out of control, but still I didn't stop. I slowed enough to make the left turn on Lake Shore Road. No going in the lake this time. I picked up speed again kept pedaling and finally turned at Market Street, then cut over to Main.

I found Carlee and Fletch giving a report to Chief Holden. Fletch looked up and said: "Oh, here comes Danger Man now."

I looked around to make sure there were no state police near. I didn't know which of them could be trusted.

"Raccoon Man is down," I said. "His horse stopped; he didn't." Only Fletch gave me a 'nice work' smile.

Then we told every detail. I said Fletch made a great shot pinning that guy's sleeve to the tree.

Carlee leaned toward Fletch: "Where were you really aiming?" she asked in a whisper.

Fletch looked to the sky and said nothing.

Finally, Chief Holden closed his notebook and said, "Good job, kids."

"Is anyone out looking for these guys?" I asked.

"We'll find them," he said with confidence I didn't share, and holstered his notebook and marched off. I called after him: "Look for a guy with half his face scraped off."

Then we three just stood there in silence catching our breath.

~~~

"Fletch, tell me one thing," I said. "I thought you said your parents took your bow and arrow away when you were seven."

"They did," he said. "I took it up again when I was nine."

"Then you got a bigger one, apparently," I said.

Carlee sidled over. "That was really brave," she cooed. I thought she was talking to Fletch, but then she looked at me.

"Walter, there's something I've been meaning to give you." She pulled out a flat little box from Snoopy's saddle bag. It was gift wrapped. I must have looked nonplussed.
~~~

"It's your birthday present." she said, as if it was something obvious. "I couldn't come to your party because my parents took me to Bermuda. But I picked this out."

I opened it. It was a mathematical slide rule inside a leather case that had a pocket clip.

"'Cause I think you're going to need it to figure out how to get us to Mars."

A sudden awareness came over me. While I thought Carlee talked only about horses, she thought I talked only about going into space.

~~~

It was the next day before I remembered to tell Mom about the deliberately spooked carriage horses. That child broke his arm. It could have been worse. Mom went right to Chief Holden and he said he was going to show me pictures of different state police officers to see if I could spot the culprit.

We finished the telescope on the 22nd of June. The Lilac Festival tourists had gone and new ones had come to the island. Timing it for the next full moon, Mom put a notice in the newspaper that everyone was invited to a skywatch party at Arch Rock. There was a viewing platform there and we set up the telescope on it. We put dozens and dozens of little white candles along the walk leading up to it. Mom bought refreshments out of the newspaper's promotion budget.

Everyone thought the magnified view of the surface of the moon was fascinating. When Ashe came up I had to give her a little boost. She looked at the craters of the moon, thought they were really cool, then I put her down. She looked around at the sky and then said, "Point it over there, Waltie, point it over there." She was pointing at what I thought was a very bright star.

"No, no," Ashe," I said. "That's just a star. You won't see anything. Just light. We're looking at the moon."

"I want you to point it there," she insisted. "Point at that."

I sighed. "Okay, but it's going to be just a bright light."

I turned the telescope a bit and adjusted the tube, then tightened it aimed at the light she was so insistent upon. I looked myself first.

I lifted my head suddenly.

"What is it?" Fletch asked.

"It..." I said. "I …..only Saturn. It's Saturn!"
~~~

“With the rings?”

“Yes, with the rings. You can see the rings!”

I looked in the eyepiece again. “Wow. I never thought I would see the rings of Saturn for real.”

I let him look.

“Mom...” I yelled for her. She came. “Look at this!”

“MY, oh my,” she said. “This is so much more fantastic than any picture.”

We all thought that.

“I want to look!” Ashe screamed.

“Of course,” I said. “It's Saturn, Ashe.” I picked her up so she could reach the eyepiece. “Be careful not to bump it,” I said. “It will go out of range. Any movement is magnified, too.”

She looked.

“And I found it,” she said, grinning.

“Yes, you did,” I said.

I should have remembered what Mom told me the day we arrived. Stars twinkle, planets glow.

29 – RAID

After a while people were wondering why Dr. Mongabay and Dr. Fychenko's attackers hadn't been caught. Downstate newspapers were making a big deal about it. A racist attack on two doctors, one still in the hospital.

Mom described it pretty well in her newspaper, but people were asking if these guys were the same ones that were trying to bribe Governor Romney to act against racial integration.

The state police got agitated all over again. I fingered the theology professor, Jasper Tarpoff, a.k.a. Raccoon Man, in the beatings, so certain state police – the ones at the bribery discussion – pretty much figured out I was the source of the attempted bribery story. Lots of people were gunning for me now.

Tarpoff was the least worrisome of them. He had to disappear, especially with the scraped face that would corroborate my report. His absence made the story just more believable to everyone. He would have been better off if he'd stayed on the job and just denied it. But I think he was afraid Dr. Mongabay, and Dr. Fychenko, if he recovered, could identify him and their testimony about the assault would go further than mine. Still, a lot of people in the community preferred to believe that Tarpoff, a white "man of God," was innocent. A lot of them were from the college, where they were morally sure of themselves.

Dr. Mongabay wasn't badly hurt, but Dr. Fychenko was in a coma at Mackinac County Hospital in St. Ignace. There was the possibility of a murder or manslaughter charge if he died, an assault charge if he survived. I felt especially bad about Dr. Fychenko. He understood my defense of space exploration.

Meanwhile, the state police and governor's staff filed another "order to show cause" demanding Mom and Freya name the source of the story that accused them – or at least some of them – of attempted bribery or go to jail.

This time the Circuit Court acted swiftly. Mom and Freya were subpoenaed. They went to court and said "no way."

Mom came back to the office and said she wondered why they weren't taken into custody on the spot.

"Maybe the judge is going to drop it," Mr. T suggested, tapping out his pipe. "More publicity will only make them look worse."

"Unless they really think we made it all up."

"Well, we didn't," I said. "And we have the tape to prove it."

"We can only wait and see," she said.

We didn't have to wait long.

They came on a Sunday.

Mom was in her glass-walled office, otherwise known as the Teddy Bear Clinic. She still took people in there for private talks and she was in there with Laura Kelly. I was dipping my finger tips in the hot wax, Fletch was sitting on the floor in the morgue reading a Superman comic. He had just said: "Hey, how come I never see see Lois Lane worrying about protecting her sources" when the daylight coming in the front window lessened with the approach of a blue tidal wave. Cops.

I quickly moved beside Fletch and spread out homework. We were on the floor, legs extended, leaning against the wall. Opposite us were slant top tables with old bound volumes of the newspaper and filing cabinets of old pictures and clippings and generally obsolete papers.

First they asked who everyone was. A cop kicked me in the foot and did the same to Fletch.

I told them who I was and said Fletch was a classmate here to do homework with me.

"About what?" the police officer asked.

"The Forties," I said.

"The Forties?"

"Yeah," I said. "The Forties. World War II, the Manhattan Project, Detroit as the Arsenal of Democracy. All that stuff."

"What of democracy?" one asked, confused. I didn't enlighten him. He looked at Fletch. "Where do you live, kid?"

Fletch told them he lived in Harrisonville and they told him to go home.

Fletch picked up his notebook and I said to him: "Don't forget your notes. You know, File Forties."

I pointed at my Waverly Ring.

"Oh yeah," he said and opened the drawer. "File Nineteen Forty-ies."

He pulled out the folder and quickly wrote in a little 's' after the number 40, so it read "File 40s." The cop looked at it and said "Go!" Fletch hurried out.

That was a relief.

Then the cops started to pull the place apart, looking for the recording tape that just went out the door.

They moved to every corner of the office and inside Mom's bear clinic/office and Mr. Trivelpiece's. One trooper, who seemed to have the most authority, said:

"We have a subpoena for the notes and tapes you used to write about an attempted bribery of the governor and same that were used by the *Detroit Free Press*. Please hand them over now."

"Ah, no, I will not!" she said. "They are protected by the First Amendment to the Constitution of the United States, the highest law in the land. Have you read this document?"

"I don't have to read anything, lady," he said. "The judge reads. I carry out his orders."

They were looking for anything that would lead them to the identity of the informant and the alleged tape recording of the bribery attempt.

It's not that we didn't have a copy of the tape elsewhere far away. We just didn't want them to have it because they might be able to get someone to identify my voice.

The bear clinic seemed to bother them.

"What's all this?" the leader-cop asked.

Mom explained, but they didn't seem to get the idea of a Teddy bear clinic in a newspaper.

"Open them," the trooper said to another trooper, tilting his head toward the bears.

What did he mean, "open them?"

The second trooper reached in his pocket and flipped open a knife. Then another came and did the same.

I inhaled suddenly. Mom looked grim but didn't say a word. I couldn't believe it. They started cutting open the hospitalized bears!

"Hey those aren't even ours," I said. Since there wasn't enough room in there for more than two cops slashing things, Mom backed away. While all the cops' eyes were focused there, she motioned to Mr. Huggins with her two hands lifted, as if holding a camera and clicking it. He sidled over and raised his camera just as I saw one of them reach for Naomi's panda. I covered my eyes for a second. When I opened them, Mom was motioning for Mr. Huggins to get back. I could tell she didn't want the troopers to notice him and confiscate the camera or film. But those guys were so into slicing up stuffed toys, I didn't think they would have noticed if a T-Rex was taking pictures.

Bear after bear they picked up, cut open, and threw down. Seeing it revealed nothing, a trooper threw the last one down on the floor and ground it with his foot like one would do putting out a cigarette.

Then they went to file cabinets.

"Where's Fletch?" Mom quietly asked me.

"Oh, ah, he had to go home and finish his homework. You know, that File 40 stuff."

She nodded, smiling. The cops were clueless.

"Please reconsider," one of the troopers said to her. "You will not like being locked up."

"Maybe so," she said. "But my favorite journalism professor always said, 'maximize experience.'"

"Who was that?"

"My father! Hey..."

Men were throwing files and mail and proofs and other stuff all over.

"We HAVE a warrant."

"Not to destroy the place," she said. They continued tossing. She threw her hands in the air. "But since when do fascists need warrants anyway?"

She was about to look at it resignedly, then one of the officers went behind her and started in on her desk. He grabbed one of Grandpa's AP award plaques, she said "Hey" while tugging it back, he resisted, and she "fell" into him with it. Another one of the men grabbed her arms from behind and started to put handcuffs on.

"You're under arrest for not cooperating with a legal warrant and, and... assaulting a state trooper," he said.

"Assaulting? What? I just tripped and fell," she said, playing innocent.

The officer turned the corners of his mouth down. "It doesn't matter. You're also under arrest for violating a court order to reveal the source of information used in a story about an attempt to bribe the Governor of Michigan."

They made her sit while they talked in another corner of the office. We all were ordered to sit.

I heard the officers arguing about someone named Miranda. "In custody, Miranda," one said. "Miranda schmanda," another said.

Some minutes went by and one troopers said to Mom: "Okay, let's go." And he muttered, "You have the right to remain silent..."

"Let's go?" she interrupted. "I need to talk to my staff and give them instructions for my absence and..."

"No you don't. And anything you say can be used against you..."

"But you just can't..."

"...in a court of law. We can."

"I can't leave without..."

"Not our problem. But you get a lawyer if you..."

"Well, this might be your problem," she said. "I have to be allowed to make arrangements for the care of my son in my absence. I don't think the *Free Press* coverage of this arrest will neglect mentioning how the Michigan State Police wouldn't let a mother provide for the safety of her child."

The head guy scowled at her. "All right. One phone call."

"And I need to talk to my staff!"

"No."

"Mom..." I said, getting nervous.

"Then I need to talk to my son."

"You can talk to him. Nothing stopping you."

"In private."

"No."

First, Mom elected to make her call. She figured she would leave the lawyers up to Freya and the *Free Press*. She called Uncle Brian – I know because I had to dial for her. She talked fast – holding the phone only by pinching it between her shoulder and cheek – and from the one side of the conversation I heard, he agreed to come up right away and stay with me.

The troopers got bored and left us in private anyway.

"Okay, Walter," Mom said in a low tone. "There's nothing to be concerned about. I'll get bailed out pretty quick. Soon as Freya writes this and the *Free Press* hits the streets with it."

She looked in my eyes. "You okay? I can't hug you because..."

"Yeah, Mom." I said. I turned her halfway around and looked at her cuffed wrists behind her back.

"Do you want me to tell you about the Kuryakin maneuver?"

30 – I'M IN CHARGE

We had only a few minutes more. Mom kept giving me instructions. "Stay safe. Cooperate with Mrs. Kwashneetski at home and obey Uncle Brian when he gets here. Don't go anywhere but home unless you are escorted by Uncle Brian. Don't talk to anyone about this. Run the newspaper."

"Yeah, okay I got it all. I'm okay without you Mom, really..."

"You said that when I dropped you off one day in First Grade," she said. "I still haven't gotten over it."

"But run the paper? You haven't even taught me to count headlines yet."

"Oh, that's easy. All letters are one, except f-j-i-l and t are a half and m and w are one and a half. Unless capitals, then it's one and a half for most letters, one for f-j-i-l-t. And two for m and w. Britt and Laura both have charts that show the maximum count allowed per column in various type sizes."

I just stood there.

"Yes, you can do it," she said. "Just remember it's important to tell people what happened, but even more important to tell them what's going to happen. So keep Britt and Laura doing advances on everything anybody is planning to do. Then tell the readers what they did. And who voted what way. Remember the five W's and H. Start each story with the most important one. Pictures – crop to the faces. That's all there is to it."

I inhaled. "Okay, but I'm not going to run the Teddy Bear Clinic."

She sighed. "Well, somebody's going to have to do triage in there...."

We put our cheeks together. I think we were both crying when they came for her. An officer grabbed her by the shoulder. She looked back at Miss Kelly and Mr. Niagara.

"Walter's in charge," she said as they pushed her along.

"But..." Mr. Niagara stopped, looked at me. "Oh great," he said.

~~~

Freya did, indeed, write about Mom's arrest – from her own jail cell. Then it was headlines all over. Even the *New York Times* wrote about the *Detroit Free Press* reporter carted off to the slammer for not revealing a source. Doug and Frank called to tell me their parents read about it and told them: "Walter's mom's in jail."

The publicity didn't get Mom and Freya out of jail, however. It just made the judge more determined to get their source. They didn't even get bail – not at any amount.

Marblecliff had been searched, too. Ransacked, really. Apparently when they saw my unopened boxes they thought they had found the mother lode of secret seditious documents. They were all opened and dumped. I would love to have seen their faces when they discovered nothing but *Superman* comic books, *Hardy Boys, Tom Swift,* and classics like *Gulliver's Travels* and *The Prince and the Pauper.* Yankees Baseball cards must have really turned them on. I wonder if they examined each one for microdots!

Before I repacked them and taped up the boxes, I looked in Mom's bedroom and stuff was strewn about there, too. Stuff was even pulled out from under the bed. And one box that was still half under there had its cover torn off and there was a bear pulled partly out. I noticed its hat first. It was one of those with the ribbons hanging down the back. I knelt down and looked carefully. He sure had an expression, one of terror. I picked him up. He also had a tire mark across his body from his right foot to his left chin.

Uncle Brian arrived in the morning. He hugged me and assured me that everything was going to be okay.

He stuck with me like a bodyguard. After I went to bed and couldn't sleep I eventually tiptoed out into the hall. I looked down from the stairs and there he was sleeping on the couch in front of the fireplace, just like Mom often did. He went with me to the newspaper office the next day.

The staff was having a budget session when I got there. There was the ongoing Mongabay/Civil Rights story, but other news had to be covered. Advertisers would expect their little promotions to be covered in exchange for
~~~

buying ads. "Miss Judy's Victorian Hat Emporium was having a hat making contest," that sort of stuff. And we'd cover it and she'd put in a business card size ad. Oh, it wasn't acknowledged quid pro quo, but it was understood.

Mr. Niagara said he had police reports and the mayor's office to check, and Miss Kelly was to do the coming events calendar and write about winners of a hot dog-eating contest. I listened, let him finish.

"Mr. Niagara," I said, trying to sound like Mom. "Somebody's got to call the hospital every day to get the condition of Dr. Fychenko. He was in critical condition. If he dies, it will be a murder charge."

"I'd like to see ole Raccoon Man get the chair," he said.

"There's no death penalty in Michigan, dolt," Miss Kelly said.

"Maybe they'll change that," he said.

"Unlikely," said Uncle Brian from the back of the room. "We're the only state that has that prohibition written into its constitution."

"Furthermore," I said, expanding my chest and trying to sound adult, "State government needs to be monitored for anything that pertains to the case."

"Kid," he said, "I do the island news. We're not in Lansing. We don't have access..."

"Work the phones," I said. "Mom put me in charge, so there may be some changes made during the emergency. You continue to cover the towns – St. Ignace and Mackinaw City. And start making contacts in state government."

"Fine," he said, swishing a reporter's notebook off the desk and into the air with his right hand and catching it with his left. "I'm off to Mackinaw City."

"Oh, and while working your beats," I said, and he had to stop, "don't forget to write those advances. We don't want any council or board taking a vote on anything unless we tell people far enough in advance so they can speak up about it if they want to."

Just then the police scanner came on talking about a bear in Mackinaw City. In town. They were chasing it. Mr. Niagara continued to stomp toward the front door.

"I hope it finds him," I muttered.

"I'll make some calls about it," volunteered Miss Kelly, jumping up sprightly.

"And somebody needs to cover the ribbon cutting for the restoration of the blockhouse at the fort...." I yelled after him.

"Sounds like a good one for you kid," he yelled back as he went out.

~~~

Mr. Niagara didn't find the bear, but he did come back with a story. He wrote:

> *MACKINAW CITY – A black bear died Friday, June 27, after it eluded Department of Natural Resources officers and invaded the city.*
>
> *It was chased by the officers and police after they failed to stop it with a tranquilizer gun and water hoses near the Old School Park.*
>
> *The bear was found inside the Up North Records store on Main Street. Officers shot it with a second tranquilizer and, when it passed out, dragged it from the store.*
>
> *There had been a plan to take the bear back to a wilderness area, but it died of internal injuries. Police speculated that it might have been hit by a car before being captured.*

– 30 –

I read that and said: "Well, I think this leaves the reader with a lot of questions. Like where did it come from?"

"I didn't get to ask the bear," Mr. Niagara said. "It was dead."

"What kind of damage did it do in the record store? And, did anybody see it? Did it really get hit by a car or was that a cover-up for police brutality?"

He scowled at me. I continued.

"Was anybody scared?"

"All right, all right," he said. "Maybe a few more...But it answers the Five Ws and H. **What**, a bear; **When**, June 27; **Where**, Mackinaw City and in a record store; **Who**, DNR and police officers; **How**, with a stun gun; and as for **Why**, God knows."
~~~

"Well I don't think that's ever an answer to a 'Why'" I said.

Miss Kelly came in on her klicky high heels. "Here, maybe this will help." She handed me four typed pages.

Aloud, I read this:

> *MACKINAW CITY –   Fifteen-year-old Andrew Dodzik thought a big dog had entered the record shop, but he quickly looked again when he heard people from outside shouting: "Get out of the store!"*
>
> *The intruder was a black bear.*
>
> *Moments before, a visitor from Switzerland had to scurry out of the bear's path as it charged into the commercial strip of Mackinaw City and she wondered if things like that happen often in America.*
>
> *Dodzik didn't even stop to grab the crutches he was using that day. Earlier, he had torn a calf muscle running. The running practice, evidently, came in handy.*
>
> *He exited the store in a hurry. "I was pretty fast, they said."*
>
> *Annalice Compton, of Geneva, Switzerland, said in her rush she fell and came out on her hands and knees, according to Big Bay Point Lighthouse Bed and Breakfast owner Linda Bianchi.*
>
> *The B & B was the next stop for Compton and her companion, Betty Tobachnek of Minneapolis. Bianchi said Compton writes postcards home every day telling friends how beautiful it is here.*
>
> *"Then she said: 'I'm going to write I was chased by a bear, but nobody will believe me.'"*
>
> *Dodzik clerks at Up North Records. It was about 2 p.m. Friday, June 27, when*

he got the surprise visitor.

The bear, ahead of public safety officials chasing him, went straight to the back of the store, where he knocked over a free-standing display of Johnny Mathis records, climbed wall-mounted shelves and broke some 45 rpm records.

Outside, Dodzik said he could hear police, using a megaphone, tell people to clear the streets.

Trailing the bear, but coming up fast, were Mackinaw City Police Chief Patrick Wyatt, Cheboygan County Animal Control Officer Mark Swain, Department of Natural Resources Conservation Officer Terry McAllister, and two other police officers.

They had been chasing the bear for about two and half hours.

It was first reported seen at about 11:30 a.m. near the LaSalle Park in Mackinaw City, in the center of the residential area.

Wyatt said the bear, about 130 to 150 pounds, treed itself in a backyard adjacent to the park.

The animal control officer shot it with a tranquilizer gun. The amount of drug was apparently insufficient, however, because the bear did not pass out, Wyatt said.

They then called for a fire truck, thinking a powerful spray of water would get the bear down.

"But when the fire truck drove up the engine noise scared the bear and it climbed down and ran off," he said.

Officers tried to keep the bear from heading to the business district, but, perversely,

that's exactly where it went, crossing
Central Avenue and going down Main.

Wyatt said he doesn't know how fast
a bear can run, "but he was faster than we
were."

There were a lot of people in town
that day and the officers' first concern was
public safety, Wyatt said.

The bear went directly into the
record store, he said. People joked that
maybe the bear wanted some music.

"We were hoping Ballad of Davy
Crockett, *" Wyatt quipped.*

It was in the store about 15 minutes
before officers arrived and took aim
with the second tranquilizer shot. Before
the drug took full effect, the bear clawed
its way up shelves. The shelves collapsed and
the bear fell on and broke a variety
of records. Claw marks were found on
the wall and ceiling.

When the bear collapsed, officers
dragged it out of the store, along with some
of the records it fell on. DNR Officer
McAllister decided to take the bear to
Wilderness State Park, where he could later
be released, but the bear died.

A veterinary examination revealed
internal injuries.

"They think he was possibly hit by a car
prior to when we found him," Wyatt said.

The bear was a 2-year-old male, and
conservation officers surmise it may have
been looking to establish its own territory.
("Hmmmm, Britt. A '**Why**'...." I said.)

Mother bears have new cubs to take

*care of, Wyatt explained, and bears of that
age are being kicked out on their own.*

*Up North Records owner Denise
Partridge said she hasn't seen the damage
yet, but by its description, thinks the
notoriety from the event will bring enough
new business into the store to offset
the breakage and repair costs.*

*"It was a fun story until the bear died,"
she added.*

*Wyatt said Swiss visitor Compton can
rest assured it was an unusual incident in
America – at least in Mackinaw City. He
said he hasn't heard of a bear coming into
town for 15 years.*

*The first person to come back out on the
street in front of the record store looked down
at the face of Gale Storm on her album
"Sentimental Me."*

*As for Dodzik, who will be a junior
next year at Mackinaw City High School, the
incident filled his quota of excitement for the
summer.*

*"Last month," he said, "I was in a car that
caught fire on the Mackinac Bridge."*

– 30 –

Everyone was silent for a moment.

"What a waste of words!" Mr. Niagara exclaimed.

"Britt," I said (at that moment I decided to stop calling him Mr. Niagara), "This is human interest. And it looks like she did some real reporting." I handed him the copy.

He took the papers from my extended hand but didn't look at them. "Well, thank goodness no Beatles records were broken," he said. "THAT WOULD HAVE BEEN NEWS."

No one said anything. "She didn't even go to Mackinaw City...." he said.

Where'd she get all this crap? It violates everything about Inverted Pyramid style!

"She's not telling you the bear died until page three!" he continued indignantly. "That's the news. You're supposed to get the important stuff in the lead. In-ver-ted Pyramid. That's Journalism 101: the most important fact, then other stuff in declining order of importance. In this case, the most important thing is, the bear died."

"No," Miss Kelly said. "The most important thing is nobody was injured. That would be the lead if you wanted to write it inverted pyramid style. But there are *other* styles. This situation lent itself to storytelling. Telling the dramatic parts. You didn't give the reader any of that."

"So what do you call this piece of drama?"

"Suspended interest." she said, snatching the pages from him and handing them back to me. "You learn all the styles and then pick the best one for the particular situation. In this case, you get them absorbed in the drama and they want to read on to find out what happened."

"And they might see some ads along the way," said Mr. T as he walked away under a puff of pipe smoke.

I started to say something, then Britt said, "How did she even get all that? I went to Mackinaw City. She didn't even go..."

"I worked the phones, jerk," she said. I think Laura was finally tired of his acting superior to her.

There was really no doubt about it. Her story was interesting. She did get lots of facts, talking to witnesses as well as officials. Britt talked to one person.

I put my feet up on the desk. "Well," I said slowly, "I don't like the use of the word 'perversely.' I don't think you can describe a bear's actions as being perverse. Perverse is a human trait."

They were both looking at me. "But we'll run Laura's version. I think she's right."

Laura smiled and winked at me and sashayed back to her desk.

"Britt has learned something," I said under my breath.

"Arrrgh," he said, tearing at his hair. "I'm going for coffee."

~~~

The next crisis was a crime at the Grand Hotel. A hotel maid was grabbed and dragged into a room and assaulted by a guest.

Britt wrote it up as a police brief and handed it to me. "Done. Unless you
~~~

want me to get the size and brand of her under garments.”

“No, this will do,” I said.

But when Mr. T saw it typeset and on the page, he called me over. “I know your mother left you in charge young man, but you may not have learned yet that crime does not happen at the Grand Hotel.”

“That's what they told me about all of Mackinac Island,” I said. “And so far I've been beaten up, came near death under deliberately spooked carriage horses, and was chased down British Landing Road by a man calling me 'dead meat.' A doctor is in the hospital fighting for his life...”

“But none of that happened at the Grand,” he said, narrowing his lips.

“No, but this maid was attacked there.”

“No, she wasn't,” he said, pulling the item off the page so swiftly its wax offered no resistance.

“No one was.”

I looked at him.

“Because if anyone is ever attacked at the Grand Hotel,” he said, waving his finger at me with the offending paragraph stuck to its tip, “the Grand Hotel will not advertise in this newspaper! Your grandfather knew that and toed the line. The Grand's advertising supports this operation. Without it…”

“Don't you think it's about time we stopped being afraid of the Grand Hotel and tell the truth? Everybody will know the story anyway. How will our readers respect us if we ignore it?”

He took the item off his finger and put it on the light table. He pointed down at it. “Do what you want,” he said. “You are your mother's son.” And walked off.   I put the paragraph back in its place on the page.

 I signaled Uncle Brian and we walked home. I went up to my room to pet cats. You know, a purring cat on your lap can be very relaxing. I never needed that before.

Then I looked out the back window and saw Aunt Yoshiko hanging up laundry. Why did I think Uncle Brian had come alone? I opened the window. She looked up at me. “*Konnichiwa*,” she said, giving me a thumbs up. What was that on her nose? She was wearing a clothespin. Ah, yes, that phobia she has about horse poop smell. Anyway, her smile was comforting. But it meant Jeffrey and Alyce were probably in the annex. That was all I needed!

Then somehow I kind of got a warm feeling thinking how they all dropped everything in their lives to come up here and be with me. Families could sometimes be all right.

<center>~~~</center>

A couple days later, Fletch came in. I wasn't going anywhere unless Uncle Brian came with me, so I mostly stayed home and at the newspaper office, so Fletch had to visit me.

"I asked Carlee to come," he said, "but she took Snoopy to some equestrian contest in Petoskey."

"She and that horse..." I said.

The paper came out. It was Tuesday. Wednesdays we had a tendency to relax. In reality, we didn't have time to waste on Wednesdays. It was an illusion. If we didn't dive right in on the next week's paper soon as the previous one was off the press, we'd run out of time. Nevertheless, muscles tend to relax with that first proof in hand. I asked Uncle Brian if he would take me to the Beaumont exhibit at the fort on Wednesday. He said, "Why not?"

Fort Mackinac was practically just next door and I'd never seen the Beaumont stuff, or knew it existed. Only when we met outside the cottage it was Uncle Brian with Alyce, and Jeffrey. I didn't think I'd invited them, but I just maintained my silence. We walked over from Marblecliff in just a few minutes.

I eyed the tea room. "Hey, can we get some ice cream?" I asked.

"Yeah, yeah," seconded the evil duo. I wished I had some Reptile Ripple.

"We just had breakfast. Later." Uncle Brian said. "Follow me."

We did and he got us attached to a tour that just started. The young guide, who introduced himself as Kenneth Potter, got our attention right quick.

"Imagine," he said, sweeping his arm indicating the town below, "fur sellers carrying bundles, New England buyers, store clerks on errands, wives carrying laundry, and the usual number of soldiers are milling around. The grounds are virtually packed with people. Then, at the fur trading post, pop!"

He said "pop" so loud we all jumped. He intended that. "The unmistakable but unexpected sound of a shot-gun blast."

Potter looked at his audience and grabbed his stomach.

"Alexis St. Martin's hands go to his belly. He can feel his own warm blood seep through between his fingers...." Potter peeked under his hands as if he expected real blood to be there. He continued:

"He peeks underneath his hands at a fist-size hole...and falls! He's been hit from less than three feet away by a load of buckshot."

Potter paused.

252

"He's French, from Quebec... 'Docteur!' his friends call. 'Avet!'

That means hurry.

"And here's where fate stepped in. The 'Army surgeon' in charge at the fort is William Beaumont, a 37-year-old New Yorker with more farming expertise than medical training. He's had one year of medical apprenticeship in the Army, courtesy of the War of 1812."

"It's June, 1822. 1822!" Potter continues. "Do you imagine there's an ambulance or an emergency room waiting? A wound like that would be fatal and Beaumont knows it. Still, he's obligated to try."

Alyce then pinched me on the butt.

"Stop it," I said and shoved her.

"Hey!" she said. Uncle Brian put his finger over his lips. "He started it," she whispered. I focused on Potter:

"The wound is so large he can see the lower edge of a lung, burnt and sticking out. St. Martin's last meal is oozing out of his stomach."

I think Potter was trying to gross us out so I remained expressionless.

"Okay, so Beaumont thinks it's all futile, but cleans the wound. He cuts off a bit of one St. Martin's ribs with his penknife to allow him to push the lung back inside. Then he applies a poultice."

"What's that?" I ask.

"Poultice: It's something they put on a wound," Potter says, "to cover it up."

One for my word collection.

He continues: "Then they wait. Everyone's expecting him to die. And after 24 hours it looks bad, indeed. St. Martin has pneumonia and a fever from the trauma.

"Beaumont, a product of the medical knowledge of the time, bleeds him with leeches, which we know did more harm than good, and administers some kind of medicine he thought would be cathartic."

I was going to ask what 'cathartic' meant, but I figured I'd gone past my excusable interruptions limit. Uncle Brian could read me, though. "Cleansing," he whispered.

"But it goes in his mouth and spills out the hole in his stomach," Potter says.

"Of course, feeding him has the same result, so Beaumont administers food through anal injections –

"OH GROSS!" Alyce blurted. There was a wave of similar remarks and groan sounds from the group.

" – for two weeks," Potter continued. "Until the wound is healed enough for the hole to be stopped up with bandaging. Then the man can eat."

He paused for effect. "Six months later St. Martin is still alive!"

"But the wound – well, it's healed, but there's a gastric fistula," Potter says. This time I didn't have to ask. "That just means his stomach remains open," he explained.

"St. Martin has to block the opening to keep his food in, but Beaumont starts thinking: 'What an opportunity!' That is his leap of genius. He can look in and study the workings of the stomach. People must have known by 1822 that the stomach does SOMETHING... something to the food. But what? Beaumont seizes the opportunity and makes history."

"And that medical history," says Uncle Brian, "impacts the entire world."

"Yes!" Potter says, pointing at him. You can just tell he loves telling this story.

"So what does Beaumont actually do?" I ask. "And how big is the opening?"

"It was described as the size of a shilling. That's a little smaller than a quarter," Potter says.

He continues: "First, he spoons in food, then siphons it out later and looks at what has happened to the food. He attaches meat to a string, dangles it through the hole and pulls it out for observation."

"And St. Martin just lets him do this?" I ask.

"Apparently. Maybe there was payment involved. Because Army Surgeon General Joseph Lovell encouraged Beaumont to continue and he did so right here on Mackinac Island through 1823 and 1824."

"And what does he actually discover?" I ask.

"Gastric juices my boy! The effect of gastric juices! That a major part of digestion takes place in the stomach.

"And the experimentation didn't stop here. Beaumont moved on to other postings in New York, Wisconsin and Washington D.C., and St. Martin traveled with him."

"That guy must have been a glutton for punishment," said a parent, shifting a toddler from one hip to the other.

"Well, I don't know if he was a glutton for punishment or what he was,"

Potter said. "But thank goodness he was whatever it was. Beaumont's work on digestion was credited on both sides of the Atlantic and was the definitive word on digestion for ages. You see, many doctors at the time thought digestion was purely a mechanical process, a grinding in the stomach perhaps. Some doctors, of course, thought there was chemistry involved, but Beaumont settled the question showing the solvent properties of gastric juice.

"He detailed it all in his book, *Experiments and Observations on the Gastric Juice and the Physiology of Digestion*, including the surmise that gastric juice was largely hydrochloric acid. Beaumont became a celebrity. Hospitals were named after him –we have one in Detroit."

I made a mental note. If I ever saw old Mongabay again I'd tell him he was right on this one. Something did happen right here on Mackinac Island.

"The interesting thing is," Potter continued, "Beaumont was not one of the elite doctors from rich families. Yet he became the father of American physiology."

"Once again proving," put in Uncle Brian, "The wisdom of meritocracy over aristocracy."

"Yes... yes," Potter agreed.

"What about St. Martin?" I asked.

"Well, he was a Voyageur," he said, emphasizing the French pronunciation. "Army officers, even those of humble beginning like Beaumont, tended to look down on the Voyageurs as worthless vagabonds. Consequently, Beaumont didn't treat St. Martin all that well. He virtually ignored his physical and emotional well being despite experiments that would often leave the man faint, nauseous, constipated, or with headaches.

"Their relationship, however it was maintained, was maintained until 1834. Twelve years. Beaumont, of course, continued to make a living off his stomach studies. He died in 1853 after hitting his head on an icy step on a visit to a patient. St. Martin outlived him by 27 years! He died in 1880, age 86."

Death by slipping on ice? I thought fondly of my thick sheepskin hat.

"Well, okay then," Uncle Brian said after Potter was clearly finished. "Who wants to go get that ice cream?"

It was a surprise how quickly we turned from green to gluttonous and dug in to big sundaes, but it was Britt who surprised us next.

31 – THE STAKEOUT

AFTER THAT TRIP TO the fort, I didn't go anywhere but to the *Herald* office and home. Highlight of my evenings seemed to be watching Cronkite and Canveral, and Jules, a.k.a. Sevaried, jump at fireflies in the grass. I don't think they ever caught one.

Britt got out of "the attic" of Northern Michigan on occasional weekends to visit his parents downstate and on those weekends we didn't expect him to be right on time Monday morning. In fact, his being missing was not unusual.

One Sunday there was a backup of traffic waiting to cross the Mackinac Bridge. Weekenders needing to get home. Only they were doing roadbed repairs and only one lane was open for a short stretch. At that point, cars going south had to take turns with cars coming north.

"There was a massive backup on the bridge," I announced rather loudly as I walked in Monday.

"No, there wasn't," said Mr. T, looking over his glasses at me.

"Oh, sure," I said, "Grand Hotel?"

"No," he said. "The Tourist Bureau wouldn't like it."

~~~

Mom's absence was entering its third week, Jasper Tarpoff still missing. Britt walked briskly into the newsroom and slapped himself in the face.

"What's the matter Brr-ritt," Uncle Brian said, "you discover you've been a bad boy?"

"No," he said. "I just have to slap the stupid mindless stare off before it freezes in place."
~~~

"What?" I asked.

"I've been to college," he said.

"That must have been a novel experience for you," I said.

"I had to fit in....look like I'd been had by the body snatchers ...to listen in on Tarpoff's class."

"But he's gone, in hiding somewhere. The police still want him for the Mongabay/Fychenko beating."

"Yeah, but somebody's teaching his class and that somebody acts like more than a friend of ol' Raccoon face."

"Who is he?"

"She."

"How do you know this?"

"I went to his class."

"You mean you surreptitiously infiltrated a college classroom?"

"Syrup nothin', kid. I snuck in."

"Means the same thing."

"Yeah, but this is community journalism. We write on the Third Grade level. No one uses words like 'surreptitiously.'"

"Most people can't," I said haughtily.

"That's the point. We write so people can read us. Third Grade level."

"Obviously, since that's the last grade you apparently attended. I can't imagine how you managed to be in a college class."

"Boys! You're getting loud," Mr. Trivelpiece said. "What is this all about?"

Uncle Brian pulled up a chair. Britt strutted around his desk, put a book and a notebook down and sat. Staring at us, he turned his right wrist and bent his knuckles towards himself. He then huffed on his fingernails and wiped them on the front of his button-down shirt. He looked up as if amazed. He put his wrists on the desk and raised his palms, gesturing with finger wiggles.

"It was like when Horst Buchholz snuck into Calvera's camp in *The Magnificent Seven...*" He grinned at himself, then paused for effect. "He's got a yacht parked down there."

He gestured toward the lake shore with a backward thrust of his thumb.

We all gaped. "What?" I asked.

"Yeah. His substitute/friend Miss Godliness of 1967 was saying how she might just 'borrow' it and enter it in the Port Huron to Mackinac yacht race."

"First she has to get to Port Huron," I said.

"Yeah, well, whaddya wanna bet Tarpoff is going to be aboard and make his exit off the island – whoosh – gone."

I stroked my chin. Mr. T cocked his head. Uncle Brian sat up straight.

"And she didn't see you, this substitute teacher? Someone new in the class?" I asked.

"Big class. Philosophy of Religion. Sat in the back... and she doesn't know everyone yet. Get this, the yacht is called *The Apostle.*"

"If you're right," Mr. T said, "she'd have to leave for Port Huron in a few days if she's going for the race. If it's just a ruse to spirit Tarpoff away it's smart, less attention leaving among other yachties. But don't you think the state police will check all boats leaving Mackinac?"

"Why? They couldn't find Mickey in Disneyland," Uncle Brian said. "What's one wanted man when you have an unsolved aggravated assault, possibly a murder?"

"Are they aware that yacht is his?" I asked.

"I don't think so," Britt said, "but let's find out." He picked up the phone and dialed. "Yes, could I speak to Chief Holden please?"

<div align="center">~~~</div>

In a few days, we got word to Mom and Freya. Freya called – apparently her *Free Press* status got some jailhouse phoning privileges – suggesting some forensic accounting. And Mackinac College was the likely place to start. Freya said "follow the money" was great advice in investigative reporting and in this case, we had a whole lot of money – the $500,000 bribe – and we didn't know where it came from.

"Freya, Mom said the phones..." I started to say.

"Yeah," I know, "they might be tapped. That's okay, kid, I'm not telling them anything they don't already know. First, you ask for an institution's Schedule of Accounts," she said. "That tells you all the ways they keep track of money. Then you hire an accountant who knows what he's looking for."

The *Free Press* was happy to pay for that. Mackinac College was a private school, so they would be allowed to keep their finances private, except that they accepted financial aid from the state of Michigan. "That threw their ledgers open," Freya said.

In the end their legal affairs account gave them away. Way too much money was spent there for it not to be suspicious. The attorney general

258

subpoenaed the school's chief attorney. Turned out to be one John Assilli, the troll in the bribery confab.

Chief Holden brought his picture to the newsroom. I recognized him immediately. He was the bearded guy with the big nose. "He was in the room! He was in on the bribe!" I blurted.

"First kill all the lawyers," Mr. T said.

"What?" I asked.

"The business manager is quoting Shakespeare," Uncle Brian said.

~~~

We met several times with Larry – Chief Holden. They were now looking for Tarpoff and Assilli. The *Free Press* hadn't written a story on the Assilli connection yet.

Freya called and said the paper's lawyers were reviewing it.

We all thought it was a case of lawyers protecting another lawyer. But then they got the go ahead.

A lot was riding on my witnessing, Freya said. But Karl Lovekey, her city editor, said they could go ahead with the story. "He said it's okay," she said, "even if it turns out to be wrong, as long as we're 'absent malice.'"

Oh yeah, that *Times v. Sullivan* ruling. We could make a mistake as long as we didn't do it deliberately because we hate the guys. I was pretty much hatin' them, but what do I know?

Well, I'm the only one who saw how they looked. The bearded guy told that cop to chase me. Then Tarpoff chased me himself on a horse. Heck, I could hate him just on his looks, but I wasn't going to say so. And, I thought, when could we talk about the young man in the room? The one who liked to borrow troopers' uniforms?

Nothing was happening to get Freya and Mom out of jail, but we had a plan we hoped would catch Tarpoff.

~~~

We put the telescope tube across Snoopy's saddle and tied it around with sleeping bags cushioning each side. Fletch and I steadied each end while Carlee led the horse by its reins. Slowly we walked the horse from Marblecliff to the Grand. We were careful. Dropping the tube would ruin the optics. I had the stand sticking out of a rucksack on my back. The eyepieces were carefully wrapped in dishcloths and put inside, too. Carlee started in on that tune again – Do do do doot doot do, do do do doot doot do.....

"What is that song?" Fletch asked.

"Yeah, what is that tune you're always humming?" I asked.

"Oh that," she said. "It's the theme from *Maverick*."

"Does it have any words?

"Sure, don't you remember?"

We didn't, but then it seemed familiar. So before long the three of us were singing along:

> *Who was the tall dark stranger there*
> *Maverick is the name.*
> *Ridin' the trail to who knows where,*
> *Luck is his companion*
> *Gamblin' is his game...*

As soon as we did that a few times, she taught us the rest of it and we sang it over and over.

After a while Uncle Brian, who was shadowing us, said "sing something else..." We did a little "I wannna hold your ha -a- a- a- nd..." and he said "Go back to *Maverick.*"

So we started over on that. It got us to the Grand much faster. I now know what Mrs. Kwashneetski said about singing is right. Puts joy in your heart and lessens your cares.

Uncle Brian said we looked like the Canterbury pilgrims as we ascended Cadotte Avenue and turned at the Grand entrance. We saw Tenacity standing at his post at the central staircase – his red jacket, white gloves. He nodded for someone else to take over for him and he helped us carry the tube to the elevator and up to the fourth floor. We still had to carry it up the stairs to the cupola.

We set it up right away.

Others arrived with their sleeping bags or blankets. Alyce and Jeffrey with Aunt Yoshiko wearing a swimmer's nose clip; Naomi, Bobby, Britt and Laura, Megan, Vince, and Mr. T.

After dinner, Mrs. Kwashneetski climbed the stairs, pulling herself up by the handrail. Miss Suzy came and Mrs. Nelsen with her daughter, Michele. Eighteen of us. We thought that was all, then MontesQ's reader, Molly, rolled out of the elevator in her wheelchair. Fletch and I gladly carried her, in her chair, up the final steps to the cupola.

Chief Holden stopped in. "Okay," he said. "I shouldn't be letting you do this, but we don't have the manpower. You just spot 'im and then call me on this." He hooked up a phone from a line Tenacity ran through the ceiling of the the fourth floor. "I got the warrant for his arrest right here." He tapped his breast pocket. "You call. I don't want any confrontations. Promise me."

Everyone was quiet. Aunt Yoshiko leaned forward.

"Chief-*san*, what is con-flon-tation?" she asked in a voice altered by her pinched nose.

"It means you don't go out and try to nab him yourself. It's too dangerous. We don't know what he's capable of."

~~~

Sleeping bags and blankets filled the round room. We didn't know how long this siege was going to go on.   We had a card table in the middle for eating pizza and any snacks Tenacity could send up from dining room leftovers once in a while, and for setting up board games. Surprisingly, Alyce took charge of scheduling. She grabbed a reporter's notebook from me and a pencil.

"Okay," she said, putting the pencil through the top of her teased up hair, "if we have 19 people and work two-hour shifts, with four people needed per shift, everyone gets a couple shifts a day...."

Naomi was put in charge of alarm clocks and making sure people were ready for their shifts. Fletch took the first watch, I the second, Carlee the third. Then it was Jeffrey's turn, then Uncle Brian's. The rest of us were reclining on our sleeping bags and rolled up blankets. Aunt Yoshiko unpacked her hamper filled with foil-wrapped pork and shrimp tempura. We told her there was no horse poop smell inside the Grand Hotel and she removed the nose clip.

We dug into the food, then heard from the doorway:

"Can I have a shift?"

We all turned to see MontesQ. He had one hand across his stomach and another gripping the wall, hair coils still untamed, but he, who hadn't stepped outside his room in years, had apparently walked down the hall and up the cupola steps all by himself.

Alyce just took it in stride and nodded and recomputed the shift times and handed him a slip of paper with his shift on it. He nodded and turned back.

We resumed eating.

"Who is that guy?" Alyce asked.

"Now we're 20," I said.
~~~

~~~

On the third day of the stakeout, Fletch took the first watch after dinnertime – pizza this time – and the people who were "on deck" were awake too. Me, Uncle Brian and Carlee. Carlee was reading a book on dressage – some kind of horse riding, of course – Uncle Brian was reading *Conan the Adventurer.* (School was out for the summer.)

I sat on a stool near the window with my forearms and forehead leaning against the glass. You could see the lights on the Mackinac Bridge in the distance competing with the stars. "The Little Dipper's there," I said.

Uncle Brian put his hand on my shoulder. Fletch moved to look in the eyepiece.

"I usually see Orion first," I told Uncle Brian. "Mom, she always sees Cassiopeia first. 'Cause it's my initial, she says. Why did I see the Little Dipper..."

"Maybe because it leads you to the North Star," he said. "The fixed star. The only fixed star in the sky. And moms are our fixed stars. You miss your mom."

"Of course I miss her," I said. "Why'd she have to go get herself arrested anyway?"

"What would you have her do?" Uncle Brian asked. "She's protecting her source. And, in ordinary times that would be enough. She thinks that journalism keeps us free, that it's necessary to have a "watchdog" sniffing out corruption and injustice in government and that's the press. You know, she's always quoting Thomas Jefferson. His preference, he said, if he had to choose between government without newspapers or newspapers without government, was to choose newspapers. Well, your mom feels that way."

I sighed.

"But in THIS CASE, you're the source," he said. "And if there's one thing your mom puts above freedom of the press and the importance of the press is the importance of you. As important as journalism is, you're more important."

"Yeah?"

"By a few million parsecs at least," he said. "And that's why I'm here. 'Cause you're my nephew and that's important, too."

"Thanks, Unk," I said.

Fletch lifted his head from the telescope eyepiece. "People walking on the dock..."
~~~

Uncle Brian looked. Then I looked.

"It's him," I said. "It's Raccoon Man. I can't see his face, but I can tell."

"Call Chief Holden," Carlee said, reaching for the phone.

We paced. Then:

"He said he's on his way," she said.

~~~

Through the telescope we watched the chief arrive. For a few minutes he stood talking to Tarpoff.

"Isn't he going to arrest him?" Carlee asked.

They kept talking. Then Tarpoff pushed the chief backwards and he tripped on a docking cleat. Tarpoff then picked up something that looked like a canoe paddle and hit him with it. The chief tried to dodge a second blow. There was a scuffle. Chief Holden was knocked down a second time and wasn't getting up. No backup appeared.

"He needs help!" I said. "Call the police station."

"No one would be on duty now," Uncle Brian said, hitting his head to encourage an idea.

"They don't have that many officers, do they?" I asked.

"No!" Carlee said and bolted out the door before anyone could say anything else.

"What's she....?"

Uncle Brian dashed out and then the rest of us followed, but she was running faster. She got downstairs and down the central Grand Hotel steps and leapt onto Snoopy, who'd been tied up on the street level. She gave the rope one strong tug and it freed him.

 We watched grass divits fly in the air as she rode the horse at a gallop down to the dock. Unk and I ran down the grass until we were out of breath. He stopped and bent over with his hands on his knees. Then we heard Snoopy's hooves clomp onto the dock's slatted wooden surface.

The man we thought was Tarpoff was untying the boat. Chief Holden was on the ground. Carlee made Snoopy rear up at Tarpoff. He started backing away, but Snoopy didn't let up. We started a fast walk towards them.

Tarpoff swung a chain and it looked like he hit one of Snoopy's front legs. He kept swinging the chain and hitting the horse. We yelled at Carlee to get back, but she and Snoopy kept pressing him. Tarpoff backed away until he fell. And still he whipped that chain at the horse.
~~~

The Apostle

Finally, Snoopy put a hoof on his chest and Tarpoff knew he was defeated and that's when we all got to the dock. Chief Holden got up on his knees, groaned, but said he was okay. He shook his head, stood, and pulled out handcuffs.

"Turn around, smart guy," he said.

Jasper Tarpoff was jailed and multiple charges brought against him. They included several assaults and attempted murder, as well as the attempted bribery. John Assilli was found hiding on the boat and similarly charged.

Their associates were not found. However, they got a message to Chief Holden warning that I would never testify against any of them. Even though I was still unidentified publicly as the source for the bribery story, the bad guys knew. And I was also the primary witness to the beating of Dr. Mongabay and Dr. Fychenko.

The good news was that Dr. Fychenko was now expected to make a full recovery. The bad: The state police wanted to put me in custody as a material witness.

32 – RESCUE

CHIEF HOLDEN TRIED TO argue for local custody. State police were insisting on taking me to Lansing to answer questions. One trooper in particular was insisting on it. The chief, suspicious, showed me the trooper's picture. Sure enough, he was one of those state cops in the room when I recorded the bribery conversation. Uncle Brian thought he might be a threat to me.

Friday morning Chief Holden called the newspaper office and said there were several state troopers coming to take me into custody.   But he had a call from someone else who said he was a friend of mine and I should meet him "at the Maiden of Norway" right now. Holden said he didn't know what that meant.

But I did. Fletch must have sent that message. It could only refer to the clue, "Marry the Maiden" from the *Finny Foot Affair,* the U.N.C.L.E. episode we acted out. We had used Anne's Tablet as a stand-in for the Maiden of Norway statue. Sure, that must be it. I needed to go there. He knew if anybody heard, or the phones were tapped, he couldn't say Anne's Tablet. They would know what that meant. Time was short if the state police were on their way. I didn't have time to explain all this all to Uncle Brian. And if he didn't know where I went he wouldn't have to lie to the police.

I ducked out when he wasn't looking. I went behind the buildings on the opposite side of Market Street to get to Fort Street, crossed it and entered the bushes. I knew the route. I ran it when Jeffrey and Alyce tormented me and when Raccoon Man's goons were after me the morning of the Bridge Walk. Yeah, it was still full of horse poop like that I used so effectively on the second occasion. It wouldn't do me any good now. I didn't know if I was going to be followed or what was waiting for me at Anne's Tablet – if anything. But I trusted Fletch would try something.

I got there and crouched down behind it. I kept my head down. I waited about half an hour. Then I heard an approaching motor and it got real loud real fast. A helicopter was overhead. It dropped low, facing me head on. At first I thought it was state police after me, then I recognized Mrs. Hart in the cockpit. She threaded that chopper perfectly between two clusters of oak and pine trees. One moment I thought the rotor blades were going to hit tree limbs, but she landed it precisely. She leaned out and hollered "Walter!" and motioned for me to come with repeated inward gestures of her arm. "We've got to get going."

I had plenty of questions, like why was she there and all that, but I only managed to ask: "Is this thing safe?"

Mounted troopers came up the road and saw me. What should I do? I had a split second to decide. She really wanted me to get in. She kept waving and the state police were watching, kinda open-mouthed, but still... I couldn't delay until they thought of something. I blew out my cheeks and ran, hoping I'd be faster than state police on horseback.

I didn't have time to let fear stop me. I got to the chopper first because troopers' horses were balking and rearing up at the sound of the chopper motor. I climbed in.

"'Coupla guys who don't know how to handle their horses," Mrs. Hart said, chuckling. She lifted off. If I got killed I hoped my mom would forgive me.

"Strap in," she said as she pulled the lever that elevated us. I watched wide-eyed for a few seconds and then I closed my eyes. She hovered and reached over and made the belt click for me.

I tightened my lids. "I am not in a helicopter," I said. "I am not in a helicopter... I am not in a helicopter..."

I said it about a dozen times. Then Mrs. Hart said: "You are in a helicopter, Walter, but everything is just fine. You're perfectly safe."

At that I opened my eyes to peek. I saw Arch Rock to the left and then the Mackinac Bridge underneath me. I closed my eyes.

"We're past the bridge," Mrs. Hart said in a few seconds. I peeked. Sure enough, Fort Michilimackinac was underneath us. "You'll be FINE," she repeated. "President Kennedy trusted me to pilot his mother from Mackinac to Battle Creek during his campaign in 1960. She survived... Whoops... little air

pocket there.”

My stomach was back on the elevator.

“...And,” she laughed, “I've six more years experience since then.”

I didn't see the humor.

“Think about giving that testimony in Lansing and how proud your mom will be that we nailed the bad guys,” she said. “Your mom's a pretty good organizer you know. She called Fletch and called me. She orchestrated this whole thing. We could use her on the NOW board.”

“The key was in making it a federal case,” she added.

I kept my eyes closed. Then there was only the loud sound of the rotor blades. Then she said:

“Uh oh...”

“What! Are we going down?” Panicked, I grabbed the seat.

“No, relax on that score, will you,” she said. “It's just that...”

“I opened my eyes. There was a blue state police helicopter on the right.

“I think that guy wants to stop us,” I said.

“Guys,” she said, nodding to the left. There were police choppers on both sides. I saw the pilot of one of them gesture to Mrs. Hart, pointing down.

She shrugged like she didn't understand.

He pointed to his headphones. She put hers on.

I don't know what the police pilot said, but I heard her reply:

“Do you want to explain to the newspapers why you forced down the wife of a United States Senator? How about we call the *Free Press* right now?”

There was a pause as she listened. Then she said:

“I intend to get my federal witness to Lansing. And this is a federal case now, sir. A matter under the Civil Rights Act of 1964. So if you can stand the publicity of being on the wrong side...”

There was another pause. We rode three abreast for several long minutes. The pilot on my right was clearly talking to somebody. Then the state police choppers veered off.

~~~

Later we radioed Chief Holden to relay a message to Uncle Brian that I was okay. In Lansing, we landed on the State Capitol grounds. I saw Mom before we actually touched down. When we landed, Mrs. Hart tipped her head indicating I could get out. I unbuckled. I stepped down and looked back at her.

“Mrs. Hart,” I said. “I really hope you get to be an astronaut.”
~~~

33 – RETURN TO THE ISLAND

July 18, 1967

I RAN TO MOM. I could see a crowd of other people in front of the Capitol building steps, but Mom was in a smaller group closer to the chopper. She had her arms open and I ran right into them. No Grinching!

"How did you get out?" I asked.

"Bail. They finally set it," she said. "The *Free Press* hired the lawyers."

I hugged her again.

~~~

There were a couple days worth of legal depositions before we could drive back up north. We stayed at Uncle Brian's house while he and his family stayed at Marblecliff. Soon we found out several state troopers were going to be indicted in both the bribery and beatings cases. They would stand trial for those state crimes and federal civil rights violations, as would Tarpoff and his cohorts. Mr. Huggins' picture of a state trooper cutting open the belly of Naomi's big panda not only made a great front page picture in the *Free Press,* but was picked up by the Associated Press and ran in papers around the world.

By the time we started up the bridge ramp we sang "I AM NOT ON A BRIDGE" louder than ever. The sunset was beautiful when our ferry docked in view of Marquette Park. When I stepped off the ramp I looked up and said:

"I AM NOT ON AN ISLAND."

Mom shook her head in that exasperated way mothers have perfected for
~~~

centuries. We both laughed though. Once home, we all had a fancy dinner out and then hired a carriage with a fringed top to take Uncle Brian, Aunt Yoshiko, and the kids down to the ferry dock.

"Thanks, Unk," I said. He patted me on the back.

Aunt Yoshiko bowed and called me Walter-*san*.

Jeffrey offered his hand.

"Stellar job, Cuz," he said.

As they all they walked up a ferry gangplank, Alyce looked back.

"You're okay, kid," she said.

They all went inside the boat, but in a few seconds Jeffrey appeared on the top deck. I saw him rummage in his knapsack. As the ferry pulled away from the dock, after it cleared about three feet, he pulled something out and then raised it above his head like he just won an Oscar. It was my skateboard!

I started to think of Reptile Fudge again, but quickly forgot the matter. I would get that skateboard back next summer.

We planned to hurry and sew up casualties and reopen the Teddy Bear Clinic. Naomi's panda showed a scar because the nap of its fur was worn low, but she considered it his badge of honor in the fight for freedom of the press.

A number of kids I knew from school came by and seemed like they wanted to spend time with me even if I didn't ride horses. Except Carlee. Fletch said she had to give up riding her beloved Snoopy. One of his shin bones had been splintered in the fight on the dock and she was spending most of her time nursing him.

Things were the same at home, but the future may be different. Mom and I had talked in the car for 100 miles or so as we approached the Mackinac Bridge. This much was settled: next winter we'd live on the mainland in St. Ignace and she'd go to the island only when weather permitted. We'd spend Christmas with Frank and his parents in New York. And when I got to Eighth Grade, depending on my grades, we'd talk about my testing for a good college prep school.

"Like Cranbrook," she said facetiously. "Mitt Romney went there."

I snarled. "Like Brooklyn Tech?" I said.

She didn't know how she'd manage without me, she said, but she'd think about it. I knew I had to find Parker Ripley and find out what he knew about my dad, but I was keeping that mission to myself until next year.

HURON

Later, when she went into her library, she saw Little Lost Fauntleroy propped up on the rolling ladder.

"You found me out, 'eh?" she said.

"Your dad did turn the car around and rescue the bear," I said.

"Of course," she said, "parents always do."

The day after my aunt and uncle and cousins left, Fletch came over and we watched news on TV about rioting in Detroit. It was getting bad. We were all wondering why Governor Romney hadn't yet called in the National Guard. I was glad the burning and looting was far away from our peaceful island. Yeah, I said "peaceful" gratefully. We decided to play chess.

Fletch and I both felt we'd better learn and understand it before it became multi-level, like on *Star Trek*.

"Ice cream?" Mom asked.

"Thanks, Mom," I said. "Can we take it upstairs? I have a few things to do in my room."

Fletch and I filled big bowls with fudge ripple and went upstairs. We started opening boxes, hanging clothes, and putting things in drawers and books on shelves.

"Carlee's grandfather bought her a new horse," Fletch said, offhandedly, shelving the *Tom Swifts*. I shrugged and didn't reply.

"It's a white stallion," he said.

"Yeah, so what?" I said.

He shelved a few more books, then said:

"She named it Pegasus."

– 30 –

By the year 2000, we will undoubtedly have a sizable operation on the moon, we will have achieved a manned Mars landing and it's entirely possible we will have flown men to the outer planets.

--Wernher von Braun

*"How many times have we heard the mantra:
Why are we spending billions of dollars up
there in space when we have pressing problems
down here on Earth? Let's re-ask the
question in an illuminating way: What is the
total cost in taxes of all space borne telescopes,
planetary probes, the rovers on Mars, the
space station and shuttle, telescopes yet
to orbit and missions yet to fly? Answer: less
than 1% on the tax dollar—7/10ths of a penny,
to be exact. I'd prefer that it were more, perhaps
2 cents on the dollar. Even during the storied
Apollo era, peak NASA spending amounted to
no more than 4 cents on the tax dollar. At that
level, NASA's current space-exploration
program would reclaim our preeminence
in a field we pioneered... With 99 of 100 cents
going to fund the rest of our nation's priorities,
the space program is not now (nor has it ever
really been) in anybody's way. ...We are
a sufficiently wealthy nation to embrace this
investment for tomorrow—to drive our
economy, our ambitions, and, above all,
our dreams.*

--Neil deGrasse Tyson

Historical Notes

After the January 1967 fire that claimed the lives of three astronauts, the Apollo program grounded itself to investigate and fix problems. It lost twenty months, but the successful October 11, 1968 launch kept alive the the goal of landing on the moon before the end of the decade.

Thousands of Americans and visitors from other countries lined the streets of Cape Canaveral for each successive launch. Their cars and campers brought traffic jams and parking woes and awe in the eyes of parents, children, and grandparents.

Wally Schirra flew the first Command Service Module. The moon was still in our sights and the end-of-decade deadline reachable.

Detroit erupted into a race riot on July 23, 1967. The result was 43 dead, 1,189 injured, over 7,200 arrests, and more than 2,000 buildings destroyed. According to surveys done by the Detroit Free Press, the main issue in the minds of Detroit's Black residents was police harassment and police brutality, which they identified in a Detroit Free Press survey as the number one problem they faced in the period leading up to the riot. The Free Press won a Pulitzer Prize for its coverage of the riot. As rocks were thrown, fire erupted, and gunfire killed rioters and firefighters and police, women reporters were told to stay in the office and work the phones. Then reporter Barbara Stanton kicked over a wastebasket and demanded an assignment covering the mayhem outside.

During the time of this story, 1966 to 1967, the US increased its troop strength in Vietnam by 100,000. In 1966, the US had 385,300 troops in Vietnam and 6,143 were killed in action By 1967, troop strength was 485,600 and 11,153 were killed in action. The final toll would be 58,220; for Michigan 2,654.

Apollo 8 astronauts would use Silly Putty to hold down their instruments. Today, however, Silly Putty will no longer copy comics out of the newspaper. Newspaper ink changed.

Unbekownst to Jane Hart and her fellow would-be astronaut, pilot Jerrie

Cobb, after they had met with President Johnson in 1962 urging the inclusion of women in the space program, the president acted to thwart them. LBJ's secretary, Liz Carpenter, had drafted a letter supporting the women, but Johnson returned the letter to Carpenter unsigned. He wrote at the bottom: "Let's put a stop to this!" It would be another 21 years before the flight of Sally Ride, America's first woman in space.

Astronaut John Glenn was also instrumental in delaying women's entry into space. He said it was not the way our society was organized.

Media bore some culpability as well. They asked mocking, frivolous questions of women aspirants, like "Who will make coffee on board?"

Mackinac College closed in 1970 after graduating just one class. Its president, S. Douglas Cornell, was a strong supporter of the space program. He graduated Magna Cum Laude from Yale in 1935 and went on to earn a Ph.D. in physics there in 1938. In 1952, after a career with the Department of Defense, Cornell became executive officer of the National Academy of Sciences and the National Research Council in Washington. Over the next 13 years, as chief of the staff of the NAS/NRC, he worked closely with numerous scientists and federal agencies on new scientific and technological developments, including early planning for the exploration of space. He is the author of The Mackinac Concept of Education, *1966, and* A World in Crisis, *1967. The college's promised "New Age in Education," however, never materialized.*

Despite his Mormon faith's tenet that Blacks were "cursed by God," Governor George Romney proved to be a stalwart supporter of housing integration. After his plans to run for President in 1968 collapsed (a failure due in part to his statement that his early support of the Vietnam war came after being "brainwashed" by U.S. military and diplomatic officials), he was appointed Secretary of Housing and Urban Development by President Nixon. During his HUD tenure he fought to withhold federal money from any state practicing discrimination in housing, but his efforts were thwarted by the Nixon Administration.

Some would call his son Mitt's defeat by a Black man in the 2012 race for the presidency of the United States "divine" retribution for Mormon racism. Mitt Romney had been an active missionary in the church for more than a decade during which the negative view of Blacks was strongly maintained.

Glossary

Abernathy, Rev. Ralph David

(1926-1990) Rev. Ralph David Abernathy Sr., civil rights leader, also led a national march against the Apollo 11 moon launch. He was Martin Luther King Jr.'s closest friend and considered King's successor after his assassination in 1968. As co-founder and later president of the Southern Christian Leadership Conference, Abernathy objected to government spending on space exploration. On the eve of the Apollo 11 launch, he arrived at Cape Canaveral with several hundred members of the Poor People's Campaign, to protest, based on his belief that "the key to the salvation and redemption of this nation lay in its moral and humane response to the needs of its most oppressed and poverty-stricken citizens."

At the Cape, Abernathy and his supporters said space flight represented an inhuman priority and funds should instead be used to feed and clothe the poor, tend the sick, and house the homeless.

NASA Administrator Thomas Paine countered: Not flying to the moon, he said, would not serve humanity and the problems Abernathy cited were much more complex than going to the moon. "If we could solve the problems of poverty by not pushing the button to launch men to the moon tomorrow," Paine said, "then we would not push that button."

Abernathy was unconvinced. On the launch day, he led his protest group to the restricted guest viewing area of the space center and chanted, "We are not astronauts, but we are people."

Agoraphobia

A psychological malady manifest in extreme or irrational fear of crowded spaces or enclosed public areas. These cause the sufferer acute anxiety sometimes leading to panic attacks, feeling of entrapment, and/or embarrassment. With agoraphobia, a person's fear is actual or anticipated and they can have a hard time feeling safe in any public place, to the extent that they can become unable to leave home. May be caused by a traumatic event.

Aldrin, Buzz

Ya gotta love him. Not only was he on the first manned mission to the moon, not only did he figure out space rendezvous and how to successfully work in space, at age 72 he slugged a guy who said the moon landing was faked. Buzz (born Edwin Eugene Aldrin, Jr., 1930) is at this writing working to promote space exploration, especially a mission to Mars.

Anne's Tablet

A bronze plaque in a secluded spot on the East Bluff of Mackinac Island, adjacent to Fort Mackinac, installed in 1916 as memorial to author Constance

Fenimore Woolson (1840-1894) by her nephew Samuel Mather. More than a yard long, the plaque leans into a mound of rocks and is accompanied by benches from which visitors may contemplate the glorious view over the Straits. The Art Nouveau relief sculpture depicts a girl in swirling dress, reaching for a branch of spruce. Engraved are poetic words from Woolson's novel *Anne*:

> *"She loved the island and the island trees; she loved*
> *the wild larches, the tall spires of the spruces bossed*
> *with lighter green, the gray pines and the rings of the*
> *juniper. Hear the rustling and the laughing of the forest*
> *and the waves of the waters on the pebbly shores."*

The first half of *Anne* is set on Mackinac Island, where Woolson, grandniece of James Fenimore Cooper, spent some summers. She spent most of her writing life in St. Augustine, Florida, and Europe. One of the interesting things about Woolson is that she was widely considered, during her lifetime, as one of the most important American fiction writers of the 19th Century and yet, today, she is hardly known. This would seem to be unfortunate, since most of our knowledge of 19th Century womanhood comes through the writings of men. Some comfort may come from the fact that her novels survive and her life and personality are memorialized by the writer Henry James, her long time friend. His novels *Beast of the Jungle* and *Wings of the Dove* are said to enshrine her memory, and Woolson, herself, felt reading *Portrait of a Lady* was like looking into a mirror.

The exact nature of her relationship with James remains a mystery, since both destroyed their numerous letters — they corresponded daily for years. James may have disappointed Woolson, since her death in a fall from a Venetian window is a suspected suicide. But one can imagine her ghost sitting on the benches at her shrine on Mackinac looking out over the harbor - realizing that she sold more books than he did.

Woolson's novels include *For the Major, Miss Grief, Castle Nowhere, Horace Chase, Jupiter Lights* and *East Angels*, usually depicting female dilemmas of the Victorian era. She was among the few females who dared to live independently at a time when that choice was typically only a male prerogative.

Armstrong, Neil

(1930-2012) First man to set foot on the moon. He was an aerospace engineer, naval aviator, test pilot, and professor. The safe landing of Apollo 11 on the moon is partially credited to Armstrong's cool nerves. He vetoed a planned landing spot, seeing it strewn with boulders, and took semi-automatic control to lead the ship to a safer spot - with companion Buzz Aldrin calling out altitude and velocity data. They made it with 25 seconds left of fuel.

He once said, "Mystery creates wonder and wonder is the basis of man's desire to understand."

Arsenal of Democracy

Before United States' entry into World War II, President Franklin Roosevelt urged Americans to become the "arsenal of democracy" by arming democratic nations against the looming totalitarian threats of Nazi Germany and Imperial Japan. According to the Detroit Historical Society, Detroit stood out in answering this call, producing 30 percent of the war material generated in the United States before the end of the war in 1945.

Art Deco

Visual arts style in décor and architecture characterized by streamlined forms and sleek surfaces — said to pay homage to the machine age with its uniform nature. The Chrysler Building in New York (built 1928-30) is considered a prime example. Art Deco was first displayed at an exhibition in Paris in 1925. It was carried around the world in the design of the ocean liner Normandie. In the 1930s, Art Deco was considered to be a sign of sophistication and wealth.

Asimov, Isaac

(1919 or 1920-1992) One of the "Big Three" science fiction writers, he also wrote non-fiction. In fact, his approximate 500 books appear in 9 of the 10 major classifications of the Dewey Decimal System (a method of library classification). He wrote The Foundation series, Galactic Empire series and the Robot series. In the latter he penned the often quoted Three Laws of Robotics:

> *A robot may not injure a human being or, through*
> *inaction, allow a human being to come to harm.*
> *A robot must obey orders given it by human beings*
> *except where such orders would conflict with the First Law.*
> *A robot must protect its own existence as long*
> *as such protection does not conflict with the First or Second Law.*

And, by the way, he coined the word robotics. Asimov said he thought *Star Trek* was a fresh and intellectually challenging science fiction show. He was afraid of flying. He lived to write. He was one of the signers of *The Humanist Manifesto*. He was an atheist. He said:

> *"It took me a long time to say it. I've been an atheist for*
> *years and years, but somehow I felt it was intellectually*
> *unrespectable to say one was an atheist, because it assumed*
> *knowledge that one didn't have. Somehow, it was better to say*
> *one was a humanist or an agnostic. I finally decided that I am a*
> *creature of emotion as well as of reason. Emotionally I am an*
> *atheist. I don't have the evidence to prove God doesn't exist, but*
> *I so strongly suspect he doesn't that I don't want to waste my time."*

Asimov died after contracting HIV infection from a blood transfusion.

Bergman, Jules

(1929-1987) Covered the space program as Science Editor for ABC News from 1961. He was the first network correspondent assigned to report on science and space. He covered all 54 manned American space flights from the first Mercury launching to the Challenger disaster in 1986. As quoted in the *New York Times*, Bergman said he wanted to give his audiences "not an ivory-tower discussion of science, but an on-the-spot report of discoveries, which are changing the lives of human beings daily."

Blacklist

Otherwise known as the Hollywood Blacklist. But actually any list of people who became untouchable simply because they brushed up against communism or communists in some way. They could also have been members of the Communist Party. But many were just intellectual explorers being punished for thinking. Americans have a Constitution that says they have the right of free speech and free association - but a lot of people forgot that while possessed by their fear of communism. The Hollywood Blacklist began about 1947 and lasted until 1960. It cost actors, writers, producers, directors, and others their jobs. Sometimes all their savings, their families, and even their lives. For more details, see the movie *Trumbo*. Read about the life of actor John Garfield.

Blue Moon

A lilting ballad to listen to while dreaming about space. Written in 1934 by Richard Rodgers and Lorenz Hart, the song was a hit twice in 1949, but became an international number one hit in 1961 with the revved up version of the doo-wop group The Marcels. Not to be confused with *The Blue Danube*, a waltz by Johann Strauss II written in 1866 and prominently used in *2001: A Space Odyssey*, the tedious Stanley Kubrick film released in 1968. In the movie, the waltz is heard as a space plane approaches and docks with a space station, and then again while another spacecraft travels from the station to the Moon.

Bosco

Chocolate syrup kids clamored for in the Sixties. First produced in 1928 in Towaco, N.J., Bosco was pushed on children's TV shows in the late Fifties and Sixties. At that time, children recognized it by its chubby glass jar. Bosco is still made; now, alas, sold in a plastic squeeze bottle.

Brian-san

Why does Yoshiko call her husband Brian-*san*? Adding *"san"* to the end of a masculine name is a sign of respect in Japanese. Not generally used with children's names.

Bribery

...*is* defined by *Black's Law Dictionary* as the offering, giving, receiving, or soliciting of any item of value to influence the actions of an official or other person in charge of a public or legal duty.

Brokaw, Tom

(1940-) Television journalist, author. Anchor of the NBC Nightly News from 1982 to 2004. He wrote *The Greatest Generation*, a history of those who fought World War II.

Brothers, Dr. Joyce

(1927-2013) American psychologist, author and writer of a popular advice column for 43 years. Dr. Brothers, who graduated from Cornell and Columbia, was at home with a baby and a husband earning $50 a month as a medical resident when she looked to TV quiz shows to supplement the family income. She noticed that *The $64,000 Question* preferred unlikely pairings of persons and topics. So she studied pugilism (a.k.a. boxing). When she won week after week, finally taking the top prize, she became part of an investigation into corruption on the show. Were contestants fed the answers? Dr. Brothers repeated her outstanding performance on the witness stand in court and emerged with no taint of scandal. She became a ubiquitous guest on talk and game shows - the "mother of mass media psychology."

Buchman, Frank Rev.

(1878-1961) Buchman got young people together at Oxford, England, to rev-up their religiosity and promote theocracy as a solution to the world's problems. He founded The Oxford Group that became known as Moral Rearmament from 1938 to 2001. In 1936, he was quoted as saying he thought Hitler was doing a good job in saving Europe from anti-religious communism. He thought every country needed a (Protestant) moral and spiritual awakening. He had lots of followers. Critics, like American theologian, ethicist, and public intellectual Reinhold Niebuhr thought the whole thing was more than a bit naïve. Niebuhr said, "In other words, a Nazi social philosophy has been a covert presumption of the whole Oxford group enterprise from the very beginning. We may be grateful to the leader for revealing so clearly what has been slightly hidden. Now we can see how unbelievably naïve this movement is in its efforts to save the world. If it would content itself with preaching repentance to drunkards and adulterers one might be willing to respect it as a religious revival method which knows how to confront the sinner with God. But when it runs to Geneva, the seat of the League of Nations, or to Prince Starhemberg or Hitler, or to any seat of power, always with the idea that it is on the verge of saving the world by bringing the people who control the world under God-control, it is difficult to restrain the contempt which one feels for this dangerous childishness."

Buchholz, Horst

(1933-2003) German actor most recognized for his role as the young follower in *The Magnificent Seven.* Buchholz played Chico, the kid who tags after the hired gunmen and whose speech to the villagers at the beginning of the movie leads Yul Brynner's character to say, "Now we are seven." During a siege of the village they are hired to protect, Chico sneaks into Calvera's camp to find out how things are going for the bandits, and to find out their plans. The film is a remake of a 1954 Japanese film, *The Seven Samurai.*

Calvera

Fictional leader of bandits in *The Magnificent Seven,* a classic film from 1960. The role was played by Eli Wallach who later said, if he had known the theme music was going to be so powerful "I would have rode my horse better."

Canaveral, Cape

A city in Brevard County, Florida, and name of a headland or a promontory of land extending into the Atlantic ocean from the central Florida coast, site of rocket launches of the National Aeronautics and Space Administration since the early 1960s. Known as Cape Kennedy from 1963 to 1973, it lies east of Merritt Island, separated from it by the Banana River. It was discovered by the Spanish explorer Ponce de Leon in 1513. Cape Canaveral, The Cape Canaveral Air Force Station, and Kennedy Space Center are all part of what has become known as the Space Coast.

Cap Com

Shorthand designation for the Capsule Communicator, the person who communicates between flight control on the ground and the astronauts.

Carson, Johnny

(1925-2005) Comedian, most popular *Tonight Show* host ever, serving in that capacity for 30 years, 1962-1992. Carson did a variety of recurring skits, including "Karnak the Magnificent" for which he wore a fanciful turban and would give "the question" when the answer was read by his sidekick on the show, Ed McMahon. The Carson show tackled controversial topics and launched many show business careers.

Cassette

Self-contained magnetic *recording* tape in a closed plastic case, 3.96 inches along the recording edge and 2.5 inches deep. The cassette was announced by Philips in 1962 and was released as the Norelco Carry-Corder 150 recorder/player in November 1964. By 1966, 250,000 cassette recorders had been sold in the United States alone. The cassette soon supplanted the 8-track tape cartridge and reel-to-reel recording in non-professional settings. Pre-recorded cassettes became a popular alternative to 12-inch Long Play (LPs) vinyl records. Cassettes could be used on both sides and the user never had to handle the tape. Once played on one side a mere flip over would have the cassette at the start position for the other side.

Cat's Cradle

String manipulation game between two players (although there is a single-player version). Players make a sequence of string configurations with the string looped around both hands. The game begins when one player, with a loop of string, makes the iconic "Cat's Cradle" configuration. You'll need to look up an illustration. Second player takes hold of each side, altering the previous figure. After each figure, the next player manipulates that figure and removes the string figure from the hands of the previous player with one of a few simple motions and tightens the loop to create another figure.

Cernan, Eugene

(1934-1917) Last man to have walked on the moon as of 2017. Asked why NASA didn't send women to the moon he replied: "None were qualified." Jane Hart and rest of the "Mercury 13" thought otherwise.

Chaffee, Roger

(1935-1967) Born in Grand Rapids, Michigan, Roger Chaffee was a Navy pilot and aeronautical engineer chosen for NASA's Astronaut Group 3. He was part of the ill-fated Apollo 1 crew that perished during a "plugs out" test when the capsule caught fire. He died with Ed White and Virgil "Gus" Grissom. Chaffee had just replaced Donn Eisele as mission pilot after Eisele dislocated his shoulder aboard the weightlessness training aircraft. Investigators of the Apollo 1 fire believe it is Chaffee's voice that declared "We've got a fire in the cockpit." For twenty-three seconds the fire was fed by pure oxygen at slightly greater than atmospheric pressure. It was Chaffee's job to maintain communication in an emergency. He stayed strapped to his seat on the right of the craft. White was in the center seat, reaching over in an attempt to open the hatch. Pressure prevented the release, until its increasing strength burst the inner cabin wall. The fire put itself out, but produced billowing smoke, which is what killed the astronauts.

Channel D

"Open Channel D" was the phrase men from U.N.C.L.E. used when they talked into their cigarette boxes (first season) or pens (thereafter because they didn't want to look like smokers) and hoped to be connected to Mr. Waverly or, at least, the girls at headquarters. What was Channel D? Probably a reserved radio frequency, but who knows? Freya Firestones's car phone was not "cellular" but a radio-based phone with dial, mounted on the dashboard. It required a big transmitter/receiver in the trunk and a battery under the hood, all interconnected by cable to the "phone" on the dash. Calls were expensive and operator assistance was required.

Checker, Chubby

(1941-) American singer-songwriter known for popularizing the dance craze known as The Twist with his 1960 hit album "Twistin' U.S.A." It marked the first time adults danced to teen music.

Civil Rights Act of 1964

Landmark legislation that outlawed discrimination based on race, color, religion, sex, or national origin. 1960s folks hated Lyndon Johnson for continuing the Vietnam War, but he wheeled and dealed for the common man in Congress. This is one of his greatest accomplishments. It was, of course, opposed by the southern states. Speaking for this "Southern Bloc," Senator Richard Russell (D-GA) said: "We will resist to the bitter end any measure or any movement which would have a tendency to bring about social equality and intermingling and amalgamation of the races in our (Southern) states." History wasn't on his side.

Clarabell

Mute clown with a horn and a seltzer bottle on the *Howdy Doody Show.* See *Howdy Doody.*

Clarke, Arthur C.

(1917-2008) A lifelong proponent of space travel, Clarke joined the British Interplanetary Society as a teenager. Considered one of the "Big Three" in science fiction, he was also an undersea explorer, television host, and futurist. In 1945 he came up with the idea of geostationary satellites for communication. In 1959 he predicted global satellite television and "personal transceivers so small and compact that every man carries one" and that "the time will come when we will be able to call a person anywhere on Earth merely by dialing a number."

He said, "Any sufficiently advanced technology is indistinguishable from magic."

British born (and knighted) he chose to live in Sri Lanka from 1956, a decision attributed to that nation's more tolerant laws regarding homosexuality.

Clarke's science fiction novels include *Childhood's End, Rendezvous with Rama, Glide Path, The Sands of Mars, A Fall of Moondust* and many others. It was one of his short stories that inspired the movie *2001: A Space Odyssey*, but don't hold that against him.

He identified himself as an atheist. He was honored as a Humanist Laureate by the International Academy of Humanism.

"One of the great tragedies of mankind is that morality has been hijacked by religion," he said. He was quoted in *Popular Science* in 2004 as saying of religion: "Most malevolent and persistent of all mind viruses. We should get rid of it as quick as we can."

Click Clack Blocks
Classic folk toy, also known as Jacob's Ladder, or tumbling blocks. Made in plastic or wood segments, the blocks are attached to each other by ribbons or strings. When grasped at one end and tilted, the blocks appear   to cascade down the strings. It's only a visual illusion, the result of one block after another flipping over. The blocks don't really change position. It was all explained in *Scientific American*, October 1889.

Communism
A form of political organization that terrified Americans in the 1950s and 1960s. After the dissolution of the Soviet Union in 1991, there are, at this writing, five remaining communist countries: China, Cuba, Laos, North Vietnam and North Korea.
Depending on what definition you read, communism is terrible, more or less.
It can be, *"A social organization based on the holding of all property in common, actual ownership being ascribed to the community as a whole or to the state,"* or, *"A system of social organization in which all economic and social activity is controlled by a totalitarian state dominated by a single and self-perpetuating political party."*
Communism derives from the intellectual writings of German philosophers Karl Marx and Friedrich Engels. Marx believed a person should contribute to the best of his ability and receive according to his needs. He predicted that growing wealth inequality will cause the working class to become aware of itself as an exploited group and overthrow capitalists and establish collective development and collective ownership of the means of production. At this point society will have achieved socialism, ruled by the working class during transition to a classless society called "the dictatorship of the proletariat." Russia and its satellite nations tried this from 1918 to 1991, when controls loosened by Mikhail Gorbachev apparently went too far and unglued the Soviet Union. Under capitalism the incentive for hard work and entrepreneurship is profit and the possibility of becoming one of those people who needs to hide money in the Cayman Islands. Incentive has always been hard to come by under communism, unless one can profit by being a member of the Communist Party and take graft under the table.

Coon
Offensive slang. Used as a term of disparagement for a Black person.

Cooper, Leroy Gordon "Gordo" Cooper, Jr.
(1927- 2004), One of the first group of astronauts, the Mercury 7, Cooper,

an Air Force Colonel, piloted the longest and final Mercury spaceflight in 1963. It was a 34-hour mission and he became the first American to sleep in space and the last to be launched solo. In 1965 he was Command Pilot of Gemini 5. Known as Gordo, Cooper was observed to be the most laid-back and relaxed of the astronauts. So relaxed, in fact, that he fell asleep waiting for his first launch. Post NASA, Cooper became an outspoken believer in UFOs and charged that the government was covering up its knowledge of extraterrestrial activity.

Counting Headlines

When type was a physical piece of metal or a photographic image, before computers could squeeze in just about anything because type sizes became infinite, headline writers had to know if the words they wanted to use would fit the space allotted by the layout editor in the size the layout editor requested. There was no automation for this. Headline writers had to count letters. But not all letters were the same size. The system devised gave a value of one to all lower case letters, except for f, j, i, l, and t, which were counted as a half, and m and w which were one and a half. Capital letters were one and half, except F,J,I,L and T were one and M and W were two.

The headline writing procedure went like this: A layout editor would decide, based on his page design and the importance of the story, what size headline was wanted, over how many columns, and how many lines.   This was expressed in three numbers. A headline order calling for 3-30-2 meant a headline over three columns in type size 30 and two lines deep. 2-60-4 would call for a headline over two columns in 60 point type, 4 lines deep. The headline writer would compose a possible headline, count it, and then look at a chart of maximum counts per column in each of the type sizes used by the newspaper to see if it would fit. Sizes usually ranged from 18 pt., very small, to 72 pt., reserved for when Martians land. Commonly used sizes were 24 pt, 30, 36, 42, 48 and 60. If it didn't fit, the headline writer would have to get creative: shorter verbs (like nix or pit, nicknames, etc.   One column-wide headlines were usually the most challenging. This is how "Ike" and "JFK" became popular. A layout editor assigning 1-48-3 might be considered a sadist.

Cronkite, Walter

(1916-2009) CBS news anchorman for 19 years between 1962 and 1981, well known for his coverage of NASA and the race to the moon. In 1969, during the Apollo 11 mission, Cronkite received the best ratings and made CBS the most-watched television network during the missions.

And few who saw it could forget the Nov. 22, 1963 news clip of Cronkite taking off his eyeglasses and announcing that "President Kennedy died at 1 p.m. Central Standard Time."

During much of his tenure as the CBS news desk, Cronkite was known as "the most trusted man in America." It is said that President Lyndon Johnson decided to resign when he "lost Cronkite."

Cronkite was well known for his end-of-newscast departing catchphrase "And that's the way it is," followed by the broadcast's date.

Cronkite was one of Edward R. Murrow's recruits. He covered the Nuremberg trials, Vietnam War, Watergate scandal, the Iran Hostage crises, Dawson's Field hijackings and the assassinations of John F. Kennedy, Martin Luther King Jr., and John Lennon.

Detroit Free Press

Still the largest newspaper in Michigan, but a smaller, leaner version. The former Knight-Ridder newspaper is now owned by the (expletive deleted) Gannett Company. In the 1960s things were a little different. *The Free Press* was a COMPETITIVE newspaper, competitive with the *Detroit News* and *Detroit Times* (which ceased publication in In 1960) and the world press.

The paper was founded in 1831 as the *Democratic Free Press and Michigan Intelligencer* by John R. Williams and his uncle, Joseph Campau, both of whom have Detroit streets named after them ("John R" and "Joseph Campau"). In 1940, the Knight Newspapers (later Knight-Ridder) purchased the *Free Press* and for the subsequent 47 years the *Free Press* was an award-winning newspaper fighting for justice, truth, the American family, and the environment in the southeastern Michigan market and statewide. *The Free Press* was delivered and sold as a morning paper while the *News* was sold and delivered as an evening newspaper.

The *Free Press* has received ten Pulitzer Prizes, two in 1968 alone. One of those went to publisher John S. Knight for excellence in editorial writing. The other went to the team that covered the Detroit Riots of 1967, "recognizing both the brilliance of its spot news staff work and its swift and accurate investigation into the underlying causes of the tragedy."

The *Free Press* motto was once expressed in its page one nameplate as "On Guard for XX Years," whatever the number might be. It is now simply: "On Guard Since 1831."

Detroit Riot

Forty three persons were killed in the civil disturbance that began in the early morning hours of July 23, 1967, when a police raid on an unlicensed after-hours bar, known as a "blind pig," met resistance. Confrontations with patrons and observers on the street exploded into one of the deadliest and most destructive riots in the history of the United States. It lasted five days, involved the Michigan Army National Guard and the U.S. 82nd and 101st Airborne Divisions. In addition to the 43 dead there were 1,189 injured, 7,200 arrests, 2,509 stores looted or burned, 388 families rendered homeless or displaced and 412 buildings burned or damaged enough to be demolished. Dollar losses from arson and looting were $40 million to $80 million, with more than 2,000 buildings destroyed. In the

U.S., the scale of the riot was surpassed only by the July 13-16, 1863 draft riots in New York City and the Los Angeles riots of 1992.

Devil's Kitchen

To imaginative minds, two Indentations in the rock wall along the southwestern shore of Mackinac Island evoke a human face with open mouth. Locals say Native Americans considered the spot inhabited by evil bad spirits, perhaps cannibals who would capture those who came too close to the spot. Blackened inside, like a well-used oven, hence the name.

Diller, Phyllis

(1917-2012) American stand-up comedian, actress known for her wild white hair, eccentric stage presence, and self-deprecating humor. Frequently appearing on the *Tonight Show* with Johnny Carson, Diller was the first solo female comedian to become a household name. She often wore wrist-length gloves, ankle boots, and held a long cigarette holder, punctuating her humor with a loud laugh. She believed making people laugh was a powerful art form. Comedian Joan Rivers said Diller spoke for all women sitting home with five children and a husband who didn't work.

Eclectic

Style (or ideas) derived from a wide and diverse range of sources. Polite way of saying mish-mash.

ERA, the Equal Rights Amendment

A proposed amendment to the United States Constitution stating that civil rights may not be denied on the basis of one's sex. It was passed by Congress in 1972, then was submitted to the state legislatures for ratification with a deadline of March 1979. The amendment received 35 of the necessary 38 state ratifications by 1977. Championed by U.S. Rep. Martha Griffiths of Michigan, the amendment was ratified by Michigan in 1972. Then there was some push back by women convinced they'd have to share bathrooms with men. Five states later rescinded their ratification before the 1979 deadline. In 1978, a joint resolution of Congress extended the ratification deadline to June 30, 1982, but no further states ratified the amendment and it died. Several organizations continue to work for the adoption of the ERA. Michigan conservative activist Phyllis Schlafly argued the amendment would cost women their privileges. (Like doing the dishes, what?)

Faith, Percy

(1908-1976) If he'd recorded only *The Theme from a Summer Place* he'd be immortal. Toronto born, Faith was an orchestrator, composer, and conductor credited with popularizing the "easy listening" format. He emphasized strings, smoothing out the brassy sound of the 40s. As a movie, 1959's *A Summer Place* is

fairly forgettable. But the theme song captivated audiences indelibly and was recorded by many, but none so perfectly as Percy Faith. Faith's orchestral arrangement was released in September 1959 - not an immediate hit, but by 1960 it was launched on its historic path to number one for nine weeks on the Billboard Hot 100 chart, a record not broken for 17 years. The melody was ubiquitous in homes and at social gatherings throughout the Sixties.

Fate, Professor

Comedic, outrageously evil fictional character played by actor Jack Lemmon in the 1966 movie *The Great Race*, also starring Tony Curtis, Natalie Wood, and Peter Falk.

Fife, Barney

Fictional character in the beloved Sixties sit-com, *The Andy Griffith Show*. As actor Don Knotts played him, Fife was a lovable, skinny misfit as a sheriff's deputy. He looked like you could knock him down with a feather. Fife was an ironic icon, in that his small stature and lack of dexterity made it unlikely he would ever nab a bad guy. *TV Guide* ranked Fife 9th in its list of the 50 greatest TV characters.

Fort Mackinac

Garrison on the East Bluff of Mackinac Island, built by the British during the American Revolution to control the strategic Straits of Mackinac. The British did not relinquish the fort until fifteen years after American independence, then they tried to take it back again in the War of 1812. They captured it by sneak attack before word of the war had reached the American soldiers on the island. British Captain Charles Roberts and about two hundred soldiers came from Fort St. Joseph in Ontario and landed on the north end of Mackinac Island, two miles from the fort, crawling up what is now British Landing Road. They trained two cannons on the fort. The Americans, under Lieutenant Porter Hanks, were taken by surprise and Hanks perceived his garrison was badly outnumbered. He had but 60 men. Fearing that the Native Americans on the British side would massacre his men and allies, Hanks accepted the British offer of surrender without a fight. (While they were getting ready to court martial him for cowardice in Detroit, a British cannonball saved them the trouble. It ripped through the room where Hanks was standing, cutting him in half and killing the officer next to him as well.)

On July 26, 1814, a squadron of five United States ships arrived off Mackinac Island, carrying a landing force of 700 soldiers under the command of Colonel George Croghan. Due to strategic disadvantages, even they failed to wrest the fort from the British. Following the Treaty of Ghent, American forces reoccupied Fort Mackinac in July 1815. The current museum at the park includes 14 historic buildings, including a depiction of Dr. William Beaumont studying the gastric juices in the stomach of Alexis St. Martin, a 19-year-old French Canadian.

Fort Michilimackinac

Not to be confused with Fort Mackinac on Mackinac Island, this fort is at the tip of the mitten of Michigan, just west of Mackinaw City. It was built as a trading post around 1715 by the French, who got along fairly well with the local Indians. When the British took it over, the Indians found it necessary to massacre everyone there.

It happened on a warm June day in 1763. The Indians were playing Baggatiway, a game similar to LaCrosse, played with a bat and ball. Ojibwa squaws were watching draped in heavy shawls and blankets. (Someone should have noticed that was inappropriate for the warm weather.) Indians kept hitting the ball into the fort. When the troops opened the gate, the squaws opened their shawls to reveal hatchets and knives underneath, which they handed over to the players who began furiously cutting down and scalping every Englishman they could find. French civilians inside were not harmed.

Alexander Henry, a fur trader who kept a diary, apparently escaped the massacre by canoeing over to Mackinac Island and hiding in what later became known as Skull Cave. He wrote:

> *On going into the cave, of which the entrance was*
> *nearly ten feet wide, I found the further end to be rounded*
> *in its shape, like that of an oven, but with a further*
> *aperture, too small, however, to be explored. After thus*
> *looking around me, I broke small branches from the*
> *trees and spread them for a bed, then wrapped myself*
> *in my blanket and slept till day-break. On awaking,*
> *I felt myself incommoded by some object upon which I lay,*
> *and, removing it, found it to be a bone. This I supposed*
> *to be that of a deer, or some other animal, and what might*
> *very naturally be looked for in the place in which I*
> *was; but when daylight visited my chamber I discovered,*
> *with some feelings of horror, that I was lying on nothing*
> *less than a heap of human bones and skulls which covered*
> *the floor!*

The Fort Michilimackinac site is now a National Historic Landmark, preserved as an open-air historical museum, with several reconstructed wooden buildings and palisade. The LaCrosse game of 1763 is re-enacted each year - but without bloodshed.

Friedan, Betty

(1921-2006) American activist and feminist, author of *The Feminine Mystique*, 1963) and first president of the National Organization of Women, strong supporter of the Equal Rights Amendment, which ultimately failed. (See *ERA.*)

Friedan's ground-breaking book showed how women were held back by a "feminine mystique," but, in reality, were as qualified as men for any type of work or career path.

Gagarin, Yuri
(1934-1968) The first human in space, Gagarin was a Russian Soviet pilot when his Vostok spacecraft completed an orbit of the Earth on April 12, 1961. It was his only flight. But he became a celebrity and a Hero of the Soviet Union. Gagarin died in 1968 when the MiG-15 training jet he was piloting crashed.

Glenn, John
(1921-2016) First American to orbit the Earth as Mercury 7 astronaut in Friendship 7 on February 20, 1962. Marine Corps aviator and engineer, U.S. Senator. Fifth person in space. But he didn't want to share, opposing women in space as antithetical to American society. (Depicted as a nauseating moralizer in the 1983 movie *The Right Stuff*). Oldest person in space, at age 77, after serving as payload specialist on shuttle Discovery STS-95 in 1998. Senator from Ohio from 1974 to 1999. Made a bid for the Democratic nomination for president in 1976, but failed to impress delegates and lost to Walter Mondale, who, ironically, a decade earlier, was seen to threaten the space program by leading a Congressional investigation into the Apollo 1 tragedy.

Grand Army Plaza
The entrance to Prospect Park in the Park Slope neighborhood of Brooklyn, New York. Its massive 80-foot high arch provides memorial to "The Grand Army of the Republic" of the Civil War era.

'Grip and Grin'
A staged photograph in which people are shaking hands (grip) and smiling (grin). Sometimes combined with another banal form: the check-passing picture. People who donate money to good causes want to have their picture in the paper for doing so, so these are very hard to avoid diplomatically. The best newspaper photographs are unstaged pictures of people doing something, faces clearly shown.

Grand Hotel
A Mackinac Island landmark since 1887. A 660-foot long front porch that became a "flirtation walk" as early as early as the 1890s. Lounge chairs and 2,500 or so potted geraniums make up the atmosphere. The Straits of Mackinac, Mackinac Bridge, and passing freighters provide the long view. Exquisite gardens are just below. The cupola in this story is now The Cupola Bar. Two Hollywood movies were filmed here: *This Time For Keeps*, a 1947 vehicle for swimmer Esther Williams, which made use of the dog bone-shaped pool, and *Somewhere in*

Time, starring Christopher Reeve and Jane Seymour, which, despite an insipid script and generally unfavorable reviews, became a cult classic with fans who meet at the hotel every October. It's just that time travel fans usually like to have a Time Machine in their time travel stories. It doesn't have to be a DeLorean.

Grissom, Virgil "Gus"

(1926-1967) Second American in space. Air Force test pilot, mechanical engineer and one of the original Mercury 7 astronauts, Grissom flew in the second one-man Mercury flight in July 1961. Then he was command pilot for Gemini 3, the first manned flight of the two-seater Geminis, on March 23, 1965, with John Young. The flight made Grissom the first American astronaut to fly into space twice. Grissom and Young orbited the Earth four times in 4 hours, 52 minutes and 31 seconds.

Grissom almost drowned on his Mercury flight. At splashdown, emergency explosive bolts unexpectedly fired and blew the hatch off, causing water to flood into the spacecraft. Grissom jumped out, but water starting filled his spacesuit and he was rescued in the nick of time. For awhile Grissom was under a cloud, suspected of having done something wrong to make the hatch blow, but NASA officials determined Grissom had not necessarily initiated the firing of the explosive hatch, even though the flooded capsule was not recovered until 1999.

Ironically, an "improved" hatch may have kept Grissom, Ed White, and Roger Chaffee locked in the Apollo 1 capsule when it caught fire during the plugs-out test on January 27, 1967. See: *Plugs-Out Test*

Gulag

The penal system of the former U.S.S.R., consisting of a network of labor camps.

GUND

Upscale soft stuffed toys manufacturer founded in 1898 in Norwalk, Connecticut. One of the oldest manufacturers of soft toys in America, one of the first to produce Teddy bears in the 1900s. Recognized for quality and innovation.

Hans Brinker

Fictional character from Mary Mapes Dodge's *Hans Brinker, or The Silver Skates*, first published in 1865. The novel takes place in the Netherlands and is a colorful fictional portrait of early 19th-century Dutch life, as well as a tale of youthful honor, altruism, and love for a parent. A great children's classic.

Hardy Boys

The Hardy "boys," Frank and Joe, are characters in many mystery books between 1927 and 1979. The first 38 books and the *Detective Handbook* were revised and dumbed down between 1959 and 1973. Get the old ones. Frank and

Joe's father is a detective and the boys get involved in his cases unrealistically, to the point of being in gun battles, but otherwise the books are good, clean fun. (Despite the Franklin W. Dixon pen name, the characters were created by Edward Stratemeyer, founder of the book-packaging firm, Stratemeyer Syndicate. *The Hardy Boys* were written by many different ghostwriters over the years.)

Harris, Sydney
(1917-1986) Columnist for the *Chicago Tribune*, later *Chicago Sun Times*, appearing in the *Detroit Free Press* ala syndication. His daily column "Strictly Personal" also appeared in about 200 other newspapers. He was "down home" but intellectual. His opinions favored women's rights and civil rights. He also wrote 11 books. Although he's been dead more than thirty years, check out these Harris quotes for timelessness:

> *"Superior people are only those who let it be*
> *discovered by others; the need to make it evident*
> *forfeits the very virtue they aspire to."*

> *and*

> *"Terrorism is what we call the violence of the*
> *weak, and we condemn it; war is what we call*
> *the violence of the strong, and we glorify it."*

When Walter's mom said he should be reading the columns of Sydney Harris and Drew Pearson, Harris was probably the better choice.

Hart, Jane "Janey" Briggs
(1921-2015) Larger-than-life Jane Hart was as depicted here, except for a few imaginary conversations extrapolated from her biography. Heiress, pilot, first female helicopter pilot in Michigan, competitive equestrian and sailor, outspoken feminist, anti-war activist and one of the Mercury 13 (women who passed the same physical and psychological tests given the Mercury 7 males) at age 40. She was the wife of Michigan Senator Philip A. Hart and gave birth to nine children. Summer resident on Mackinac Island. In the Sixties and Seventies, she flew her husband to his campaign stops. She was 93 at her death in June 2015.

Mrs. Hart was an activist and outspoken at a time when women were expected to be silent and merely decorative. A founding member of the National Organization for Women, and a Roman Catholic, she once told *The Chicago Daily News*, "The Catholic Church is racist, and its position on birth control is ridiculous." For attempting to hold an ecumenical Mass for Peace inside the Pentagon in 1969 she was arrested along with seven companions. The purpose, she said, was "to bring the idea of peace and love of God into this house of death."

Jane Cameron Briggs was born on Oct. 21, 1921, in Detroit, where her father, Walter O. Briggs, was an industrialist. She attended Catholic academies before enrolling in Manhattanville College in Westchester County, N.Y., which she left before earning a degree. She earned an anthropology degree from George Washington University in 1970 at age 49. Jane Hart was audacious in sports, from riding against top professionals in equestrian jumping competitions to sailing the Port Huron to Mackinac boat race. At 73, she crewed a sailboat crossing the Atlantic. She earned her pilot's license at 18. During World War II she joined the Red Cross Motor Corps and drove trucks from Detroit's auto plants to military bases and ports. She married Phil Hart in 1943, just before his deployment overseas with the Army's 4th Infantry Division.

Hart, Phillip

(1912-1976) Michigan Senator from 1958 to 1976, Hart became known as The Conscience of the Senate. "It's easy to vote your conscience when you wife's an heiress," he once quipped. (Jane Hart was heiress to the fortune of Walter O. Briggs, an industrialist who owned the Detroit Tigers.) In his book *Inside Congress*, author Ronald Kessler lauded Senator Hart as one of the few truly honorable men who served in the Senate. Hart was re-elected by overwhelming margins in 1964 and 1970. His opponent in 1970 was Lenore Romney, wife of George Romney and mother of Mitt.

Hart was a graduate of Georgetown University and the University of Michigan law school. He was ahead of his time in suggesting the decriminalization of marijuana and reasonable gun control laws. He was proudest of his work as floor manager of the 1965 Voting Rights Act and the 1968 Open Housing-Civil Rights Bill, his championing of the legislation to make Michigan's Sleeping Bear Dunes and Pictured Rocks national lake shores, and his sponsorship of consumer-related legislation (e.g. truth-in-packaging, truth-in-lending, and truth-in-spending).

In its eulogy, the *Washington Post* said Hart "battled for Civil Rights, a better break for the consumer, and reductions of the giant concentrations of economic power by huge corporations." We sure could use him today.

Heinlein, Robert A.

(1907-1988) Four-time Hugo Award-winning science fiction author, Heinlein was called the "dean" of science fiction writers and, with Isaac Asimov and Arthur C. Clarke, one of the "Big Three." His book titles are too numerous to mention, but his *Stranger in a Strange Land* was a notable favorite on college campuses at the time of this novel. His *Future History* series is another notable favorite, involving the long-lived Lazarus Long. One of his many books for young readers, *The Rolling Stones*, introduces flat cats, who are astoundingly similar to the Tribbles writer David Gerrold contributed to the *Star Trek* lexicon. Like his peers, Heinlein anticipated many scientific developments, including the cell phone, 30 years before Motorola. Within his fiction, Heinlein shows a true iconoclast's preferences for free love, individual liberty, and self-reliance and warns about the influence of organized religion and the tendency of authorities to repress nonconformist thought. In *The Notebooks of Lazarus Long* (1973) he tells us:

> *God is omnipotent, omniscient, and omnibenevolent -*
> *it says so right here on the label. If you have a mind*
> *capable of believing all three of these attributes*
> *simultaneously, I have a wonderful bargain for*
> *you. No checks, please. Cash and in small bills.*

and:

> *Men rarely (if ever) manage to dream up a God*
> *superior to themselves. Most Gods have the manners*
> *and morals of a spoiled child.*

Hippies

A counter-culture movement that blossomed in the mid-Sixties, lasting well into the 1970s, generally among young people from college campuses whose disdain for the Vietnam War set them against society and government. They felt alienated by middle-class materialism and repression. Hippies preferred long hair, casual dress, psychedelic colors, and chanted "make love, not war." Females wore granny dresses, men wore flares, both wore rimless glasses. Flowers were their universal sign. They tended to approve of free love and recreational drug use. They adopted *The Whole Earth Catalog* (pub. 1968) as their handbook. Some lived in co-ops and adopted vegetarianism. Hotbeds of Hippie-ism were Greenwich Village in New York City and Berkeley, California. For *The Man From U.N.C.L.E.'s* take on Hippies, see *The Pop Art Affair*, 1966. Although Hippies seemed to define Sixties' changes, some say the real thrust for change came from NASA and the astronauts who would take us to the moon. At any rate, general Hippie values, such as diversity, love outside of marriage, and draft resistance, went mainstream in time.

Hippies play no part in this book. However, since it is a book about the Sixties, it would be remiss not to mention them.

Howdy Doody

Iconic freckle-faced boy marionette with a big toothy grin, unforgettable to Fifties and Sixties kids who ran to their TVs when they heard "It's Howdy Doody Time!" Operated by Buffalo Bob Smith, the puppet was a fixture of children's television programming from 1947-54, when it was shown in black and white, and from 1955 to 1960 when it became a pioneer in early color television at NBC. As early as 1948 there was a demand for Howdy Doody dolls and related merchandise. (You didn't think show-related merchandising began with *Star Wars* did you?)

Howdy Doody emphasized circus and western pioneer themes. Buffalo Bob had a fringed leather jacket and a mute sidekick, Clarabell-the-Clown. Most kids of the era will never forget Clarabell's honking horn and squirting seltzer bottle as they were invited to participate in songs, comedy routines, and games.

The original Howdy Doody puppet resides at the Detroit Institute of Arts.

Howe, Gordie

(1928-2016) The most consummate hockey player of all time, with a career from 1946 to 1980. A Canadian, he played his first 25 seasons with the Detroit Red Wings. His nickname, "Mr. Hockey," is a registered trademark.

Hubbard, Elbert

(1856-1915) A writer best known for his philosophic, entertaining multi-volume *Little Journeys to the Homes of the Great* series and the short publication *A Message to Garcia*. Hubbard was also a publisher and founded the Roycroft artisan community in East Aurora, New York, where he was an influential exponent of the Arts and Crafts Movement.

Jiffy Pop

Self-contained pan of popcorn and oil with an aluminum foil cover that expands like a balloon, but stays attached as the corn pops. Made on the stove top, in a "jiffy," of course. Launched in 1959.

Kipling's poem

...sometimes thought of as the origin of the journalist's 5Ws and H mantra, *I Keep Six Honest Serving Men*, by Britisher Rudyard Kipling. Here's how it opens:

> "I keep six honest serving-men
> (They taught me all I knew);
> Their names are What and Why and When
> And How and Where and Who.
> I send them over land and sea,
> I send them east and west;
> But after they have worked for me,
> I give them all a rest.

The rest of the poem is some kind of slam against Queen Victoria, but we don't need to go into that here.

Knight, John S.

     (1894-1981) Fiercely independent newspaper owner and publisher whose chain in its heyday (which included the 1960s) owned the *Detroit Free Press*, *Akron Beacon Journal*, *Charlotte Observer*, *Philadelphia Inquirer* and *Miami Herald*. He became the first publisher to win three Pulitzers in one year, 1968. One was for his editorials criticizing the Vietnam War and speaking up for freedom of speech. One was for the Charlotte paper's editorial cartoons by Eugene Gray Payne. The third went to the *Free Press* for reporting the Detroit riot (See *Detroit Free Press*) Knight papers were principled, feisty, unpredictable, and compelling.

Konnichiwa

     Often used as "Hello" in Japanese. Technically "Good-afternoon."

Ku Klux Klan

     A hate group dating back to 1860s, favoring white supremacy, white nationalism, and curtailed immigration, supported by terrorism in its various incarnations. KKK members would like to "purify" American society. Right wing extremists if there ever were any.

Kuryakin, Illya

     Fictional Russian secret agent working for U.N.C.L.E. in the 1962-1964 hit TV series The Man From U.N.C.L.E. Played by British actor David McCallum. See *Solo, Napoleon* and *McCallum, David*.

Lansing Riot

     The Lansing riot of August 7, 1966 happened exactly as depicted in this narrative, except for the parts played by the fictional characters.

Liuzzo, Viola

     (1925-1965) Michigan civil rights activist, mother of five, part-time Wayne State University student who attended Selma to Montgomery, Alabama, marches and was driving fellow activists to the Montgomery airport March 25, 1965 when she was shot dead by members of the Ku Klux Klan, ostensibly outraged that she was sitting in the car near a Black man. She was shot twice in the head and died instantly. The Black male, Leroy Moton, then 19, pretended to be dead, bullets missed him and he survived. At the time, male civil rights activists who were killed were recognized as heroes; Liuzzo was criticized for bringing death upon herself. Before leaving for the marches she told her husband the civil rights struggle "was everybody's fight." Her legacy suffered a smear campaign by the FBI, possibly to protect the agent they had in the car, but no allegations were ever proven. It was surmised by many that her death helped spur the 1965 voting rights act to passage.

LOR - Lunar Orbit Rendezvous

Key concept for getting man to the moon, LOR was actually, for a time, the minority preference among the alternatives. Those included EOR, Earth Orbit Rendezvous, wherein various components of a spacecraft needed to go to the moon are assembled in Earth orbit, and direct ascent -all the way in one big rocket.

LOR was approved 1962. It is believed to have been first proposed in 1916 by Ukrainian rocket theoretician Yuri Kondratyuk, as the most economical way of landing humans on the Moon. This method saves on "dead weight" because the propellant necessary to return from lunar orbit back to Earth need not be carried as dead weight down to the Moon and back into lunar orbit. The method was nearly ruled out until it was championed by Dr. John Houbolt of Langley Research Center.

Lorre, Peter

(1904-1964) Actor with a sort of flat face and bulging eyes, whose voice, instantly recognizable, might be described as nasal, raspy, effeminate, or simply unique (and often imitated on Looney Tunes). He was usually hired to play the loner, the schizophrenic murderer, or bad guy (as in *Casablanca* and *The Maltese Falcon*), but with exceptions (such as the professor's sidekick in *20,000 Leagues Under the Sea*). His one-time wife, Celia Lovsky, played T'Pau in the *Star Trek* epsiode *Amok Time*, officiating at the marriage challenge of Spock's assigned wife.

Lovell, James

(1928-2025) Only person to fly to the moon twice without making a landing, Lovell was command module pilot for Apollo 8, the first NASA mission to enter lunar orbit. While scheduled to be the sixth man on the moon via the Apollo 13 mission, fate intervened. The Apollo 13 capsule suffered a critical failure and almost did not make it back to Earth. But we all know how it got back thanks to Ron Howard's great 1995 movie, *Apollo 13*. Lovell didn't actually say "Houston, we have a problem," but close.

Lucky Strikes

Still killing people after all these years - Lucky Strikes started out as a chewing tobacco in 1871, became a cigarette brand in the early 1900s. Popular probably due to sponsorship of radio and television musical shows beginning in the 1920s. Sports figures touting the brand added to its cache.

MacGill, Elsie

(1905-1980) Not only a top aeronautical engineer and the first female in the world to hold those credentials, Elsie MacGill was such a heroine in Canada that they wrote a comic book about her in 1942. It was called *Queen of the Hurricanes*. That's because the Hurricane was an important fighter plane during

World War II. When thousands of blueprints for the plane came from England, MacGill designed machines to manufacture the required 60,000 parts. Part of her innovative input was to make interlocking parts that fit together Lego-like. That made the plane easier to repair under wartime conditions. She also designed the Maple Leaf Fighter II, known for its high altitude performance.

Michigan plays a role in her expertise. After becoming the first woman to graduate in electrical engineering from the University of Toronto, she worked for an airplane production plant in Pontiac, Michigan. That sparked her interest in aviation. She received her master's degree in aeronautics from the University of Michigan.   And all that was after she overcame a bout with polio and defied doctors' predictions that she wouldn't get out of a wheelchair.

MacGill was born in Vancouver, British Columbia. For good measure, her mother was the first female judge in the province and her grandmother was a well-known crusader for the female vote. In 1967 she was appointed to Canada's Royal Commission on the Status of Women.

Mackinac College

Private liberal arts college, backed by the religious Moral Rearmament movement, opened on Mackinac island in the fall of 1966. It had 350 students over four years; 36 staff, one graduating class. S. Douglas Cornell, an optical physicist, quit as executive officer of the National Academy of Sciences to be its president. The idea was to get "the right young men" into positions of influence in public affairs (where they would offer moral leadership to the rest of us.)

Mackinac Bridge

Built between 1954 and 1957, the Mackinac Bridge is the longest suspension bridge in the western hemisphere; 8,614 feet suspended, 26,372 total. Including approaches, the bridge is 4.995 miles long. It links Michigan's Lower and Upper Peninsulas. The roadway is four lanes, 54 feet wide; 200 feet above water at mid-span. It is held up by 42,000 miles of cables. A suspension bridge is designed to accommodate wind, temperature and weight changes.

Five men died during the construction of the bridge and, at this writing, five babies have been born on it; three in ambulances and two in taxis.

In 1989 a young woman and her car, a Yugo, a small compact, were blown off the bridge. Since then, drivers are given high wind warnings.

The Mackinac Bridge deck may move as much as 35 feet to the east or west in high winds. If Walter's mother had known this, she would never have driven across it!

Mackinac Island

Mackinac in all cases is pronounced Mack- (short)i-naw. In its entirety, a National Historic Landmark in the Straits of Mackinac; 3.8 square miles, 8 miles in circumference; its early days included Native American settlement, French missionary presence, an Army garrison, and headquarters for Great Lakes fur trading, including John Jacob Astor's American Fur Company. Fort Mackinac was involved in two battles of the War of 1812. In the late 1900s, the island began to emerge as a resort area, first for the families of nouveau riche industrialists.

Mackinac Island banned all motorized vehicles in 1898. Although 80 percent is preserved as a Michigan State Park, hotels and tourist venues abound, including golf courses, riding trails, souvenir shops, bicycle rentals, and the renowned Grand Hotel. Tens of thousands of visitors come by ferry in the summer months. Year-round residents number under 500.

Mackinaw City

City at the tip of Michigan's Lower Peninsula, just east and in sight of the Mackinac Bridge. The city is a tourist mecca, offering two ferry lines' services to Mackinac Island, Star Line and Shepler's. After 138 years, Arnold Line ceased service in November 2016.

Magic Markers

What the Sixties generation called felt-tip pens.

Malcolm X

(1925-1965) American Muslim (Moslem was the preferred spelling in the first half of the 20th Century) minister and human rights activist, often cited as one of the most influential African Americans in history. His family moved to Lansing, Michigan, shortly after he was born. There they were harassed by white racists and their home was burned in 1929. He is considered influential primarily for his ideas of racial pride and Black nationalism. He was a follower of Nation of Islam leader Elijah Mohammad until he became disillusioned by him/it. The feeling was mutual. Three members of the Nation of Islam shot him to death in 1965.

Malcolm X said: "You can't separate peace from freedom because no one can be at peace unless he has his freedom,"

"Education is the passport to the future, for tomorrow belongs to those who prepare for it today," and

"If you don't stand for something you will fall for anything."

Malice

In *Times v. Sullivan* (1964) the United States Supreme Court ruled that actual malice must be proved by a public official/plaintiff before he or she can succeed in a lawsuit for defamation and libel. This harks back to the Founding Fathers' determination to give the people the right to criticize government. *Times v. Sullivan* is considered the most forceful defense of press freedom in American history.

Absence of Malice, a screenplay by Kurt Luedtke, former *Detroit Free Press* executive editor, was made into a movie in 1981 starring Paul Newman and

Sally Field. The movie shows how sticky it can get when you're "absent malice" but your reporting injures innocents. Sally's character makes ethical mistakes, including getting involved with her source, but heck, it was Paul Newman.

Manhattan Project

During World War II (1942-45) the massive research and development project in the United States which produced the first nuclear bombs.

Marquette, Father Jacques

(1637-1675) French Jesuit missionary explorer who, with Louis Jolliet, traveled down the Mississippi River and reported the first accurate data on its course. Marquette arrived in Quebec in 1666, founded Michigan's first European settlement, Sault Saint Marie, and later founded St. Ignace, Michigan. He is immortalized in a larger than life bronze statute on stone pedestal on Mackinac Island. The statue and park were dedicated in 1909. The blackened bronze Father Marquette seems to be looking out over the Round Island Channel harbor, east of downtown Mackinac. The park is a favorite gathering place for island visitors.

Material witness

Someone who's testimony is likely to be important enough to influence the outcome of a trial.

Maverick

Beloved American television western series (1957-1962) with a comedic bent, Maverick told the tale of brothers Bret and Bart, played by James Garner and Jack Kelly, respectively, and sometimes British cousin Beau, played by pre-James Bond Roger Moore. Bret didn't drink. The boys were gamblers, but nice; spiffy dressers, but not dandies; fond of women, but not predators. If you can watch only one episode, catch *Shady Deal at Sunny Acres*, and watch for Efrem Zimbalist, Richard Long, Regis Toomey, J. Pat O'Malley and Diane Brewster in cameo roles. Then you'll understand the true meaning of "I'm workin' on it."

Maypo

Maple-flavored oatmeal created by the Maltex Corporation in Burlington, Vermont in 1953, famously sold on television using the catch-phrase "I want my Maypo!" A host of child actors as well as sports figures Mickey Mantle, Wilt Chamberlain, and Johnny Unitas have uttered the cry.

McCallum, David

(1933-2023) If you didn't know him as U.N.C.L.E. agent Illya Kuryakin, you might know him as forensic pathologist Dr. Donald "Ducky" Mallard on *NCIS*. Scottish born McCallum began his active acting career in 1947, became a sex symbol with his blond Beatle-like haircut playing enigmatic Russian agent Kuryakin between 1962-64. Although he worked steadily after U.N.C.L.E., including a stint as an inter-dimensional secret agent in *Sapphire and Steel* opposite Joanna Lumley, McCallum did not enjoy as much fame and glamour - until after his 70th birthday when his role as Ducky Mallard took off. See *Kuryakin, Illya*; *Solo, Napoleon* and *U.N.C.L.E.*

McMahon, Ed

(1923-2009) Sidekick of Johnny Carson on the Tonight Show, often the straight man for Johnny and pitch-man for advertisers.

Mercurochrome

A dark red topical antiseptic containing mercury. Few people under 40 have ever heard of the stuff. Somewhere along the line (1998) its permits got pulled for not being "generally recognized safe," despite kids having it dosed on their skinned knees since WWI. Its antiseptic qualities were discovered by a Johns Hopkins physician in 1918. While still important in developing countries, the antiseptic was banned in the U.S., France, and Germany because of its mercury content.

Mercury 7

After rigorous physical and emotional fitness tests, first men chosen to be astronauts by the National Aeronautics and Space Administration (NASA). Their names were announced on April 9, 1959: Alan Shepard, Virgil "Gus" Grissom, Gordon Cooper, Wally Schirra, Scott Carpenter, John Glenn and Donald "Deke" Slayton.

All made it into space. Slayton's trip was delayed about a decade. Grounded in 1962 due to an irregular heart rhythm, he was cleared to fly in 1972 and named docking module pilot for the Apollo-Soyuz test project in 1975. He was 51 and the oldest man to fly in space until John Glenn flew again in 1998 at the age of 77.

Mercury 13

Group of women pilots who passed the same tests given the Mercury 7: In addition to Michigan's Jane Hart, Jerrie Cobb, Myrtle Cagle Janet Dietrich, Marion Dietrich, Wally Funk, Sarah Gorelick, Jean Hixson, Rhea Hurrle, Gene Stumbough, Irene Leverton, Jerri Sloan, and Bernice Steadman.

They were faulted for not having military jet pilot experience at a time women were banned from Air Force training schools and that was the only place you could get such experience. John Glenn said women couldn't become astronauts as a consequence of "our social order."

Sally Ride became the first American woman in space in 1983. Eileen Collins commanded the space shuttle in 1999 and 2005. See: *Women in Space.*

Miranda - Miranda Warning

We've all heard this on TV cop shows for decades now. But it wouldn't have been that familiar to Walter when his mother's newspaper was raided in 1967. It was on June 13, 1966 that the United States Supreme Court decided that people being arrested or under interrogation should be informed of their right not to incriminate themselves under the U. S. Constitution, specifically the Fifth Amendment. Also, they should be informed of the Sixth Amendment right to counsel. The case stems from *Miranda v. Arizona*. When police forget to "Mirandize," their suspect's statements can be ruled inadmissible in court.

No precise wording is required, but the warning must state they have the right to remain silent and that anything they do say can be used against them in a court of law; the right to have an attorney present before and during the questioning; and, if they cannot afford the services of an attorney, the right to have one appointed at public expense.

Mondale, Walter

(1928-2021) Walter Fredrick "Fritz" Mondale was a senator from Minnesota during the Apollo 1 tragedy and he was serving on the Aeronautical and Space Sciences Committee. He put the screws to NASA fairly deep. In 2001 he explained that he thought NASA was being lax in safety precautions and getting it all out into the open "forced NASA to restructure and reorganize the program in a way that was much safer."

Mondale, a Democrat, later served as 42nd Vice President of the United States under President Jimmy Carter. Carter and Mondale were renominated in 1980 and lost to the Republican's Ronald Reagan and George W. Bush. In 1984, Mondale won the Democratic Party's nomination over challengers such as the Rev. Jesse Jackson (who won the Michigan primary) and Gary Hart. Mondale was the first major party candidate to choose a female running mate, U.S. Rep. Geraldine Ferraro of New York. They campaigned for a nuclear freeze, the Equal Rights Amendment, reducing the federal debt, and an increase in taxes. They lost big. That pledge to increase taxes just didn't warm hearts. Reagan/Bush won 49 states. Mondale/Ferraro won only his home state of Minnesota and Washington D.C.

Monkees, The

American rock band active between 1965 and 1971. Members Peter Tork, Micky Dolenz, Davy Jones, and Michael Nesmith started out as actors in a TV show playing band members who aspired to be like the Beatles.

That wasn't wildly successful, so they became a real band and outsold the Beatles in 1967. "Hey, hey we're the Monkees!" for real: 75 million records sold worldwide from such hot tunes as *Last Train to Clarksville, Pleasant Valley Sunday* & *I'm a Believer* and *Daydream Believer.* Oh, those 1967 sales? They exceeded those of the Beatles and Rolling Stones combined.

Moon Pie

A dessert made of two oversize round graham cracker cookies, with marshmallow filling in the center, dipped in a flavored, usually chocolate, coating. Moon pies were invented at the Chattanooga (Tennessee) Bakery in 1917, reportedly when a miner was asked what kind of snack he would like and replied with the graham cracker and marshmallow ingredients and asked for it to be "as big as the moon."

Moral Rearmament

An international moral and spiritual movement founded in 1938 by the American minister Frank Buchman's Oxford Group. That year Buchman spoke in London, calling the crisis before mankind "fundamentally a moral one." It was based on four absolutes: absolute honesty, absolute purity, absolute unselfishness, and absolute love.

Catholic theologians found the movement naïve, since it claimed it could solve problems that have plagued mankind since the beginning of civilization. The Nazis didn't like it, seeing it might undermine National Socialism. Russians thought it would supplant the inevitable class war. Buchman led the group for 23 years, gathering support of right wing, wealthy followers. He died in 1961. In 2001 the group was renamed Initiatives of Change.

Mormon Religion

"Mormon" most often refers to members of The Church of Jesus Christ of Latter-day Saints (LDS Church) because of their belief in the Book of Mormon, though members often refer to themselves as Latter-day Saints or sometimes just Saints. The faith began with Joseph Smith in upstate New York and his desire to marry as many women as possible.   He taught and practiced polygamy during his tenure. Due to their high birth and conversion rates, the Mormon population has grown significantly in recent decades rising from around three million in 1970 to over 15 million in 2015.

The Mormons health code bans alcoholic beverages, tobacco, coffee, tea, and other addictive substances. Males dominate. They tend to be very family-oriented, and have strong connections across generations and with extended family, reflective of their belief that families can be sealed together beyond death. Mormons also have a strict law of chastity, requiring abstention from sexual relations outside of marriage and then only the opposite-sex kind. Strict fidelity within marriage is required (except for the multiple wives, of course).

A full list of nutty Mormon beliefs would take too much space here.

Mumy, Billy

(1954-) Child actor in the Sixties, Mumy is best know for the *It's a Good Life* episode of *The Twilight Zone,* first aired November 3, 1961. Mumy, then age 7, played dictatorial 6-year-old Anthony Fremont, a kid with extraordinary powers who terrified a town, including his own parents, with his ability to transform objects, and wish anything and anyone "into the cornfield." Actress Cloris Leachman played his mom. This scary tale was voted one of the 100 best-ever television episodes. Mumy and his daughter joined with Leachman for a sequel in 2004, *It's Still a Good Life*. The original story was based on a 1953 short tale by Jerome Bixby.

Look for him as a kid genius named Erasmus in the charming movie *Dear Brigitte* (1965) with James Stewart playing his father and an appearance by Brigitte Bardot.

Mumy was also in television's distressingly stupid sci-fi offering, *Lost in Space*, which lasted 83 torturous episodes from 1965 to 1968. To be fair, at least they resurrected Robby the Robot, who appeared in *Forbidden Planet (1956)*.

NAACP

Now a "household word," NAACP is one of those few acronyms that newspapers decide don't need to be spelled out, like FBI. But to spell it out, NAACP stands for the National Association for the Advancement of Colored People. Obviously founded before they decided they preferred to be called Blacks.

Nader, Ralph

(1934 -) Consumer advocate, lawyer, author. Ralph Nader's *Unsafe at Any Speed: The Designed-In Dangers of the American Automobile*, was a bestseller in 1966. The book accused automobile manufacturers of stonewalling on safety features such as seatbelts and stability to save money. The chapter, "The Sporty Corvair - The One-Car Accident," showed how the General Motor's compact car had been frequently involved in accidents involving spins and rollovers, resulting in more than 100 lawsuits. GM tried to discredit Nader by hiring private detectives to tap his phones and investigate his past, and prostitutes to try to trap him in compromising situations. Nader sued the company for invasion of privacy and settled the case for $425,000.

Nader inspired hundreds of young people to come to Washington D.C. to help him with other work. They came to be known as "Nader's Raiders" and, under Nader, investigated corporate malfeasance and government corruption, publishing dozens of books.

In 1971, Nader co-founded the organization Public Citizen to oversee such projects.

While Public Citizen continues to work for consumer protection and worker safeguards, in 2024 it took on fighting for democracy and the rule of law. Its paid membership hovers around half a million as of 2025, with another half million in its cheering section.

Unsafe at Any Speed was one of the most influential books of the 20th Century, doing for consumerism what Betty Friedan's *Feminine Mystique* did for feminism and Rachel Carson's *Silent Spring* did for the environmental movement.

NOW - National Organization of Women

Founded in 1966, NOW is a feminist organization with 550 chapters among all 50 states. Founders, including Betty Friedan, were frustrated by the federal government's lack of enforcement of anti-discrimination laws.

Jane Hart was one of the original backers.

Offset Printing

In this method, pages are paste-ups of paper headlines, columns of type, and photos. Finished pages are photographed and, using the negative, "burned" onto a thin metal plate. The image is inked and transferred (or "offset") from a plate to a rubber blanket for printing by an inking technique that relies on the fact that oil and water do not mix. After the 1950s, many newspapers switched from "hot lead" raised type to offset printing.

Hot metal typesetting involved injecting molten metal into molds in a linotype machine. The operator would enter text and each line would be cast as a single piece (a line-o-type) called a slug. Pages were composed of slugs and tightened together in a frame to be printed from. The slugs would be melted down again after use. It was an improvement over the earlier method of composing letter by letter from a drawer of raised letters. Linotype production was the industry standard for newspapers, magazines and posters from the late 19th Century to the 1960s and even later. The *Detroit Free Press* was still using hot type in 1966. Our fictional newspaper was offset.

Ovaltine

Developed in Berne, Switzerland, exported to Britain in 1909, Ovaltine is a milk flavoring product. Originally it consisted solely of malt, milk, and eggs, flavored with cocoa. The formulation has changed over the decades, and today several formulations are sold in different parts of the world --   with malt extract, except in the blue packaging in the U.S.; sugar, except in Switzerland; and whey. Some flavors still have cocoa. Ovaltine, a registered trademark of Associated British Foods, is now made by Nestle (the people who extract our water and sell it back to us in plastic bottles at massive profit) in the U.S. and Australia and Twinings elsewhere. Children's radio programs in the Thirties and Forties, and later television shows, were sponsored by Ovaltine. Listeners could save proofs-of-purchase from Ovaltine jars to obtain "secret decoder ring" badges or pins that could be used to decode messages in the program. "Ovaltine" is an anagram for "Vital One" Kids loved it in the 1950s and 1960s, whatever it was made of then.

Parsec

A unit of measurement for interstellar space, 3.26 light years. According to Isaac Asimov in his *Guide to Science*, "a parsec is the distance at which a star would show a parallax of one second of arc; it is equal to a little more than 19 trillion miles or 3.26 light years.

Pearson, Drew

(1897-1969) One of the columnist's Walter's mother thinks he should be reading. Pearson's "Washington-Merry-Go-Round" was sold to a syndicate and the column first appeared in the *Washington Herald* in 1932, but its pro-Roosevelt stand didn't sit well there. It was picked up by the *Washington Post* and Pearson's investigative go-for-the-jugular style made him the most famous columnist in America. Pearson also gave commentary on NBC radio. Critics note Pearson used the sensational and salacious with little restraint. In 1950 he began a series of articles attacking Senator Joseph McCarthy, who was by then finding a communist under every bed (205 in the State Department alone). By the time of his death, Pearson's column was syndicated in 650 newspapers. It was credited with sending four congressmen to jail and the resignation of President Dwight Eisenhower's chief of staff, Sherman Adams. In the final analysis, Pearson was revealed as someone who saw journalism as a weapon against people he didn't like and played fast and loose with facts. Washington-Merry-Go-Round was continued by Pearson's associate, Jack Anderson, then others, to become the longest running column in American history.

Petoskey Stone

The stones are recognized by their distinctive six-sided mottled pattern with darker nucleus. They are often made into jewelry and decorative objects.

No surprise, Petoskey stones are often found on Petoskey beaches; sometimes in Charlevoix, occasionally inland.

Ringworm sometimes manifests as similar-looking small circles with a nuclei, albeit without six sides.

Pitts, Zazu

(1894-1963) American actress and comedian from the silent era to 1963. Sixties kids knew her as the goofy sidekick of Gale Storm in Storm's popular 1956-60 TV show, also known as *Oh, Susanna*. Pitts played Elvira Nugent or Nuggie, shipboard beautician, constantly involved in scrapes with Ms. Storm, the social director on board.

Plugs-Out Test

This vital test makes sure a spacecraft can run on its own internal power and all its systems can be operated without the umbilical connection to the launch tower. On January 27, 1967 a plugs-out test of the Apollo 1 capsule ignited a fire that killed Astronauts Ed White, Gus Grissom and Roger Chaffee. NASA attempted to find the cause of the fire and some procedures were changed, but the plugs-out tests still must be carried out for all missions. In the Apollo 1 case, a board of inquiry was not able to determine the specific cause of the fire, but identified these conditions as contributory: a sealed cabin, pressurized with an oxygen atmosphere, an extensive distribution of combustible materials in the cabin, vulnerable wiring carrying spacecraft power, vulnerable plumbing carrying a combustible and corrosive coolant, inadequate provisions for the crew to escape, and inadequate provisions for rescue or medical help.

Prospect Park

Brooklyn's 585-acre public park designed by Frederick Law Olmstead, who also designed Central Park in Manhattan, by comparison 778 acres. Prospect Park is situated between the neighborhoods of Park Slope, Lefferts Gardens, Ditmas Park, and Windsor Terrace. Next to the Brooklyn Botanic Garden and Brooklyn Museum, the park includes a zoo, a nature conservancy, bandshell, baseball diamonds, tennis courts, playgrounds, and Brooklyn's only lake, covering 60 acres.

Psychedelic fashion

'Psychedelic,' with its vibrant colors and bold swirls and geometrics, was the number one adjective used to describe fashion and décor in the Sixties. Why? Chemical stimulants that became popular, like LSD, increased sensations and appreciation of colors, textures, and lines. But rest assured, it wasn't necessary to take drugs to reject bland and conservative dressing and to have fun with the wilder, freer fashion of the Sixties. It's harder to explain the absurdly thick black eyeliner. Liz Taylor as Cleopatra? Twiggy?

Raisin in the Sun

A 1959, now immortal, Broadway play by Lorraine Hansberry that tells a Black family's experiences in Chicago as they attempt to "better" themselves with an insurance payout following the death of the father.

Eventually the mother puts some of the money down on a new house, choosing an all-white neighborhood over a Black one for the practical reason that it happens to be much cheaper. A white representative of the neighborhood they plan to move to makes a generous offer to buy them out. He wishes to avoid neighborhood tensions over interracial population.

Ripples of Hope

Robert Kennedy considered his anti-apartheid speech, given at the University of Cape Town, South Africa, June 6, 1966, his best. Its most memorable line: "...each time a man stands up for an ideal or acts to improve the lot of others, or strikes out against injustice, he sends forth a tiny ripple of hope, and crossing each other from a million different centers of energy and daring, those ripples build a current that can sweep down the mightiest wall of oppression and resistance."   Many writers worked on the speech, but primarily Richard Goodwin and Adam Walinsky.

Rolling Stones, The

Before the rock group, the most famous Rolling Stones were the intrepid space-faring Stone family, conjured up by science fiction writer Robert A. Heinlein. *The Rolling Stones*, beloved classic published in 1952, focuses on twin 17-year-olds Castor and Pollux, who live in the lunar colony with their mom and dad, sister, little brother, and grandmother. When the twins decide life is too dull on the moon and attempt to buy a spaceship to travel and go into business for themselves, their father is supportive, but contrives for the whole family to go along. (Mom's a doctor and shows courage - ahead of its time in fictional depictions of women; Grandma led the Lunar Colony revolt a generation back.) The twins learn a few things about business trying to sell bicycles where the market is glutted, and face a tax evasion charge. Then they decide to sell a peculiar animal they call flat cats, but find they reproduce too fast to be money makers. These flat cats are clearly role models for Star Trek's future Tribbles.

Romney, George
   (1907-1995)   43rd Governor of Michigan from 1963 to 1969, George Romney was born in Mexico of American parents who were in Mexico on account of their parents, polygamous Mormons fleeing U.S. federal government enforcement of laws forbidding multiple wives.   Romney's parents practiced monogamy and returned to the U.S. in 1912 to avoid marauders from the Mexican Revolution. Romney grew up in humble circumstances, working in wheat and sugar beet fields at the age of 11, then later becoming skilled at lathe and plaster work. He didn't graduate from any of the several colleges he attended, but eventually ended up in Detroit as spokesman for the American Automobile Association. From there he went on to become CEO of American Motors, gaining entry into politics via serving on the panel rewriting the Michigan Constitution in 1961 and 1962.
   Romney's advocacy of civil rights brought him criticism from his church.
   In January 1964, Council of the Twelve (apostles) member Delbert L. Stapley wrote to him saying a proposed civil rights bill was "vicious legislation" and because the Lord had placed the curse upon the Negro, mere men should not seek its removal. He said the Negro is entitled to considerations but "not full social benefits" nor intermarriage privileges with whites nor should the whites be forced to accept them into restricted white areas. And he agreed with Prophet Joseph Smith that they should have been resettled back in Africa. To Romney's credit he basically ignored that; to his discredit, he didn't make a public peep in objection to it.
   Later, when he observed that proponents of the Equal Rights Amendment were uninterested in discriminating against homosexuals, he called them "moral perverts." When criticized for that he called them moral perverts again.
   In 1967, he announced a bid for the Republican nomination for President. A later announcement that on a trip to Vietnam he "had the greatest brainwashing that anybody can get" about the necessity for military intervention there, didn't sit well with GOP party leaders or those who respond to pollsters, apparently. He became an anti-war candidate, reversing his earlier opinion that the war was

justified. His candidacy died shortly thereafter.

Richard Nixon went on to win the Republican Nomination and the Presidency. We all know how well that worked out.

Before that though, Nixon made Romney his Secretary of Housing and Urban Development. In 1968 the Fair Housing Act mandated a federal commitment towards housing desegregation and required HUD to orient its programs in this direction. When Romney tried to move Blacks from inner-city ghettos to Warren, Michigan, where whites had "fled," he didn't make Warren residents happy. Nixon made him back-off. The two men rubbed each other the wrong way in many ways. Romney finally handed in his resignation in November, 1972

In his latter years Romney dedicated himself to promoting volunteerism, but he encouraged his son, Mitt, to challenge Edward Kennedy for his Massachusetts Senate seat in 1994. Kennedy won.

Romney, Lenore

Gave up a MGM movie contract to marry George and have kids, Mitt Romney among them.

Romney, Willard "Mitt"

(1947-) Raised in Bloomfield Hills, Michigan, he went to Cranbrook prep school there, Brigham Young for his B.A., and then Harvard. He became a rapacious businessman who specialized in putting companies out of business and destroying jobs while banking the profits off-shore (net worth $190 to $250 million). As a teen, Romney taunted and abused other students at Cranbrook, liked to dress up in state police uniforms (a felony) and follow girls in his car with a light on top. While his peers were protesting against the Vietnam War and their draft numbers, he was protesting the protesters and speaking out for the war. But he planned to access a religious deferment by becoming a Mormon missionary in France for his two and half most vulnerable-to-the draft years.

He helped his mother lose her bid for Michigan Senate against Phil Hart in 1970. He was pro-choice before he was against it. As the 70th Governor of Massachusetts from 2003 to 2007, he backed health care reform that involved state-level subsidies and mandatory participation - two elements he disdained in the Obama plan when campaigning for President in 2012.

Unlike John F. Kennedy, who said he would not put any tenet of his religion above the law, Romney said he would be "informed by" his, in a belief that "Freedom requires religion." He lost.

Sagan, Carl

(1934-1996) Rock star-magnitude space science popularizer, astronomer, cosmologist, astrophysicist, astrobiologist, author, Sagan promoted the search for extraterrestrial life. He assembled the first physical messages sent into space: the Pioneer plaque and the Voyager golden record, both with universal messages designed to be understood symbolically and mathematically, without needing common languages.

Sagan wrote *Cosmos* (1980) and hosted the popular television show of the same name.

In 1996, a man wrote to him asking about the distance to heaven. Sagan replied: "...Nothing like the Christian notion of heaven has been found out to about 10 billion light years." (One light year is almost six trillion miles.) He said he would rather know than believe.

Smithsonian magazine writer Joel Achenbach wrote in 2014 that no one will ever match Sagan's talent as the gatekeeper of scientific credibility or be able to so elegantly explain space in "all its bewildering glory." (But Neil deGrasse Tyson is gaining on him).

Some of Sagan's books include *The Pale Blue Dot, The Demon Haunted World: Science as a Candle in the Dark, Billions and Billions, The Dragons of Eden* (which won a Pultizer Prize), and *Broca's Brain*.

Sagan died without changing his mind about religion or hearing an extraterrestrial's reply from anywhere in universe. But he would have known the odds on that: there ARE billions and billions of stars.

Saint Ignace

You can be called a "Yooper" if you live in St. Ignace, city just off the north end of the Mackinac Bridge, Upper Peninsula (U-Per.....).

Usually written St. Ignace, the town was founded by Father Marquette in 1671, and was named for St. Ignatius of Loyola. St. Ignace has a rich Native American history and was once the bustling hub of 17th Century fur trade. In the mid-1800s, the population swelled as logging and commercial fishing went into full swing. Now St. Ignace is known for its annual antique car show and as a port of departure for Mackinac Island.

Schirra, Wally

(1923-2007) One of the original seven Mercury astronauts, Navy captain, test pilot, aeronautical engineer. Schirra flew the Mercury-Atlas 8 mission October 3, 1962. He was the first to achieve a rendezvous in space on the December 1965 Gemini mission and became the only person to fly in all three early space programs: Mercury, Gemini, and Apollo.

Sevaried, Eric

(1912-1992) CBS news journalist and commentator, WWII radio correspondent in London during the Blitz, having been hired by radio news pioneer Edward R. Murrow. During the Vietnam War, known for his fearless, perspicacious, and incisive commentary. His 1946 biography, *Not So Wild A Dream*, is a true wordsmith's personal recollections of WWII. Sevaried was first to report the Germans' march into Paris. He survived his aircraft being shot down over

Burma, and, when 18 years old, a dicey canoe trip with a friend - 2,250 miles from Minneapolis to Hudson's Bay.

Schlafly, Phyllis

(1924- 2016) This constitutional lawyer, conservative activist, author and speaker, believed women shouldn't have careers - except for herself. She was an ardent anti-feminist and in her last days an adviser to Donald Trump. During the 1970s, the Schafly opposition might have dealt the Equal Rights Amendment its fatal blow. She argued the ERA would take away gender-specific privileges then enjoyed by women, including separate restrooms and exemption from the military draft. With restrooms seemingly up for grabs and Congress considering including females in the draft law, she won, but she lost.

Shepard, Alan

(1923-1998) First American in space on May 5, 1961. Missed being the first human in space by less than a month. The Soviet Union's Yuri Gagarin flew April 12. Shepard missed the Gemini program due to an inner-ear problem, but got back in time to command Apollo 14 and walk on the moon.

Silly Putty

A moldable, silicone-based substance that was taken into lunar orbit by the Apollo 8 astronauts in 1968, apparently to hold things up. Before that kids knew it makes a cool toy, since it bounces and sticks and leaves no residue. Back then Silly Putty could also be pressed on petroleum-based newspaper ink and retrieve the ink, providing a copy of the text or picture on the flattened putty. Children everywhere copied the faces of comics characters and had fun stretching them out of shape. Non-transferable soy-based ink put the kibosh on that source of amusement.

Initial discovery and/or invention of Silly Putty is in dispute, but in 1949 a toy store owner named Ruth Fallgatter brought the basic substance to the attention of marketing consultant Peter C.L. Hodgson and together they marketed it in a clear case. Hodgson saw further potential. He borrowed $147 to buy a batch of the putty to pack 1 oz (28 g) portions into plastic eggs for $1, then naming it Silly Putty. Initially sales were poor, but after a *New Yorker* article mentioned it, Hodgson sold over 250,000 eggs of Silly Putty in three days. The Korean War put a damper on things when the main ingredient was rationed, but soon silicone was back up for grabs. Initially, the eggs were marketed to adults, but by 1955 it became a real cool item for the 6 to 12 set. In 1957, Hodgson produced the first televised commercial for Silly Putty, which aired during *The Howdy Doody Show.*

In 1961, Silly Putty went worldwide, becoming a hit in the Soviet Union and Europe. Peter Hodgson died in 1976. A year later, Binney & Smith, the makers of Crayola products, acquired the rights to Silly Putty. As of 2005, annual Silly Putty sales exceeded six million eggs.

Slide Rule

Carlee put some thought into that gift of a slide rule for Walter's birthday. The scientists who figured out how to put man on the moon used pencils and paper and slide rules. A slide rule is a 6- to 12-inch ruler-like gizmo with a sliding middle section. The top and bottom are fixed and the act of sliding the middle section reveals relationships between numbers that allow adding, subtracting, multiplication and division, finding square roots, and other sophisticated calculations, including those using logarithms, which provide a simpler way to make computations. In fact, the first slide rule was built by William Oughtred, a math teacher in England in the 1600s, basing it on John Napier's discovery of logarithms. A slide rule was an essential part of daily life for engineers, architects, builders, technicians, and scientists of all types for generations, until suddenly supplanted by the hand-held electronic calculator. That was about 1972. So Walter won't use that slide rule for long, but learning how to operate it will give him an intellectual advantage. That's because, while computers do the math for us, they do it without us having to think about how they do it. When you're using a slide rule, your mind is in gear, you actually understand the process. A bit of folk lore has it that Buzz Aldrin took a slide rule with him to the moon on Apollo 11 and used it for last minute calculations before landing. At any rate, we couldn't have got him there in 1969 without them.

Sojourner Truth

(1797-1883) By saying "Aren't I a journalist?" Freya Firestone is recalling the immortal 1851 speech "Aren't I a Woman?" by abolitionist/feminist Sojourner Truth, in which she showed, by what they do, that women should have the same rights as men. The former slave died in Battle Creek, Michigan in 1883.

Solo, Napoleon

Napoleon Solo is a fictional character from the 1960s TV spy series *The Man from U.N.C.L.E.* Originally, Solo was intended to be the only man from U.N.C.L.E., but as David McCallum's depiction of Russian Illya Kuryakin, with his golden bangs and modish clothing, took off and all but stole the show, Kuryakin became the second "Man from." McCallum was elevated to co-star status, and the chemistry between Kuryakin and Solo is credited for the show's success.

Named and imagined by James Bond creator Ian Fleming, Solo was intended to be an American James Bond, a womanizer, but in a gentle way. And as a man, Solo was more laid-back, more at ease, a Cary Grant type.

Solo is Number One in Section Two (Operations and Enforcement) at U.N.C.L.E. (The reason he wears badge number 11 is never explained in the show). Solo is rarely caught entertaining the idea that he might not succeed, especially in wooing. When Kuryakin bests him at it, he has an adorable pout. Solo is urbane, cool, and unflappable, even when tied up and about to freeze, be shot, or be sliced by a giant pendulum blade.

Sonny and Cher

Sonny Bono (1935 in Detroit -1998); Cher (1946-) Pop singing duo catapulted to fame in 1965 with the million-seller single "I Got You Babe," followed by "The Beat Goes On" in 1967. Cher's career is legendary. Bono would go on to be congressman for California's 44th district from 1995 until his death.

Sources, protection of

Why are journalists willing to go to jail to protect the identity of their sources, as does Walter's mom in this story? Yes, it could be for their safety, if the people who didn't want the information divulged to come out are violent types. But, generally, if journalists couldn't give whistleblowers assurance their identities could be kept secret, many things wouldn't be found out. It's in the interest of democracy, public safety, and fairness to find things out. We want to know if our politicians are corrupt, our police operate within the law, our corporations are doing what's right for their customers and the environment, and our public servants operate within standards of decency and justice. Often inside sources let us know when they are not. And when the public knows the truth, the bad stuff can be corrected. "Such sources," according to the Associated Press, "make available to the public more than the sanitized 'spin' of government and corporate press releases."

This is what helps keep us free: Information provided on condition of confidentiality from workers fearful of bosses, citizens fearful of government, those 'inside' criminal organizations, and those knowledgeable about corruption, plots, and imminent threats.

Sputnik

Tiny Soviet satellite that caused big fears in the United States when it was launched October 4, 1957. It was the first artificial Earth satellite. In low orbit, it could be seen with the naked eye going around the Earth every 96.2 minutes. It only survived 92 days, but it launched the space race with the Russians.

Stanton, Barbara

Detroit Free Press reporter/editor, another Michigan woman with eyes on space. In May 1986, Stanton was one of 40 finalists in the Journalist-in-Space competition and the only one from Michigan from a field of 1,703 applicants. The planned five finalists were never chosen. Following the Challenger disaster in January that year, in which teacher Christa McCauliffe and six crew members died, NASA decided to scrap the idea. Originally, a journalist was to follow the Teacher-in-Space within a year.

Stanton helped bring a Pulitzer Prize to the *Free Press* for its coverage of the Detroit Riot in 1967. After she had to fight to "get out there" amidst the mayhem, Stanton covered the infamous Algiers Motel Incident in which three men were killed by Detroit police. The men were among a group of friends who were being "interrogated" by Detroit police, state troopers, National Guardsmen, and private guards. The *Free Press* team also investigated each of the 43 deaths that occurred during the riots.

Stanton worked for the Free Press for 40 years as a reporter, copy editor and its first female associate editor. Her editorials are remembered as "passion seasoned by reason." Through her writing she worked unstintingly to help preserve Michigan's environment and natural resources.

Starr, Brenda

(1940-2011) Fictional newspaper comic strip and comic book character, a female journalist who travels to exotic places - often more in search of her "mystery man" than a good story, but heck, she was made to look like movie actress Rita Hayworth (who ran off with Prince Aly Khan). The important thing to know about Brenda Starr is that she (along with Superman's newswoman friend Lois Lane) probably made many thousands of young girls from the 1940s to 1960s believe they could be newspaper reporters or just have careers when societal norms said otherwise. *Brenda Starr, Reporter* was created by a female artist, Dale Messick, who started out working for greeting card companies. She created Brenda Starr (after her female pirate comic strip was rejected) for the Chicago Tribune Syndicate but it did not initially appear in the *Chicago Tribune*. *Tribune* Editor Joseph Medill Patterson was against it because it was created by a woman! Eventually, however, Brenda Starr appeared in the *Tribune*, the *Detroit Free Press* and about 250 other newspapers at the height of its popularity in the 1950s. Messick retired as Brenda Starr's artist in 1980 and the strip was continued by other artist/writer teams until 2011.

Sugar Loaf

Dramatic 75-foot high stack of limestone breccia created by post glacial erosion. Situated within Mackinac Island State Park.

Swift, Tom

The fictional boy genius in more than 100 volumes of American juvenile adventure stories that emphasize science and invention. Created by Victor Appleton, the Swift novels began in 1910.

Tang

Fruit flavored powdered mix for making beverages by adding water, first sold by General Foods in 1959. Use of Tang on John Glenn's Mercury flight and later Gemini missions gave the little known product a sales boost, but it wasn't invented for the space program. "Tang sucks!" said Buzz Aldrin, reportedly.

Teasing (hair)

Also known as ratting or backcombing. By using a comb or brush backwards near the roots of your hair, in sections, you can create height or volume. The top layers are smoothed out over the "rats." Popular in the 1960s, this technique helped some movie stars and copycats achieve the era's "big hair."

Television tubes, 6SN7

Little vacuum tubes, three or four inches tall, were a basic component of early television sets - like the 50s-made Dumont the Hudson's have at their Mackinac Island cottage. The tubes controlled various aspects of the television's performance, but often when just one went bad it ruined viewability. A tube might control the horizontal hold, for instance, or the brightness, or focus. It was up to the TV owner to find out which tube needed replacing. Most drug stores of the time had "Tube-Tester" consoles and sold replacement tubes. On most tubes, the leads, in the form of pins, plug into a tube socket for easy replacement. The in-store testers would offer up the various sockets and the old tube could be tried in the one it fit.   The 6SN7 tube was often used as an audio amplifier in the period 1940-1955. From the mid-50s though, transistors gradually replaced tubes, which allowed electronic items to shrink in size. But the 6SN7 was one of the most important components of ENIAC, the first programmable digital computer. It contained several thousand.

Tereshkova, Valentina

(1937 -) First woman in space. Yes, really. The Soviets sent her up on June 16, 1963. She was 26 at the time, a member of a skydiving club. From more than 400 applicants and five finalists, she was chosen to pilot Vostok 6. She orbited the Earth 48 times in almost three days in space. With that single flight, she logged more flight time than all the American astronauts who had so far flown, combined.

She also kept a detailed log and took photos of the horizon, which were later used to identify aerosol layers within the atmosphere. (Aerosols are fine solid particles in air or gas, natural or artificial. Fog and geyser steam are natural aerosols; smoke, dust, and air pollutants are artificial ones.)

Before her flight, Tereshkova was a textile-factory assembly worker. When the female cosmonaut corps was disbanded, she became a prominent member of the Communist Party of the Soviet Union. She also studied at the Zhukovsky Air Force Academy and became a cosmonaut engineer. Tereshkova is regarded as a hero in post-Soviet Russia. In 2013, she offered to go on a one-way trip to Mars if the opportunity arose. She is also the mother of Elena Andrianovna Nikolaeva-Tereshkova, the first person to have both a mother and father who had traveled into space.

Thirty (- 30 -)

Why did Walter feel professional using "- 30 -" to indicate the end of his story? Because it's a tradition in journalism dating back to the days of telegraph operators.   After tapping out their messages in Morse code, a "- 30 -" meant they were taking a break and would be back in 30 minutes.

THRUSH

Fictional organization of ne'er-do-wells, world domination conspirators, and all-around bad guys (and plenty of women) who are antithetical to U.N.C.L.E. in the television show *The Man from U.N.C.L.E.* While U.N.C.L.E. exists to keep peace and order in the world, THRUSH stands for narcissistic self-interest; the personal acquisition of money and power with total disregard for everyone and everything else. Sounds familiar.

Tonto

Fictional Native American character-companion of the Lone Ranger, the masked hero created by G.W. Trendle and Fran Striker. Tonto was Comanche or Potawatomi. According to the story line, Tonto and the Lone Ranger roamed the west defending the helpless against the forces of evil. At the end of each tale their benefactors ask: "Who was that masked man?" Televised from 1949 to 1957, *The Lone Ranger* became a western icon for a generation of American children, ABC's first "hit" show. Actor Jay Silverheels played Tonto in the TV series. On radio, Tonto made his first appearance in the 11th episode, which originated on WXYZ in Detroit.

Don't even consider the Disney version.

Twilight Zone

Ground-breaking television show (1959-1964) whose very name has become a household word for odd, unusual, or just plain creepy. As in "I felt like I was in The Twilight Zone." Who can forget that *To Serve Man* was a cookbook, the waiter in the diner had three eyes, or being scared by the 6-year-old who could wish people into the cornfield? More than 50 years later, the episodes remain compelling. Shape-shifting, time travel paradoxes, sentient machines, android relations, time moving at different speeds - it was an idea box for *Star Trek* scripts to come. And it all came about because a network didn't want script writer Rod Serling writing about real stuff like lynchings and The Holocaust. So he had a leap of genius: make aliens do it and then it's okay to talk about it. When will we realize the Monsters Are (really) Due on Maple Street?

Tyson, Neil deGrasse

(1958-) Space science popularizer in the Carl Sagan tradition. Astrophysicist, cosmologist, science communicator, author of *Death by Black Hole*, Tyson hosts the new *Cosmos* television series. Just like fictional Walter, he began his interest in astronomy at the age of nine after visiting the sky theater of the Hayden Planetarium in New York. "So strong was that imprint [of the night sky] that I'm certain that I had no choice in the matter, that in fact, the universe called me," he said. During high school, Tyson, who grew up in the Bronx, son of Puerto Rican and African American parents, attended astronomy courses offered by the Hayden Planetarium, which he called "the most formative period" of his life. Tyson was speaking on astronomy by the age of 15. Carl Sagan failed to entice Tyson to come and study at Cornell, but his hosting young Tyson's visit to Ithaca was also formative. Tyson said he knew he wanted to be a scientist, but Sagan's friendship, he said, showed him the kind of person he wanted to become.

He studied physics at Harvard. Tyson has argued that many great historical scientists' belief in the intelligent design theory of the creation of the Universe limited their scientific inquiries to the detriment of the advance of scientific knowledge.

When asked if he believed in a higher power, he said: "Every account of a higher power that I've seen described, of all religions that I've seen, include many statements with regard to the benevolence of that power. When I look at the universe and all the ways the universe wants to kill us, I find it hard to reconcile that with statements of beneficence." Tyson said he was interviewed about a plasma burst from the sun on a local television show in 1989. "I'd never before in my life seen an interview with a Black person on television for expertise that had nothing to do with being Black. And at that point, I realized that one of the last stereotypes that prevailed among people who carry stereotypes is that, sort of, Black people are somehow dumb. ...I said to myself, 'I just have to be visible, or others like me...' That would have a greater force on society than anything else I could imagine." Likewise, Tyson responded to a question about whether genetic differences might keep women from working as scientists. He reflected on battling societal forces of such resistance.

"My life experience tells me, when you don't find Blacks in the sciences, when you don't find women in the sciences, I know these forces are real and I had to survive them in order to get where I am today. So before we start talking about genetic differences, you gotta come up with a system where there's equal opportunity. Then we can start having that conversation."

U.N.C.L.E., The Man From
Smash hit TV series, 1962-1964. America's answer to James Bond. "The first successful spy show on American television," according to Craig Henderson, who published the first U.N.C.L.E. fanzine, *File 40*, beginning in 1970. "It was one of the first TV shows to become an international phenomenon."

In the show, U.N.C.L.E. (the United Network Command for Law and Enforcement) employs secret agents from many countries to keep justice and order in any part of the world. Headquartered in New York and other major world centers, U.N.C.L.E.'s frequent adversary is the evil, greedy organization known as THRUSH. Out of the New York office, hidden behind the street level facade of a tailor shop, U.N.C.L.E.'s principal agents are American Napoleon Solo and Russian

Illya Kuryakin. It was determined by the producers that each episode would involve an "innocent," someone from the everyday walk of life who somehow got embroiled in the plot.

Solo was played by actor Robert Vaughn, who took it good-naturedly when what was intended to be a bit part, that of Illya Kuryakin, was transformed into an essential, irresistible, and outrageously popular one by actor David McCallum. In public appearances, McCallum was mobbed like we wouldn't see again until the Beatles came to America.

The agents' boss, Alexander Waverly, was played by Leo G. Carroll of *Topper* fame. Each episode was an "affair," such as *The Waverly Ring Affair* and *The Finny Foot Affair*.   No cocktails were "shaken not stirred," but Vaughn played the lothario with taste and light-hearted humor.   And in Kuryakin, Americans found a communist they could take to their hearts.

Unsafe at Any Speed

Ralph Nader's 1965 book that became a bestseller by 1966.   It exposed the automobile industry's utter disregard for consumer safety and kicked off the consumer movement. The book, full title *Unsafe at Any Speed: The Designed-in Dangers of the American Automobile*, showed how auto executives ignored safety issues and covered up known problems.   The public was aghast and the book spurred passage of the National Traffic and Motor Vehicle Safety Act in 1966, which created a regulatory agency empowered to set design standards for automobiles, such as mandatory seatbelts.   In 2005 conservatives gave it honorable mention in a list of "Most Harmful Books of the 19th and 20th Centuries" published by *Human Events* magazine. Beyond the auto industry, Nader was really trying to show how harmful it is for elites to control business in general. See *Nader, Ralph*.

Vaughn, Robert

(1932-2016) Actor who played Napoleon Solo on T*he Man from U.N.C.L.E.* Breakout role: alcoholic in *The Young Philadelphians (*1959), earning an Oscar nomination. He also gave a stunning performance as the gunslinger consumed by fear in *The Magnificent Seven*. Later he played a Solo-type character in the British series *The Protectors*. When the Beatles came, they wanted to meet Vaughn.

Vietnam War

Millions of people died on both sides of this two-decade-long (1955-1975) conflict been communist and anti-communist forces. The United States became involved to prevent the communist take-over of South Vietnam and as part of a larger plan to stop the spread of communism (...the "Domino Effect").   U.S. advisers were sent to the region as early as 1960.   Fighting escalated when U.S. and North Vietnamese ships got into a scuffle in the Gulf of Tonkin in 1964, or were reported to have. The whole incident may have been made up. Anyway,

Congress then passed the Gulf of Tonkin Resolution, which gave the President (then Lyndon Johnson) authority to increase military presence. Soldiers kept dying, and for the first time Americans could see the agony of war on the evening news at home while they ate dinner on TV trays. A huge war-protest movement began. President Nixon began troop withdrawals and "Vietnamization" in 1969, but the war went on, Black soldiers being killed in disproportionately higher numbers than whites. Paris Peace Accords officially ended the war in January 1973, but the killing continued. The Americans evacuated South Vietnam in chaos. Saigon was captured by the North Vietnamese in 1975 and many civilians died because of the American pull-out. Unexploded ordnance and Agent Orange and similar chemicals continued to kill for years after the shooting stopped.

Von Braun, Wernher

(1912-1977) German aerospace engineer who created the V-2 Rocket for Hitler and the Saturn 5 for the United States. Von Braun was a member of the Nazi Party. Clearly he loved rockets more than he loved Nazis, but just as clearly he worked on rockets over the corpses of tortured concentration camp slaves. He was aware of the slave labor, cruelty, and bestiality around him, but said he was unable to change those conditions. Still, there is no record of his ever trying. After the war he surrendered to the United States, became a space-exploration star in Disney films and helped the United States reach the moon.

Voyageur

French Canadian travelers - usually a term applied to those who worked the fur trade via canoe. Used primarily for Canadians and those in the upper mid-west states in the 18ᵗʰ and early 19ᵗʰ centuries. Legendary folks to French Canadians. Celebrated in folklore and music. Not as well respected on Mackinac Island judging by Dr. Beaumont's treatment of Alexis St. Martin. It was a hard life.

War of 1812

The Americans and the Brits went at each other again between 1812 and 1815. This time the British burned the White House and the Americans threatened to take Canada. Americans didn't like English trade restrictions and the impressment of maybe 10,000 or so men into the Royal Navy. The Brits wanted to keep Canada under the Crown.

The war was fought here and there with many famous skirmishes like the Battle of Lake Erie and the Battle of New Orleans (which was actually after the war was over). But the pivotal battle was the lesser known Battle of Plattsburgh. Plattsburgh, N.Y., is situated on Lake Champlain. Champlain flows into the Hudson River, which takes shipping into New York City.

Had the British won Lake Champlain they would have won the war by controlling such a vital link. In the 1814 Battle of Plattsburgh the Americans were out-manned against a larger, more formidable British naval force. But 31-year-old

Commandant Thomas Macdonough knew how to turn his smaller ships swiftly by shifting the anchors, thus being able to present fresh guns to the enemy and that technique proved decisive. Americans took the victory.

On Mackinac Island, July 18, 1812, a mixed force of British regular soldiers, Canadian voyageurs, and Native Americans captured the island's fort before the American defenders knew that war had been declared. They came from the north and crawled up what is now known as British Landing Road. Fort Mackinac was taken without casualties. Americans got it back, eventually.

Waverly Ring

Introduced in *The Man from U.N.C.L.E.* episode *The Waverly Ring Affair*, we find that a Waverly Ring guarantees the wearer is on the up and up and commands an U.N.C.L.E. agent's obedience to the wearer. In the *Affair*, when secret "File 40" documents turn up outside headquarters, Waverly assigns Napoleon Solo and Illya Kuryakin to find out if agent George Donnell is playing a double game and to help places a Waverly Ring on Napoleon.

In paying homage to the ring story, Walter and Fletcher forget a Waverly Ring is explosive. After being placed on the finger, it can only be safely removed by Mr. Waverly himself. If true to the tale, Ashe couldn't have "lost" it.

Wawashkamo Golf Course

This 9-hole golf course off British Landing Road has been played continually since it was laid out in 1898 and that's a Michigan record.

White, Edward

(1930-1967) One of the Mercury 7, Edward Higgins "Ed" White II earned his aeronautical engineering degree at the University of Michigan in 1958, following up on a Bachelor of Science degree from West Point in 1952. He was also a test pilot for the U.S. Air Force. On June3, 1965, as a crew member of Gemini 4, he became the first American to experience EVA - extravehicular activity - a walk in space.

White died with Gus Grissom and Roger Chaffee when fire engulfed the Apollo 1 cabin during a "plugs-out" test (see *Plugs Out Test*). White's job was to open the hatch cover in an emergency, which was impossible because the door design required relieving slightly greater than atmospheric pressure and opening inward. The fire's heat raised the cabin pressure to the point where the cabin walls ruptured. The astronauts were killed by asphyxiation and smoke inhalation.

White was awarded the NASA Distinguished Service Medal for his flight in Gemini 4 and the Congressional Space Medal of Honor posthumously.

Women in space

Soviets could take credit for the first woman in space in 1963, Cosmonaut Valentina Tereshkova (see entry under her name). Americans didn't have a woman in space until Sally Ride's flight in 1983, but that was not before the Soviets sent a second woman, Svetlana Savitskaya in 1982. Savitskaya also became the first woman to walk in space in 1984.

At this writing, 59 women have flown in space out of the 536 individuals who have left the Earth's atmosphere. Forty-four American women have gone into space, four Russians, two each from Canada, China, and Japan, and one each from France, India, Italy, South Korea, and the United Kingdom.

Notable women astronauts include Ride, who was the first astronaut to operate the robot arm, and:

Shannon Lucid, who made five trips and spent 838 hours in space, plus 188 days on the Russian Space Station Mir between 1985 and 1996, at one time holding the space endurance record for an American astronaut, male or female;

Eileen Collins, first female Shuttle pilot in 1997 and first female Shuttle commander in 1999; commander of the Shuttle Discovery, the Shuttle program's first flight 29 months after the 2005 Columbia disaster;

Anna Lee Fisher, chemist, emergency physician, and first mother in space, 1984;

Judith Resnik, who gave her life for the cause of space exploration - a victim of the Challenger explosion in 1986;

Kathryn Sullivan, first American woman to make a spacewalk, 1984;

Mae Jemison, first African American woman in space in 1992;

Ellen Ocoha, first Hispanic American woman in space in 1992;

Roberta Bondar, first Canadian woman in space, 1992;

Kalpana Chawla, first Indian woman in space who also gave her life for the cause in the 2003 Shuttle Columbia disaster, which also killed Laurel Clark;

and Peggy Whitson, as of April 24, 2017, held the record for most days off planet - 534 - not to mention eight space walks totaling 53 hours and 22 minutes. She was also the first woman to twice command the International Space Station.

On Shuttle Discovery Flight STS 131, four of the seven crew members were women.

Brains, tenacity and bravery. Nothing left to prove.

Woodfill, W. Stewart

Owner of the Grand Hotel on Mackinac Island. He began work at the hotel as a desk clerk in 1919, eventually becoming manager and buying the place with two partners in 1925. Except for two years when it was sold to others - he bought it back in '32 - Woodfill ran the hotel until 1972, when he sold it to his nephew, R.D. Musser. He resisted change and collected old carriages. He died in 1984 at the age of 88.

Woolson, Constance Fenimore
See *Anne's Tablet*

Acknowledgments

The author wishes to note her incalculable thanks to:

"Blythe and Lloyd Poor, Brooklyn, N.Y., for three years of listening to stories with patience and discernment, 2005 - 2009.

"Editors Laura Clark, Bill Parsons, Luke Schafer and Jim Tremlett.

"Buzz Aldrin, not only for going to the moon, but for figuring out all that counter- intuitive space rendezvous stuff and inventing tools to make space-walk work feasible.

"My father, for steering a course to the planets and beyond in his heart.

"My brother for pointing his telescope at Saturn, even though he thought it was 'only a star.'

"My grandmother, Anna, for her intrepid journey to America at the age of 17.

"My son, for a little bit of witty repartee whenever needed.

"Also Jonah Magar and Julie Taylor at the Michigan State University library; Mackinac Island librarian Anne St. Onge, Capitol Area reference librarians and the tech volunteers at the city library in Stratford, Ontario.

"And, of course, The United Network Command for Law and Enforcement."

About the Author

A Michigan native, Diane Petryk attended Michigan State University where she earned both bachelor's and master's degrees in journalism.

Petryk has worked on newspapers of all sizes in eight states and abroad. She was a copy editor at the *Detroit Free Press*; sub-editor on *The Dominion* in Wellington, New Zealand; assistant city editor of *The Savannah Morning News*; and news editor of the *The Herald* in Sanford, Florida. She also edited a weekly in Michigan's Upper Peninsula, and reported for newspapers from the Canadian border to Central Florida.

She has been honored for investigative reporting by the New York Associated Press, the New York Newspaper Publisher's Association, the North Carolina Press Association, and the Georgia Associated Press.

"Invasion of the Child Snatchers," her probe of child protective services nationwide, is published in *Abuse Your Illusions, A Guide to Media Mirages and Establishment Lies*.

This is her first work of fiction.

Lake Superior
Lake Michigan
Mackinac Island
Lake Huron
Michigan
Lansing
Detroit

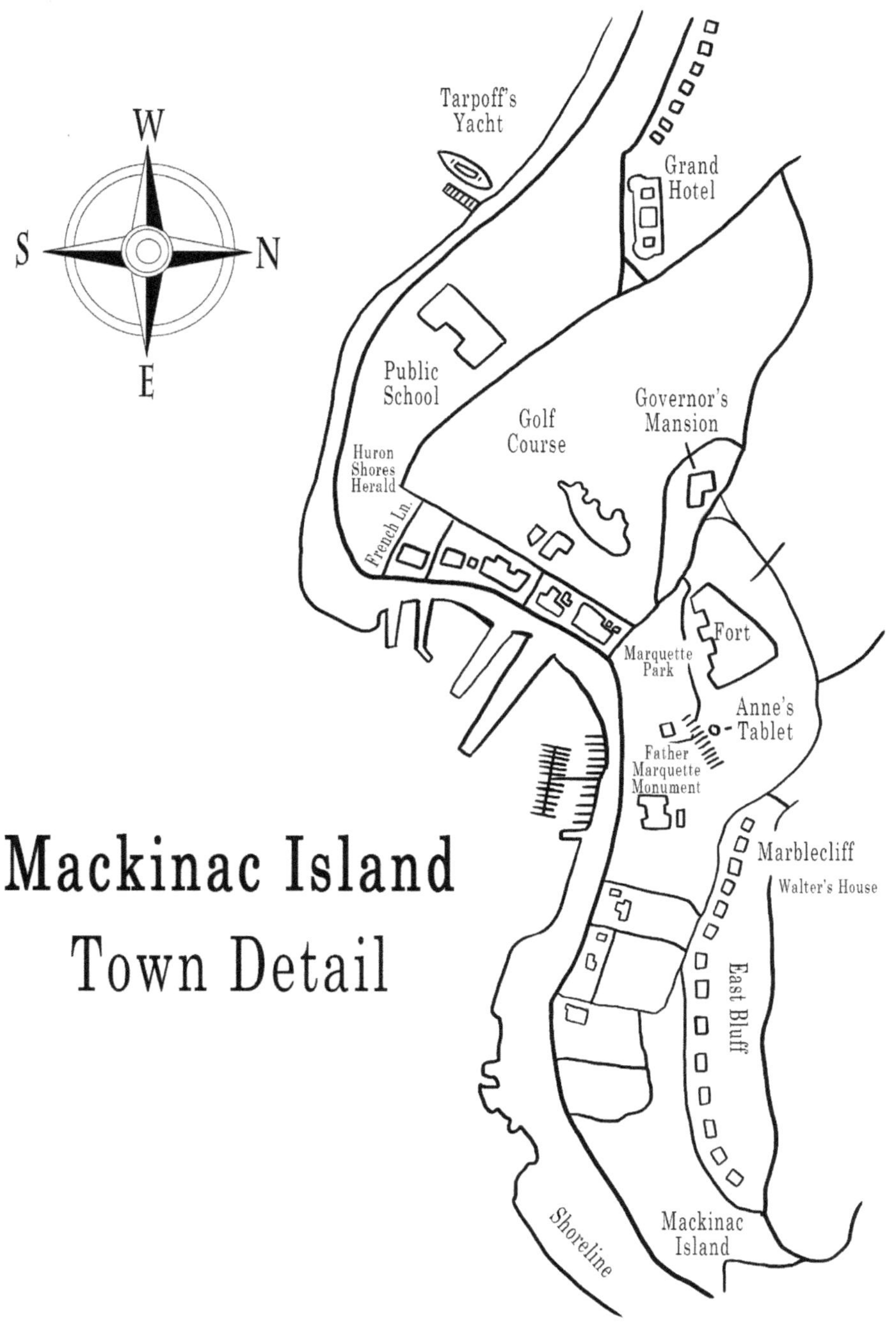

Mackinac Island
Town Detail

Walter Hudson will return in *The London Underground Affair*

www.ingramcontent.com/pod-product-compliance
Lightning Source LLC
Chambersburg PA
CBHW042012120726
47911CB00028B/762